Dragon Blade

DRAGON BLADE

WAR OF THE BLADES: BOOK TWO

J.D. Hallowell

SMITHCRAFT PRESS

Smithcraft Press
1921 Michels Drive NE
Palm Bay, FL 32905

SmithcraftPress.com

ISBN 978-1-62927-008-1

Also by J.D. Hallowell

DRAGON FATE
WAR OF THE BLADES: BOOK ONE

Praise for *Dragon Fate*

"Excellent . . . really well-written and compelling."

—Geoffrey Kabaservice, author of *Rule and Ruin* and
the National Book Award-nominated *The Guardians*

"If you are a fan of fantasy and dragon-lore, it would be hard to go wrong with *Dragon Fate*. . . . Action, adventure, and, of course, dragons. You will not be sorry for getting this book."

—Adam Byrn Tritt, author of "Ezekiel's Wheel";
Tellstones: Runic Divination in the Welsh Tradition;
The Phoenix and the Dragon; and *Bud the Spud*

From Amazon.com and Amazon.uk readers:

"This book took me on an adventure-filled journey full of magic, intrigue and excitement. Overflowing with likeable and believable characters, Hallowell successfully depicts a traditional fantasy story that I thoroughly devoured in just a few days."

"*Dragon Fate* is a well-paced, enjoyable story with consistent characterisation. . . . The characters are swashbuckling from the start in a way that keeps the interest levels sparked! . . . Some of the imagery is truly magnificent, as is the way some of the ideas develop throughout the story—and I liked the detail very much at these times. Overall, I found myself wanting to know more . . . bring on the sequel!"

"The plot was not only brilliantly revealed and constructed, but original and interesting to boot. The plot and the story as well as the depth to the characters is really what makes this book such a fantastic read."

"*Dragon Fate* is a rollicking good story, with an ending which I am sure has been designed to leave room for a sequel."

"One of the most delightful stories I have read in a while. I found that I was really drawn into the story and I could only put it down when my battery died."

DEDICATION

DRAGON BLADE is dedicated to my family, especially my wife, Jennie, my son, Connor, and my daughter, Rashel, for giving me the motivation to write this in the first place and the encouragement to continue once I'd started, and to my readers, without whom writing these books would be a useless gesture.

Acknowledgements

I WOULD LIKE TO thank everyone who has been involved in the process of bringing this to publication, particularly Craig R. Smith of Smithcraft Press for his design work, editing, and friendship; my son Connor, and my wife, Jennie, for their discussions, critiques, and patience; my brother Jim and my niece Kimberly for their comments and encouragement, and last, but certainly not least, the other authors and readers from Reddit, Goodreads, Mythic Scribes, and the Amazon forums who have been a wellspring of feedback, information, camaraderie, and support.

Contents

CHAPTER 1

THE OLD MAN walked up behind Delno and hit him on the back of the head with the wand he carried everywhere.

"Ow, damn it, that hurts!" Delno yelled.

"Then pay attention to me," Jhren responded.

"I was paying attention. You said to watch the clouds outside the window, and then see if I could cause them to move. I was doing that and had all of my concentration on the effort when you snuck up and attacked me for no reason!"

"You weren't concentrating on the lesson; you were trying to use telekinesis, not magic," Jhren replied. "I want you to use the words I've taught you and move the cloud with magic."

"I've used your *system* of magic and I've used mine. . . ."

"Your *system* is telekinesis, not magic," the old man said before Delno could finish.

"I've done both, and they both feel the same to me; what's the difference?" Delno asked belligerently.

"The difference, in this case, as I've explained before, is the amount of power you can summon and how fast you can summon it." Jhren shouted as if he were trying to get the words into his pupil's head by sheer force of volume.

Brock walked in at that moment. "Well, it appears you two are getting along just fine," he observed dryly.

"Oh, yes," Delno said, "so well, in fact, that I'm contemplating killing this old conjurer quickly and putting him out of my misery."

"At least if you did that, you would be doing something new and different," Jhren spat back.

"You two need to learn to work together," Brock observed.

"Tell that to him: if he hits me with that damned stick one more time, I'm apt to put it in a storage place he will find extremely uncomfortable."

"Spare the rod and spoil the child," Jhren sing-songed.

"First, I'm not a child," Delno responded. "Second, I've always been taught that that adage refers to the curved rod of the shepherd used to gently guide the sheep. It does not refer to a bludgeon held by a sadistic tyrant and used to beat the poor animal senseless."

Jhren shook his head and then said, "Get out; you're useless this late in the afternoon anyway."

Delno got up to leave. He grabbed the book he was studying from, and the paper he would need to make notes. Then he left the room.

Jhren stood for a moment before turning to Brock and saying, "He really is learning, he just has trouble seeing the difference between magic and mind tricks because at his level of experience, the two are nearly the same."

Brock asked, "Was I any different?"

Jhren chuckled and said, "Yes, you were twice as thick-headed."

Brock smiled and replied, "You just don't like teaching adults. I'll speak with him about the magic if you think it will help, but you can help by remembering that he's not a child who can be bullied. He was a seasoned warrior before he became a Rider. Then he managed to get a dragon who wasn't even two months old from Larimar all the way to Orlean on his own. One thing I've learned about him is that he is sharp, and harsh teaching methods have to be used sparingly."

Jhren looked at Brock and said, "I know, my friend. The problem is that I not only like this young man, I owe him my life. He deserves the best training, and I am old enough now that I may not be around long enough to give him that."

"What are talking about, Jhren? You're not that old."

"I'm not a Dragon Rider, Brock. I am ninety-four years old, but it's not just the age; people live to be over one hundred all the time. Those two years under the tender care of my former apprentice have taken their toll. It's late summer, and I don't think I'll see another spring. I have to teach that young man a lifetime's worth of magic in a few months so that he is prepared for what awaits you all in Horne."

Brock didn't like talking about Jhren's mortality, so he accepted the switch in subjects. "I wish you knew more about what's going on down there. All you've given us so far are vague hints."

The news they already had about Horne, though limited, was disturbing. The Roracks' attacks were becoming more frequent, and they were well organized. Of the three Riders who normally stayed in Horne, Quincy had been killed. The report mentioned that magic was used, but was vague about the method, and there was no mention of anyone seeing the person or persons responsible. It simply said that the dragon was hit and forced down by magic, and once on the ground, she and her Rider were overwhelmed by Roracks.

What little Jhren had overheard during his captivity was limited to what his apprentice had let slip on the occasions he had come to question the older mage. The most disturbing part of all was the hint, confirmed by Orson, that someone, or something, was using the Roracks as an organized shock force, which would logically mean that this was just the first stage of a much more involved strategy.

"I've given you what I have," Jhren replied. "I was their prisoner, not their honored guest."

Brock gripped the old man's shoulder and smiled, then without another word he left the room. Delno was waiting for him, and fell into step beside the older Rider. They walked in silence for a few moments until they were well away from Jhren's quarters.

"I didn't mean to eavesdrop, but you and Jhren weren't exactly trying to be quiet," Delno said. "I had no idea that he was still in such poor health; I wish he would allow Nat to examine him."

"Don't bring that up to him again, please," Brock replied. "He doesn't trust elves and as far as he's concerned, a half-elf is just an elf who will make the world a better place by dying young."

"I don't understand what his problem is with elves," Delno responded.

"Mages and elves tend to mistrust each other. Elves believe that mages tend to act without due respect for the natural world using magic for their own selfish ends, while human mages tend to think of elves as frivolous dabblers in magic only interested in flowers and trees. I personally think the problems go all the way back to the mage wars. I also believe that both sides tend to blame each other for being limited in how much magic one person can wield. The elves blame the mages for casting the spell that forever limited magic use, but history also tells us that the elves were instrumental in the development of the spell itself. It seems that now neither side has much use for the other."

"Well, I won't promise not to try to get him to see Nat; I think it would do him a great deal of good. No man lives forever, but dying before his time because he is just being stubborn is ridiculous."

"Well, if you are going to bring it up again," Brock replied, "do it when I'm not around."

One of the two "prisoners" walked around the end of the hallway. Seeing Delno and Brock, he saluted as he approached.

"Lawrence," Delno said tiredly, "you don't have to salute me; I'm not your commanding officer."

"But you are my keeper," the man responded. He looked to be about twenty-one, but in reality he was nearly forty, and, therefore, Delno's senior by over a decade.

"I am only your keeper in so far as you have to report to me or be remanded to the custody of the local jailer until we can decide what to do with you. That doesn't mean you have to salute me."

Simcha had chosen his subordinates more for their ability to obey orders than for any ability to think for themselves. They weren't stupid by any means, but they were definitely followers, not leaders. Once it had been ascertained that they had not had anything to do with the theft of the Dragon Blade or the kidnapping of Jhren, their only real crime against Palamore was the negligible act of being Simcha's messengers, which was only counted as a crime so they could keep the two men under observation until they were sure the pair wouldn't fly off and join the other side in Horne. So far, both Riders denied having any but the most superficial knowledge of what was going on in Horne, and Delno and Brock tended to believe them. Once they were out from under Simcha's influence, they seemed to be pretty decent fellows.

"However we put it," Lawrence replied, "you have been put in charge of us, and we must seek your permission to do anything."

"If this about you being allowed to fly, the answer is still no," Brock stated flatly.

The look on the Rider's face showed his disappointment. Delno placed his hand on the man's shoulder and shook him once gently, "Lawrence, we've been through this, it's only been three weeks since you and Adamus, under Simcha's orders, engaged us in a heated battle over control of this city and country. People need a little more time than that to forget. There are those who have called for your execution. It is only because the Queen, at our request, has declared that your crimes are against Brock, Jason, Rita, and me that the government of Palamore hasn't put you on trial."

"But dragons need to fly." He sounded more like a sulky boy than a grown man of forty years.

"Your dragons are allowed to fly; they just have to do it under supervision and without you on their backs." Delno replied without sympathy. After dealing with Jhren all morning, the man's whining was nearly intolerable.

Brock, hearing Delno's tone of voice and sensing the problem, said sharply, "Lawrence, you're forty years old; stop acting like you are twelve." The man stood up straight as if he had been slapped. "You participated in an attempt to overthrow the rightful rulers of this country, and they have placed you our custody. Until we can be absolutely certain that you are rehabilitated, we cannot allow you to fly around the countryside free." Then he softened his tone and continued, "It's only been three weeks, man, and you've already been given freedom to walk about as you please. You're going live at least two thousand more years; give it a little time."

Lawrence looked at him openly and said, "I just miss Rhonna, and Adamus misses Beth. We talk to them in our minds, but it's not the same as being able to actually reach out and touch them."

Delno could understand the sentiment. Even though he and Rita were getting closer all the time, they both still needed time alone with their dragons. Just being able to talk to Geneva wasn't enough; he felt the need for close contact if they were separated.

"I will give you this much, Lawrence," Delno responded. "You and Adamus may go to your dragons and be with them. You will not be alone though; Leera, Fahwn, Gina, or Geneva must be there; one of our dragons for each of yours." The other Rider smiled and nodded, but before he could speak, Delno cut him off and added, "If either of you tries to mount your dragon during the visits, you will not be allowed to visit again. If you actually get off the ground, you will be forced down by whatever means necessary, and, if you survive, your dragon's wings will be permanently clipped."

Lawrence was obviously horrified at the thought of such drastic measures, but he nodded and said, "We have no intention of trying to escape; we won't abuse your trust."

"Good," Delno replied, "I'm giving you another bit of freedom. It's one more step in the process of redeeming yourselves."

As Lawrence went off in search of Adamus to tell him the news, Delno reached out telepathically to inform Geneva of the change and of the dragons' responsibilities regarding it.

"*That's nice, Love,*" she replied. "*They get to spend time together while we get to watch out here alone.*"

"Please, Geneva," he responded, "*I've had a very hard day, and I could use your support, not your sarcasm.*"

"*I am sorry, Dear One,*" she said contritely, "*it's just been over a week since you and I have had any time together ourselves, and then you give the privilege to our enemies.*"

"*Former enemies, Dear Heart, former enemies. I'm hoping that these two Riders will not only prove themselves to be friends, but in the long run, I'm optimistic that I can actually teach them to think for themselves.*"

"*You are a kind, generous, and highly intelligent man, Love, but you can't save the whole world by yourself.*"

He laughed out loud and said, "*No, Love, I can't save it alone, that's why I need to grow my allies rather than harvest my enemies.*"

"*Come out soon, Dear One; I miss you.*"

He took leave of Brock and went in search of Nat. He had made one decision; Jhren would at least meet the half-elf. He found Nat with the king's healer and asked him to come to Jhren's apartment. Nat was skeptical but agreed to meet him there in two hours.

That being done, he went off in search of Rita.

"*She is with Fahwn,*" Geneva answered. She was obviously peeved that the only way she would be seeing him was that he was looking for Rita; the jealousy issue still hadn't been completely resolved. He made a quick side trip to the apartment that he and Rita shared.

He found all three of them in the courtyard. Geneva and Fahwn were perched on the walls watching as Lawrence was spending time with Rhonna. Rita was on the catwalk, her head resting against Fahwn's shoulder. He walked into the courtyard and headed for the stairs that led to the top of the wall.

Lawrence looked up almost dreamily and saw him. He waved and said, "Thank you, sir, this works just fine. Rhonna will leave in a few minutes, and then Adamus can visit with Beth."

Delno just waved and continued walking, wanting neither to intrude on their communion, nor to get into a conversation with the man. He reached out mentally to Geneva: *"Whose idea was it to have them take turns in the courtyard?"*

"Mine," Geneva said. *"They need time together; they don't need the temptation of meeting in an open field."* Her tone was gruff, and he knew she would be hard to placate with everything that had happened.

Since Rita was between him and Geneva, he stopped and kissed her lightly, then said, "We need to talk—after dinner tonight."

She shrugged and said, "All right, Handsome. We'll talk after dinner." He ignored her puzzled look and moved quickly to his Bond-mate.

He walked right up and put his head on her shoulder. He just stood there like that for several moments, and then he said, *"How long do you think it would take you to fly to the lake between the two fields east of the city?"*

"It's less than a league away, only a few minutes if we hurry, why?"

"I want to be alone with you. I've worked hard today, and I want to just be together for a few minutes where no one will bother us, but I also have something that must be done here in less than two hours."

They were interrupted as Rhonna vacated the courtyard so that Beth and Adamus could visit.

"Well," she observed, *"we won't get there any faster if we just stand here talking about it."*

He mounted; he wasn't accustomed to riding without a saddle but the position was nearly made for it, and they would not be doing any aerobatic maneuvers. Gina landed on another section of wall, apparently summoned by Geneva to take over watching the "prisoner's" visitation.

Flying without a saddle made him feel even more strongly bonded with Geneva, and he was doubly glad they had decided to take a little time for themselves. It was also exhilarating being three hundred feet off the ground with no security straps; not exactly dangerous, but still thrilling.

After a few minutes, Geneva landed lightly by the water's edge. Delno had been carrying a bundle, and he showed her the contents. He had stopped briefly at his quarters and now carried a brush and oil and even a large bar of soap.

"I figured it was time to own up to my debt and wash your back, Love," he said.

"I was beginning to wonder if you even remembered that promise you made to me in Llorn," she replied.

"I always remember promises I make to ladies in jailhouses, Dear Heart."

They both laughed as she waded into the lake and began rolling to wet herself all over. Then he stripped down to just his trousers and literally climbed up on her back and bent to the task of applying soap and brush to her scales and hide. They talked and joked while he scrubbed. Though he worked quickly, it was still over an hour before he was satisfied he had gotten her whole back. Then he used the oil to smooth out a couple of flaky spots where she had recently shed some scales. Finally, he just lay down on her back between her wings and held her as best he could for several moments.

Geneva sighed contentedly and then said, "Dear One, I could stay just like this the rest of the night, but you said you had something to attend to, and you may already be late."

"Damn," he said, "I had actually forgotten, but I have to meet Nat at Jhren's apartment."

"I suddenly wish I were much smaller; I'd like to go to that meeting," she said sarcastically. Then she added, "You'd better take a shield with you."

He grabbed the clean pants he had used to bundle the brush and other supplies in and changed quickly. Then he threw on his tunic and the slippers he had taken to wearing around the palace. Once the other items were bundled up in his damp trousers, he mounted up and Geneva flew him back to the palace. Since the courtyard was now empty, he had her land there. Once down, he threw the bundle in the direction of the nearest servant saying, "Take these to my apartment," as he turned and ran in the direction of the mage's quarters.

As he skidded to a halt outside the mage's door, he could hear Jhren's angry voice coming from inside. "Damn it, I said I don't want you here, you pointy-eared meddler."

"Well, I certainly didn't want to come and listen to your verbal abuse either, you cantankerous windbag," Nat's voice shot back.

"You can just leave," Jhren replied.

"I could," Nat responded, "but I promised Delno that I would try and see you."

"You've seen me; now go; your promise is fulfilled."

"I promised to see you as a healer."

"I don't want any of your elven magic practiced on me," Jhren shouted.

"I don't practice elven magic; I practice medicine by scientific methods." Nat retorted just as loudly. Delno had never heard the half-elf raise his voice like this.

"Really," Jhren spat out, "what do you know about scientific method?"

"I have been studying and practicing medicine by scientific method most of my life," Nat responded.

"When you pass your ninetieth birthday we can talk about how long that is," Jhren retorted.

Nat laughed out loud.

"What's so funny?" the mage demanded.

"I passed my ninetieth birthday nearly fifty years ago," Nat replied. "Furthermore, I have been studying medicine since before you were even a twinkle in your father's eye, *old wizard*."

Just as Delno was about to intervene, Jhren said, "Since before I was born, huh?" The old man sounded skeptical but not nearly so angry. Delno decided to wait to interrupt.

"I am one-hundred-thirty-seven years old; I started studying medicine at my father's side when I was four. I didn't take up the profession formally until I was twelve, so, *technically*, I have been practicing medicine for 125 years."

Jhren was silent so long that Delno feared the old man had just discounted what Nat had told him and simply turned his back on the physician. Then Jhren said, "Well, I guess it would be a shame to waste all of that time practicing. Let's move over here and see if you've practiced long enough to have gotten any of it right."

Delno decided that Nat had the situation well in hand, so he moved on without letting them know he had even been there.

Chapter 2

ALL CONVERSATION STOPPED at the dinner table as Jhren and Nat walked in together and took seats next to each other as if they had been good friends for years. Up until this evening, the mage had opted to take his meals in his own apartment because he had refused to sit at the same table with the half-elf. Even the Queen hadn't been able to persuade him to join them.

"What are you all staring at?" Jhren demanded.

There was no immediate reply from anyone. Finally the Queen said simply, "It's good of you to join us, Jhren; we have missed your company at the table these past weeks."

"Well, I can't stay in my room forever," Jhren replied, "and the healer here has helped me get some of my energy back, so I thought I would join you all tonight."

"Just don't overdo," Nat said.

"Don't get fussy over me," Jhren replied, "I said you could be my healer; I didn't marry you."

Most of the people were able to contain their laughter, but Brock had to cover his by pretending to cough, while Rita nearly choked on her wine.

"Of course, my friend," Nat responded. He looked across the table at Delno and winked.

Jhren said, "This man has quite a bag of tricks." He looked at Brock and asked, "Did you know that he can tell how your bowels are doing by feeling your pulse?" Jhren had a habit of simply saying whatever was on his mind.

"I haven't had the opportunity to observe him while he's practicing," Brock replied, while Rita tried desperately not to fall out of her chair laughing. Delno was doing only slightly better than she.

Fortunately for all concerned, the main course arrived and everyone was silent, as was the custom in the palace while the servants were present. By the time dinner was served and the servants had withdrawn, Jhren was happily eating, since this evening was the first time he'd actually felt hungry since his rescue.

Once they had eaten, Delno waited only as long as politely necessary before excusing himself and asking Rita to join him for a stroll in the palace garden. They left quietly as the others around the large table continued their conversations. The garden was really a large atrium in the same wing as their quarters. It had been converted some time in the past when one of the rulers had decided to take up horticulture as a hobby. There were many different kinds of plants from all over the known world, some of which, from the coastal marshes in the extreme southwest, actually digested insects that they lured in with various strategies.

As they walked among the plants, Delno said, "I've noticed that our presence is becoming the accepted norm here in Palamore rather than the novelty it should be."

"Yes," she replied, "I've noticed that same thing. I've been asked to do everything from settle disputes between craftsmen to oversee the opening of a new trade hall. Those aren't Riders' responsibilities."

"You're right: I know that the Queen is tired and would like to put the place in order and retire, but I'm beginning to fear she may have plans to put us in charge in her place. I found myself helping her decide the fate of a soldier who had gone home without leave because his wife was having their first child. While I've been a soldier and I could sympathize with the man, I shouldn't have been the one to decide his fate." Then he added, almost as an afterthought, "I docked the man two weeks' pay, and then had two week's food and some cloth sent to his wife."

She kissed him and said, "You're pretty soft-hearted for a tough old campaigner."

He chuckled and replied, "Soft-hearted? Probably more soft headed. I hope my leniency because of the situation that precipitated the event doesn't make every damn fool out there think he can take an unauthorized vacation." Then he looked her in the eye and added, "The point is though, I shouldn't have been the one to make the call. The commanding officer should have, but since they all credit me for sending Llorn packing, they've been bringing me this day to day nonsense for the last three weeks. I almost wish I had stabbed that idiot commander from Llorn for handing me that blade and all but surrendering to me on the spot; now everyone believes I run the army as well as half the rest of the kingdom."

"What does Brock think about all of this?" she asked.

"Brock has been busy with duties of his own and hasn't noticed it yet. I've kept him running quite a bit trying to gather intelligence about the situation in Horne because I have to devote so much time to training and can't do it myself. Also, the Queen is very subtle; I think she purposely keeps him at a distance from all of this. I have a feeling that she is using our relative youth, and my sense of family duty to manipulate us."

"Well, Handsome, this is usually the point when you come up with some plan to extricate us from the jaws of peril. What do you have up your sleeve?"

"Well, I certainly don't want to do anything to jeopardize our position here." As she looked at him with a raised eyebrow, he explained. "I don't think the Queen is doing these things out of malice; I think she is just tired of running the country and would like a break. Unfortunately, we have other duties ourselves. The problem is that I need the Queen's continued good will so that we keep our living quarters while I continue to study under Jhren, and Geneva matures."

"So, your big plan is to just keep letting her put more and more of her duties off on us? I have to tell you, Handsome, I'd come to expect more out of you up until now."

He shook his head and smiled, "Relax, Beautiful. Have I let you down yet? I have a plan in the works, but I need to talk to Nat and Jhren first. If all goes well, you and I will be taking a trip soon."

No matter how much she pleaded or threatened, he wouldn't tell her any more as they walked to their apartment. Finally, she said, "If you don't tell me, you can sleep somewhere besides the bed tonight."

"If you impose that, you can wash your own hair and back," he retorted.

"That's not fair," she responded.

"A fair is a carnival with lots of make believe. This, Beautiful, is real life." She began to pout, which Delno was now sure she did because she knew he found it so attractive, and he added, "I'll tell you what. You draw the bath and get in to soak while I go find Nat and Jhren. If all goes well with that meeting, I'll come back and join you in the tub and explain it while we scrub each other's backs."

CHAPTER 3

"WE'VE MADE IT *to Orlean, Love,*" Geneva said as she began to glide down toward the city gates.

"*It seems like we left it so long ago,*" he responded. "*Has it really only been a month?*"

"*Give or take a few days.*"

"Hold tight, Nassari," Delno told his friend, who was riding with him at the moment.

She landed gently; Rita and Fahwn landed a few seconds later and Adamus and Beth were right behind them. Nassari grunted and muttered under his breath. The Riders were taking turns carrying him as a passenger, and Delno got the honors on the third part of the trip from Palamore. It was early afternoon, and between Nassari's constant chatter and his nearly constant complaining about flying, Delno was beginning to wonder about the wisdom of bringing the man along.

Since Delno's magic lessons had reached the point that he needed to practice what he'd learned before he could move on, and since Nat had felt that Jhren needed to do nothing more strenuous than walk in the garden and drink the herbal tea he had prescribed for the mage, Delno had organized the Riders into two groups. Brock, Jason and Lawrence were to go south and gather information about enemy activity and try to recruit more Riders to their cause. Delno and his group would head north with the same mission. Granted, there were few if any Riders north of Trent, and none north of Orlean, but the potential to add Corice to their list of allies was a possibility that needed to be explored.

That was why they had decided to carry the extra burden of a passenger; Nassari's political connections should be quite helpful if they could put up with him until they reached Larimar.

Delno and the others dismounted, and he led the way to the garrison. They would go and see Pearce and Connor after they had seen Robbie and delivered Winston's message. The message wasn't really all that important; Delno knew the exact contents since he had been right there when Winston had dictated it: just an account of what had taken place since their departure.

"Colonel Eriksson," Robbie said after he had read the letter. "That will most likely mean that he will be moved to a larger posting."

"Well," Delno replied, "I can't say for sure, since I have no connection to the Ondarian military other than my friends from the garrison here, but it could mean that he will be moving men to Horne to assist the troops already down there."

"More men to Horne?" Robbie asked. "Nearly half our army is already down there. Are things really going so badly that we need to send more troops?"

"All we have are vague reports and the continued call for more men and arms." Delno answered. Then he brightened and said, "Cheer up though, man. Winston didn't want to put it in writing since it's not official, but he told me to tell you that he's put you in to be captain of this post, and he believes that it will be confirmed."

"Captain," he said softly. "That is good news, if it's confirmed." Then he smiled somewhat sheepishly and said, "Do you remember that young woman your friend introduced me to, Jennie?" At Delno's nod, he went on, "Well, she is everything I've ever dreamed a woman should be; bright, pretty, considerate, just everything." Then he looked Delno in the eye and said, "I've asked her to marry me, and she's agreed. With this promotion, I'll be able to set her up properly in a house without having to ask my father for an advance on my inheritance."

"That's wonderful news, my friend; when is the wedding?"

Robbie's face fell slightly, "Well, that would depend on how soon the promotion goes through."

"I wouldn't worry, Robbie," Delno responded, "Winston seemed to think that we could have brought it with us if we had waited another few days to leave. He just sent the letter requesting your promotion two days ago."

"I'm afraid things don't work quite that fast in the Ondarian army," Robbie said. "It could take months before that goes through the proper channels and the actual orders are cut."

"Even with recommendations and requests to expedite the process signed by two Dragon Riders and the commanding general of the Ondarian Army?" Delno asked.

Robbie was speechless. Rita walked up to him and said, "It's all true; I was there when they got the general to sign the letters. It might be a bit early, but congratulations, Captain." She stood up on her tip toes and kissed him on the cheek.

Seeing the petite Dragon Rider kiss the young man, the senior sergeant said, "That's confirmation enough for me. Congratulations, sir," then he saluted.

They stayed and exchanged news for about an hour before Delno said they had to find Pearce, and they all walked out of Robbie's office. Connor was coming in the garrison gate as they were going through the door. Delno could tell the boy wanted to run up and greet them, but he restrained himself and reported to Robbie. Finally, after giving a full report about his morning patrol, he saluted and turned to them.

After the Riders exchanged greetings, Robbie said, "I certainly hope that if they aren't going to send me more men when they send that promotion letter, they authorize the funds to keep this young Rider here. He's good at his job: it's mainly due to him that travelers are safe on the roads; my men have had nearly all they can do keeping the city from falling to disorder."

Connor straightened at the praise. "I just do my job to the best of my ability, sir."

"Your best is quite impressive, young Rider," Robbie replied. "Now, if you will all excuse me, I must see to patrols."

As Robbie walked away, Delno said to Connor, "Why don't you stow your saddle and meet us at the healer's house? We'll catch you up on what has happened."

As Connor ran off to put his gear away, they walked slowly towards the gate of the garrison; by the time they reached it, the boy had rejoined them. Delno and Rita filled him in as they walked.

Missus Gentry was pleasantly surprised when she opened the door and found them on the stoop. Pearce was treating a patient, so she showed them to the sitting room and went for refreshments. By the time she returned with drinks and cakes, the physician had joined them.

They spent the next hour and a half bringing the man up to date on everything.

"The thing Nat is finding a lack of in Palamore is a reliable supply of herbal ingredients," Delno informed him. "That should pick up some now that the threat of impending war is no longer looming large, but he wants to be sure he has a good supply before we move on."

"So, he really is planning to accompany you all the way to Horne, then?" Pearce asked while looking over the list of herbal supplies that Delno had handed him.

"He won't be talked out of it," Delno replied. "He has become convinced that he is fated to go. Personally, I'd feel better if he'd stay in Palamore or return here until this is all over."

"One thing I've learned about my former master is that once he has made up his mind to do something, he sees it through," the physician replied. "I'll see to it that these items are packed and ready to go when you are."

"No, I'm afraid you'll have to send them by courier," Delno responded. "We will be leaving for the north in the morning and won't be back in Palamore for at least a fortnight, maybe more."

"Leaving in the morning?" Connor exclaimed, "I thought you'd at least stay a few days."

"I'm sorry," Rita replied, "I thought we explained that we have to get to Corice as quickly as possible."

"Yes," Delno added, "we were going to wait until the trouble in Horne had been dealt with to go and try to open diplomatic relations with Corice, but events are not going well in the south, and now, with the death of a Rider down there, we decided it would be best to try and get all the help we can."

"I was just hoping to spend a little time flying with other Riders."

"Oh, not getting on well with the men at the garrison?" Delno asked.

"Oh, don't get me wrong; the men are good to me, and my sword practice is going very well. However, they don't seem to know how to treat me. I'm a Rider and earn my pay, and they've been taught all their lives to respect Riders, but I'm still a fourteen-year-old boy, so we don't get chummy. Pearce is the only one in the city who isn't a bit standoffish, but I rarely see him." Then he added quickly, so as to not slight the healer, "He's great company, but his healing skills are much in demand. When he has time, we talk quite a bit."

"What about Tom and Jim?" Delno asked. "They're closer to your age; don't you spend time with them when you aren't working?"

"They spend as much time as they can around me, but I just don't like the way they either hero worship me, or show off to their friends when they're around me," Connor answered.

Delno laughed and said, "I had a conversation about such things as hero worship with a very wise man once. You may have heard of him; his name is Brock." At the mention of his father's name, Connor sat straighter and paid closer attention. "What you need to remember concerning those two is that they come from two of the poorest families in the area. They have little of worth in their lives, yet they need to feel that they do. Showing off their friendship with a Rider gives them status they could not have otherwise achieved. You don't have to like it; in fact, it's better if you don't get to like it, but you should accept it for their sake."

"I try, but it just irritates me," the boy replied.

"Don't worry about it so much; if you spend more time with them the novelty of being around a Dragon and Rider will wear off. I'll bet that if you got couple of stiff-bristled brushes, the boys would be willing to fly to one of the streams with you and help you wash Jenka. Just remember to make sure they are strapped on before you get airborne."

Connor wasn't the only Rider in the room looking at Delno as if he'd suddenly taken leave of his senses.

Rita said, "You've got some purpose in mind other than making sure the boys all get along and have a good time, Handsome, but I'll be darned if I can figure it out."

"Well," he said, smiling, "as you know, we are now caught up in Corolan's grand scheme. However, I see no reason not to start implementing Delno's grand scheme."

"I suppose that's why you and Brock sequestered yourselves for several hours before we left?" Rita asked.

"Of course," he responded, "Brock and I had a great deal to discuss. We talked about Horne quite a bit, but that is just one of our problems, and it's more of a symptom than a whole disease itself, and ultimately it's we Riders who are responsible for it all." He paused for a moment then said, "You see, in a way, Simcha wasn't entirely wrong."

Rita nearly jumped to her feet to make a retort to such a notion, but he quickly said, "Calm yourself, Beautiful, and let me explain. The Dragon Riders have become complacent. We expect to be treated well, and be given what we need for our services, but most of us do nothing to earn it. We're little more than figureheads in most places. For all of the complaints that have come out of Horne about the Riders down there taking herd beasts or other goods without payment, those three were the only ones who regularly earned their keep doing what Riders claim to be pledged to do; protecting others."

"And scant thanks they got for their troubles," Adamus spat out.

Delno held up his hand and spoke before he, or either of the others, could get wound up. "Yes, scant thanks, until the Roracks once again began attacking in large numbers. For several generations those Riders flew patrols and kept the people so safe that those same people didn't even realize they were in any danger. Things have changed and we've lost a good Rider and Dragon in the process, but that all just gets back to my point; people become complacent whether they are Riders or just average folks."

He paused while he sipped his drink.

"So, this is the part where you tell us how that and Connor making friends with two local boys comes together, right?" Rita prompted.

"Exactly," he responded. "The whole thing comes together because we don't have any binding oath that Riders take." They all started to object at once, but he held up his hand and said, "Let me finish. I have heard parts of a *code* that Riders are supposed to follow, but no one can recite this code. That's because it doesn't really exist; even Brock admits that. So, once the trouble in Horne is dealt with, Brock and I intend to remedy that situation."

"You're going to ask Riders to swear an oath?" Rita asked.

"Partly," he replied, "but this is where we get back to the beginning, and I tell you what the boys have to do with this." He deliberately paused while he again sipped his drink before continuing. "Most candidates are presented because of their parents' political connections. It's been that way for a very long time. Brock was one of nine candidates and only two of those boys had even the slightest chance of bonding: the rest were the sons of influential men. The problem is that most of those influential men aren't connected to the Riders at all. They simply want to use the hatching as a way of gaining influence politically. That is what Brock and I intend to put a stop to."

"So you're going to select Riders from impoverished families?" Adamus asked.

"No, not necessarily from poor families," Delno replied. "When I was here I noticed that the dragons liked those boys, even spent time talking with them without the Riders around. I asked Geneva about this when we were together in the Dream State, and she said the boys had potential to be candidates. Now that's no guarantee that they will bond, but it means they have a chance if they are presented to a hatchling. The boys like us and have a chance to become friends with a young Rider. Those are the kinds of candidates that Brock and I are looking for; young boys with no political connections to anyone, but who are already our friends. Interestingly enough, we have two boys who are potential candidates, and Gina is carrying two female eggs; quite a coincidence, wouldn't you say?"

"I've got to stop leaving you and Brock alone for hours at a time," Rita said, shaking her head.

"You don't think it's a good plan?" Delno asked.

"Oh, the plan is fine; I just don't like you and him going off and rearranging the social structure of the world without me at least being there to watch," she replied.

"Haven't you forgotten one little point?" Pearce asked.

"The boys' parents?" Delno replied, and the physician nodded. "Well, my friend, that's the last reason that we stopped here before moving on to Corice. Brock and I were hoping to enlist your aid in getting them to agree."

"Now tell me that Nat wasn't in on all of this," Pearce said.

"Right up to his pointy ears," Delno responded. "He's the one who suggested you help, since it was you who arranged for the boys to become orderlies at the garrison in the first place."

"How long do I have to convince these people to allow their sons to be presented?" Pearce asked, more amused than annoyed.

"Well," Delno answered, "Gina is close to her time. Brock, Jason, and Lawrence are going to swing up this way within a fortnight so that she will clutch here in Orlean. Ideally, the boys should have the chance to see the eggs as soon as possible after they are laid."

Later that night, Delno found himself sitting with Geneva on a large ledge, looking out on a reddish sky of swirling cloud shapes. He was always amazed at how real everything felt. He put his hand on Geneva's side and he actually could feel her scales. "It's good to be here tonight, Love," he said.

"I'm happy you came. I would bring you more often, but you are usu-ally preoccupied," Geneva replied.

"I am sorry, Dear Heart; there have been so many demands on my time lately that I just haven't had as much opportunity to indulge myself. I know that you are jealous of Rita, but my relationship with her is quite different from my relationship with you. It's not her who keeps us apart; it's all of the rest of my life."

"I understand, Love," she responded. "I'm actually getting over my jealousy towards her, and I have grown quite fond of Fahwn and the other dragons, as long as we don't have to compete for food and atten-tion. The rest of it isn't your fault, or mine. We were not born to this world to be mediocre. We were born to grand families, and fate has put us in a time that requires us to take charge and help reshape the world."

"Geneva, I do believe that you have grown up," Delno observed. "That was a very mature sentiment."

"Thank you, Dear One," she replied. "I really think that the knowledge my mother passed on to me, coupled with the strength of our bond, has indeed matured me." She looked at him suddenly and said, "Fahwn and Rita approach, so I need to tell you this quickly. I spoke to the old female again just before you joined me. I asked her name, and she didn't answer. When I told her I would not speak to her again until she told me her name, she still refused, and accused me of being childish. Then she said something quite disturbing. She said that I would learn my place and that you and I would both learn respect for her and her rider."

"That is interesting, Love, but she didn't give any hint as to who she is?" Delno asked.

"No, she didn't; in fact she got so upset that I would continue to ques-tion her that the other dragons ejected her for her outbursts. She had just left when you arrived. I feel that we have a powerful enemy, Love; don't neglect your magic practice."

"Yes, a very powerful enemy and I have a feeling about who that dragon really is," he replied.

As Delno finished speaking, Rita and Fahwn came into view. They didn't land; it was as if they had been standing there all along, and he couldn't see them. He suspected that Geneva had prevented them from making contact until she had finished what she had to say. He quickly filled Rita in on Geneva's revelation.

"Looks like you've managed to make a powerful enemy, Handsome. Better work hard at that magic practice; you may need it," she said. "Hey, what's so funny?"

As she had spoken, he had started laughing out loud. "It just seems that all of the females in my life tend to think alike; you just repeated Geneva's sentiment almost word for word."

"Geneva is highly intelligent and shows great wisdom. You should listen to her." Rita responded.

"Thank you, Rita," Geneva replied.

They sat for a few moments and then Rita asked, "So, care to fill me in on the rest of your plan, Handsome?"

"I told you my plan," he answered.

"You told me the part of your plan you want the other Riders to know right now. You haven't told me the rest of it yet," Rita said flatly.

"There is more, but even Brock doesn't know all of it," he said.

She waited a moment and then said, "Well?"

He sighed before answering, "I don't want to lay it all out right now, especially because much is still a work in progress, but I suppose you won't let it go until I do." He looked at her and said, "This stays strictly between me and you." At her nod, he continued, "I've been coming to the Dream State a lot since I bonded, though not so much in the last couple of weeks."

"I knew that, but what does that have to do with your plans?"

"Everything, beautiful but impatient one, everything. I have actually made some tentative contact with several of the wild females." At her astonished look, he said, "It's true; they have come to accept me here, and a few have been willing to have limited contact."

"I don't believe that any rider before you has made contact with the wild females here," she said.

"My grandfather did." He was again rewarded with a surprised look from Rita. "You know that there are about a hundred bonded female dragons, right?" At her nod, he went on, "Well, there are around three hundred wild females in the Dream State most nights. Now, we also know that not all wild females come here all the time. I've been doing the math, and I figure that there must be at least six hundred wild females, and perhaps as many as a thousand. I figured there had to be quite a few from my talks with Nat about breeding pools. Even with magic involved, you still need enough viable adults to prevent inbreeding."

She pondered the numbers for a bit and then said, "But with that many dragons around, wouldn't we see wild dragons more often?"

"That's part of my point. We don't see them because they live so far away from inhabited lands," he replied.

"Where do they live, then?" she asked.

"Well, my sweet, from talking with the wild females, I've come to realize that there is a big world out there. I believe that the world we live in is much larger than any of us imagined. Think of it this way; we just came from Palamore this morning. We left just after dawn and arrived in Orlean not long after noon, and we made two stops to shift our passenger so we didn't tire the dragons. That same distance took a week for Winston and his troops to travel at about eight leagues a day."

"Well, dragons fly much faster than draft animals can walk. . . ." she began.

"That's not the point. The point is that we tend to think of such distances as far because it takes so long for the average person to travel because he is limited to riding a horse, or going on foot. The distances involved aren't as great as we think. When you actually do the math, eight leagues times eight days, it's only sixty-four leagues, give or take a few miles. That works out to about two hundred miles."

"I know you are going somewhere with all of this, but I'm having trouble following," She said.

"Well, since we know that there are a hundred bonded dragons, and they pretty much use most of the territory we have available, then the thousand or so un-bonded females must take up a proportionately larger amount of land. There is a lot of space out there that is uninhabited."

"Inhabited by trolls and Roracks, you mean," she snorted.

"No, it isn't. In the first place, dragons wouldn't tolerate Roracks in their territory, or trolls either, for that matter. The Roracks are hemmed in pretty well. To the north is a range of very high mountains that are barren and extremely dangerous to climb; the rest of their territory is mostly bordered by Horne." He paused for a moment to collect his thoughts. "According to the wild females to whom Geneva and I have been speaking, there are a number of somewhat dangerous animals in the unknown lands, but most are not intelligent, and only a few are active hunters. There are vast stretches of land that have been ignored since the end of the mage wars."

"But why have these lands been ignored? We see that more land is needed. It seems to me that people would have claimed these lands long ago if they were viable," she responded.

"Ah, but they don't know they are there. The mages who waged war on a scale that threatened the very existence of all life on this world nearly destroyed those lands. The territories we inhabit now are what were saved from those wars by the elves and those mages who did work for the common good, but they are also ringed all around with mountains, which makes them isolated from what is beyond those boundaries. The boundaries were raised incidentally as a result of the powerful magic used in that war, but they have served to keep our lands and people safe from the devastation that occurred beyond those barriers. However, it's been tens of thousands of years; I believe those other lands have healed."

"So you intend for the Riders to take those lands?" she asked.

"No!" he answered quickly. "A nation of Dragon Riders would be a very bad idea. Dragon Riders are too powerful to become an independent force with their own country. I think it's good for Riders to remain at least marginally dependent on those they are sworn to protect."

"So, what then, just turn the lands over to whoever wants them? You keep twisting and turning, Handsome. Where are you going with this?"

"At first, I thought turning those lands over to any who would chance moving to them would be the way to go, but knowing that I face a two to three millennium life span gives me a different perspective on the situation as a whole. Before, when I thought of long term I tended to think of decades; now I tend to think in centuries. We have shortages all over. Here in Ondar, crops have failed. . . ."

"That's because of drought," she interjected.

"Partly, but it's also due to over working the land. Fields should be allowed to spend a season sitting fallow every so often to recover. There are also things like crop rotation that aren't happening. You can only get so much back into the soil by piling manure on it and growing the same crop year after year. It won't be that long, by our life spans, until there will be shortages that will bring famine to entire countries."

She was thoughtful for several moments before asking, "So how do we fix this problem?"

"Hopefully, we can. If not, a lot of these people's children and grand-children are going to die. The problems in Horne are slight compared to what is coming if we can't work together for the long term. We need to start by getting as many Riders behind us as possible, including making sure that we control who is presented at hatchings. Then we need to begin to start fostering the idea among the people that everyone is responsible to future generations for how they leave this world in their own time. Finally, we need to help open up new lands to those who will work those lands as stewards, not control them as kings." He drew a deep breath and added, "In the long run, we need to bring people around to a new way of thinking. Seeing themselves as part of the world as a whole and using it responsibly. We have to convince people to think ahead for generations, not just a few years. They have to realize that what they do now will affect their great-grandchildren. As we help them explore and settle new territories, they need to understand that those territories aren't inexhaustible. And finally, we have to do as the dragons have done, though they don't really understand why they've done it, and realize that only so many of us can live on the world without overcrowding it."

She whistled and said, "That's a big job you've set for yourself, Handsome. Come to think of it, it's a big job you've set for us."

"That's why I've worked so hard to make contact with the wild females; I intend to make more eggs available for bonding." Then he smiled and said, "When I pass on my Dragon Blade to new leaders a couple of millennia from now, I want to know that I did everything I could to ensure the survival of our species."

He let that hang in the air as he bid her goodnight and faded from view.

CHAPTER 4

TOM AND JIM were smiling like they had just been told they were getting extra birthday gifts as they climbed onto Jenka behind Connor. They were very crowded, and the ropes that had been rigged for their safety looked a bit uncomfortable, but the two boys were oblivious to such inconveniences. Delno helped Connor inspect the safety lines one more time and admonished him not to forgo the procedure on the return trip, then he bid them farewell. He surveyed the crowd as Jenka gathered herself and pushed skyward. The boys' parents were watching with a mixture of pride and trepidation, but pride was obviously the more prominent of the two emotions; he was sure there would be no problem with presenting the boys as candidates.

He walked over and greeted Pearce. The physician returned his greeting and then said, "Rider, may I present the parents of those two boys. This is Mary, Tom's mother, and the boy's father, Robert. And this is Jim's father, James." Then he turned to the parents and said, "This is Delno Okonan, Rider to Geneva, and grandson of Corolan, who was Rider to Geneva's mother who bore the same name."

As he clasped arms with them, Delno was almost startled by the formality of the introduction. He would have preferred to be on a simple first name basis with these people, but Pearce had insisted that this was best, since it would lend credence to their request. After all, they were asking these people to turn their sons over to the Riders; they needed to know that they were dealing with someone of real authority and responsibility.

The three parents were nearly in awe of being so close to the Rider and could only stand mute while they were torn between the honor of meeting him and trying to watch their sons fly away on the neck of a dragon. To save them any embarrassment, he turned and watched with them until Jenka was just a tiny speck in the sky. Then he said, "Even Brock, who is over five hundred years old, says he still gets a thrill out of watching dragons fly; it's something you never get used to."

Jim's father James was the first of the parents to speak. "I'm sorry my wife couldn't be here; she broke her foot t'other day and couldn't make the trip to town this morn," he drawled. "Healer says you want to get our boys on dragon back as Riders. Why's that?"

"Well, let me say that I'm sorry to hear about your wife's injury. Perhaps, if you will let me, I can stop there and heal it for her."

James looked at him suspiciously, but Pearce quickly added, "Delno is very good at doing magical healings; if he looks at her, she will be as good as new within a few minutes rather being off her feet for two months."

James nodded and said, "I don't want to put you out; it's a two-hour walk, and Healer says you have to leave this morning."

"A two-hour walk is only a few minutes' flight; it will be no trouble. If you will fly with me to show me exactly where we're going, I can even save you the time of having to walk home."

Geneva relayed a message from Rita: "I thought you were in a hurry to be off this morning."

"I am," he replied, "but I am also in hurry to set these people's minds at ease. Taking a few minutes to fly them all home and do a simple healing won't put us out and will go a long way towards making them friends. We are asking them to give us their children; we can give them a little of our time."

Rita smiled and nodded almost imperceptibly.

James spoke again, "That's mighty kind of you, Rider, but you still haven't answered the important question: why did you choose our boys and not some others?"

The other parents looked shocked that the man would speak so bluntly to a Rider. Delno laughed and said, "You are a straightforward man who doesn't mince words, James. I like that."

Mary and Robert relaxed as he continued, "We didn't exactly choose your boys; the dragons did." At their perplexed looks, he explained, "Your boys have been helping us with our gear and such since Brock's arrival over two months ago. They have never shied away from the dragons, and the dragons enjoy their company. It is unusual for a dragon to talk to someone who isn't a Rider unless her Rider requests it, yet the dragons talk freely with your boys. When questioned about this, the dragons say simply that they like the boys and that the boys would make good candidates at a hatching."

"That's all there is to it, then?" Robert asked.

"Pretty much," Delno replied. "I can go out into the village and look for candidates for weeks and not be sure I have anyone the dragons would consider likely. Therefore, we felt we should take the dragons' recommendations into consideration."

Mary stepped forward and said, "I want to thank you, Rider. We are poor people and you are giving my son more opportunity than we could have dreamed possible." Her eyes were wet as she spoke.

Delno held up his hand and stopped further comment, "Before we go any further, let me be clear about one thing. No one is making promises here. Your boys will be presented as candidates, and, if chosen, they will become Riders with all of the duties and privileges that go with it. However, you have to understand that being presented to the hatchling doesn't ensure bonding. The only one who can make that decision is the hatchling; she will choose as she sees fit." Then he chuckled and added, "Of course, so far, we've two candidates and two eggs."

James snorted and then said, "That's still a better chance than it looks like I'll be able to give the lad: he's got my blessing to give it a try." Then he looked at Delno and added, "I suppose that since you are willing to come help my missus, we'd best be off and not delay you any longer."

Delno nodded and said goodbye to the other parents; Mary actually hugged him. Then he helped James get mounted behind him on Geneva while Rita helped Mary mount behind her. Adamus was a bit put out at having to ferry passengers, but he said nothing about it as he helped Robert get seated. Delno would heal Jim's mother's broken foot and then meet them all back at Orlean where they would pick up Nassari and their supplies.

Later that day, after they had been flying for nearly three hours, Nassari was complaining to Delno about anything and everything that seemed to come to his mind, including his disagreement with Delno's plan to present Tom and Jim as candidates to Gina's eggs.

Finally, Delno had had enough. As they set down on their first break, he all but threw Nassari off of Geneva's neck and then jumped down so close to the man they were nearly nose to nose. "Nassari, I've had all of your complaints I'm willing to take. First you don't like flying, then you don't like stopping. Now you don't like that I have taken time to ensure that two perfectly acceptable candidates are presented at hatching. If you don't stop complaining about everything, I will put you down in the next village we pass and you can make your own way, whether back to Palamore, or on to Larimar, as best you can!"

Nassari looked at the other two Riders, who had heard the whole exchange, for support and found them purposely busying themselves to avoid being involved. He looked at Delno hoping that the lecture wasn't serious, but found his friend's attitude was unlikely to change. Then, in typical Nassari fashion, he shifted his own position so fast it was almost dizzying to watch.

"You're right, Del," Nassari said, "I've been a rather large pain in the arse since we left Palamore." He paused for a moment, then seeing that none of the Riders had any interest in disagreeing with him, he continued, "I'm just a bit peeved at being sent on this mission in the first place. Then that whole business with the eggs puts me in a bad position if and when I return to Palamore, but I shouldn't take it out on the three of you."

At Delno's sharp look, he asked, "Now what have I said to upset you?"

"What do you mean that the business with the eggs puts you in a bad position when you return to Palamore?" Delno asked.

"Well," Nassari replied, "the Queen was a bit put out when you commandeered her Rider right out from under her nose. . . ."

"Her Rider? You mean Jason?" Delno was getting more upset by the moment.

"Yes, him, but if you are going to keep interrupting me I will never get around to answering your first question."

Delno glanced at Rita and then said, "Very well, Nassari, continue."

As Rita moved closer so that she could hear better, Nassari went on, "Well, once you had put Jason under your own command, she was a bit put out, but she consoled herself with having the other two Riders who flew with Simcha. She thought that they could be easily controlled." Adamus started to say something, but Delno held up his hand for silence. "Then, when you put them in the air under your control, she consoled herself with the fact that Gina would be clutching soon. You see, she hopes that at least one of those eggs will be presented to a candidate of her choosing; someone whose first loyalties lie with Palamore, not with the riders. It seems that our fair Queen has gotten it into her head the best way to insure the safety of Palamore is to have as many Riders and magic-users as loyal subjects as she can possibly get."

"That woman's scheming never ceases to amaze me," Delno said. "After everything I've told her about the need for the neutrality of the Riders, she plots to virtually steal two eggs out from under our noses."

"You can't really blame her, Del," Nassari responded. "She's only trying to ensure the safety and sovereignty of her country. She really does expect to pass on the leadership soon, and she wants to make sure that if the troubles in Horne spill out on the rest of the world, Palamore is protected."

"Ensure the protection of Palamore against the trouble in Horne? By dividing the loyalties of the Riders?" He shook his head. "Besides, if I wanted to use those eggs for political purposes, I would have sent Adamus with Brock and Lawrence and taken Jason and Gina to Larimar with me so that she could clutch there. I'm sure that between your connections and mine we could have found suitable candidates. However, I am not interested in cementing relationships that way."

"Well, if you would let me in on your plans, the way you used to do," Nassari replied, "I might be able to help you, but you are keeping your hide tiles close to your waist these days. You could try letting your friends in on what you are doing once in a while."

"What I am trying to do," Delno responded, "is ensure that individual kingdoms do not gain control of the Riders. While doing that, I want to keep the Riders somewhat dependent on the generosity of the kingdoms so that we don't end up with another Rider who believes he can govern better than those chosen to do so. I want to do all of that without myself becoming the undisputed leader, whether self-appointed or voted into office, of the Dragons' Riders. I intend that the Riders will be governed by consensus among their own ranks. While I'm accomplishing that, it would be nice to deal with the trouble in Horne in such a way that we don't end up dead with the entire world under the rule of the mad-man who is using the beast-men."

Nassari started to speak, but Delno silenced him. "What I want to do right now is have some lunch and get back into the air," Delno said. He turned to Rita: "It's your turn to carry the passenger when we leave."

"I'll do it, Handsome, but this time he'd better trust in those safety straps and keep his hands to himself, or I'll throw him off and see how well he glides."

Delno looked at Nassari with a raised eyebrow and Nassari said, "Hey, there was some rough air up there. I was just scared, honest."

CHAPTER 5

"**D**ELNO! WAKE UP!"

At Geneva's desperate cries, he came fully awake. He didn't wait to ask what was wrong or even put on his trousers; he grabbed his Dragon Blade and climbed from the tent. Rita, having been similarly alerted by Fahwn, was right behind him. Adamus climbed from his own tent only seconds later. The sound of someone snoring softly came from Nassari's tent.

"*There are two of them, Love, sneaking towards the camp from behind you,*" Geneva told him.

They pivoted towards the intruders. Delno began simultaneously chanting and drawing energy with his mind. He pushed the energy he was drawing directly into the fire that had died down. Apparently Adamus had a similar idea because he grabbed a bundle of wood and threw it on the coals. With the energy Delno was pouring into it, the wood flared immediately, throwing light in a large circle.

"*There is a dragon trying to remain hidden not far away, Love,*" Geneva said, "*Should we do something about her or should we stay near you?*"

"*Stay near until we know more. If they wanted us dead, they could probably have flamed us while we slept,*" he responded, "*but stay ready in case we need to move fast.*"

Just then two figures stepped into the light. One was a young-looking man of about twenty-two; the other was definitely cat-like in appearance. Delno stepped slightly forward and held his Dragon Blade at the ready; he also made sure that all their minds were shielded.

"There's no need for all of that," the young man said.

Delno noticed that the newcomer was quite distracted and seemed more interested in looking at Rita, who was standing there naked, than in talking with either of the men. He nearly stepped into the way to block her from view, but then decided that any distraction to the young Rider was most likely an advantage to themselves. Delno also noticed the faint magical glow of a talisman of some kind the younger man had on under his tunic.

"Just give them the message, and let's get out of here," the cat-man hissed.

The Rider looked at the cat-man with obvious annoyance and Delno said, "So, this is what it has come to on your side of this war; Dragon Riders taking orders from these beasts."

The blonde Rider bristled at the comment and said, "He is my traveling companion, not my superior."

The cat-man growled and said, "I'll show you who is superior when I tell Warrick how you preferred to stand here staring at that naked female rather than delivering the message like you were told."

The rider blanched and said, "You fur-lined idiot, you should never have said that name." The cat-man's eyes went wide, and the youth continued to berate him. "When your species was altered, most of that hair must have grown inward into your pathetically small brain. We'll see who is in trouble when we get back."

He was about to say more when Rita's movement caught his eye. She stepped forward, completely unashamed of her nudity, and said, "So, Warrick isn't dead as had been suspected." She looked at Delno and said, "That explains who that old female was in the Dream State."

Delno only nodded as if this were no real news to him.

The young man couldn't seem to take his eyes off of Rita. Delno asked him, "Who are you, boy?"

"His name is unimportant; you will listen to the message he carries or suffer," the cat-man spat.

"The last of your kind who attacked me ended up with his guts hanging down around his ankles before I finished the job, kitty, so I wouldn't be so quick to make threats if I were you."

The creature nearly screamed in rage and crouched to launch itself. The blonde Rider grabbed its shoulder and said, "He's trying to bait you, fool, settle down, or you will get us both killed." To Delno he added, "Know this, Rider, I am young, but I have been taught well. I have a full-grown dragon who is over two years old, and your dragon has no flame yet. Attacking me would be unwise."

Delno snorted his laughter, "Then you should know this, boy; Geneva may or may not have her flame yet—that is for you to find out—but she has twice already bested a dragon with over seven hundred years of flying experience, and she did it both times without fire." The boy's eyes widened, and Delno continued, "And do not forget, also: Geneva isn't the only dragon you would be facing here tonight if this meeting goes awry. There are two other fully mature dragons here, both with enough flame to make up any deficit on Geneva's part, a fact that one of your furry friend's relatives could attest to if he weren't a pile of ash right now."

"You'll pay for that, human," the cat-man made the word sound like an insult.

Before the youth could stop the beast, it launched itself at Delno with incredible speed. Geneva roared and began moving toward them. Delno got his Dragon Blade up in time and caught the creature in the left shoulder while it was still in the air and then used the momentum of the cat-man's flight to guide it away from himself. Another dragon screamed in the night. Delno didn't recognize the voice, and figured it was the boy's dragon trying to get to the fight.

The cat-man had yowled loudly as the blade bit into its shoulder. The last of these creatures he had fought had chewed narcotic plants to deaden any pain and give itself courage; apparently this one wasn't drugged. Still, though, it did recover somewhat and got to its feet. Before it could attack again, Delno threw his hands forward and jumped, executing a forward roll that covered the distance between him and the cat-man in one move. Much to the astonishment of the beast, Delno came out of the roll with the Dragon Blade pointing forward and stabbed his opponent right through the upper abdomen at the solar plexus. The tip of the sword penetrated all the way through and severed the spine as it did. The man-beast's legs collapsed, almost taking the Dragon Blade out of Delno's hand. As he withdrew the saber, the cat-man tried weakly and in vain to claw him.

Delno turned to the sound of another scuffle behind him, and found Adamus had disarmed the boy and Rita was holding her sword to the young Rider's throat. A quick check with Geneva told him that once the scuffle had started, they had simply informed the boy's dragon that they would kill him if she tried to intervene. She had screamed once in despair and then given up.

At that point, Nassari came out of his tent and said, "What's going on here? You people are making enough noise to wake the dead." Then seeing Rita standing there naked and threatening the younger man, he whistled appreciatively and said, "If you are going to have one of those kinds of parties, you could at least invite me."

Several moments later, with Delno and Rita now dressed, and the young Rider, Paul, tied up, and his dragon, Mariah, under the watchful eye of the other three dragons, they discussed what to do now.

"I say give me a little time with him, and I'll get some useful information from him," Nassari said.

Delno had never quite seen his friend like this. "Nassari, I won't have the man tortured, not even threatened," Delno replied. "He came as a message bearer; it wasn't he who attacked me."

Paul looked at Delno and said, "You already know the name, so I might as well use it. Warrick won't be happy that you have taken me prisoner. You're right; he sent me as a messenger. We came to you under a truce, and you killed one of his emissaries."

"Under a truce!" Rita exclaimed. "You walked into our camp like you owned the land we're sitting on and brought that abomination with you. When you couldn't control it, it attacked Delno for its own reasons, and he had no option but to kill it or be killed by it."

"He goaded the Felanx into attacking him. He obviously knew they are hot-tempered and high-strung," the young man responded.

"The only thing we know about those beasts is that they have attacked us every time they have been given the chance to do so," Rita spat back.

"Enough! This is getting us nowhere," Delno said. Then, turning to Paul, he asked, "What is this message you have brought?"

"Let me go and I will tell you. You can't keep me prisoner; I am under the truce of parlay. That's a rule of war, in case you hadn't noticed."

Delno walked over and knelt beside the young man. "Boy, I was a seasoned veteran of war before you were a Rider. When you enter an enemy camp under truce there are rules, the first of which is don't try to sneak into their camp in the dead of night like assassins, as I believe that beast originally intended," Delno pointed at the corpse of the Felanx. "By rules of war, you make it obvious that you want to talk by getting your enemy's attention with a white flag, and wait for an invitation to come ahead before you do so." Under Delno's harsh stare the younger man began to sweat with fear. Delno continued, "Now then, let's stop all of this nonsense and you just tell me your real purpose here."

"Well," the youth swallowed and said, "We were supposed to scare you, not kill you. We really do have a message from Warrick, though you weren't supposed to have heard that name yet."

"Forget the damned name, boy," Delno replied, "I had figured who was running the show on your side of this long ago. Get on with the message."

The young Rider flinched as though Delno had threatened to slap him, "All right. I was to make it look as though the Felanx was barely under control long enough to scare you. Then I was supposed to tell you that if you travel south and join us, you will be made a commander. If you choose to ignore the offer, he will hunt you down and destroy you."

"How were you supposed to intimidate us with just one of those beasts when four of them couldn't destroy us the first time they were sent in the dead of night?"

"Well," he replied, "we were supposed to take you unawares. The talisman you took from me was supposed to keep your dragons asleep while the Felanx tied you all up before you could stop him." Then he looked a little sheepish and added, "We figured you would be afraid of the Felanx because you'd never seen one before. I guess you ran afoul of some of the six of them that Warrick helped Orson create in Llorn. They were all supposed to be kept a strict secret."

Delno looked at the talisman for a moment, and then he examined it with his magic the way that Jhren had taught him. At first it just glowed with magic the way it had when Paul had been wearing it. Suddenly, he felt as though he were riding a dragon in a head-long dive. There was a rushing in his ears and a feeling of falling, and then he was looking at the back of a man who appeared to be about fifty to sixty years old. The place seemed to have a familiar feel; then he realized this was very similar to being in the Dream State with Geneva.

The man said, "Well, report. Since you're here, that idiot Felanx must be dead, not that I'll miss him, but what went wrong? Did you deliver my message? You didn't kill Corolan's grandson, did you?"

The man shot the questions out rapid fire before he turned around to face the intruder. When he saw Delno, he froze and much of the color drained from his face. He just stared for a long moment.

"Well, from your questions and your reaction when you saw me, I take it you hadn't planned on encountering me here. Since I already know your name, and I'm pretty sure you know mine, I guess we can dispense with the false pleasantries. This is rather interesting" he continued while looking around at the changing hues of the landscape. "Took a lesson from the dragons, I see; created your own little Dream State."

"Oh, it's like the Dream State, except that here I control everything. Only those I permit may come here, and I control what happens," Warrick replied.

As the man spoke, Delno felt something trying to get into his mind; he clamped down hard and Warrick visibly flinched as he was rebuffed. Delno began to look for a way out of this place. At first there appeared to be none; then he remembered the talisman. It was the gateway. He felt for his body and could sense that he was still standing in camp holding the talisman in his hand.

"Well," Delno replied, "like so many other things you have thought to be under your control, I doubt that control is as absolute as you believe it to be."

"We will see, young Rider, we will see," Warrick responded. "I know much of what you have done. You have beaten that fool Simcha; he always was such a worthless rider; self-righteous and totally sure of himself to the end, no doubt. Of course, he was also very easy to manipulate. I will admit that you, on the other hand, have been a bit of an enigma, up until now."

"Only up until now?" Delno asked. "Have me all figured out, do you?"

As he spoke, he continued to use his magical sense to examine the talisman. If he concentrated hard, he could see the portal that brought him here. If he could keep the man talking, he should be able to figure out how reverse the flow at will. The only other option would be to destroy the thing, but that could be dangerous. Also, by applying his will to the object, he could see around himself in the physical world. It was a bit distracting and strange, as if this Dream State was overlaid on his normal vision and he could see and hear both at once.

"Oh, I've had you figured out for some time now," the older Rider said. "You are simply like your grandfather: you have some noble idea that you can twist and shape the world a little at a time and control events in the long run to suit your desires. You see, we're more alike than we are different, you and I."

"Really? I don't see it that way. You seek total control by any means possible, even if it means using the beast-men to slaughter half of the population of the world, and you have no regard for the dragons, either. There is no creature you won't callously use and then cast aside when they are no longer needed. You have no allies, just tools."

He had it now. It was a matter of blending the magic that Jhren was teaching him with the psychic abilities he gained from his connection with Geneva. He could not only reverse the flow and leave when he wanted, he could project the image he was seeing and allow the others gathered to see and hear what was going on. He decided to do that and keep the connection open for a little longer.

"We are all just tools, my young friend," Warrick answered. "You and I are tools of fate. Those I use are just extensions of that; their lives only have what meaning I give them. On your side, you have taken the role of leader in opposition to me. You would sacrifice your allies as willingly as I if the need arose."

"The way you are so willing to sacrifice the young Rider you sent to kill me? Tell me, Warrick. Do you even know the boy's name?"

"I know his name, though that is completely unimportant because his true name, the name I have given him, is Sacrifice. If he is not sacrificed now, to the task I have assigned, then he would simply be sacrificed later in the same cause. However, you have mistaken my intentions; you were not to be killed. My message to you was simple: join me, serve me for the greater good of the world, and we can spare many of your *friends'* lives in the process."

"The greater good of the world?" Delno said. "After all of the death and destruction you've helped bring about, you will forgive me if I am somewhat skeptical of that assertion."

"You are just like your grandfather: you claim to look to the long-term good, but you fail to see what is right under your nose. Do you realize that the food sources of the countries you are trying to protect will decline and fail over the next few generations? That if drastic measures aren't taken, human beings will cease to exist on this world?"

"I've seen the signs of such collapse. I don't see how killing off half the population and allowing the Roracks to live on unchecked to prey on the survivors will solve the problems, though. I prefer to find a solution that is less violent and more aimed at ensuring the survival of the human species rather than supplanting that species with one that shouldn't even have been created in the first place."

Delno could see his companions watching. They were completely unsure of what they were seeing. Rita looked as if she wanted to do something, and he held up his hand to keep her from making any attempt to interrupt or interfere.

"Oh, I have no intention of allowing the Roracks to take control. They are merely tools, as I have said. When they have served their purpose, I will make them turn on each other. Then when they have nearly killed themselves off, I will eliminate the survivors." Warrick smiled and continued, "You see, my very young Rider, I have had over a thousand years to think about this problem; ever since Corolan took me into his confidence concerning how affairs were going among the people of this planet." At Delno's look of uncertainty he said, "What, you didn't know that Corolan had taken other Riders into his confidence concerning his grand plan to bring parliamentary rule to the world? I believe I was the first, but he also confided in Brock, and together they were planning to bring others in. You see, most of Corolan's plans have come to fruition: that's why I ordered him destroyed and had his Dragon Blade brought to me."

Delno tried not to let his surprise and anger show on his face and almost succeeded.

"Does it upset you that I had your grandfather killed? Well, I wouldn't worry too much about it; he was old and would have died soon anyway. I believe that he may have been getting a bit senile, too. He refused to see that the population had to be thinned and those in power needed to be brought under the control of the real ruling class: the Riders."

"And the Riders, of course, need to be under your control," Delno replied.

The sarcasm was lost on Warrick. He said, "Of course they need to be under my control. I am the oldest and wisest Rider. I have Corolan's Blade. I am the one who has learned how to use the compelling stone that controls the Roracks and other semi-intelligent beasts." He paused and then added, "I am obviously the rightful ruler of the world."

Delno laughed and responded, "Well, that is certainly a nice speech, but your plans seem to be going a bit off, from my perspective."

"Oh, I admit that I underestimated you, but it won't happen again. In a way, you did me a favor anyway. By eliminating Simcha, you merely saved me the trouble that he would have caused later. This way I can blame you and not have to explain to the other youngsters under my influence why he had to die. Saying that our enemies killed him goes down so much better than trying to explain that he was too self-righteous to be allowed to remain a living threat to my power. You see, he had the ridiculous idea that he could restore the individual kingdoms to their former state of monarchy. I couldn't allow that idea to settle in after all of the work that I put into pruning the power and purity of the ruling families in the southern kingdoms."

They stood looking at each other for several moments. Warrick finally spoke. "Well then, youngster, what's it to be? Will you join me and save us both a lot of trouble, or am I going to have to kill you?"

"Well, you may find that I am much harder to kill than you suspect, and as for joining you, I've seen how you treat your allies. So, since I face death either way, I think I'd prefer to do things on my own and continue with the immediate plan of stopping you."

Warrick shrugged and said, "So be it."

He pointed at Delno and energy shot out of his hand and hit the younger man right in the sternum. Delno felt an almost crushing weight in his chest. He felt as if his heart might explode. Warrick smiled and said, "You see, boy, I really do control everything that happens here."

Delno didn't even take a second to ponder how the old Rider could make a physical attack in a psychic realm—he simply reacted. He looked for energy to use to repel the attack. The only energy he found was the energy that Warrick was using against him. Desperately, he reached for that and was rewarded by a lessening of the pressure on his chest. Then he turned the energy around and sent it back at Warrick, hitting him full in the face with it. It worked; the older man was so surprised that the attack abated completely.

Warrick was hurt; Delno could see a faint trickle of blood coming from the man's nose. The older man quickly recovered, though, and Delno didn't waste time waiting around to see how this contest would go. There would be another time when he was more ready for a fight. He reversed the flow of the portal and was pushed out of Warrick's psychic realm. Warrick tried desperately to stop him but failed. Delno found himself standing near the campfire with the talisman still glowing in his hand. Rita rushed to his side.

He looked at the talisman and realized that something was wrong. It was not only still glowing with energy, it was beginning to pulse like a malevolent heartbeat, and the energy within it was still growing. Delno became alarmed and looked for a way to dispose of it quickly. He was a bit disoriented, and so wasn't even sure of what direction he could throw the thing. He quickly stepped to the body of the Felanx and shoved the talisman under it. Then he threw his arms around Rita and pulled her down on to the ground on the other side of a fallen log near the fire. Everyone else followed his example and sought what shelter they could find. The talisman exploded, raising the body of the Felanx off the ground almost a foot and nearly blowing it in half. As Delno had hoped though, the body had absorbed most of the explosive force, so no one was injured.

He got up and checked Rita, then himself. Once he was certain that they were both all right, he checked everyone else. The young Rider, Paul, was the most shaken of them all.

"That bastard," Paul said. "He told us how we would usher in a new age, the age of the Riders, when Riders would rule the lands and all would live in peace," he said. "What he planned was for himself to rule the Riders and the rest of us to be his enforcers. Named me "Sacrifice," did he? Well, I'll show him a sacrifice."

Delno let the man wind down. He decided that he would question Paul later concerning all that Warrick had said. The idea of some kind of stone being empowered to help him control the beast-men was a bit of news that he had a feeling Warrick would come to regret revealing. Geneva was looking over the remains of the cat-man.

"*Killing it wasn't good enough, Love? Had to blow it up as well?*" she asked.

"*I had to do something with the damned rock or that could have been any one of us,*" he answered. "*Too bad the talisman was destroyed; I would have liked to have Jhren take a look at it.*"

"*I would like you to have Jhren with you next time you have to deal with that maniac. Also, in the future we only deal with things like this together; don't go off alone like that. You could have been killed,*" she admonished.

"*Next time I have to deal with a maniacal tyrant bent on world domination in close quarters, I will be sure and take you with me, Dear Heart,*" he replied.

"So," Rita asked, "what now, Handsome?"

"Well," he answered, "now we have to keep moving."

"What about our *new friend*? I've been listening to his rantings, and he seems more angry at how he was treated than surprised that he was on the wrong side."

He thought about her question for a few moments and then said, "We have two choices: we can either take him with us, or take him back to Orlean and leave him in the care of the garrison. I'm in favor of the former over the latter."

"I know you tend to look for the good in all people, Handsome, but not all people are good. I believe he will betray us, given half a chance."

"Who will he betray us to, Warrick?" he asked. "Warrick just told him that he was only worth anything as long as he was willing to sacrifice himself to Warrick's schemes. He appears to have had a change of heart in that respect. No, Beautiful, rather than place him in the care of men who have been taught to revere Riders and in the company of a young impressionable boy who might be swayed by the lure of adventure, I think we are all better off if he comes with us. We can watch him closely, and we have three dragons to keep track of his dragon."

As she opened her mouth to protest, he added, "Besides, as punishment for his transgressions, we can make him carry Nassari as a passenger."

He winked, and she shook her head and laughed.

CHAPTER 6

"I DON'T LIKE HAVING that man, Paul, come along with us," Nassari said. "It's dangerous. Suppose that whole thing was nothing but a charade to get you to bring him along so that he can report on our activities?"

"That is precisely what I think he is here for," Delno replied.

It had been one full day since the whole incident that left Paul in their custody. One more full day of travel should see them at the city of Larimar. Nassari had spent the entire flight with Paul on Mariah. Apparently, the young Rider hadn't been much on conversation, and Nassari didn't trust him.

"If that is what you think, then why are you bringing him along?" Nassari was incredulous.

"Do you remember the old saying in Corice, my friend? Keep your friends close . . ."

"And your enemies closer," Nassari finished for him.

"Exactly," Delno replied.

Rita added, "We couldn't just kill the young man in cold blood, and we didn't want to risk leaving him with only one young Rider, Connor, to watch over him and his dragon, not to mention that taking him back to Orlean would have cost us a day's travel time."

"This way," Delno said, "he can't get into much mischief because what we are doing isn't a secret. Also, with Geneva and Fahwn keeping constant watch on both of them, even when they are asleep, they will have a hard time contacting Warrick and telling him anything, especially with the talisman Warrick gave them for that purpose destroyed. In the meantime, he may let something slip that could possibly give us an edge against Warrick."

"I still don't understand. How has he managed to get those dragons to work with the Roracks?" Rita asked. "In all other instances, they are mortal enemies; they kill each other on sight."

"I've asked Geneva to find out about that for me. Her powers have been growing at least as rapidly as my own. There is little one of our dragons can hide from her now if she puts her mind to finding out, and they all seem to obey her without thinking about it."

Later that night as he found himself in the Dream State with Geneva, everything was as he remembered; the reddish changing hues of the cloud formations, the soaring dragons, and the mountain ledge. The only difference was the female dragon sitting near them. She had a distinctive marking that Delno had seen when she was soaring before. He had met her once, very briefly. She was a wild female. Geneva had told him her name; he strained to remember it so he wouldn't appear disrespectful.

A few moments passed then he turned to the wild dragon and said, "Hello, Marlo, it's good to see you. How are you this evening?"

"Lonely, as always." Wild dragons didn't have a knack for human pleasantries, and while they enjoyed the interaction, they tended to answer questions about their state of being honestly rather than using a standard social response such as *'I'm fine, how are you?'* "You are very polite, human. It has been several weeks since we met so briefly. It is good of you to remember my name."

"Marlo has been telling me some troubling news," Geneva interjected. "Now that I have been talking to them about the trouble in Horne, many of them have been telling me about something disturbing."

There was a *ripple* through the Dream State: almost as if Delno had been watching the clouds through imperfect glass and the glass had moved. He had come to recognize that as a warning that their emotions were upsetting the nearby dragons who were communing here. If it continued, he and Geneva would be ejected.

Geneva looked around and then said, "Marlo is close by and would allow you to approach enough to speak with her if you would be willing. You must not bring everyone: she hasn't accepted us completely yet."

"If it makes you feel more comfortable, you may bring the small female human who sometimes accompanies you here," Marlo added.

"You are showing great trust by meeting with me, Marlo; I would dishonor that trust if I brought someone else along. Geneva and I will meet with you by ourselves," he replied.

He tried to disentangle himself from Rita without waking her and failed; the woman tended to sleep lightly as of late. She followed him out of the tent and said, "Now that I'm awake, could you try repeating that? It sounded like you said you were going to meet with a wild dragon, but that couldn't be right; no one has ever met with a wild dragon face-to-face."

"I told you that my grandfather has, and now I shall do so, too," he replied.

"Then I'm coming with you." She stopped to put on one of her boots.

He turned and said, "Rita, I need you to stay here. If you recall, the only two Riders here we can totally trust are you and me. I need you to stay with the others and keep the camp in order."

"I don't mind so much now that I haven't earned your complete trust, Delno," Adamus said from the darkness. "After all, it's only been a few weeks since I flew with a group that tried to kill you, but Rita is right: if you are going to meet with a wild dragon face-to-face, you shouldn't do it on a dragon who still can't breathe fire. You should take Rita with you. If you don't feel that you can trust me enough to watch Paul and Mariah, then leave Rita and take me along."

Delno smiled and said, "You are rapidly earning my trust, Adamus, but I still have to decline your counsel. This female, a little over one hundred years old, has agreed to meet with me. It would be an insult if I abused her trust by bringing someone else. Besides, Geneva may not have flame, but she is a lineage holder and that gives her great authority in Dragon Society even though she is young." He placed one hand on each of their shoulders and whispered, "Stay and watch the camp, both of you, I need to know how, if at all, Paul reacts to me going to meet this wild dragon." To Adamus, he added, "I'm sorry for the subterfuge, my friend, but it serves our purpose right now to have Paul think that I trust you less than I do."

Adamus smiled and nodded, realizing that he had just been brought even closer to Delno's inner circle. He saluted and walked to the fire.

Rita looked like she was about to continue the argument, so Delno took her in his arms and whispered so quietly that someone standing right next them wouldn't have been able to hear, "This is the chance we have been looking for. We know that there are riders working against us in the southwest. This is our chance to start making alliances with the wild dragons which could very well give us the allies we need to end this conflict quickly and decisively." He looked down into her eyes and then added, "I have to do this alone, but you don't have to be left out; I will have Geneva relay what is happening to Fahwn. We'll only be about a league away."

She smiled and stood on tip-toe and kissed him. "Be careful, Handsome, it's taken me over a month to housebreak you; I wouldn't want to have to start all over again with someone else."

He swatted her playfully on the fanny and she clubbed him gently on the shoulder in return as he walked away toward Geneva. Paul was climbing from the tent he shared with Nassari, and he said to Delno's back, "You're insane meeting with one of those wild females alone; Warrick lost two riders trying to establish dialogue with them."

"That's probably why I've had so much trouble arranging such a meeting in the first place. Stay in camp and behave yourself. I want to talk to you about Warrick's attempts to contact the wild dragons when I return."

Delno was pleased at the look of despair on Paul's face. Obviously the young man wasn't supposed to have mentioned Warrick's attempts to contact the un-bonded dragons.

Geneva was ready to fly when he reached her, and he decided against the use of a saddle. He didn't want to take the time to rig it on her, and he didn't want to show up at this meeting looking like he was ready for combat. If this meeting didn't go well, he would simply leave, not fight.

"I have given Mariah strict orders that she is not to fly while we are gone, with or without her rider," Geneva said.

Delno shook his head and said, "It amazes me how easily you and I slip into the role of leaders. Before we bonded, I would have thought that Dragons and Riders were more independent and less easily led."

"You must remember the basics about being bonded, Love," she responded. "Each partner shares everything with the other: emotions, pain, joy, everything. You are bonded to a lineage holder. That is so very much more than just a title of honor among my race. It is also a position of great authority. It is akin to being born a queen among your people. Since I have that authority among the bonded dragons with whom we travel, you tend to have that authority with their Partners."

"Yes," he replied, "I do tend to forget such basics about the bond. I suppose I shouldn't find anything surprising when magic is involved, but it has only been such a short time since I even considered magic in my everyday dealings *with the world around me. Before I met your mother, which was such a very short while ago, I wasn't even sure I believed in dragons, let alone the magic surrounding them and everything they do."*

Geneva launched herself, and they gained altitude rapidly. As always, he was thrilled and somewhat in awe of Geneva's power, grace, speed, and agility. He fervently hoped that he would never lose that sense of wonder at flying with her.

It seemed that they were only in the air a few seconds before Geneva angled her flight in what he had come to recognize as a landing glide. Within a few moments they were on the ground not more than fifty yards from Marlo. Delno dismounted and slowly approached her.

When he was within ten feet of her, she said, "It is good of you to come, Rider of Geneva."

Geneva hadn't informed him of any particular etiquette so he responded to the formal greeting with, "It is good of you to meet with me like this, Marlo."

Marlo seemed satisfied with the return greeting and said, "I have much to tell you. First, know this: your attempts to contact the un-bonded females haven't been met with great success because your enemies have tried such in the recent past. They came to us in the Dream State and talked us into meeting with them. At the first meeting, they tried to convince us of the nobility of their cause, and at the second meeting they tried to use magic to force us to be obedient to them. They received flame for their efforts. We won't be used like they use our beast-men enemies."

"As you have noted," he said formally, "those men were our enemies. I believe them to be the enemies of all intelligent creatures everywhere. They seek only power for themselves and will use whatever means they can to get it. That is why they tried to coerce you with magic. You have my promise that I will do no such thing. If I seek your aid, then I will ask for it and not hold it against you if you refuse for your own reasons. I simply come to you as a friend."

She suddenly looked pained, and, thinking he had erred, he quickly said, "If I have offended you, I apologize. I meant no disrespect."

"I am not offended, Rider. You have come to me with an open mind. You have spoken your thoughts, and I can see them to be true, and you have offered me friendship. Mine is a solitary race by necessity, not choice. Most females feel the need for companionship. That is why some choose to bond and the others choose to dwell as much as possible in the

Dream State. I feel the loneliness more than most, and you have offered me real friendship. It makes me happy, but it makes me more aware that I am alone."

"I am sorry; I would never intentionally cause you pain of any kind." He had moved closer while she was speaking, and he placed his hand on her snout like he had with Geneva's mother.

"That I believe," she responded, and allowed the touch, reveling in it.

Geneva had to fight down the urge to challenge the older dragon for being so openly affectionate with her Rider. She spoke softly, "Marlo, there is still much you must share with my Partner, and daylight will come soon."

Marlo drew her head back away from Delno's hand a bit reluctantly and said, "You are right, Mother of Your Line, we have much to discuss, and I am taking liberties with your hospitality."

Geneva nodded, but said nothing.

"I travel the world and watch your kind closely," Marlo said to Delno. "I am one of the few of what you call wild females who doesn't keep to a specific territory. I avoid the territories of others and hunt on the fringes of human lands. I am careful not to be seen. In fact, the last time I was seen was near the city your people call Larimar. I have always liked watching the people of that city: that time I was distracted watching the young lineage holder finding her wings and was seen by someone who was hunting."

Delno exclaimed, "Then it was you who was seen and not Geneva. That's very interesting, but how come Geneva didn't know you were there?"

"Her powers weren't great enough at the time to penetrate the shield I used to block myself from her. I knew that if she found me, she would be upset that I had inadvertently invaded her territory," she answered. At a slight prompt from Geneva, she went back to the original subject. "Since I travel so extensively for one of my kind, I am in a position to know much about what is going on in the world around me. Nearly a month ago, two dragons and Riders came out of Horne to the city you call Larimar. They kept themselves hidden, but nearly two weeks after they left, a sickness began to sweep through the municipality and people began dying. The sickness continues to devastate Larimar even now."

"Did these Riders use some form of magic to cause this sickness?" Delno asked.

"I do not believe so," Marlo answered. I observed them closely and could sense no extraordinary magic about them. I believe that they brought some sickness with them and released it in the city somehow. I was able to watch them, but not able to get close enough to hear them when they talked to each other."

Delno asked, "How are you able to observe other dragons so easily without being seen?"

"Since I must occasionally cross the territories of others of my kind in my travels, I have gotten very good at avoiding being caught," she replied. "Otherwise, my urge for companionship would get me into trouble quite often."

Delno smiled as he thought about that, and then said, "Well, what you say makes sense. If our enemies thought we might look to the north for help, plague in their biggest city would certainly prevent them from sending men and arms. The Riders could have been carrying something as a vector without fear from the disease because the magic makes them immune. Since the plague is not magical in origin, magic will be less effective against it."

"Something must be done," Marlo exclaimed. "I am fond of watching your species, and it pains me greatly that those people suffer and die like this."

"Is there nothing you can do to heal the sick, Love?" Geneva asked.

"I will do what I can," he replied, "but sickness is different than a broken bone or a cut. It is more of a foreign invader and harder to find and eliminate." He slammed his right fist into his left palm and said, "Damn it, we should have brought Nat along with us."

Marlo asked, "What is Nat? Can it help these people?"

"Nat is a 'who,' not a 'what,'" Geneva explained.

"Nat, or Nathaniel, is perhaps the best healer in the kingdoms right now," Delno added. "There may be a better healer among the elves, but not among the humans."

"Where is this Nat now, and why can't he be brought here?" Marlo inquired.

"He is in Palamore, and the reason he can't be brought is that we are escorting a prisoner as well as trying to carry out a diplomatic mission," Delno answered.

He quickly explained about their mission, and about Paul, to her while he paced impatiently. She watched him and listened until he had finished, and then she was silent for several moments, deep in thought.

"You are right," Marlo said at last. "It would take you over a week to get your whole party to Palamore, and then you would have to collect the healer and return, which would take at least another week."

"Not to mention the time spent there dealing with the myriad problems that the Queen will lay on us that will further delay our return trip," Delno said disgustedly. "In the meantime, this plague will continue to sweep through my homeland."

Geneva added, "We can't even contact Brock and ask him to fetch Nat because he is so far away, and we need to keep Gina away from Palamore until her eggs are laid."

They were all silent for several minutes, and then, suddenly, Marlo said, "I will go and fetch this healer from Palamore."

Geneva and Delno were both stunned. They knew that Marlo liked humans, but to put herself in direct contact with them like this to save the people of Larimar was totally unexpected.

Geneva said, "Are you sure of this, Marlo?"

"Yes," Delno added, "you will have to go to Palamore and deal directly with the people there, and once you have found Nat, you will have to fly him back here."

"I understand what I must do," she replied, "and while it frightens me, I am willing to do it to try and save the people of this city."

"I wouldn't have asked it of you," Delno said, "but since you have offered, I am happy to accept your assistance, and I thank you and applaud your actions. If you would be willing to fly with us to our camp, I will write a letter to Nat so that he will be assured that this isn't some trick of our enemies."

In camp later that day, Nassari asked, "How long will it take for her to return with the healer?"

"The same amount of time as it would take the last three times you asked that," Rita answered, obviously annoyed.

"Well," he retorted, "perhaps it is easy for you to sit idly and wait; you have no relatives or friends in Larimar."

As Rita was about to make a heated reply, Delno intervened, "Peace, both of you. Nassari, I know you want to go and help our people. However, we are not healers. I might be able to help one person at a time magically, but that is a slow, drawn out process and would be a drop in the bucket. We need Nat's skills. Hopefully, he will be able to come up with some herbal remedy that can be widely distributed."

"And what if he can't find a cure?" Nassari asked irritably.

"Then the delay won't make that much difference either way," Delno responded. Then he put his hand on his friend's shoulder and said, "Nassari, I have family and friends there, too. I find myself in the unique situation of having to leave those who are already at risk in their current position to bring aid that might save the greater number. Also, I can't take you to Larimar because unlike us Riders, you don't have any special immunity to this plague. If you hadn't refused to go so adamantly, I would have happily sent you back to Palamore with Marlo to keep you safe."

"It just seems like it will take so long to get help here," Nassari complained. "It took us days to get here; how long will it take for one dragon to return?"

"I know," Delno replied. "However, without a passenger to slow her, Marlo can soar on the winds without stopping. She doesn't even have to stop for nightfall the way we did. She will reach Palamore sometime toward early morning. When she finds Nat, who will be at the palace where she will land, she will explain the situation and give him the letter I wrote. I included things in the letter that only he and I know, so he should have no problem trusting Marlo. They should be on their way back no later than the day after tomorrow and here within two days of that." Then he gave Nassari a sad smile and added, "It's the best we can do, my friend."

Delno needed a break, both from the monotony of waiting in camp and from Nassari. He went to Geneva. *"How are you holding up, Dear Heart?"* he asked.

"I am less impatient than your friend," she responded. *"If he doesn't stop pacing around the camp like that, he will wear a rut in the ground."*

"He is anxious to go and help our people in Larimar. I can't really blame him; I would like to rush there and do something myself."

"You aren't worrying everyone else with your impatience, Love," she replied.

"Unfortunately, Love, I'm a veteran of enough military campaigns that I've learned to hide such anxiety, even when people are dying while I have to wait. I have to say, there are times I wish I had never learned that lesson."

"I know, Dear One, and I would change that if I could, but it is part of what makes you who you are."

He leaned against her side and just let the feeling of closeness take away some of the anger, guilt, and helplessness that he felt.

After a few moments, she asked, "Did you learn anything from Paul when you questioned him?"

"Concerning his knowledge of this plague or his knowledge of Warrick's failed attempts to control the wild dragons?" He answered her question with questions of his own.

"Either," she replied. "Does he know anything?"

"Well, he claims that he only knows that Warrick sent emissaries to the wild dragons twice. He also claims that those emissaries were flamed without provocation at the second meeting. It's more likely the wild dragons took the attempted use of magic to coerce them as an attack and rightfully defended themselves." He sighed and took a moment before he continued. "As to the plague, he says that he has no knowledge of that at all. I actually tend to believe him; not because he is trustworthy, but because Warrick wouldn't trust such information to him knowing that he would most likely be questioned by us once he had been captured."

"Well, I have been thinking about how Warrick gets the dragons to work with the Roracks, and I have a theory," she said. "I have questioned Mariah about this and she says that, although it went against her inner feelings, she did so. She and the others simply did as their Bond-mates desired, but now that she has been away from Horne for a few days, she again feels the hatred my race has for the Roracks. I believe that Warrick uses that stone he mentioned on the dragons. I think that he tried to use it on the wild dragons, and it failed because we are so resistant to magic. However, he can use it on the bonded dragons of the Riders who follow him because the Riders' compliance to his will makes the difference."

"That does make sense," he responded. "Now that she is no longer under the direct influence of the compelling stone, and her contact with Paul is limited, she has reverted back to her inborn enmity toward the beast-men. Perhaps the stone has range limits as well, and that played a part in why it failed to control the wild dragons. Warrick sent emissaries, but he didn't go himself, and he isn't likely to let that stone out of his possession. All of this is conjecture, but it is probably close to the mark and could be helpful." Then he shook his head, "There are still too many 'maybes' involved when the fate of so many is at stake. I wish we knew more about this compelling stone that he uses."

"You will put it all together when the time comes, Love," she said. "But for now, you are tired and distraught. Rest while you can; I have a feeling that you will be very busy in Larimar."

Delno didn't argue, or even comment; he simply lay down with his shoulders and head resting against her front leg, closed his eyes, and let sleep take him.

CHAPTER 7

IT WAS A good thing that dragons could go for several days without sleep. Marlo had not stopped to rest since the Rider had given her the letter to carry to Palamore. As the sun was coming up the next morning, she glided down toward the city. She had been warned that she might be feared when she showed up at the palace without a rider, but she would be patient and would not make sudden moves. She also resisted the urge to fill her flame bladder. She did not intend to show any aggression when she landed.

As she touched down in the central courtyard, several servants at first looked for her Rider. Seeing that she not only bore no human, but didn't even wear a saddle, they hurriedly ran to get someone in authority. It wasn't long before nearly a dozen humans approached in a group. Some were armed with spears, which she had been told to expect. The armed guards seemed to be especially protective of the female human in the group. They stood in front of her with their weapons ready.

Everyone stood stock still and waited. Neither the dragon nor the people even spoke; they just watched each other. The men with spears held them ready but didn't overtly threaten the dragon with them. The dragon was careful not to show her teeth or click her claws nervously on the paving stones. Several minutes passed.

Finally the woman said sharply, "This is ridiculous. If this dragon meant me harm, we would all be dead by now. Stand aside so that I can talk with her and see what she wants."

Marlo was impressed with this female; she showed good sense. The men reluctantly lowered their weapons and let her through.

"Are you the Queen of Palamore?" Marlo asked.

"I am," the woman replied. "Do you bring message from your Rider? I'm sorry, but I don't recognize you."

"I am a friend of the pair you call Delno and Geneva. I am what you refer to as a wild dragon; I have no rider."

Marlo could sense the human's confusion, but she was pleased that the Queen didn't react badly to her being un-bonded.

"I have a message for one called Nathaniel," Marlo said, using Nat's proper name to show respect. "If he is present, I will give it to him."

"He is in his quarters," the Queen replied. "I will send for him."

The humans were obviously confused, but sent for the physician. Marlo waited patiently. After several moments, a man came into the courtyard who matched the image of Nat that Geneva had put into her mind. "I am Nathaniel," he said as he approached.

"I have a letter from the one you call Delno," she responded. "It is tied to my wrist; you will have to cut the cord to retrieve it. Approach slowly, and I will not harm you."

Marlo quickly decided that she liked this man; he approached her without fear, and she had a sense that he liked dragons as much as she liked humans. That was good, since they would be traveling together for a time. Nat used his sickle-shaped herb blade to cut the cord, and then he stood right next to the dragon while he unrolled the letter as if doing so was the most natural thing in the world.

Nat noticed the Captain of the Palace guards trying desperately to get his attention. "What is it, Captain?" His annoyance at being kept from the communication was obvious in his voice.

"That's a wild dragon; you should come back over here," the man said, then looked ridiculously scared because he realized that the dragon could hear and understand every word he'd just said.

"Really, Captain," Nat said, still annoyed, "if this person wanted me dead, I'd either be a pile of ashes or a mushy spot on the pavement by now; a few more feet one way or the other wouldn't make much difference. Now, if I may do so in peace, I will read this letter from Delno." Then he turned his back dismissively on the rest of the humans assembled in the court yard: the whole interaction impressed Marlo with Nat's good sense and his courage.

To put the humans more at ease, Marlo had laid down on the paving stones so that she wasn't standing as if ready to fight. This put her front legs out in front of her. Nat, as was typical for him, was so engrossed in reading Delno's letter that he simply sat down on the nearest thing that was even close to being high enough to use for the purpose. That thing just happened to be Marlo's foreleg. He settled down right at the crook of her elbow and finished reading the letter. Marlo wasn't sure what to make of this contact. It wasn't offensive, so she just let him stay there.

The rest of the people all gasped when the physician sat on the leg of the wild dragon. They had heard stories of people being attacked by wild dragons. It was said that wild dragons were wild by choice and had little tolerance for people. Of course, it was also said that wild dragons kept to themselves and avoided human areas as well.

Nat finished reading the letter. It was certainly authentic; it contained information that only he and Delno knew about their first few days in each other's company. Since it was authentic, he had to conclude that the call for him to come was equally genuine. He looked around thoughtfully and suddenly realized where this nice couch had come from.

He stood and turned to face the dragon. "I am sorry for taking the liberty, my dear, but I get distracted when something catches my attention. I hope I didn't offend you by sitting on your leg."

While his apology was real, he still showed no fear. Marlo found that rather refreshing for some reason and said, "It's all right. I took no offense."

The two stood regarding each other for several moments, and then Marlo said, "Since you have read the letter, you know that Delno wants you to accompany me. How long will it take you to be ready?"

"At least a couple of hours, I'm afraid," Nat replied. "How much weight can you safely carry? I have some supplies I would like to bring."

"I can easily carry your weight plus that much again in supplies if you have some way to rig them in place. It may be hard to fly if the weight shifts around much."

"Very well, I will make arrangements and see what can be found to use to rig my supplies to your satisfaction, if you don't mind waiting here while I go get everything taken care of," Nat said and turned back to the group of people who were watching in amazement.

Nearly two hours later, Nat was ready to go. They had found an old dragon saddle in the livery. The straps were a bit dry rotted, but it only took the livery's leather worker a little over an hour to make it serviceable. With Nat strapped on and his supplies tied in place, Marlo was ready to fly. Nat had asked Marlo if she would be bothered by him carrying his long knives on his back and she had said that she would not mind.

"I haven't ever flown before," he said.

"Does the prospect scare you?" Marlo asked.

"Certainly not! I'm thrilled with the very idea of it. I am sure that I will enjoy this immensely," he said with a huge smile on his face.

"Very well," she replied, "here we go."

She crouched down and launched in typical dragon fashion. Nat was absolutely thrilled with the sensation of flight and the feel of the dragon beneath him. He had remembered what Delno had said about the temperature at higher altitudes and had dressed accordingly.

It was difficult to talk with the dragon while flying, and, since they weren't bonded, she didn't speak directly in his mind. Therefore, there wasn't much to do except enjoy the ride. After about three hours, he began to feel the urgency of nature's call and shouted to Marlo to land. She obliged and began gliding down in a spiral toward a small clearing.

Once in the clearing, Nat didn't take time to walk out into the bush. As is typical of elves and physicians, he was not shy about his bodily functions, which is what saved his life. He was just finishing when Marlo said, "There are two creatures sneaking up on us. They have separated and appear to be hunting us."

Nat had just drawn his long knives when one of the cat-men leaped at him from the edge of the bush. If he had been bashful and gone further away from Marlo, he would have been killed. The initial attack was fierce, but the creature misjudged the distance slightly, so Nat was easily able to use his left blade to block the heavy weapon that the cat-man was trying to decapitate him with while he slashed out with his other long knife. Nat's right blade found its mark and opened a long, deep gash in the cat-man's side that began just below the armpit and continued all the way to the creature's waist. The beast screamed in agony but rolled back to a fighting crouch as it hit the ground.

Nat barely noticed the movement to his left and slightly behind him. He needn't have worried though; Marlo plucked the second cat-man out of the air mid-leap and slammed it to the ground hard enough to break nearly every bone in its body. The creature didn't have a chance to scream as the air was knocked from its lungs by the force of the impact. It tried feebly to rise, but Marlo slammed her front foot down on the beast, piercing its torso with her claws and pinning it to the ground. It was quite dead.

The first cat-man, despite the terrible wound Nat had given it, recovered and attacked. The attack was clumsy though, and Nat simply blocked the roundhouse swing with one blade while using the other to stab directly into the creature's throat; then he twisted the blade and slashed to one side, severing the major vessels on that side of its neck. It stumbled for a moment trying desperately to continue the fight, but its struggles only made it bleed to death faster.

Nat made sure both creatures were dead, and then examined Marlo to ensure that she had taken no hurt. Then he examined himself to ensure that he was also still completely intact.

"Can't you feel it if you have been wounded?" Marlo asked.

"Usually, but the body produces substances that help give humans a burst of energy in such situations; sometimes those same chemicals cause a reduction in the ability to feel pain. I've seen men who were grievously wounded but didn't know it because their bodies had secreted so much of the chemicals that they could not feel the pain of their injuries. So, it's always best to check and make sure rather than assume."

"And you checked me first," she replied. "I thank you."

"What? Oh, sorry; I was looking at the creatures, I'm afraid. They are quite an abomination, but that doesn't make them any less fascinating," he responded, and then added, "Now then, what were you saying?"

"I was thanking you for making sure that I wasn't harmed," she said smiling at him.

"Oh, yes, well, you're quite welcome, my dear; it's the least I could do, since you saved my life, and, thank you, by the way."

Marlo chuckled at Nat's mannerisms and said, "Well, if you are through, we should probably get back into the air. We still have a long way to go."

"Yes, I'm quite through, and I could happily spend the rest of my life flying with you. It is such a wonderful sensation. I do thank you so very much for carrying me. I must admit, as enamored with dragons as I am, I never dreamed that I would actually get to fly with one."

Within a few moments they were airborne. This time they didn't stop until Marlo felt Nat lying forward on her neck and realized that the man was asleep. She was mildly surprised that he hadn't asked her to set down for a rest break. She glided in and landed near a large stream. Nat woke only long enough to disengage all of the gear so that Marlo could be comfortable. Then he couched himself with his head resting on her foot and slept.

When they woke, Nat quickly prepared a meal and hot beverage. He added herbs to his drink that would help his immune system keep him from catching this plague he was going to treat. Marlo was curious about all of his doings, so he explained everything to her. She expressed her amazement that he would put himself at such risk to treat people he didn't even know, and he simply explained that sometimes healers did that. She was still impressed with his courage.

The sun had been up for over an hour as they lifted off the ground. As Marlo circled, they hit a sudden cross wind that caused her to nearly roll over. Nat laid forward and clutched her neck, the way that Delno had been told to do by Brock, and let dragon's instincts take over. He was facing the sun and it was unusually bright until she righted herself and turned away from it.

They flew nonstop this time until they reached the camp where Delno and his party were waiting for them: it was late evening and the sun was setting. Marlo had flown slightly more leisurely on the return trip for Nat's sake, but even so, they made it back by the end of the third day since she had left. The Dragon had pushed hard and wanted nothing more at the moment than to go to sleep. She glided down and landed near the other dragons. Once on the ground, Delno and Rita quickly filled Nat in on all that had happened since they had parted company.

"Well, since there were only six Felanxes *made* in Llorn and we killed four while still in Ondar, the two that you and Marlo killed are quite likely the last of them in the north," Delno said.

As Nat sat near the campfire drinking some of the herb tea he had made for himself and Nassari, he kept rubbing his chest. "What's wrong, my friend? Were you hurt by the Felanx that attacked you?" Delno asked.

"No," the half-elf replied, "Marlo was buffeted by a strong cross wind, and I think I abraded my chest on her scales while I was hanging on."

"Better let me take a look," Delno responded, "We'll be moving on to Larimar tomorrow, and I don't want you treating contagious patients if you have any open sores."

Nat felt a little foolish being so concerned over a minor inconvenience, but he also recognized that Delno was right. He removed his shirt and Delno examined the injury.

"Nat," Delno said in an astonished voice, "I can't heal this."

"You can't? But I've seen you heal injuries that were much more severe than this," Nat responded.

"That is no injury, my friend," Delno replied. Then he put his hands on the physician's shoulders, looked him and eyes and said, "That, Nathaniel, is a Dragon Mark."

Nat's eyes went wide, and he simply stared at Delno, unable to make coherent speech. Then he examined the mark much more carefully. Delno was right. It was a reddish color, like a wine-colored birth mark. It was dragon shaped in the vaguest, most abstract way.

"Soon, my friend," Delno said, "That mark will begin to take on Marlo's orange color with that distinctive yellow star shaped mark on her chest." As Nat still stared at him incredulously, he added, "You're a bonded Rider now."

It took nearly two hours before Nat was ready for more conversation. He had walked to the edge of camp and stood staring at his Partner almost that whole time; not moving, just watching her sleep. Then he simply turned around and walked back to the campfire as if nothing had happened.

"Marlo told me everything she knows about the plague in Larimar while we were traveling together," Nat said as if there had been no break in their conversation. "She apparently doesn't know much; she could only get so close to observe without being seen. She really did try her best, though." He added the last part almost defensively as if he didn't want anyone thinking less of her because she hadn't put in enough effort.

"Marlo has made an extraordinary effort at helping us." Delno replied. "Just forewarning us was worth much, and then for her to go and retrieve you was more than we could have hoped for."

"Of course, she bonded with him," Paul spat out, as if doing so was some kind of insult.

"Yes," Delno said, "she bonded with him. I find that a very happy coincidence for both of them. Why do you find it so distasteful?"

"It's not natural that he should bond with a mature dragon, and he's an elf," Paul was able to make the last observation because Nat had taken to wearing his hair in a ponytail since leaving Orlean.

"Half-elf; the eyes would be slanted if I were a full elf," Nat replied, as if instructing an idiot.

Paul glared at the physician and said, "There has never been an elf Rider."

"I've heard that," Delno stated. "It's about time there was. I think Nat is a natural Rider, and I'm quite pleased with the fact that he and Marlo have bonded."

"Two unnatural acts in one," Paul replied, "a half-elf bonding with a wild adult dragon. Only humans should bond with dragons, and then only with hatchlings."

"Really?" Rita said, "Then how did humans first bond with dragons? Do you think some wild female simply surrendered her eggs? I find that hard to believe, and legends suggest that the first riders went into the mountains during the earliest wars with the Roracks and emerged onto the battle field weeks later on dragons, flaming their enemies to ash." Then she wrinkled her nose and added, "That would be a neat trick for a dragon only a few weeks old."

Paul started to make a reply, but Nat cut him off. "I have to say that, at this moment, I don't really care about any of this. We were discussing the current situation in Larimar. Now whether this man's," he indicated Paul, "interruption was planned to disrupt our conversation, or whether he is just a racist isn't important at this time: what is important is that I believe that I have an idea of what is afflicting the people of Larimar and how to cure it."

Paul stared at Nat open-mouthed.

"You already know?" Delno said, "That is good news. Tell us more."

"Well," Nat replied, "as I was saying, Marlo told me of her observations. They weren't made up close, but dragons can see many times farther than humans. From the markings caused by the disease, I believe it is a sickness common to Roracks. They catch it the way humans catch the common cold. However, when it spreads among humans, it causes death in more than half of those afflicted. Those who survive will have some immunity from further infection. There hasn't been a serious outbreak in Horne for nearly a century because most of those in that country have developed some resistance. If it has returned, then we must work fast here and then send word to the healers who are in Horne."

"Oh, yes," Paul said belligerently, "we must drop everything and rush to Horne to our deaths. If the plague is no threat to the people of Horne, why do you seek to send your friends to their deaths trying to warn them, Half-elf?"

"Because," replied Delno, "the men who have been sent to Horne to assist in the fight against the Roracks will have no such protection. Why would you want to keep us from contacting the healers there and saving those men, Rider from my enemy's camp?"

Paul shot to his feet and reached for his sword, then remembered it had been taken from him. "I have given you information; I have stated my hatred for the leader of your enemies, yet you give me insult in return for my assistance. Now either give me satisfaction, give me leave to go my own way, or give me death. I will no longer tolerate such treatment."

Delno looked at the man for a long time. Finally he said, "Go, and do not rejoin our enemies. I have spared your life once; if we meet again and you oppose me, I will not hesitate to kill you. You may take your possessions, other than your weapons, and Mariah may not fill her flame bladder within a day's flight of this camp."

The young Rider looked hard at Delno and then said, "I go, and I will not report to Warrick on you. I was supposed to be captured and spy on you; that you know. What Warrick doesn't know is that I heard what he said about me. I do think that he is not the just man I had first believed him to be. I am also not ready to give my aid over to the camp of one who would readily take in half-elves as allies. I will go away and await the outcome of the coming conflict. When that is decided, I will make a more permanent decision concerning you and your plans."

"Remember one thing," Delno replied, "if you do not return like a beaten dog to your master, and I am not successful, Warrick will not forgive you for deserting him. If you do not go back, then I suggest that it may be in your best interest to aid my cause rather than simply await the outcome. But that is for you to decide; I merely give you the freedom to make that choice on your own. But know this: If you do prove false and return to your master, then I will kill you the next time we meet."

Delno turned his back on the man in final dismissal. He didn't stop Paul from taking what supplies he owned, and Paul didn't try to retrieve his weapons. Then the younger Rider walked to his dragon, and Delno informed Geneva that Paul and Mariah were free to leave, and the dragons need only ensure that Mariah didn't fill her flame bladder.

Marlo was a bit angry that the enemies were allowed to leave peacefully, but Nat was in contact with her and quickly quieted her down. Then he went to her, and they stood together for a long time.

When Delno asked Geneva what was going on with Nat and Marlo, she informed him that the two were simply finding their own space with each other, and all would be well. Geneva approved of the bonding, too.

CHAPTER 8

THE NEXT MORNING Delno awakened everyone early. They ate a quick breakfast, and Nat prepared an herbal tea for Nassari. The tea would help keep Nassari from contracting the plague when they got to Larimar.

"What about you?" Delno inquired. "Aren't you going to drink some of that tea, too? You haven't been bonded long enough to be immune to disease. That part of the bond can sometimes take up to a year to become effective. That's why Rita got that infection that your father had to treat even though she and Fahwn had been bonded for six months."

"Oh, don't worry about me, my friend," Nat replied, "I get some immunity from being part elf, and I have been exposed to this sickness enough times in the past that I am already fully immune. I will be fine."

Delno felt compelled to double-check Nat's saddle before he would allow his friend to mount. Then, after ensuring that all of their supplies and equipment were secure, they got airborne. The dragons always seemed to revel in taking flight in the early morning as the sun was just coming over the horizon. They each stroked their wings hard to gain altitude as if trying to get higher than the others to be the first to actually see the sun appear on the crest of the world.

"You are in high spirits for one who is flying into a tragedy, Dear One." Geneva said.

"Nat will set Larimar right in short order, Dear Heart, and it is delightful to see him with Marlo; they are a good match."

"Yes, they are, and it doesn't hurt that her bonding with Nat will help your plan to enlist the aid of the wild dragons, either."

"I didn't plan it this way, Love, but I'll take any advantage I can get at this point," he responded.

"Hers was a particularly tragic case, Love," Geneva replied. "She was meant to be bonded and has lived just over a century in total loneliness. However, don't expect that all wild females will wish to join up and bond with riders."

"I don't expect that. I do hope, however, that some of the wild dragons will see the sense of helping us and will join our cause. With their help, we gain allies of incredible power. I would like to force Warrick into submission, but failing that, I would like to defeat him with as little loss on our side as possible, and the way to ensure that is to have overwhelmingly superior numbers."

"We shall see, Dear One, we shall see. It should be easier to get the wild females to aid your cause now that Marlo has joined. At least they will listen without prejudice."

They flew on through the morning and only stopped very briefly for a mid-afternoon meal. An hour or so later, Nat spotted something that made him land. He and Marlo had located herbs that would help the plague victims. It was a relatively common plant that grew wild in the wetlands of Corice. Nat had all of the Riders gather and carry as much as they could. Then they flew on and didn't stop again until Larimar was in sight.

Delno could tell right away that something was wrong, and not just the plague. The fires on the walls were lit and there was a large force of men and equipment just out of bow range on the fields outside the city. As they got closer, it was clear that the force was a besieging army, and they were building siege engines to blast holes in the city walls. Delno recognized the colors that the army on the field was flying. Apparently, Bourne had once again renewed hostilities against his homeland.

He had Geneva relay orders that Fahwn and Beth were to flame the ground far enough in front of the siege engines to avoid casualties but close enough to get the message across that they shouldn't attack the city. As Beth went down to flame near one of them, Fahwn did the same with another. Just then Geneva said, "Hold on, Love." There was a strange sensation behind him, and then he realized that she had filled her flame bladder and was preparing to make a strafing run at the third siege engine. Delno managed to make sure that Geneva firmly impressed on

Marlo the importance of keeping Nat out of such activities, and then he was lost in the marvel of riding a flaming dragon.

The result of the display was just about what Delno had expected. The soldiers of Bourne were scurrying around like ants when you kick an ant hill. He had Geneva and the rest land close enough to the walls of the city that they would be out of bow range of the Bournese. He really hoped that his own people didn't open fire on him.

The archers of Larimar held their fire, but watched the dragons and riders warily, ready to launch a hail of deadly missiles. The riders all sat motionless for a long time, and then Delno rummaged through his pack until he found his white shirt. He then waved the white shirt at both camps. It took nearly a quarter of an hour before he saw white flags being waved from either side. Seeing that both agreed to parlay, he dismounted and instructed the other Riders to do the same.

They still had to wait for over an hour before the diplomats from both armies appeared and began to make their way to the center of the field. The men of Corice and those of Bourne stopped nearly a hundred feet short of actually approaching the dragons. Finally, Delno, Nassari, and Nat walked to a spot that was midway between the two groups and about hundred feet to the side of where the dragons had landed. This seemed to satisfy the others and they approached the Riders.

The first thing that Delno realized was that he recognized the military officers from both armies. The two officers from Larimar had been commanders when he had been promoted, and the two from Bourne had both been present at the signing of the peace treaty between the two countries at the end of the last war.

Delno greeted the officers from Larimar first. The one wearing Colonel's insignia had been a captain the last time Delno had seen the man; his surname was Dreighton. The other, now a captain, had been a lieutenant and his surname was Porter. Both men were astounded to find Delno Okonan here under such circumstances and wanted an explanation. Delno promised they would get that later.

Delno then turned to the group from Bourne. "As you can see, Gentlemen, I am from this kingdom. I am a veteran of the last war between our two countries . . ." he began, but was cut off by the Bournese general.

"I know perfectly well who you are, Delno Okonan. Even those in Bourne who don't know your face have heard your name. You are the man who led fifty Corisians and held Stone Bridge against nearly six hundred of our troops, and all you got for your effort was a promotion to lieutenant. If you joined the Bournese Army, you would be given a position commensurate to your worth."

"I arrive, it seems," Delno responded, ignoring the attempt to sway his loyalty, "in time to lend assistance to my countrymen when they are in the middle of a crisis of plague, only to find an army from Bourne besieging my home as well. Why has Bourne attacked Corice?"

One of the officers of Bourne answered, "We seek recompense from Corice for the expense of the last war. We were never compensated for the losses we suffered in men, material, and money during that time. We have come to collect that debt."

The officers and delegates of Larimar started to speak up, but Delno held up his hand for silence. "You seek recompense?" Delno asked. "Recompense for a war that you started without provocation? You swept down out of the north and attacked this land, and we spent two years of bloody hell repelling your armies. You created a war which nearly bankrupted both countries, and now you seek reimbursement?"

"We don't see it that way," the Bournese officer said flatly. We merely moved into disputed lands; lands that belong to Bourne. We lost much in that war, and in the end we were forced to give those disputed lands to Corice in order to have peace. We have realized that doing so was a mistake and have come to rectify that situation."

"Oh," Delno replied, "and the fact that the treaty your king signed states clearly that there are no disputed lands doesn't mean anything?"

"The king signed that treaty as much for the benefit of Corice as for anything else. It was a magnanimous gesture that he has since come to regret." The man's mannerisms were beginning to wear thin on Delno.

"Larimar is not situated in, or even near, any of those places. Are you quite sure that you haven't been advised by outside parties that Corice has been weakened and is ripe for the taking?" Delno asked.

The man suddenly became uncomfortable. He shifted from one foot to the other, and he was no longer willing to look Delno in the eyes. "Our sources of information and our purposes are none of your concern," he said. "What is of your concern is that I have more than enough men to bring this city to its knees. You will either surrender or be conquered."

"And what is of your concern," Delno spat back, "is how many of your soldiers you are willing to see killed by dragon fire if you don't pack up and leave Corice immediately. That little demonstration we gave you this afternoon is nothing compared to the devastation we will wreak on you if you choose to pursue your present course."

The Bournese general sneered at Delno, and said, "Dragon Riders are neutral in such affairs. They don't get involved in such wars. There hasn't been a dragon involved in a war in over two thousand years. You, sir, are bluffing."

"A bluff is, quite simply, a lie, and I have never been any good at lying. If your armies are not withdrawing by tomorrow morning, then they will do so by tomorrow afternoon. That is no bluff, sir; that is simple truth. You and your men have not had the opportunity to see what dragons can do to ground troops. I have, and it is not a pretty sight."

The men of Bourne withdrew to their lines and Delno turned to the officers from Larimar and said, "Now then, Colonel Dreighton, Captain Porter, I believe I promised you an explanation."

The explanation took over an hour and then subsequent questions took that long again. When it was over, Delno was given permission to have Nat meet with the team of healers who had been trying to combat the sickness that was sweeping through the city. The group from Larimar, especially the civilian diplomats, were reluctant to allow the dragons closer, but Delno's word that they would create no problem provided that they themselves, or their Riders, weren't accosted was enough for the military commanders in the end. The dragons were given leave to perch on the walls of the city and the Riders were invited in to talk with the city council and the king.

It was decided that Nat and Nassari would accompany the Delegates back to the city on foot while the rest of the Riders and the dragons would wait for a signal that the men manning the walls had been told they were coming so that there wouldn't be an inadvertent panic.

While they stood watching for the signal, Rita asked somewhat testily, "How long have you known that Geneva had her fire, and when did you plan on telling the rest of us?"

"That sounds more like an accusation than a question," Delno replied. "I wasn't withholding vital information from you, I promise," he added a bit annoyed her tone.

Adamus stepped into the argument before it could get out of hand. "We simply felt that we should have known. You see, we've been flying a protectively tight formation on you since we disarmed Paul. If we had known, we would have given Geneva a bit of room and not worried over you so much."

"I see," Delno responded a bit chagrined that he had taken offense, "well then, to answer your question," he looked directly at Rita, "the first

I knew of it was when she filled her flame bladder in preparation for making that strafing run. I found out about fifteen seconds before you did."

Both of the other Riders just shook their heads.

"Well," Adamus said, "I have to admit, it was a pretty good run for a first attempt."

"For a first attempt?" Geneva was indignant. "That makes it sound as if there is considerable room for improvement. That was a pretty good run, period. I may lack practice, but I have observed the others, and I believe I have the basics figured out."

All three Riders laughed while Geneva continued to stammer out her anger at such a comment. Finally Delno said, "Let that comment stand as punishment enough for the transgression of not telling us you had acquired flame."

"I wasn't sure until I filled my flame bladder if I had," she responded. "So much has been going on. I was going to make a practice run to see first, but didn't get the chance."

"Well, Love," Delno spoke, "no one is really angry with you. We just tend to forget that you are still maturing because you have come so far so fast."

"She doesn't have much more maturing to do now that she has her flame," Rita responded. "The only thing left is mating; let's hope that doesn't happen in the middle of a battle somewhere."

Geneva scowled as the Riders shared another laugh at the prospect. "At least I can control my urges," she said to Delno.

Delno gave her a stern look and said, "Don't say that out loud, Dear Heart; I had just gotten you two on good terms, and for my sake I would like to keep that peace intact."

"Notice, Love, that I didn't say it out loud. However, I would like the humor at my expense to be curtailed, especially since I acquitted myself rather well this afternoon."

"Yes, you really did, Love; I am quite proud of you," Delno replied in a tone that left no doubt as to his sincerity. "They are merely letting off their tension. They know we may face real war tomorrow, and they are afraid. They are afraid both of the prospect of injury or death to themselves or their comrades, and that they may have to be the instruments of death to hundreds of men. Both of those outcomes are terrifying. Forgive them for taking that out on you; you are just convenient."

"I hadn't thought about it that way, Dear One. I had thought that my actions deserved praise, and I got the opposite; it is confusing."

"Yes, it is," he said, "but we are the leaders of this little army of ours, and it is up to us to provide them with a place to vent their frustrations so that they can continue to function. I'm sorry, Love, that's part of being in command. You will have to get your praise from me and allow the others to have their emotional outbursts from time to time."

"I guess I am learning as I go," she replied. "I will keep that in mind."

"There's the signal," Adamus said as he watched a man standing on the wall waving a torch back and forth.

The four dragons took off together and flew to the walls of Larimar where they perched and set up their own watch.

As Delno dismounted, Nat came up to him and said, "I was right; they had no idea what was killing them. They have been doing well for their level of skill with herbs, but I have my work cut out for me if I intend to get this plague under control quickly." Then he turned to the group of men who had followed him up the stairs and onto the wall. "Well," he said irritably, "what are you waiting for, an engraved invitation? Help us get this stuff off of the dragons so that we can get to work."

The men were clearly afraid of the dragons. In fact, Delno had his suspicions that some of them were afraid of the half-elf. Finally, two young men moved to help him divest Marlo of her burden of herbs and physician's tools.

Delno and the other Riders helped remove the gear and the remaining raw plants from the dragons. "Leave the saddles on Geneva, Beth, and Fahwn," he said, "we may have to be in the air quickly, and it takes time to rig them."

Then he added mentally to Geneva, "Relay my apologies to the others about the saddles, Love. I wish we could remove them and just let you rest, but that army out there may have other ideas, and I want fighting straps in place if I have to take to the air in hurry."

"We understand, Love," she replied. "That's why the saddles were designed not only for your comfort over long use, but ours too. Marlo wants to know why her saddle has been removed; she is willing to defend this city with us."

"Tell her that I know she is willing, and I have no doubts of either her bravery or Nat's, but his job in the city is of at least equal importance as our job outside the walls. In fact, his task is more important, and while she must be ready to take him anywhere he needs to go if the situation calls for it, they will not be directly involved in any fighting. While I would like to field four

dragons, I cannot risk interfering with the mission set for her and Nat. With-
out them, we defend a tomb!"

Marlo straightened with pride and nodded once to Delno. Nat suddenly stopped in his work while he spoke mentally with Marlo and she
relayed Delno's orders. He nodded and smiled at his friend, then went
immediately back to work.

Colonel Dreighton approached him then and told him that the city
council and the king were waiting to speak with them.

Just then a lieutenant came up and said to Delno, "Sir, we have a problem with the dragons."

Both the colonel and Delno turned to the man and Delno asked,
"What kind of problem, Lieutenant?"

"Well, sir," the man replied, "the dragons have taken up so much of the
wall that we have no one watching that whole section. The enemy could
sneak right up to the base of the fortification with no one to notice."

"No one to notice?" Geneva said sharply. "Do I look like a sparrow
perched here looking for crumbs?"

The man was startled by being spoken to directly by the dragon. He
was completely speechless and could only stare mutely at Geneva.

Delno laughed out loud and said, "Peace, Geneva, these people are not
steeped in dragon lore like those of the southern kingdoms. He meant
no insult." At that statement, the poor man only nodded his head up
and down, still unable to utter a syllable. To the lieutenant and those
within earshot Delno said, "Dragons can see for miles, and they possess
extraordinary night vision: they see during the night better than a man
can see in full sunlight. If our enemies were holding a book out there, the
dragons could tell you what was written on the pages from here. Also,
they see heat as well as light, so they can see the body heat of a man hiding in the bushes before he can get within bow range of the wall. Lieutenant, this particular section of wall is better watched right now than it
would be if you had two hundred men manning it."

The man looked at the dragons with respect approaching awe in his
eyes. Then he finally found his voice, "My apologies, Good Dragon, I
meant no offense. I did not know that you were watching our enemies."

"Apology accepted," Geneva replied. "You may have your men bring
their weapons and set their own watch as well; we will not harm them."

"Well, that's settled," Delno said. "Bring up as many men as can fit
comfortably on the wall, and they can help the dragons watch. If the

dragons see anything, they will report it directly to your archers, which will save a bit of time over relaying the information through us."

Then he turned to Adamus and said, "I would like to have all of the Riders in this meeting, but I need one Rider to stay on the wall with the dragons just in case there is trouble on the field. You've earned your place in the meeting as a Rider, but you've earned my trust enough to leave you here alone to watch the enemy. Which will it be?"

Adamus straightened and said, "I'll stay on the wall, Delno; I'm not a big fan of meeting with royalty, and I thank you for the trust."

"Good enough," Delno replied, "you won't miss much; if anything important happens, I'll have Geneva relay it to you through Beth."

Delno motioned for Rita to join him and then turned to Colonel Dreighton and said, "Lead on, Colonel, I believe we have defense plans to discuss with the king."

CHAPTER 9

KING DORIAN OF Corice was as tall as Delno, and his reddish-brown hair had acquired a bit more grey since the last time Delno had seen him. Still, he was holding up well considering that he was sixty-seven years old.

As Delno walked in, two guards barred his way and demanded that he remove his weapons before advancing. Delno, though annoyed, began to reach for the buckles securing his blades to his belt and motioned for Rita to do the same.

"That won't be necessary," the king said. "This man is a decorated hero and a citizen of this country. I won't ask him or his companions to remove their weapons in my presence."

It was the guards' turn to be annoyed, but they stepped aside and let the Riders pass.

"Delno Okonan, the last time I saw you I placed a medal of valor around your neck for your efforts in saving my kingdom. It appears that you have once again come to the aid of your country at a crucial moment. I'm told that you not only bring those most excellent dragons to our defense, but a healer well versed in the arts of Elven herb-lore to cure this plague that is ravaging the city from within. You and your Riders are most welcome," the king stated formally as he extended his hand to Delno.

"Your Majesty, I am ever at the service of my people," Delno replied with equal formality though he didn't bow. "Let me introduce one of my traveling companions. This is Marguerite Killian."

"Please call me Rita; Marguerite is too much to say all at once," Rita gave Dorian her most winning smile as she extended her hand.

The officers exchanged worried glances and the king stiffened a bit at the perceived lack of courtesy.

Geneva relayed communication from Rita and Fahwn, "*Rita says that you may have put the man in a bad temperament by not bowing. He is used to being treated as a king, and this isn't the south.*"

"*Tell her that this may not be the south, but Dragon Riders are still traditionally equals of royalty. Neither side need bow to the other. I don't want our relationship with this man to start off as a subordinate one. I don't want him or anyone else here thinking that we are merely war engines that they can command and use as they see fit. We are in charge of ourselves, and that must be made clear right from the beginning. Also, when the current crisis is over, we still need to meet with these people to establish real diplomatic relations. I don't want them to walk into such meetings thinking of us as merely lesser diplomats; I want them to think of us as equals,*" he replied.

Then the king shrugged, looked around and said, "I was told there were four Riders; am I not to have the privilege of meeting the other two?"

"You will meet them soon, Sire," Colonel Dreighton responded, "forgive us for the slight, but we felt the healing of the people and the protection of the city should take precedence over etiquette."

Delno added, "One is the healer you yourself mentioned; he has already set about his task of tending to the sick. The other is on the wall with the dragons so that a Rider is present should the need arise for a dragon to take flight while this meeting is in progress."

"Ah, thinking like a true military man, Delno Okonan," the king responded with a smile. Then he lowered his voice conspiratorially, "You know, I wanted to raise your rank to captain, but the damned bureaucrats vetoed it so strongly I had no choice but to capitulate. If you had stayed in the military, I was going to give you a Letter of Peerage and then promote you."

Delno was a bit shocked at that revelation and only nodded. He had turned in his letter of intent to resign almost four months before his term of service ended. If he had waited and been made a Peer of the Realm, his whole life would certainly have been different than it was now. Of course, if that had happened, he would not be bonded with Geneva. He had no doubt that he was much better off that things had happened the way they had.

Delno, Rita, the two military officers, and the king walked toward a group of men and women. The group included Nassari, who seemed right at home in their midst. Delno had little doubt that this was the city council of Larimar. He also noticed that one man had a black eye and one of the women had tried to cover a large bruise on the side of her face with make-up, and none of them were carrying edged weapons of any kind. Apparently, Nassari had been telling the truth about the violence of politics and politicians in Larimar.

The council members bowed to the king as he approached the group. Then they all started speaking at once. They wanted to know what the military was doing about the army besieging the city. What was being done to stop the spread of plague, and, most importantly, what was being done about the dragons perched on the city walls? It took several moments, and still the Captain had to shout to finally get them to shut up and listen.

"I will answer your last concern first, since that is what appears to be foremost in your minds," the king said. "The dragons on the walls of this city are here to help us. What is to be done with them is that we will treat them as honored guests who have come to help us break this siege. They, and their Riders, will be shown every courtesy of visiting royalty; treatment which, traditionally, they are entitled to."

"There is no tradition for such as this in Larimar," a voice said from the back of the group. "They are demon spawn and should be banished."

The king looked over the group trying to identify the speaker and then simply said, "Dragon lore and the traditions that go with it have not been taught to the masses in this kingdom since the Exiled Kings moved north. However, it is taught to the royal family. These Riders are men and women, and the dragons, though magical, are also mortal creatures. They are not demon spawn, and they certainly aren't evil."

"We've never needed such as them to protect ourselves before; why do we need them now?" said the woman with the bruised face. "Our soldiers can defend these walls from that rabble out there."

"Never needed such before? Are you certain?" Delno asked. "You tend to forget the parts of history you find inconvenient. The Exiled Kings are revered for their fortitude and perseverance, but it has been forgotten that it was the Dragon Riders, my Grandfather Corolan in particular, who helped the Exiled Kings get out of the south and establish the two kingdoms here in the North over two thousand years ago."

Dorian raised one eyebrow and looked more closely at Delno.

"Your grandfather?" the woman spat. "If that is so, that would certainly make you a long-lived family."

"Dragon Riders share the longevity of the dragons they are bonded to," Dorian replied as if reciting a passage he had learned from a book. "The magic that bonds the pair lengthens the life of the Rider while it shortens the life of the dragon. It is not unheard of for bond-mates to live over three thousand years. So it is entirely possible that this is the grandson of Corolan." Then he turned to Delno and said, "If that is true, it makes you my great-nephew."

It was Delno's turn to be surprised. "Oh, it's true, Your Majesty." he replied. "My grandfather was slain by Roracks while in Horne. After she killed the Roracks, his Dragon Partner, who was pregnant, headed north to safe and familiar territory. I found her in distress above the falls, egg bound. I helped her deliver her one remaining egg and was bonded to the hatchling."

"As I have been trying to tell you all," Nassari said, "Delno is a fellow countryman who has brought these Dragon Riders to help us. You really need to get over your prejudices and put your superstitions aside."

"I would still prefer to rely on our own resources rather than on the whims of magical creatures," the man with the black eye interjected.

"Ten percent of my soldiers are already dead from this damn plague, and half of those remaining are sick," Colonel Dreighton told them. "We have spent our resources, and the bank is nearly empty. I am in command, not because of my age and experience, but because I am the highest ranking military officer left to take the job. At this point, I will take whatever help I can get. I welcome these Dragons and Riders with open arms."

"As do I," said a man who had just entered.

The man quickly introduced himself to Delno and Rita as Jerome Morran, master healer and physician to the king.

"I not only know the half-elf physician they brought along, I've wanted to study under the man for many years. He is quite simply the best herbalist to be found outside the Elven lands. Our people could be in no better hands: I've told all of the local physicians that they are to follow his orders to the letter or they will be permanently banned from practicing in Corice."

"That's all well and good for you, Healer," the man with the black eye replied, "but we have no intention of waiting until the desires of these elves and wizards change and they turn on us." He turned to the king and asked, "Have you stopped to consider that they could be working with the very army they say they are here to defeat?"

"Yes, I have considered it," Dorian responded, "and rejected the idea. If these Riders were in league with our enemies, why would they even bother with this pretense? By the time they arrived, the military leaders and I were already considering asking for terms of surrender. Our people are dying from plague within the walls, and death awaits us on the field outside; we were completely demoralized when those dragons swooped down and made that impressive display this afternoon." He paused for a moment and then added, "So you see, it is either trust that these Riders can help, or surrender and hope that our enemies are merciful."

Everyone was silent for several moments, and then the king continued. "Of course, if you, as the ruling council, decide that you are so terrified of the dragons that you would prefer surrender, I, by law, have to consider your request. Surrender will mean that I will most likely be taken to the King of Bourne in chains. I can't imagine that they will leave the city council intact, but you can always take your chances. Of course, the Bournese have killed the leaders of the cities they have overrun in the past." He paused for effect before saying, "Talk amongst yourselves for a while and let me know what you decide. Just in case, though, I will go over defense plans with the Riders and my military leaders."

Saying that, the king turned, and, offering his arm to Rita and taking Delno by the elbow, led them off to one side of the room. Once he had put as much distance as possible between himself and the city council he said, "They are fine when it comes to the normal business of state, but they simply hamper the operation when it comes to war. That is why I don't have to listen to them unless they directly call for surrender."

There was silence for a few moments and then the king asked, "How long have you known that you were Corolan's grandson, Delno?"

Delno was a bit taken aback by the question; he had expected to be asked about the coming war. "I didn't actually know until several months after I left Corice."

"Tell me, what of your grandmother? Is she alive?" the king looked pained as he asked the question.

Delno shook his head. "I'm afraid she died in childbirth. My mother, newborn and needing a wet-nurse, was given over to my grandfather's relatives. She was raised with the caravans and then settled in Larimar when she was old enough to make her own decisions."

"I knew the answer to that, though I didn't want to admit it," the king replied sadly. "Your grandmother and I were twins. I was the elder by nearly an hour. Our mother also died in childbirth, and we nearly died as babes because we were born premature. Much later, when we were twenty-three, my sister introduced me to a man she had fallen in love with. He was older, and I disapproved. When I found out he was a Dragon Rider, I wanted nothing more to do with him. I begged her to reconsider and go through with a marriage that had been prearranged. She and I fought about it, and she left without saying good-bye. I wish I had kept my disapproval to myself for her sake. At least then I wouldn't have gone all these years waiting for the news I knew I didn't want to hear."

Dorian was slouching and looked as though he had aged visibly in the last few moments. Delno put his hand on his uncle's shoulder. Finally, the man regained his composure and straightened. Then he smiled at Delno and said, "And here my great-nephew has lived in the same city as I have all of his life. Has served in my army and been decorated by me personally, and I never knew. I wish I had not been such an ass to your grandparents: then you would have grown up knowing your heritage. Can you forgive me, Nephew?"

"My father has always said to me, before you berate a man for making a mistake, make sure you have made none of your own," Delno replied. "There is nothing to forgive, Uncle."

Dorian quickly embraced his great-nephew and then said, "Now then, tell these guards who they are looking for, and they will make sure your family sees the healers. Then, as soon as it can be arranged, your loved ones will be brought to the palace for a reunion."

Delno provided the men with the information. The men seemed reluctant to leave the king, but Dorian said, "Be about the task I have set for you. If I am not safe in my own halls, in the company of two Dragon Riders and two of my finest military officers, then having two more soldiers won't make a bit of difference."

Delno turned to his great uncle and asked, "Shouldn't we begin planning our defenses?"

"Not on your life," the king replied. "The last war we fought against Bourne was won because I had the good sense not to interfere with my military commanders. My job is to wait here and review what you request and then see how much more I can squeeze out of the bean counters to give it to you. You and Colonel, excuse me, General Dreighton have proven yourselves in the past, I'm sure you both will do what needs to be done. I brought *you* over *here* away from the council members so that we could discuss family matters. Now, if you and the general will excuse me, I will go and play politics while you and he discuss military strategies."

Both Delno and General Dreighton exchanged glances and smiled as the king walked away.

"Well," Delno said, "at least I can congratulate you on your promotion, General."

The general shook Delno's hand. The two men discussed integrating the dragons into the defenses of the city while they walked back to the walls.

Later, back outside, Geneva said, *"You are pensive, Love; what is bothering you?"*

"I have been thinking about my heritage quite a bit. I have come to realize that fate has played a strong hand in deciding which direction I am to be pointed, but I still marvel at the number of things that could have changed all of that." Then he leaned against her and wrapped his arms as far around her neck as he could. *"I am simply glad that everything has worked out in such a way that we are together, Dear Heart, but there is a question that I would like to ask you about your heritage."*

"Of course, Dear One. Ask; I will answer."

"Very well. Corolan saved your grandmother and her Partner and was rewarded by bonding with your mother and being given a Dragon Blade, correct?"

"Yes, as I understand it, though my lineage lore doesn't include specifics about that."

"I know that your mother knew she would die and passed on her lineage to you, but how did your grandmother know and pass on the lineage to your mother? I haven't heard that she was mortally wounded in that battle."

"She wasn't mortally wounded, but she was very old. She knew that my mother would be her last daughter, and so she passed on the lineage before my mother hatched. My grandmother lived for nearly five years after my mother was born. Until my grandmother died, my mother was what you would call the Heir Apparent."

"That clears it up nicely. I had wondered how that all worked, Love," Delno replied.

"*I'm glad I could put your mind at ease, Dear One,*" Geneva responded. She paused for a moment and then added, "*There is bad weather moving in. We will have a storm by morning. You had better sleep while you can.*"

"*I think I'll sleep here on the wall with you,*" he said. He sat down in a semi-reclined position using her front leg for a sleeping couch. Rita came over from where she had been speaking with Fahwn and kissed him.

"Since we haven't been given proper quarters yet, I think I'll take your example and sleep with my draconic Partner instead of my human one," she said to him.

Usually when they spoke of their relationship they were either very playful or simply businesslike. To have Rita speak of them as Partners was as close to using the word love as either of them had yet gotten. He smiled and held onto her hand for a moment before he let her go so that she could walk back to Fahwn.

"Good night, Rita, if you need me for anything tonight I'll be right here. Just call out, I'll hear you."

She walked away toward Fahwn but it was almost as if the connection remained unbroken.

Chapter 10

GENEVA HAD BEEN right; when dawn came the next day, it was so dark and gloomy that it was difficult to tell when night ended and day began. The clouds that had been building all night now threatened a deluge, and the winds were so strong and chaotic that the dragons were unable to take flight.

Delno watched the Bournese army continue their preparations for the coming assault on the city as lightning began to flash. Finally, the rain began to fall as if the clouds had actually burst. The rain alternately fell in sheets and was driven sideways by the near gale. The dragons huddled on the walls with their wings held tightly to their backs to avoid having them wrenched around like sails in the wind.

As Delno and Geneva watched, they realized that the Bournese were using the cover of the storm to maneuver their siege engines into range. It was slow going for them because the rain, even after only such a short time, had turned the field into a quagmire. Still, they made slow, steady progress. Every time the lightning flashed he could see that they had inched forward. He couldn't help but hold a grudging respect for their persistence.

It took nearly an hour for the first siege engine to be coaxed into position. It sat there nearly three hundred yards away from the wall, about fifty yards beyond the range of the strongest bows. He might be able to hit the target, but one bow against a large trebuchet would not make any difference. The lightning flashed again and he could see the weighted arm of the machine swing down as it threw a nearly three hundred pound stone. The stone fell inside the wall. It was dangerous, but the real danger was when they finally got the range and actually knocked a hole in the stone fortification itself. He wished for thousandth time that the winds didn't have the dragons grounded.

The lightning flashed again and he could see that they were drawing the arm of the trebuchet around for another shot and that the other two were nearly in position.

The young lieutenant on the wall near him said, "I wish that lightning would strike that thing instead of the ground."

Suddenly Delno smacked the heel of his hand against his forehead and shouted above the roar of wind and rain to the young officer, "Why didn't I think of that sooner? You are a genius, and I am a fool."

The Corisian archers manning the walls near him looked at Delno as if he had suddenly taken leave of his senses as he began chanting. Just before the second stone could be launched from the big war machine, lighting struck it, shattering the throwing arm and electrocuting the entire crew of seven who were manning the machine.

Delno looked at the young lieutenant in command of his section of wall and said, "I'm not good enough to create lightning on my own, but when it is already provided by the storm, I am capable of directing where it strikes."

Some of the men looked mortified that they were in this close proximity of someone who could perform such a feat of magic. The rest of the men simply cheered. Delno didn't notice either reaction: he was busy chanting and calling on the magic. A bolt of lightning hit the next closest siege engine with the same result as the first: wood splintered and the crew died in the electrical discharge.

This time, all of the men on the wall cheered as Delno began to focus on the third trebuchet that was still being manhandled into position. The storm had covered the blast and the dying screams of the first two crews, so the men pushing and pulling the third machine into range had no idea of their fate until it was upon them. The lightning hit and the machine splintered and the resulting blast from the bolt sent several men flying like a child's toys, while many of rest did a kind of strange dance and then fell dead. There had been nearly forty men pushing the war engine into position.

One shot had been fired from the enemy's siege weapons and now all three trebuchets were in ruins and nearly fifty of their men were dead. The few who weren't killed by the lightning retreated back to their lines. There was no more movement toward the walls within the enemy camp. Though the men couldn't see through the rain, Geneva reported that it appeared that those who had been preparing to charge once the siege engines had battered holes in the city walls had left their lines and sought shelter from the storm.

Delno briefly considered calling the lightning down into the enemy camp and then rejected the idea. He wanted to send them home with as little loss of life on both sides as possible. The storm had turned the dry field into a huge mud basin. With no clear way to get inside the walls and ankle deep mud to wade through, a charge would be suicide. The enemy would at least wait until the weather cleared before they tried anything else. At that point, he would attempt once again to persuade them to go home. If they didn't, the dragons would convince them.

The rain lasted until late afternoon, then stopped as quickly as if some-one had simply turned a valve. The late summer storms in the mountains could appear quickly and do terrific damage and then disappear as fast as they had come. If it weren't for the mud and the three small patches of devastation on the field, there would be no evidence there had been a storm, or that anything out of the ordinary had happened.

The trebuchets, which had been hauled in in pieces and still taken several days to assemble, would take weeks to replace, even if the Bournese could find suitable materials for their construction locally. If not, they would have to send to Bourne for replacements. The loss would leave them three options. They would either have to make a huge ram to batter down the gates of the city, which they would have to do under fire from the walls, or they would have to build scaling ladders and get over the ramparts themselves, which would be at least equally costly in lives. The third option would be to dig in and besiege the city until hunger drove the inhabitants to surrender. Of course, once Nat cured the plague victims and eliminated that danger, the king would allow commerce to resume on the river, and the docks were quite easily defended from the safety of the city walls. And, there were always the dragons, as well.

There was no activity in the enemy camp for the remainder of the day. The dragons and men on the walls watched carefully through the darkness, but there was nothing significant to report by night's end. Delno hoped that the destruction of the siege engines had discouraged them to the point of being reasonable.

After talking with General Dreighton the next morning, Delno hung the huge white flag of parlay where it could be seen by the spotters in the enemy camp. There was no immediate reply. It wasn't until mid-morning that a group of men—Geneva was able to identify the Bournese commander among them—came toward the city carrying a white flag. Delno chose to ride out to meet them on horseback rather than have Geneva upset them. The dragons all stayed on the walls, but they remained in plain sight to deter any treachery.

As they reached a point halfway between the city and the encamped army, both sides dismounted and met on foot. The general from Bourne was the first to speak and the destruction of his siege engines hadn't lessened his audacity. "You have flown the white flag and asked for parlay; do you seek terms for surrender?"

"That isn't what we had in mind, but we will accept your surrender if you wish to do so." Delno deliberately misinterpreted the man's words.

"You know very well that I was seeking your admission of defeat," the Bournese general replied.

"Why would we admit to such utter nonsense?" General Dreighton responded. "So far you have fired one shot from your siege engines before we destroyed them and left you with no alternatives."

"Ah, so now the men of Corice take credit for random acts of nature," one of the other officers from Bourne said mockingly.

"The lightning may have been random, but where it struck was under the control of my magic," Delno responded.

The resulting shocked look from the Northern men was expected. They had the same prejudice against magic in Bourne as the Corisians did. To have someone lay claim to such an act would put them on edge, and once they returned to camp the rumor would spread through their ranks faster than wildfire through a forest. If the Army of Bourne didn't leave soon, anything bad that happened to them, from acts such as those that had destroyed the trebuchets to simple accidents, would all be attributed to the magic users of Larimar, even without the dragons to further demoralize the besiegers. If they waited to build new siege engines, by the time they were ready to make another move against the city, desertion would reduce their ranks by at least a quarter.

"All right, Gentlemen," Delno said, "let us get down to business. I have destroyed three war machines that you cannot replace. The plague that you expect to weaken us to the point of surrender is being brought under control as we speak. You cannot starve the city because Corice still controls the river and supplies are once again moving along it. The only reason I didn't call some of that lightning down amongst your camp yesterday was that I hope to end this conflict with as little bloodshed as possible."

He paused while the Bournese officers exchanged glances and thought about his words, then he continued. "If you are foolish enough to try and storm the city without your siege engines, we will use the dragons' fire and my magic to slaughter your troops. I would like to send you packing without killing any more of your men. However, if it comes down to a choice between your army or the people of my country, I will kill every Bournese on Corisian soil."

Delno was about to let them mull that over when he noticed that one of the younger officers appeared to be ill. He pointed at the man and said, "I see that the sickness you had hoped was your ally has become your enemy. As I said, our Elven healer has it under control in the city. If it has become a waiting game, it looks like we shall see who outlasts whom."

The Bournese general said nothing; he simply spat on the ground at Delno's feet and then he and his entourage left the meeting. Delno noticed that the younger officers looked as though they disapproved of their commander.

The rest of the day passed without incident; however, there was a great deal of activity in the Bournese camp far into the night. The next morning, the Bournese army had lined up, and they advanced to just out of bow range as a messenger came forward under a white flag. The messenger, a young man of about seventeen or eighteen, was allowed to approach the wall to deliver his message.

"General Thomas Andrewson has assembled his troops and wishes to engage the Army of Corice," the young man said nervously. "He bids those soldiers in the city of Larimar who have an ounce of courage to assemble and take part as willing participants. Those who do so and live will be treated as honorable prisoners of war," the man stopped and swallowed, clearly reluctant to continue with the rest.

"Out with the rest of it, lad; we are honorable men. We allowed you to get this close under a white flag; no one will shoot you for delivering your message," General Dreighton yelled from the wall.

The man relaxed a bit at the assurance and continued. "Those who, that is, the general has said, that those who insist on hiding behind their stone walls instead of engaging our troops honorably will be shown no mercy at all. Any who survive will live out the remainder of their days as hobbled slaves in the quarries of Bourne." The man visibly flinched as if expecting an arrow to pierce him at any second.

"Is that all of it, then?" Dreighton asked.

The young man was a bit surprised to find himself still alive. He smiled apologetically and said, "No, sir, there's one last bit." He drew a breath and said, "Our general has also said that if the People of Larimar would surrender now, they will be treated fairly. He has also offered that any man who wishes to defect to the Bournese Army will be awarded the rank of senior private now and given ten acres of land, either here or in Bourne, when the hostilities are ended." Then he again smiled an apology and said, "That's the last of it, sir."

General Dreighton thought for a moment and then said, "Well, do you want to take my reply back, or do you want us to lower you a rope so that you can surrender and get away from that madman? You'll be treated fairly here."

"To be honest, sir, I'd like nothing better than to surrender, but the general has my younger brother working as an orderly, and I'm afraid that he will do him an injury if I don't return."

All of the soldiers of Corice manning the walls chuckled at the statement. They weren't unsympathetic to the young man's plight; they were simply amused that the state of morale had deteriorated so rapidly in the Bournese ranks.

"Then tell your general this," General Dreighton replied, "we will consider his offer. If the king and the governing council decide to surrender, we will give him an answer by mid-day. I would rather tell you to tell the man to go and soak his fat head in a bucket of water, but letting him think we are considering his terms might save you and your brother some pain."

The men on the wall laughed outright at their general's statement. The young messenger bowed and said, "Thank you, sir. I had a feeling you wouldn't accept the general's terms. Thank you for not sending me back with news that might cause me trouble."

The man bowed again and Dreighton said, "Very well, man, off with you now. We don't want your general to think you're getting chummy with us."

The young man turned and trotted back toward his own lines. Within a quarter hour, the same youth again approached under a white flag. Again he was allowed to get near the wall.

"The general says that mid-day is much too long to wait, sir." The man spoke directly to General Dreighton as if reporting to his own commanding officer. "He says he will have an answer now or the troops will attack."

"Is that all of it?"

"From General Andrewson, yes, sir," the young man replied. "I have one more thing to say though, sir."

They stood for a moment and then Dreighton said, "Well, what is it, son?"

"Well, sir, my brother seems to have run off into the hills while the general wasn't looking, so if that offer to surrender is still open, I'd rather not go back to lines," the young man said a bit sheepishly.

General Dreighton smiled and called for a rope to be lowered. As the young man voluntarily grabbed the rope and was hauled up, there was movement along the ranks of the Bournese soldiers. Several men ran forward with bows trying to get within range to shoot their own messenger. The first man to kneel and try to draw a bow suddenly dropped the arrow he was trying to nock and grabbed at the one that had abruptly buried itself nearly up to the fletching just beneath the hollow of his neck.

Everyone who wasn't actively involved in hauling the teenager up looked to see who had shot the Bournese archer from that distance. There was Delno, standing tall, drawing back the string of his powerful bow and taking aim at another of the enemy archers. He let fly and another man fell when the shaft penetrated his chest through his boiled leather armor. By that point, the youth had been hauled up and was safely out of sight of the archers on the ground. The Bournese retreated to their ranks and Delno just stood where he was, in full view of the enemy soldiers, watching, his bow in his left hand now down by his side, and a light breeze making his cloak flair out slightly behind him.

General Dreighton pointed to two soldiers and said, "You two, take our young prisoner and see that he is put someplace safe and comfortable. He has surrendered honorably and voluntarily; see to it that he is well treated." To the young man he said, "I'm sorry that you will have to be kept under lock and key, but you won't be harmed or interrogated. As far as you are concerned, this war is over. If we can find your younger sibling and bring him to you, we will."

The young man repeatedly thanked the general and everyone else on the wall as he was led away.

*"Delno, there is activity, "*Geneva said. *"It looks as though someone is moving among the men on the lines and preparing them to charge. I can't be completely sure, but it looks like they are carrying some ladders."*

"Very well, Love, join me here." Out loud, he yelled, "Prepare to repel ladders."

The men of Bourne shrank back a bit as they saw Geneva rise from one section of the wall and move to get her Partner. Apparently, they had been kept so busy they had forgotten about the dragons. Rita and Fahwn took to the air as Delno and Geneva did; they were soon joined by Adamus and Beth.

Delno could see the senior sergeants and officers moving among the men trying to motivate them to attack the walls. Some were using whips and cudgels on the men who were reluctant to move faster. Delno watched as one man who was pointing at the dragons was stabbed in the back by an officer. Delno poured his rage at the officer into the energy he sent toward the man. Within a second, the officer was hit so hard by an invisible bolt of energy that he was literally broken into pieces. Everyone around that officer simply stood staring at the remains in stunned silence.

The initial confusion passed quickly, and a large group of Bournese charged at the walls carrying ladders. Delno had Rita and Adamus strafe the front of the line while he went for the men in the back ranks; instructing Geneva to especially target anyone carrying a whip or cudgel rather than a sword. The carnage in the front of the charge was terrible: dozens of men were incinerated outright, and dozens more were horribly wounded. The officers and the non-coms in the back had literally whipped the men into such a frenzy that many in the middle who tried to stop to avoid being burned were trampled instead. Then, when the men realized that certain death awaited them forward and they turned to retreat, they ran straight into Geneva's flame, and what had happened to the front ranks now became the fate of the rear.

Geneva was good, even without practice. She effectively targeted nearly all of the leaders of the charge. When it was over, what had started out as two hundred and fifty armed men valiantly charging the walls was now half that number desperately trying to get away from the conflagration that threatened to consume them all.

Delno called a halt and had the dragons soar up out of bow range and circle the enemy lines. He hoped that the demonstration would be enough, but apparently the Bournese needed more convincing, because another large group, at least four hundred strong, broke from the ranks and charged. This time, Delno told all the Riders to make sure to use shields, because he expected that the enemy would be ready and use arrows on them. Then he told Adamus and Rita to again target the front of the line; especially trying for the ladders, while he again targeted the leaders who were literally driving the men forward like cattle.

The result was even more devastating than the first strafing run had been because this time the men had clustered more in groups around the ladders. Again those in the lead were either killed by fire or trampled when they tried to turn to avoid it. Again the leaders and those around them died by Geneva's breath. Delno tried desperately not to listen to the screams of the dying men. He wished he could block out the stench of burning flesh.

He had been right about the enemy trying to hit them with arrows. His shield had held and Rita and Fahwn were unharmed, but Adamus had taken an arrow through his right calf. Beth was unharmed because of her scales. Adamus was more angry than seriously hurt. He was busily berating himself for not getting his shield up in time.

He watched carefully as they circled, the enemy didn't appear to be trying to ready another charge. Delno did notice one officer beating a soldier who had left the line. The man fell and the officer continued to whip the man. Delno, almost absently, killed the officer with magic. The men standing near the dead officer picked up the soldier he had been beating and carried him off the field toward the rear. Delno hoped they were carrying the man to an aid station and not to further punishment.

The men on the ground remained huddled together with weapons drawn as if they were grimly determined to deal with their fate for opposing the dragons. They waited for the Riders to swoop down and continue the attack. After the dragons had been circling for half an hour, the men started to retreat to their camp. At first it was just a few men, like a trickle of water through a hole in a dam, but the trickle soon became a torrent as more and more men hurried away from the carnage they had already witnessed. The Bournese had started the day with about two thousand troops; they would end the day with nearly one quarter of those troops dead or severely injured with nothing else to show for their commanding general's foolishness.

The rest of the afternoon was spent manning the walls. At nightfall, a group of nearly two hundred Bournese troops approached under a white flag. They bore no weapons and merely asked to be allowed to surrender. They sought only those terms the Army of Corice saw fit to offer. The gates were opened under the watchful eyes of the dragons and the men were allowed inside. About half of them were sick with the plague that Nat had already brought under control in the city. All of the prisoners were seen and treated by the physicians and then given food and water. They had to be housed in the stockyards since Larimar had no other facilities for them, but they were put in clean holding facilities and treated well. The young messenger's brother was among them. He was sick and being treated, and the two were reunited.

The next morning a group of men approached from the enemy camp. They carried a large white flag and bore no weapons. They were leading General Andrewson and his senior staff, who were all bound. They were allowed to walk up close enough to be heard.

One officer spoke for the group, "We have brought this madman and his loyal officers to offer up as prisoners. We no longer follow them and have no desire to continue these hostilities. We who remain wish to surrender to the Army of Corice. We do ask, when you dictate terms, that you remember that the man who made the earlier threats and ordered those men to commit suicide trying to rush your defenses was brought to you by us. We ask for your mercy, but we make no demands."

"I, General Dreighton, accept your surrender. Go back to your camp and have your men gather their weapons and stack them there where you stand. When your army is disarmed, we will discuss the rest of the surrender." He turned to his officers and said loudly enough so the men standing beneath the walls could hear, "Open the gates long enough to get the prisoners inside, and then give orders that the men bringing the surrendered weapons are not to be attacked so long as they make no threatening moves." Then he turned back to the men on the field and said, "Do you have any immediate needs that you yourselves cannot meet?"

The man looked as if he didn't believe his own ears. He said, "Many of our men are sick with the same plague that has affected your city, and many were injured yesterday who need healers and medicines we don't have."

"They will be attended to," Delno said. "Go back and tell your people that the healers and at least one dragon Rider will be among them shortly. They need have no fear of the Riders so long as they don't attempt any aggression. We will use every means we possess to help heal the sick and injured."

The men on the field stood with their mouths open not fully believing what they had heard. "We did not expect such compassion from those we had wrongly attacked. I will tell our soldiers what to expect and tell them that the men of Corice are a breed apart who should be praised for their mercy."

A group of Corisian soldiers relieved the men of their prisoners and the Bournese general and his staff were then housed in the city jail. They were placed there as much for their own protection as because of their status. Even the other Bournese wanted them drawn and quartered.

Within an hour, Delno and the healers were moving among the sick and injured of the former enemy camp. Delno used all of his skill to treat burns, broken bones, lash sores, and any other injuries he found, while Nat and the other physicians concentrated primarily on treating the disease and preventing further infection. By nightfall, all of the healers were exhausted but the immediate crisis was over.

Later, back in the city, Delno and General Dreighton were talking with King Dorian. The king wasn't sure whether he should be pleased that he had suddenly acquired fifteen hundred new subjects, or upset that he now was compelled by his officers' compassion to help relocate the men and settle them into Corisian society.

"We should send them back - after they clean up that mess they've made of the plain outside our gates, of course." Then, at the looks on their faces, the king added, "I know they brought up the prisoners and surrendered, but it's not like they came south under duress. They are all volunteers in the Bournese Army. The fact that they deserted should be their problem, not ours. After all, they surrendered to us under any terms we saw fit."

"Uncle, we can't send them home to a death sentence," Delno replied. "If they hadn't mutinied and brought their commanders to us, we would still be out there manning the walls. Even with the dragons, eventually some of them would have gotten through, and men would have died on our side. Besides, many of them are not volunteers; many are conscripts who had no choice but to obey orders."

"Well, that does put a new light on things," Dorian replied softly. "I just wish we could execute that insane general of theirs and send them home." Before Delno or Dreighton could object, he held up his hand and said, "I know, by treaties that have existed for centuries we can't execute officers unless we can prove that they committed crimes against civilians. The fact that the only reason we can't prove that against these men is because you didn't give them a chance to commit such crimes doesn't help convince me to abide by a treaty that they would have ignored." Then he sighed and added, "Don't worry; the officers will be taken to the Stone Bridge, and there they will be released from their chains and set free to return to their own country, and the men who remain here will be resettled." Then, almost to himself, he said, "Treaties or no treaties, we are going to build a large fort on our side of that damned bridge!"

Just then several people entered. Delno immediately recognized them all: his mother was as radiant as ever; his father was as stalwart as he remembered, and his brother looked to be in awe of his surroundings.

CHAPTER 11

DORIAN SEEMED TRANSFIXED as he watched Delno's mother approach. When she was only a few steps away, the king reached out to take her hands in his. "You look just like your mother," he said, as a single tear trickled down his cheek.

Laura Okonan attempted to curtsy, but the king held her fast and said, "You need not curtsy in my presence, Niece."

Laura was not surprised when Dorian called her "niece", but it was certainly news to her husband and younger son. John Okonan stared openly at his wife while their younger son was looking from his mother to his father to his brother, and finally to the king like his head was suddenly too loosely attached to keep it still.

"We must take refreshment and talk," Dorian said. Then to the first servant he saw he ordered, "Bring wine and food to my private dining chamber." He turned to Laura and her family and added, "If you will all join me, we can talk without interruption and get to know each other."

Delno quickly embraced his mother and father while reaching out and patting his brother on the shoulder. Then the four of them began to follow the king, accompanied by his personal guards.

When they reached the door of the king's private dining chamber, Dorian said to the guards, "You will remain out here and allow no one into this room for at least the next two hours."

"But, Your Majesty," one of the men replied, "it is our job to stay with you at all times, for your safety."

"Nonsense, man," the king shot back, "my great-nephew, Delno, is a skilled swordsman, magician, and Dragon Rider. What makes you think that you can keep me any safer than he can?"

At the perplexed looks on the faces of the two guards, Delno said, "I believe it is me they wish to keep you safe from, Uncle."

The king made a rude noise and said, "Delno Okonan is the Hero of Stone Bridge. If I am not mistaken in my Dragon Lore, that saber he carries is a Dragon Blade. Without it, he is more than a match for the two of you. With it, he is unstoppable."

The men were still quite reluctant to leave their liege lord, so Delno said, "Really, Uncle, they are just doing their jobs; jobs that you have given them to do. Can't they at least station themselves inside the door? That way they can do their jobs, and we still have our privacy."

"Oh, very well," Dorian replied, "they can station themselves inside the door."

As they all entered the door, the senior of the two guardsmen whispered to Delno, "Thank you, sir; we really aren't supposed to leave him."

Delno smiled at the men and then walked to the dining table with his family. At the king's request they chose seats. The king, Delno's brother Will, and Delno moved to pull out the chair for Laura but John, since he was already standing beside her, beat them to it.

Dorian smiled and said, "I see that manners were well taught in the Okonan House, and that they were taught by example. It's nice to know that my kin has been in good hands all these years."

John smiled at the compliment while he held the chair for his wife.

Once they were all seated, Dorian was the first to speak. "I must apologize for not finding you sooner. I had no idea that my niece and her family lived in the same city with me. I placed a medal on Delno after the war without even suspecting that he was my great-nephew."

"You couldn't have known," Laura replied. "The last time my father was here he gave me vague hints that I was related to the royal line of Corice, but he didn't tell me that my uncle was the king. It was only recently that I heard anything about my father, and that news was of his death at the hands of those foul beast-men in the south."

"Well, you are home now," Dorian said, "I wronged your mother by refusing to accept her love of a Dragon Rider. Knowing Dragon Lore, I did not want her marrying a man who would most likely outlive her by several centuries. I wanted her to marry the man who now sits on the throne of Bourne and create strong ties between the two kingdoms so that we might stop these wars that crop up every generation or so. She found the King of Bourne repugnant, and we both refused to listen to each other. She left with Corolan in the dead of night without saying good-bye. I have regretted ever since that I pushed her so hard that she felt compelled to leave her home. I should have listened, and you would have been born and raised here."

"Everything happens for a reason, Your Majesty," Laura replied. "My mother had the best healers on hand when I was born, and still she died in childbirth. I don't think she would have fared better here than she did in Palamore. If she had stayed, then I would not have been raised among the caravans and would never have met Delno's father."

Delno, sensing that his world was once again about to be tilted on its axis, stared openly at his mother as she continued, "You see Delno, you are adopted by the man you have called father all of these years."

Delno looked from his mother to his father and back again. "I had suspected that this was so at one time; you don't have a child with dark hair and eyes born to parents with fair hair and light eyes. I had put it out of my mind for quite some time. Why did you never tell me before?"

"We saw no need, until now," John Okonan answered. "If you had lived out your life here in Larimar, it would have made no difference. Since you have become a Rider, it is time that you know all of your story."

"When I was old enough to be considered a woman by the standards of the vanners I lived with, but still naive enough to fall in love with the first dashing boy who looked my way, I met the young man who fathered you. Since he was of Corolan's clan, he was a cousin, but many times removed. He was strong telepathically, and he also had some small skill with magic. His father was the Caravan Master, and he was the eldest son. He was nearly four years older than I was. He and I were making plans to get married when he died in an accident at a river crossing. His name was Timothy Moreland."

"That name sounds very familiar," Delno said. He thought about it for a moment and then asked, "Did he have a brother named Roland?"

"Yes," she replied, "do you know Roland?"

"I met him several months ago just before I left Larimar. He is now Caravan Master. I guess he inherited the position from his father."

"Well," Laura remarked, "Roland is your uncle. In fact, he offered to take me in when his brother died. He was such a serious young man, and had a well-developed sense of responsibility. It's not surprising that he is now Caravan Master."

"If Roland wanted to take you in, how did you end up in Larimar?" Delno asked.

"Roland is a good man, but I had no real love for him. I decided that my child would not be raised as a vanner. It's a harsh life and can be quite dangerous. Even your father, who was well-trained and had the advantage of magic, was killed trying to maneuver one of those over-sized wagons and protect those stupid oxen while fording a swollen river. I wanted a different life for you. Our next stop was Larimar, and I left the caravan when we arrived. I found work cooking at an inn, and that's where I met John Okonan. I was four months pregnant and just beginning to show. We were well suited to each other, and he asked me to marry him. He didn't care that he would be raising another man's child, and he has always treated you as his own."

Delno looked at John Okonan and said, "Well, that's certainly true. You have never favored the son of your own blood over me. You've treated us both equally and given us both all that you could. I've never known Timothy Moreland, and I can't even picture him. You are the man I think of as father, and always will."

John smiled at his adopted son and nodded. Will, though not stupid, was a bit confused. "So, Delno and I are only half-brothers?" he asked. "What does all of this mean?"

"It means," Dorian interjected, "that I have found my lost niece and that you and Delno are both my great-nephews. It also means that your mother and her family are welcome to move into royal quarters and live in luxury if you desire." He paused for a moment and then said, "It means that now that I have found my family after so many long years that I have no intention of losing track of them again."

"I am just a simple man," John Okonan said. "I don't think I am suited for palace life, but my wife is. She should live in luxury, and I've always regretted that I wasn't able to provide enough for her to do so. If she would like to move up here, I guess I'll have to move with her and walk back to my carpentry shop every day."

John paused and everyone smiled at him. "As for my sons," he continued, "they are old enough to make their own decisions. Will is a good carpenter, but I have seen that he would like a different life than one I've pushed him into. He enjoys working with wood, but he'd prefer it was a hobby rather than a job."

He paused while he and Will exchanged glances. "I wish I could deny that, but my father is right; I would rather be an artist, but we live in a pragmatic society. More people would rather put furniture on their floors than paintings on their walls."

"I never knew you enjoyed painting," Delno remarked.

"Well," Will responded, "you are my older brother, and I love you as such, but we have never really been friends, so we haven't paid much attention each other's interests. Perhaps we can work on changing that in the future."

"I think I'd like that," Delno replied.

There was a knock at the door, and the guards opened it just enough to see who it was. At first they said that no one was to be admitted, but then one of the guards approached and said, "I'm sorry, Sire, but the woman Rider is outside the door and wishes to speak with Delno Okonan."

At the same time Geneva said, *"Rita wishes to know if she is allowed a few moments of your time or if you intend to stay sequestered with the king for the remainder of the day?"*

"Relay to Rita that I am also with my mother, father and brother. If she has business, then it can wait. However, if she would simply like to join us as my companion, then she is certainly welcome at this meeting as far as I'm concerned."

"Rita says she apologizes for her jealousy and would very much like to join you," Geneva relayed.

Delno realized that everyone was looking at him. "Were you in contact with your dragon?" Dorian asked excitedly.

"Yes," he replied, "She was relaying a message from Rita to me. Rita's business with me can wait, but I would like to have her in here if no one objects."

The king told the guards to admit the Rider, and as Rita joined them, he asked Delno, "Can all Riders converse with all dragons on a mental level then?"

"No, at least as far as I've seen," Delno answered, "but all dragons can communicate with each other that way. Rita tells Fahwn what she wants to say to me and Fahwn relays that through Geneva. It takes a bit of time to get the messages sorted out, but when you are half a mile away from each other, it actually speeds up communication."

Dorian laughed and said, "It sounds like a good way to hold private discussions even in the midst of large groups. Wish I had something like that when dealing with the council."

Rita joined them and Delno made introductions all around. Once more wine had been poured John remarked, "A woman Rider, and so young."

Rita and Delno both laughed. At John's perplexed look Delno said, "I know that we shouldn't tell a woman's age, Father, but Rita had passed your present age before you were born."

At John Okonan's perplexed look, Rita explained, "I was born over a century ago on an island in the south. I was presented as a candidate for bonding when I was fourteen."

"You look to be no more than perhaps your early twenties," John stated.

Delno chuckled. "Men have made the mistake of believing Rita to be young and immature to their regret before, Father," he said.

Both Delno and Rita laughed. John was smart enough to know that they were sharing some private joke, so he let the matter drop.

"Are you and my son . . . attached?" Laura asked.

"Mother!" Delno said.

"Well, you may be the leader of the Dragon Riders and Corolan's grandson, but you are my son as well, and as your mother I have a right to know such things."

"Delno and I are very close," Rita answered. "Our relationship is one of mutual respect, trust, and love."

Delno cocked his head and looked at Rita. Up until now he and she had strictly avoided mentioning the word "love" when speaking of their relationship, even though they both knew it was so. He smiled at her and nodded, and she nodded to him in return. It was such a small, simple gesture that it might have gone unnoticed by any one not paying careful attention, but to them it was as if they had climbed to the heights of the walls yelled it to the whole city.

"Are the two of you married or not?" Will asked.

"Will!" Laura Okonan said sharply, "Dragon Riders are not to be held to the standards that the rest of us take to be normal." To Rita she said, "I can see that you and Delno are certainly attached and that you care deeply for each other. I didn't mean to embarrass you; I merely wished to know that my son is happy."

"There is no offense taken," Rita responded. "Delno and I are as attached as two people who will live for two to three millennia can be. Whether we will always remain so is something that only time will tell.

As you have said, Riders can't be held to the same standards as other people in such matters."

"But tell me, Nephew, if you can both use telepathy why don't you just contact each other's minds directly?" Dorian said, still thinking of the telepathic link between Dragon and Rider.

Delno thought for a moment before answering, "There are two reasons, Uncle. First, to just reach into the mind of another is not as easy as using the magical bond we already share with the dragon. The second reason is that it is an invasion of privacy."

"But surely if you and Rita are bonded as you say, Brother," Will interjected, "you have no great secrets from each other."

"Will," his mother intoned, "all people have some secrets, even from those they love. Suppose Rita was angry with Delno for something small. In her mind that would translate to hurtful things she might never say out loud. She wouldn't want Delno to know those thoughts, and he wouldn't want to be subjected to them. I think going through the dragons the way they do is a good filter for preventing hurt feelings and problems."

"Exactly, Mother," Delno replied.

The five of them sat talking for much more than the two hours Dorian had set aside for the meeting. As they realized how long they had remained sequestered, Dorian called to the servants and had them find suitable quarters for his niece and her family.

Delno and Will lingered and talked just a bit more. Delno discovered for the first time that his younger brother was much more complex than he had thought. Will even expressed a desire to meet the dragons and said he would like to get them to pose if they could be persuaded to do so.

Once he and Rita had been shown to their quarters, she had quickly found the bath tub and decided to make full use of it. Delno helped her fill the tub and watched as she undressed and got in. He then helped her wash her hair and back as he usually did when they bathed together.

While they sat, he asked, "So, what do you think of my family?"

Rita made a bit of a show of thinking it over before saying, "I like them. They are nice people, and I can see where you get your good manners from."

They sat for a moment before she said, "In my culture, you don't bother formally introducing your family to someone unless you intend that she is to become part of that family also."

"There is a similar custom in this culture," he responded. "In fact, if we were going by the customs of some of the mountain folk around here, just introducing you to my parents would mean we are now married."

"Well, then," she said mischievously, "I guess that makes the rest of my plans for this evening all right then, since we're properly married now."

Later that night as he lay in bed with Rita he reached out to see if Geneva was still awake.

"Yes, I am awake, Love; I was simply giving you your solitude."

"I never seek solitude from you, Dear Heart," he replied.

"Yes, you do, especially when you and Rita are involved," she chuckled, "but I am getting used to it. Everyone needs a bit of total solitude sometimes."

Delno considered her words carefully and realized that she was right, "I love you, Geneva," was the only response he could think of.

"I love you, too, Dear One, but you should sleep. You have a big day tomorrow since we must arrange to return that insane man to his own lands. Also, we must work out the particulars of your diplomatic mission and then make arrangements to return to Orlean." She was silent for a long moment but finally added, "Sleep now, Love, I am here with you if you need me."

"Good night, Love," he said. "I will see you tomorrow."

He closed his eyes and was asleep within a few moments.

CHAPTER 12

"**I**WOULD LIKE TO help with your problem, Nephew," Dorian said, responding to Delno's inquiry about sending troops to Horne, "but the plague has left my army at three-quarter strength. We have defeated the force that Bourne sent to conquer us, but they still have an army of over five thousand on their own soil ready to move at the whim of their king."

Delno and Rita were once again sequestered with the king in his private dining hall. Delno, realizing that they had little time to lose, took the opportunity afforded by his privilege as royal nephew and as leader of the Dragon Riders who had saved the country to press the king for aid in Horne.

"Well, Uncle, as far as the situation in Horne goes, it is a problem of fight them now, or fight them later when you will most likely stand alone."

"I understand that," Dorian replied. "I also understand that the King of Bourne has never forgiven either Corice, or me, for the perceived slight of your grandmother not marrying him. Counting that rout that you and your Riders perpetrated, the man has waged four wars on us since I took the throne a little over thirty years ago. I believe you are right, and he has acted on the advice of messengers from your enemies in Horne as regards this last campaign. But one defeat won't stop him. It is clear that he has been massing troops and equipment since your victory at Stone Bridge caused him to sign the last treaty. The intelligence gathered from those who have defected from the command of that Bournese madman confirms that there is still a significant threat just across the border. I have to move troops to the passes and fortify our own lands before I can even consider sending troops elsewhere."

"It appears that our enemies have outguessed me," Delno said. "I had hoped to come north and find neighboring kingdoms who would join forces and send reinforcements to fight those I believe to be our mutual enemies. Instead I find that Warrick has already looked to this land and taken the time to sow the seeds of dissent. I wonder how he managed to think so far ahead of me and figure out what I was about before I had tipped my hand and begun moving in this direction."

"It's possible that he hadn't figured out your plans but had his eye on these lands before you did." At Delno's puzzled look Dorian explained, "We nearly lost the last war. Our army was down by over fifty percent. The Bournese were faring little better when suddenly they began to guess our troop strength and movements with uncanny accuracy. The only way that they could have done so would be if they had surveillance methods that we didn't. That type of surveillance can only be done from the air, and since we never saw them, we must assume that they watched us at night. Only dragons can see that well at night. It appears that you have been fighting these same enemies for far longer than you realized. If you had not managed to hold Stone Bridge that day and half a thousand troops, even untried recruits, had gotten through to reinforce the soldiers already wreaking havoc on our forces, we would have been forced to surrender then. As it turned out, you forced a stalemate that allowed us to sue for peace on economic grounds. Torrance of Bourne does not care how many men die in his service, but, at least until now, he has been unwilling to completely bankrupt his country to defeat us."

"I don't understand," Delno said. "Why is the North so important to a man who is seeking first to conquer the South?"

"I can't speak with absolute authority, but I have a possible explanation for that," Dorian answered. "From what you have told me, Warrick is trying to set up a new regime that will be world-wide. He wishes to place the world under the control of Dragon Riders, but only those Riders he controls. The royal lines of Corice and Bourne have always produced the highest percentage of Dragon Riders of all of the old noble houses. His dragon, Hella, is not a lineage holder, so she has no specific authority over other dragons except possibly her own offspring. If he can control the royal lines of these two countries, and raise children to his way of thinking, he can then present them at hatchings, and the resulting bonded Riders will be under his control."

Rita who had been listening intently but remaining quiet while Delno talked with his uncle asked, "But the Northern Kingdoms left the south over two thousand years ago; why would he come here looking to find suitable candidates?"

Dorian smiled. "Rita, I may not be much of a military man, but there are two things I am quite good with: politics and history." He looked at Delno and asked, "How many Riders are there now?"

"About a hundred," Delno answered.

"Well, when the Exiled Kings moved north, there were just over two hundred. When the Clan wars started, there were nearly five hundred Riders."

Delno and Rita looked at each other in shocked silence.

Dorian smiled and said, "Yes, five hundred bonded pairs flying about the lands. There wasn't a time in those days when one didn't find at least one Rider staying as a royal guest at some noble house. It was a grand time, and there was peace. Then the feuds began to break out all over. The Riders, most of them nobly born, quickly began to take sides. It was house against house on the ground, and dragon against dragon in the sky. The numbers of all began to diminish at an alarming rate. Finally, some of the Riders realized that they needed to rise above their house allegiances, or they would all perish. Your grandfather, Corolan, was chief among them. He convinced the other Riders, or at least some of them, that the fighting had to stop; that the houses would slaughter themselves if it continued. Those Riders who flew with him worked quickly but quietly to help the two most prosperous houses, House Corice and House Bourne, to get the advantage. They had hoped that by having those houses in control, the rest would then fall into line and cease hostilities." At Delno's astonished look he responded to his nephew's unspoken question, "Yes, Corolan actually helped Houses Corice and Bourne gain the upper hand against his own House Palamore. He knew that, at the time, House Palamore wasn't strong enough to either stand alone or unite the Houses. Since, up to that point, Bourne and Corice were not nearly as antagonistic to each other, he chose them because, not only were they strong enough, but they weren't actively trying to kill each other. It was a gamble, but if it hadn't worked, all of the houses would have been destroyed."

He paused while Rita and Delno absorbed what he had said before he continued, "The two houses, with the help of the Riders, did gain the upper hand, and things began to settle down. The peace between the House Corice and House Bourne lasted for nearly three decades, though there were skirmishes among some of the other houses. Then, just when it looked as though the hostilities would end, two sons, one from House Corice, and one from House Bourne, were captured, and their minds reworked magically to turn them into traitors against their people. Each one managed to kill the leader and many other key figures of his own house before both of them were stopped. However, even with that threat gone, the two biggest Noble Houses were in complete chaos, and the others renewed hostilities and moved against them."

He paused for a moment and sipped some water. "The Riders felt some responsibility for all of this, since they had manipulated the houses into their position of authority, so they decided to try and help in the only way they could. It was through their intervention, and the distraction created by the infighting of the other houses, that the Exiled Kings were able to gather their remaining resources and move north without further loss of life. They found these lands unoccupied except for a few tribes in the mountains. Those people were friendly and showed the first settlers how to survive the harsh winters. Without them, the two houses would have perished. The differing groups quickly settled into two kingdoms, with the mountain people settling into the societies of both. Since House Corice and House Bourne would have nothing to do with magic, the number of bonded pairs declined, in part, due to the loss of the family lines that produced most of the Riders."

"Why did they cut themselves off from magic like that?" Rita asked.

"Because they had been nearly destroyed by magic! They felt that by discouraging magic and teaching the royal families about it so that they could watch for it and guard against it, they could avoid that same thing happening in the future."

"Why, then," Delno asked, "didn't the two houses unite and form one country, rather than the two we have now?"

"That is a question that many scholars have asked over the years," Dorian replied. "I have studied the history extensively, and the only reason that I can think of is simply that neither family wanted to give up any of its own authority for such an alliance. There was enough land that the two families felt they could each make their own way and live in peace. According to what I've read, it even worked for the first few centuries."

"Then how did it get to the point it is now?" Rita asked.

"Perhaps, my dear, our houses are just too arrogant to be allowed so much power," Dorian responded sadly. "At first, the two houses lived in complete peace. The people of Bourne recognized that Corice was the buffer between them and the south, who they still feared. The Bournese even assisted us in keeping our borders free from incursions. Everything we think of as facilitating trade in Corice was originally designed to defend our country from the southerners."

Delno opened his mouth to speak, but his uncle waved him to silence, fully engrossed in his role as teacher at this point. "The docks where we receive and send shipments were originally built because this is the northernmost navigable point on the river. First, the docks were built to prevent any craft from landing troops to the north and flanking us. The city of Larimar then grew up to support and protect the docks. The peace lasted for at least three centuries. However, since we were the border country between the north and our old enemies in the south, we were the ones who had contact with the southerners. Eventually we became less interested in keeping the southerners out and more interested in trade with what had become prosperous countries. Our neighbors to the north eventually became upset that they had no caravan routes and no way for trade boats to reach them. It rankled that they had to pay Corisian merchants who marked the products up to make a profit. Eventually, our enemies to the south became our trading partners, while our friends to the north became our enemies. Wars would break out about once a generation and then a new treaty would be signed and the peace would last a few decades before the cycle started again."

"It seems to me," Rita remarked, "that they brought the trouble upon themselves. If they hadn't been so quick to move farther north to keep you between them and their old enemies, they would have had trade routes available to them. It's only natural that any goods that reach that far are more expensive when they get there."

"My dear," Dorian said, "that has been pointed out to the rulers of Bourne since they first began to complain. It has also been pointed out that they should send their own merchants and buy the goods directly from the caravans, since no caravans go farther than Larimar. The reply to that was the complaint that it still costs money to move the goods whether they are transported by Corisian merchants or Bournese merchants."

"So," Delno said, "about once every twenty five to fifty years the rulers of Bourne get it into their heads that the best solution is to conquer Corice and take control of the trade."

"Exactly," Dorian replied. "Of course, Torrance seems more determined than any of his ancestors. He continues to remind us in diplomatic messages that our countries would be well on the way to lasting peace if we hadn't withdrawn our offer of alliance through marriage, and he continually tests our resolve with these incursions. There are treaties in place that prohibit the building of fortresses on the passes and especially at Stone Bridge. Those treaties were signed to prevent the hindrance of trade, but lately they have simply facilitated the attacks on Corice."

He stared at his nephew for a few moments and then said, "Since the Bournese have disregarded every treaty they find inconvenient, I intend to disregard the treaty prohibiting fortified garrisons on the border routes. We will put an end to future wars before they get to our gates."

Delno was thoughtful for a moment. Then he looked at his great uncle and said, "You could offer the men who surrendered the job of building the fortifications. That way they can earn their keep rather than clutter up the city as political refugees."

Dorian looked at Delno as if he had just been inspired. "That could solve both of our problems," he said suddenly. "You could ask those men to volunteer to go to Horne. I will see to it that any who return are given full citizenship, including voting rights, for service to Corice."

Delno and Rita exchanged looks at the suggestion.

"After all," Dorian explained, "they are soldiers. They know how to fight. We can give them their weapons, and they will also be helping their own homeland in a roundabout way. I am sure we have surmised the correct answer to who is instigating the problems coming out of Bourne. If that can be stopped, perhaps hostilities can be stopped and normal relations reestablished."

"Well," Delno said, "that would only leave one question unanswered. Why would Warrick come so far north to find allies? Why Bourne?"

"Nephew," Dorian responded, "Did you ever study your history?"

"Some, but I didn't have too much chance as a carpenter's son," Delno replied.

"Well," Dorian said, "You should know that the countries we know now are the result of the expansion of the city states that were there before. The city states were named for the Noble Families who controlled them. Corice was one family name, Bourne was another, Palamore was still another, as were Llorn, Horne, Trent and Tyler to name a few. Then some of the Houses who allied themselves with others were absorbed when those larger Houses consolidated their territories into countries and those smaller Houses lent their names to cities such as Orlean, Larimar and Karne. Even when the ruling family no longer bears the name of the country, they are from that line, though interbreeding has comingled the lineages to the point that no one could completely sort it out now."

"Well, that makes sense, but still doesn't explain why Warrick has chosen to find his friends in Bourne," Delno replied.

"Delno," Dorian said smiling, "when you have a chance, you should read the Dragon Lore we have in the library here. Not only do we have much of the ancient history, but we have bought books that contain much of the more recent doings of the world also. Warrick is a second generation Rider. His father was Lance Bourne of the House of Bourne and a very honorable man. Warrick obviously seeks to restore House Bourne to its former place as a ruling House."

CHAPTER 13

THE NEXT DAY Delno met with the highest ranking officers left among those who had surrendered. They were all still being held at the stockyard inside the city walls. While they were being treated well, they were anxious to find out what their fate would be. They understood quite well that they could no longer go home. If Corice wouldn't accept them as political refugees, they wanted to begin making their way south.

"You and your men have been given political refugee status," Delno informed the Captain from Bourne, "but that is all. You have not been given anything more than the right to try and make your own way as refugees in a foreign country."

"I understand," the Bournese officer replied. "We ask only that we be allowed to go about our way and try to find meaningful employment of some kind. We also understand that we won't be taken into the Corisian army and asked to fight against our own homeland, which is as we would prefer anyway. Most of our countrymen who now stand against Corice do so as unwilling conscripts."

"There may be a way that you can help yourselves, them, and ultimately, your homeland of Bourne, Captain."

Delno could see hope spring into the man's eyes, but he also saw a good bit of skepticism there as well.

"What are you offering?" the officer asked.

"A chance to do what you have been trained to do," Delno replied. "I am leading a group of Dragon Riders against someone in Horne who is not only making a grab for power; he is manipulating your king and his senior officers as well. He was once from the Noble House of Bourne, but his close relatives, and therefore his close ties to Bourne, are long dead. We have come to the belief that he is responsible for instigating not only the current situation, but the last war as well."

"If you are asking us to move against our own countryman, as I have already said, we must refuse," the Captain responded.

"No," Delno assured the man, "I am not asking you to take direct action against one your own. The man I speak of is a Dragon Rider who is approximately two thousand years old. He has somehow gotten the beast-men of the south to work together as a cohesive fighting force. You will not even have to work directly against him. Horne, and the Dragon Riders who fly with us, are calling for men and arms to fight the beast-men. Hopefully, once the business in Horne is put to rest, your king will realize that he stands alone and will give up his dream of conquest over Corice. However, even if your king decides to continue the fight, you, and any men with you who live through the war in Horne, will be given citizenship with full voting rights here in Corice, if you choose to accept it."

"I have heard rumors of these beast-men. They are fierce fighters and give no quarter, nor do they ask for any. They fight to the death and rarely retreat. What you are asking is nearly as difficult as fighting against your dragons. Many of my men are seasoned veterans and career soldiers, but many more are simply conscripted farmers and tradesmen with no more than basic training. I will ask them all, but I fear you may get fewer men than you would like for this campaign."

"I will take any who are willing to march," replied Delno. "A hundred seasoned veterans to add to the soldiers who have already been sent to assist in this fight would still be better than none. Tell your men that so far no dragon has flown with the enemy forces in this campaign, but we have at least five there now and six more will be joining soon. The call is out for more and we hope that our dragons will number several times that of those the enemy commands. Also, I have a few surprises still in store for our enemies. However, you should know that even though we will be trying to support them from the air, the time may come when your men will have to face an enemy dragon, but by that time we will have taught them how to at least defend themselves better from such attacks."

"You don't paint a cheery picture of victory, Rider," the officer responded.

"I won't lie to you or your men, Captain; this is not to be an easily won campaign. The stakes are high for those who go. That's why the prize is so great. Corice doesn't bestow the right to participate in politics to soldiers who are citizen volunteers until they have completed their eighth year of service, or have distinguished themselves with such deeds that their bravery and loyalty can be questioned by none. You are being offered that right for one campaign; we believe the prize fits the deed."

Delno let his words hang in the air for a moment and then said, "Speak with your men, Captain. Tell them about the campaign and paint them a realistic picture. Those who go will be accepted as citizens if and when they return. For those who do not go, nothing will change. They will still be political refugees and will have to make their way as best they can. I will return for your answer after I have seen your former commander and his staff safely across Stone Bridge."

"The men of Bourne know the name Delno Okonan. Even though you stood against us in the last war, we all know you to be a good soldier and an honorable man. You haven't tried to lure us to Horne with rosy pictures of easy victory. You deal with us honestly and we appreciate that. I will talk with the men and have an answer for you soon."

The officer saluted Delno and Delno returned the salute before walking away from the holding area.

Later, astride Geneva at Stone Bridge, Delno could see that a force of Bournese soldiers was camped just out of bow range on their own side of the chasm. A large force of Corisians was similarly camped on the southern side. The soldiers of Bourne started to approach the bridge, but Geneva sent forth a great burst of fire that reached nearly half-way across the span and they stopped their advance. Fahwn and Beth circled lazily above the spectacle but were ready to join in if a battle erupted.

A wagon was brought up to the bridge. General Andrewson and his staff were offloaded. They were all in shackles but otherwise unharmed. General Dreighton approached on horseback and said, "As per the treaties of old, since you are senior officers you are to be released here to return to your own army. You won't be harmed. But know this: King Dorian has decreed that since your liege lord disregards treaties as he sees fit, we will not honor such a treaty in the future. If you are again caught on Corisian soil, you will be executed without trial or ceremony.

Go now and tell your king that it is in his best interest to cease hostilities against Corice."

The general and his officers were released from their shackles in full view of the Bournese soldiers who were watching from a safe distance. The staff officers immediately turned to make their way across the bridge, but the general called them to a halt.

"You are in no position to dictate any terms to the officers of Bourne," Andrewson said. "The only reason you managed to overcome our forces on the field was through the treachery of rebellious troops on our side. When I return with troops who will remain loyal, we shall see who will be executed. I will personally drag that son of a dog you call king before my Lord in chains to beg for his worthless life."

Delno slid down from Geneva's neck and walked to General Andrewson. "I am beginning to believe that you are either as mad as your men think you to be, or you are such a fool that you believe that you will be allowed to get a force into Corice again. I truly do feel sorry for the men under your command."

Andrewson smiled. "Your dragons won't be here forever, fool. When they are gone, we will have little trouble conquering Corice. We have some surprises of our own."

"The future is always in motion," Delno responded. "We shall see in due time. For now though, I am done with you. Get yourself across this bridge before my patience fails, and I throw you into the canyon. He turned and strode back to Geneva without so much as a backward glance.

The Dragon Riders and General Dreighton stayed to oversee construction of the fortifications at the bridge. The first step was to be a timber palisade directly across the bridge itself. That would protect the workers while they built a stone structure that would be completed with an iron gate. Once the stone rampart was built, the timber would be removed.

Thick hard wood trees were quickly cut and put into position. As the timbers were being placed, Andrewson sent a messenger across the bridge to inform the Corisians that Bourne felt the wall was a violation of treaties with Bourne, and if construction wasn't stopped, he would have his troops attack immediately. General Dreighton told the messenger to tell General Andrewson to go pound salt up his arse.

Shortly after the messenger got back to his camp, a large group of Bournese soldiers gathered in preparation for a charge across the bridge.

General Dreighton called for archers, but Delno had them wait until he gave the order before firing. While workers continued to put the large logs into place, Delno set about constructing a magical barrier about midway across the bridge. The Bournese troops were allowed to march right up to the barrier. The front row of six men was quite surprised when they walked right into the shield and were stopped as if they had hit a wall. More and more men gathered on the other side of the shield. Many tried to penetrate it with spears and swords to no avail. The officers were yelling useless orders and frantically trying to get the men to double their efforts. Several men fell from the bridge to their deaths in the canyon. Eventually, with the Corisians laughing and jeering at them, the men of Bourne retreated. Once off the bridge on the other side of the canyon, they were able to send a volley of arrows at the men still working on the timber palisade since the shield only extended across the bridge itself; the Corisian archers returned fire. Unfortunately for the soldiers of Bourne, the Corisians were more accurate. Over a dozen Bournese fell dead, and the remaining men of Bourne retreated to a safe distance.

Delno healed the Corisian workers who had been hit by arrows. There had been one death on the Corisian side of the canyon. The men continued working for the rest of the day and far into the night. By the next morning, a large timber wall completely blocked the bridge. Then the workers started construction on the stone works that would keep the bridge impassable to the Bournese Army.

"What if they bring up siege engines to destroy the stone works like they did in Larimar?" Adamus asked. Rita nodded her head in agreement with his question.

"If they do that," Delno responded, "they will most likely weaken the bridge as well, since the stone works are anchored on the stone of the bridge itself. Our own siege engines will then destroy the bridge completely. Once all of this madness is over and lasting peace is achieved, we can build a man-made bridge across this chasm. Until then, the only other passes into Corice from Bourne are much too narrow to get siege engines into, so the fortifications we are building at those will hold. Stone Bridge is the easiest passage, and the most accessible; as in the last war, it must either be held or destroyed completely."

That night Delno concentrated on the Dream State and Geneva as he drifted off to sleep. It worked; he found himself standing with Geneva on a ledge within moments. Geneva was a bit surprised to find that he had come of his own accord.

"I don't think I could have come if you weren't here, though," he said to her.

"No, I don't think so either, Love, but it is a nice trick and has saved us time this evening. There are several non-bonded dragons who wish to speak with us. They were quite surprised to find that Marlo had flown to get Nat and even more shocked when the two of them bonded. They wish to discuss this."

He was about to answer when two females soared down to land near them. He knew they were not really this close in life; that the Dream State was a psychic creation, but he was still impressed to be in such close proximity to them.

"Hello, I am Delno Okonan, bonded to Geneva, and friend of Marlo."

"I am Sheila, and I also know Marlo," the larger, red dragon said. "I am concerned that you have spoken with Marlo, and she is now bonded. How have you done this? There are those of us who do not wish to be bonded. You must not do this again."

"I have done nothing," Delno replied. "Marlo offered to bring Nathaniel to me so that he could help with the plague in Larimar. They became bonded on the trip. It was not my doing; I had not anticipated it, but Marlo is happy with the bond."

"Yes, Marlo has always been fascinated by humans. I believe she has always wanted to be bonded but never had the opportunity," the other dragon said shyly. "She spent many days pining over the men she watched. I believe she will be much happier now that she has found a partner."

Sheila sat pensively for a few moments before she spoke. "Alright, I concede the point. That Marlo has found a way to become bonded is no great surprise, but this still produces a danger for the rest of us if we interact with humans. Suppose we find ourselves bonded when we don't wish to be?"

"That may be a danger," admitted Delno. "However, what of the dragons who aren't bonded who wish to be? If I have no right to promote this, do you have the right to prevent it?"

Sheila lifted her head and started to make a harsh reply but there was a ripple in the "fabric" of the Dream State and the other dragon said hastily, "He makes a good point, Sheila. None of us have the right to interfere either way. If a dragon wishes to be bonded then she should be allowed the opportunity. If a dragon is content with her status as non-bonded then she should not be forced into situations that would put her in close proximity with humans."

"Of course you would take that side, Saadia," Sheila replied, "the fact that you would like to be bonded is no great secret."

Saadia, a smaller dragon who was the color of a light blue summer sky with no other markings, hung her head. "I do not deny that I hate the loneliness. I also do not deny that I find the Dream State a poor substitute for actual companionship," she said softly. Then she raised her head somewhat defiantly and continued, "But the choice should be mine, not yours or anyone else's. If I choose to seek out a human, you have no right to interfere."

Delno waited for Sheila's angry reply, but was pleased that the red dragon didn't make one. Instead Sheila said, "You are right, of course, Saadia. I have no right to decide such fate for others. Legends speak of such things happening in the distant past, but it has been so long since an adult dragon has bonded that I had thought those legends were false. Even among the oldest females, who have watched this world for more than six millennia, none can remember such a thing happening, though all say that it did happen in the past. I suppose it will take some time to get used to the idea."

"I appreciate your open-mindedness, Sheila," Delno said. "I believe that we have mutual enemies who are waging war on two fronts: here in Corice and south in Horne. Those enemies seek to take any such choices from us. I believe that if our enemies succeed, they will not only seek to destroy all dragons and riders who oppose them, but all dragons who are not bonded as well. The leader of these enemies hopes to establish himself as supreme leader of the world and he knows that as long as non-bonded dragons exist, there is a chance that Riders will arise who can oppose him. He will eventually try to kill all free female dragons he cannot bring directly under his control."

"Are you then proposing that we seek to bond and commit ourselves to your control?" Sheila asked suspiciously.

"No, I am not suggesting that at all. Certainly I would help any who seek to bond with humans to do so if they ask, but that is not my goal here. My goal is to ask for aid in our fight against a mutual enemy for the benefit of us all. Those who wish to remain non-bonded are certainly welcome to the life they choose."

"And if you win this war, what of those dragons who remained neutral?" Sheila asked him.

"I don't seek dominion over them. My ultimate goal is to unite the Riders under an oath of service to the intelligent species of this world in the hope of preventing this war from being repeated with new players in the future. As for those we refer to as Wild Dragons, they are free to do as they please, just as they have always been."

Sheila sat thinking for several moments before responding. "I believe you," she said finally. "I will talk with the others of my kind who might aid you and contact you with their answer. However, don't expect too much until they have seen some proof of your loyalties. We have been tricked before by men who were Riders and should have been true to their word. Many of the dragons who were there for that will be slow to respond favorably to your plea for help."

"I am near the lands you call Corice," Saadia said, speaking up. "I will come to you and we will talk. I am willing to help you, and perhaps I might find someone worth bonding with, as well."

Sheila stared at Saadia for a long moment and then shook her head and said, "I suppose that was to be expected; you have always felt the loneliness more than I. I will not try to talk you out of this daughter, the decision is yours to make."

"Thank you, Mother; I feel that my future, even if it brings me death at the hands of our mutual enemies, lies with men."

Delno and Geneva bade Sheila farewell and then, before leaving the Dream State, told Saadia that she could find them at Larimar later that morning.

CHAPTER 14

THE NEXT DAY, with the construction of the stone works well under way at Stone Bridge, Delno told Rita and Adamus of his meeting with Sheila and her daughter in the Dream State.

"Having more dragons will certainly be a help, but can they be trusted to act in our best interests?" Adamus asked.

"As long as it is in their best interest as well, I can't see why not," Rita responded. "After all, they are reasonable beings. So long as their fate moves with ours we should make good allies."

"Yes, that's true," Delno replied, "to a point." The other two Riders stared at him while he collected his thoughts. "Dragons who are not bonded are at a definite disadvantage in battle, even against ground troops. We aren't just along for the ride when the dragons make a strafing run. We maintain shields that keep their hides free of arrows or other missiles. When fighting another dragon and Rider, we use magic while they do the flying and maneuvering. We are a team. In either case, the lone dragon is more vulnerable and we will have to take pains to help them as best we can."

"It is rare for an arrow to penetrate the hide of a dragon," Adamus remarked. "Even your bow isn't powerful enough to penetrate a dragon's scales."

"Yes, but the scales get slack if the dragon is fatigued, leaving enough space for an arrow to get between them if the angle is right. Fighting a war can be quite fatiguing," Delno replied. "Also, their eyes are vulnerable. If enough arrows are aimed at their heads when they make a pass one is bound to hit the mark. The eyelids are somewhat armored but you can't aim with your eyes closed."

"That will present a problem," Rita said, "We will have to try and maintain shields on two dragons at once. That doesn't strike me as an easy thing to do. Have you ever tried it, Delno?"

"Not yet," Delno replied, "though I have done similar acts of magic when shielding more than one person at a time from a mind probe. However, we may be putting the wagon before the oxen in this situation. Sheila has said that she will speak with the other dragons; none have joined us yet."

"You're wrong, Handsome," Rita said, "Two wild dragons have joined us so far. Marlo and Saadia have joined outright, more will come." Then she smiled seductively and added, "You can be very persuasive when you want to be."

Delno almost laughed as Adamus blushed at Rita's double entendre. Adamus was a young man and a bit embarrassed at Rita's sometimes blatant sexual references. Delno didn't get the chance to respond to any of it, however, because just then an alarm was raised; the Bournese were trying something to stop the construction of the fortifications.

The Riders quickly mounted and took to the sky where the dragons would be most effective. Once in the air Delno saw the reason for the alarm: the Bournese had spent the night constructing two small catapults and were now launching pitch balls at the wooden palisade. Archers were standing by to shoot fire arrows at the pitch once they had enough of it on the wood. Green wood had been used to frustrate the use of fire arrows, but the pitch would burn long enough and hot enough to make even green wood catch fire. Since the stone works were barely begun, this was a serious threat to the wall and could lead to another battle for Stone Bridge.

"You have to give them credit for tenacity," he said to Geneva.

"I'd rather they go away so that I can give them credit for having some good sense," she responded.

Delno quickly began drawing energy from his surroundings and concentrated on the nearest catapult. The machine was nothing compared to the huge trebuchets that had been brought to Larimar, but it didn't have to be. The trebuchets were large siege engines that used a weighted arm to hurl rocks that weighed nearly twenty stone through fortified walls. These catapults used saplings as springs to launch balls of soft pitch that weighed less than two stone. They were merely a way to get the pitch to the wood while remaining just out of bow range. Instead of knocking the wall down, they would then use flaming arrows to ignite the pitch and burn the logs.

Rather than concentrate on the catapult itself, Delno was concentrating on the pitch balls that were setting beside it. They began to bubble and smoke. The men who were handling them backed away as several of the balls burst into flame. The crew tried desperately to put the fire out before it consumed the catapult itself but they didn't have water near to hand, and beating at it with tarps and blankets only smashed the balls and spread the flames. The wood of the catapult itself began to burn a few moments later. The men manning the machine were forced back by the heat.

"One down, one to go," he said.

"Make it quick, Love; they've got the range with the second one."

Delno watched as the second catapult launched a pitch ball which sailed in a neat arch and landed with a splat right against the lower part of the palisade at the bridge. He began to concentrate as the crew hauled the spring arm of the machine back in preparation for another shot. The pitch balls around the machine began to smoke as another one was loaded into the basket ready to be fired. Before the machine could be fired, the pitch still on the ground burst into flames. This time the crew didn't even try to put it out. Delno had used so much energy so quickly that all of the pitch laid out around the machine caught fire at once, nearly exploding. The machine was quickly being engulfed by flames. The rope that held the spring arm back quickly burned through and the pitch ball in the basket, now flaming, sailed toward its target.

Delno realized that in his haste to destroy the machine before it could launch more pitch at the wall, he had inadvertently caused it to launch the flame that might well destroy a section of the palisade. He watched as the flaming orb seemed to sail in slow motion toward its target. He tried to erect a shield that would stop it, but found that the slow motion was an illusion of the adrenalin now rushing into his system; his own actions were moving just as slowly. He failed to get the shield up in time and the ball hit its mark. Within seconds the pitch that was already splattered on the wall caught, seconds after that, the flames were nearly fifteen feet high once all of the pitch was burning. Delno swore as a cheer went up on the Bournese side of the bridge.

Delno could only watch as workers climbed the palisade and began a bucket brigade to try and dowse the fire that was burning brightly on the other side of the wall. The Bournese archers quickly took position and began shooting at the men on top of the wall. One man fell with an arrow in his chest.

"*Nothing we can do for them except try and keep those archers at bay. Are you ready, Dear Heart?*" Delno asked.

"*I will be by the time we are close enough. Hang on.*"

Delno could feel the flame bladder expand as Geneva banked towards the archers. He erected a shield that would protect her from the majority of the arrows that he was sure would come. Erecting such a shield was a tricky business in itself. Put the shield far enough forward that it completely protected the dragon's head and neck, and it would block her flame, possibly even throw it back in their own faces. Put the shield too far back and he might as well not even bother. The big trick was to protect the unarmored wing membranes. Fortunately, a dragon's head is well protected with thick plates, providing she doesn't get hit directly in the eyes. Delno, thinking of trying to use two shields at once, directed a second shield in a kind of transparent cover over Geneva's eyes. He did that to see if he could maintain two shields, but it was a lucky thing he did, as a volley of arrows that were aimed at her head, and especially her eyes, bounced harmlessly off and fell to the ground.

Geneva made her pass and her fire was devastating. Over a dozen men died as she flamed the line of archers. The rest turned and ran, but this time they scattered rather than clumping together, making themselves less likely targets as Fahwn made a pass right behind Geneva. Delno had Geneva relay to Adamus to hold and wait until the Bournese regrouped rather than make his pass right behind Fahwn.

"*Thank you, Love. That second shield saved me from being blinded. It would seem that our enemies have been coached on how to fight dragons since last we fought them,*" Geneva said.

"*I was thinking the same thing,*" Delno replied. "*Tell the others to make sure their eyes are shielded, too. This is not going to be an easily won rout; it looks like we will truly have to fight.*"

"*I have already told them to shield their eyes. What I would like to do is find out who is instructing our enemies and target them,*" she answered.

"*That's a tactic they won't be expecting,*" Delno said as he watched the archers beginning to regroup. "*Can you see the enemy's command tent, Love?*"

"*I see a group of three tents with people coming and going with great purpose. Wait: there is the enemy general we released standing just inside the open flap of one of the tents.*"

"Well, then," Delno said, "*that is our next target. Tell the others to keep on the archers; we have to give the men on the wall a chance to put out that fire. It seems to be burning out of control and catching much faster than I would have expected.*"

Geneva did as he directed, then angled her flight directly towards the tent she had spotted the enemy commander in. She stayed high enough to remain out of arrow range until she had to commit to her run. On impulse, Delno examined the area magically and found that there was someone inside using magic. Whoever it was apparently didn't expect to be attacked in the command tent, because the magic wasn't directed at Geneva. It appeared to Delno that the magic user was concentrating on increasing the fire at the wall. Delno made no attempt to interrupt the magic user as Geneva dived down and flamed all three tents. The magic user and the commanders didn't know they were in danger until it was too late: the canvas was no protection at all from Geneva's fire.

At the same instant, Fahwn and Beth made simultaneous runs against the archers. On this run, however, Fahwn attacked the front rank while Beth attacked the rear from the opposite direction. It required a bit of precision on the part of the dragons, but it left the archers nowhere to run. This time, only a dozen men escaped and they fled in complete panic. The infantrymen who had been massing for an assault fell back, unsure what to do. Everyone on the Bournese side appeared to be waiting for orders that would never come. Delno had the other two Riders remain in the air while he returned to speak with General Dreighton.

As Delno dismounted, the general came to him at a trot followed by his staff. "That was a good bit of flying, Rider," he said. "We have the fire under control, but the logs are burned nearly half way through. If that display of yours hasn't discouraged them from further attempts to take the bridge before we can get the stone works into place, then we may have no choice other than destroying Stone Bridge itself. The king was quite clear: 'Either build a stonework that will hold, or destroy that damned bridge,' I believe, were his exact words."

"Well, General," Delno replied, "I can't guarantee that they won't try again soon, but they will be a bit slower to do so without their commanding general and his senior staff." Dreighton and his staff officers looked a bit shocked by that news, so Delno continued, "I believe that we also got at least one of the advisors sent by our enemies from the south as well: he was using magic and was the reason the palisade burned so hot so quickly."

He then dismounted and told Dreighton everything that had transpired during the battle. The general was at first shocked that Delno had made the attack on the command tents, but quickly decided it was for the best. It seemed that all of the old rules of engagement that Bourne and Corice had abided by had now been set aside. It also seemed that since it was Corice that had dealt two devastating blows in less than a week, the Bournese would most likely be hard pressed to field another competent commander to the bridge for several days at least. That should give the workers time to get much of the stone work done before they would have to repel another attack, since the masons were working round the clock.

Fahwn and Beth were doing fine since the air currents were good, and soaring meant they could conserve energy. Geneva relayed that both dragons felt that they could stay aloft for several hours if need be. Delno had them remain aloft until he was sure that the battle was truly over and the damaged timbers were reinforced from the Corisian side. Then he asked Adamus to stay at the bridge as air support if the need arose, while he and Rita returned to Larimar.

CHAPTER 15

A S THEY GLIDED down to the city walls, Delno and Rita both noticed that there was a light blue dragon sitting near Marlo. Geneva relayed to Fahwn and Rita that the newcomer was Saadia, who had decided to join them.

"We are much later than we had thought we would be, Love," Geneva said. "Don't be surprised at what you find when we land."

No amount of coaxing could get any more information out of her, though Delno could feel that she was quite amused at whatever the situation was.

Nat was standing near Marlo looking quite pleased with himself. Delno could tell that he had some news to share by the look on the half-elf's face. He smiled and returned the physician's wave. Then he noticed that Will was standing near Saadia. In fact, he had his hand on her shoulder, and the two appeared to be quite comfortable with each other.

He was astounded at the implication and turned to Geneva. "You could have told me that my brother had bonded with Saadia," he said aloud.

"And miss that look of surprise on your face? Never!" she replied.

Will, smiling broadly, waved at his older brother. As Delno walked over to him, he saluted. Delno returned the salute and smiled.

"Well, I see you and Saadia have met," Delno understated.

"It was the most amazing thing, Delno," Will replied. "I came out here with Nathaniel to meet Marlo, and while we were all talking, Saadia came. Marlo was in contact with her, and I was just watching her fly to the wall, thinking that she must be the most beautiful dragon in the world. She landed and introduced herself rather shyly, and we started talking. She was craning her neck around to get a better look at me when I turned to see the source of a noise behind me. There was a bright flash of light, and then I had a burning sensation over my right shoulder blade, and we were bonded."

"I was watching the whole time," Nat said. "I was actually disappointed, if you want the truth. That's two bondings I've been present for and didn't actually notice anything extraordinary. I really must work on my awareness. I'm beginning to realize how much slips past me when I am preoccupied."

"While you are certainly right about your preoccupations, my friend," Delno said through his laughter, "I believe that there isn't much for observers to see. For the most part bonding takes place between the two who are actively involved, and there isn't any real show to watch."

"That may be," Nat replied, "but if you remember, I didn't know I was bonded until you saw the mark and explained it to me. I miss far too much worrying about my medicines."

"Yes," Rita said, giving the healer a kiss on the cheek, "and the rest of us are much better for it. As Delno said before, if it weren't for you, we would be defending a tomb."

Nat smiled at the compliment. "Oh, that brings me back to my news. The plague is completely under control. Those who are still a bit sick are being treated and will be back to normal in a few days. The city is now safe from the disease."

"That is indeed wonderful news, Nat, but I am not at all surprised." As Nat's face fell, he quickly added, "There's good reason I sent for you, my friend; I had complete faith in you and your healing skills. That you have brought the plague under control so quickly only shows that my faith was as well placed, as I knew it would be."

Nat beamed.

Delno turned to the newcomer and said, "I apologize for not being here to meet you personally, Saadia, but the Bournese attacked the new fortifications this morning, and we had to deal with that before we could leave Stone Bridge."

"It is all right, Delno Okonan," Saadia replied. "If you had been here, I might not have met my Partner. I am happy with the way that things have worked out."

"Yes, and my brother also appears happy with the arrangement." Then he turned to Will and said, "I have never known you to work the slightest magic, Brother. How is it that you came to bond with a dragon?"

"Never known me to work magic? Do you remember playing hide and seek as children? Ever wonder why I always won?" Will responded. "I have always had the ability to hide if I don't want to be found. You can look right at me and not see me, even in broad daylight."

"I thought you just knew the best hiding places," Delno laughed and clapped his brother on the shoulder. Will winced a bit, but still smiled, and Delno apologized for forgetting about the fresh dragon mark.

"I would love to stay up here and talk with you and Saadia, but I must see the king," Delno said turning and striding away.

"We will have to talk much before you leave Corice, Brother," Will called out to his brother's back. "I know nothing about being a Rider, and I have a pregnant dragon to care for."

Delno stopped as if he had run into a brick wall. "Pregnant!" he exclaimed. "I had no idea she was pregnant."

"It's not as though dragons can be held to the same standards as humans," Will said defensively.

Realizing that Will had taken his words to mean he was unhappy with circumstances, he said, "You misunderstand me, Brother. This is wonderful news." He smiled at both Will and Saadia. "How many eggs, and what are the sexes of the hatchlings?"

Will looked a little confused, like a child in school who should know the answer to the teacher's question but doesn't.

"Three eggs," Saadia replied. "One male and two females. I will lay the eggs within three weeks' time, I think. I am not as sure as I would be if I were older; this is my first clutch."

"For a day that started out so tragically, it is turning out to be a day of wonderful news," Delno said. "First, my younger brother bonds with a dragon, and now I find that we are to have new hatchlings soon. We will have to make arrangements for you to clutch someplace comfortable. Tell me, what do you require?"

"When the time comes, I will require a peaceful place to lie down and lay the eggs, but that is still weeks away. I will need to hunt today or tomorrow. I flew a long way since last night and my body was already somewhat depleted from producing the eggs and their shells."

"Then you shall have all the food you require," came the king's voice as he appeared at the top of the stairs that led up to the wall from the watchtower door. All of the men on the wall snapped to attention. The king addressed Saadia directly: "How much food do you require, my dear? I will see to it that you get it."

Saadia looked at the king for a moment, and then smiled a draconic smile. Most men would have paled at seeing all of those teeth displayed at them like that; Dorian simply returned the gesture.

"I am hungry enough to eat at least one of those animals you call cows, and perhaps one or two pigs as well," she replied.

"Very well," the king responded. "Do you wish to kill your own down on the field, or would you like me to have some men slaughter the animals and bring the meat to you here?"

"I appreciate the offer to bring the meat, but bringing the animals to the field for me to kill will be fine, thank you."

The king turned to a soldier standing at attention nearby and said, "You there, corporal."

Delno didn't think the man could stand any more rigid without snapping his spine but the corporal actually managed to straighten just a bit before responding to his liege lord, "Yes, Sire."

"Take however many men you need, and secure a nicely fattened cow and two pigs, and then have them staked out in the field close enough to the wall that our new friend won't have to fly far to get to them," Dorian said, and then added, "Also, make sure they are all at least a dragon length apart, so that she has no trouble with them while she feeds."

"Yes, Sire." The man immediately turned to do his king's bidding. Dorian called out to him, "If anyone gives you any trouble, refer them directly to me, and I will deal with them. Then report back to me at the palace when the job is done; I will have more for you to do."

Dorian turned to Delno, "If he does a good job, I'll promote him and put him in charge of making sure the dragons and Riders have everything they need."

"Uncle," Delno said with some concern creeping into his voice.

Before he could finish his thought, Dorian cut him off and said, "I know, Nephew. I may not be as strong in magic as you and your brother, but I can feel the concern in you now. The Riders can't afford to feel indebted to any kingdom. I am not giving you presents here. You have done great deeds in defense of this country, and a few cows and pigs are small payment for such service. As long as I am king, Dragon Riders will be treated as royalty in Corice. I turned away from a Rider once before, and it has cost me my twin sister, and left my kingdom open to attack from our northern neighbors ever since. I can't go back and rectify that directly, but I am not a man who repeats his mistakes."

Delno nodded to his uncle and he, Rita, and Nat accompanied Dorian back to the palace to discuss the morning's events.

CHAPTER 16

ONCE BACK IN private chambers with his great uncle, Delno told Dorian of all that had transpired at the bridge. Dorian was a bit unsettled by the news that Delno had directly attacked the command tents.

"Directly attacking the commanders has always been considered *uncivilized* by both kingdoms, until now," Dorian said.

"In case no one has noticed," Delno said a bit sarcastically, "war isn't exactly a civilized activity, especially if you are one of the common soldiers who has to bear the brunt of the fighting."

"You're right, of course, Nephew," Dorian said in a softer tone. "Often commanders have to put aside personal feelings and send men to die; it is easier to disregard that awful fact if you think of the men as tools rather than individuals. Perhaps if we kept our focus on the fact that they are men, we wouldn't be so quick to wage war in the first place."

"We can take some small comfort in the fact that we aren't the ones waging this war, Uncle. We are merely defending ourselves and our country."

Everyone was silent for a long time and then Rita said, "We will have to make provision to have someone here to help train the new Riders once Saadia's offspring are hatched and bonded."

"Are we even sure she wants them to be bonded?" replied Nat. "After all, she herself was born free and made the choice later; perhaps she will want the same for her daughters."

"Oh, she wants them to bond at hatching, alright," Will said as he entered the chamber and joined them. "She has felt the loneliness of being un-bonded since she was hatched, and doesn't want her daughters to go through that. She is convinced, as are others from what she has told me, that dragons were designed to bond with humans, and that not doing so feels like an unnatural act."

"Well, that would certainly fit with all you have told me about the history of dragons, Nat," Delno said. "They are a created species that was designed from the beginning to bond with and enhance the ability of both species to use magic. I am beginning to think that the territorial solitude they impose is more in keeping with that design than to keep them from depleting an area of food. After all, dragons are an intelligent species: if they wished to raise large herds for the purpose of keeping a good food supply available, they could certainly do so."

"That's an interesting theory," Nat replied. "But why would the dragons say it was because of the food supply, then?"

"Is that question actually coming from the man who told us about humans practicing self-delusion in order to accept what would otherwise be distasteful?" Rita asked with a smile.

Nat smiled back and said, "I am merely trying to look at the situation from different angles, my dear."

"Well, theories are all well and good," Delno responded, "but they don't help us with our current problems. We have two dragons about to lay two female eggs each. We have two candidates in Orlean to present to those eggs, but none here in Corice. Even if we do find suitable candidates, we have no experienced Riders to leave with any of the newly bonded pairs if we are to field as much strength as possible in Horne."

"What about Nat?" Will asked. "He is a new Rider, but he is as well versed in dragon lore as our uncle."

"Now that the immediate danger of the plague here has been dealt with, Nat will need to leave for Horne as soon as possible." Delno looked at the half-elf and said sternly, "You are not to engage the enemy down there; you are much too valuable as a healer to risk your life fighting with some damn fool Rider who is working for our enemies."

"I thought that Riders had no clear leaders and were able to do as they saw fit," Nat quipped.

"They are," Delno replied, "so long as they are not our best healer, who I consider to be irreplaceable. I don't feel that one dragon, more or less, even one as brave as Marlo, will make that much difference, but your skills as a physician may be the difference between life and death for those who are injured in the war that is coming."

"I'm not exactly helpless, my friend, but I will do my best to avoid any direct fighting," the physician replied.

"That still leaves me," Dorian spoke up. "I have read much dragon lore over the years. It is required reading for the nobility of Corice, and I became especially interested after my sister left with Corolan. I know much about care and training of young dragons. With Saadia's help, we could begin the training of the two hatchlings here in Corice."

"That is all well and good, uncle, except that I don't want to burden Corice with that duty, especially since the Riders' loyalties must be to the dragons and not any one country in particular."

The pointed comment wasn't lost on Dorian. "I have no intention of trying to usurp the young Riders' loyalty, Nephew," he said softly, "but I do admit that my offer is not completely altruistic. Our enemies to the north have now seen two examples of what dragons can do in a battle. Our enemies to the south, and I fully believe that Warrick is the main enemy of Corice, will have their hands full trying to deal with the Riders you take to Horne. I believe that Warrick did not expect you to have so many willing Riders follow you, and he has overextended himself. Therefore, he will not be able to send Riders to Bourne, and the Bournese will be slow to attack if we have dragons watching from our walls. After all, they have no way of knowing that the dragons they see aren't fully trained and ready to breathe destruction down upon them."

"Also," Will added, "Saadia is not exactly immature, if you will recall. She is quite capable of carrying messages and scouting our borders. It will take me some time, but I am sure that I can learn to be a good Rider and assist her as needed."

"Very well," Delno answered them, "I concede the point. However," he turned to Will, "there is much you need to learn about magic that no one here can teach you. Magic is an integral part of the equation when fighting from the back of a dragon. You will at least need to understand how to erect and maintain a shield to keep both of your hides free of arrows."

"Actually," Dorian interjected, "there are books about those types of things here in the palace. I think it is high time that such books again be made public knowledge, even if they are kept under royal scrutiny. I will see to it the Riders who remain here while you are in Horne have access to them."

"Books on magic being made public, Uncle?" Delno quipped. "Won't that enrage the citizenry of a country that tends to disdain magic?"

"Oh, many of them do fear magic, but since your use of it to break the siege, most of those citizens have had a change of heart," Dorian replied. "I don't keep myself totally secluded here in the palace, Nephew; I go out and about quite regularly to see what my people think of how their country is being run. That is why I've been a popular king for so long. From what I have gathered, the old prejudices against magic are not nearly as strong as they used to be. There are a few holdouts who still think anyone who is associated with magic should be banished, if not killed, which is one of the reasons I am so glad that your mother and father have moved into the palace, since their connection with you would put them at risk. However, most people are willing to at least be open-minded on the subject."

"Especially when it directly benefits them," Will said sarcastically.

Delno shrugged and said, "We are a pragmatic people. I suppose that now they have seen magic work to their benefit they are more open-minded than I would have given them credit for being." Then, switching subjects, he added, "It would seem that our training problems, here at least, are handled. I hope we can do as well in Orlean."

"Why don't we leave the trainees under the care of Connor there?" Rita asked. "He is already familiar with the boys you have picked to bond, and they trust him."

"I had thought about that, and it is the most likely solution. However, he isn't going to like it. He is fourteen and anxious to prove himself; he will want to accompany his father to Horne. If Brock agrees with that request, I have no real right to order him to stay in Orlean."

"I doubt Brock will agree to it," she replied. "Brock has buried several of his children over the years because they weren't bonded, and he simply outlived them. He was extremely pleased when Jenka chose Connor, but he has also been worried that the two of them would be called to fight the Roracks in Horne as he has done over the years. That is the real reason he agreed to let Simcha train the boy, although he claims it was Connor's foster parents who talked him into it. He wanted to keep him as far from trouble as possible. No parent should have to bury a child; it's supposed to be the other way around."

Everyone in the room nodded in agreement with Rita's last statement. Will was suddenly stricken with the enormity of what had been said. Until that moment, he had not given any thought to any of the negatives to being bonded to a dragon. In fact, until that moment, he hadn't even stopped to realize that he would now outlive every member of his family other than Delno by hundreds, possibly thousands of years.

Delno saw the realization dawn on him, and he put his hand on his half-brother's shoulder and said, "Now you know the curse of the Riders. We have to watch our kin and our friends grow old and die as we stay young and fit, and once we have buried them all, we still must live on for many years." Then a thought occurred to him. "Brother," he said, "Do you have someone whom you had hoped to marry?"

Will looked at Delno and saw the great concern in his eyes and felt a sense of kinship they had never before shared. It was, perhaps, the most overt act of brotherly protection that Delno had ever shown him. He smiled and responded, "No, I have been so busy with my studies in both carpentry and art that I have not had the chance to form such an attachment. I have been known to attend social events with a couple of young women I know, but no one I would want to introduce to our parents." Then he looked around him and said with a smile, "Perhaps I can find a Dragon Rider who is as beautiful and charming as Rita."

Rita giggled and said, "You will certainly meet other women Riders, but everyone says that I am one of a kind."

They all laughed and continued talking about dragons and hatchlings and finding candidates for over an hour until Dorian insisted that everyone have dinner with him. The rest of Delno's family joined them. Delno's mother had finally come to terms with the fact that both of her boys were grown men. She was just beginning to acknowledge to herself that Delno was a Dragon Rider. The news of Will bonding was a bit much at first, but she accepted it with the same good grace and poise that Delno had seen of her since he was old enough to notice such things.

His father, however, was not quite as sure. He had wanted to pass his business on to one of his sons, and he was a bit disappointed at this new development. It took the rest of the evening for him to finally admit that he had already given up hope of Will taking the carpentry business anyway, since his youngest son obviously wanted to be an artist. After about a half a bottle of wine, he even began to like the idea of being able to brag that both his sons were Riders. He finally said he could give the business to his nephew who he had just recently taken on as an apprentice.

CHAPTER 17

DELNO WOKE WITH a start and reached for his Dragon Blade, which was hanging on the head of the bed. He was on his feet with the sword in his hand within a second. Rita woke, and seeing him armed and ready, jumped from the bed and drew her own blade. They both faced the door.

"What is it?" she whispered.

"I'm not sure. I was startled awake by something," he replied.

They both listened intently for any sound in the corridor. There was only one door to the bed chamber they shared. Suddenly Geneva screamed audibly, and inside his mind she shouted frantically, "Delno, the window."

He turned to the unlikely portal and saw a dark figure climbing through into the bedchamber. Rita had apparently gotten the message from Fahwn because she was already turning before he could warn her. The creature gave a low guttural growl and launched itself at him. He barely had time to register that it was a Felanx as he swung his blade up and sliced through the creature's sword arm. The arm fell to the floor and the Felanx howled in pain as it landed and rolled.

Rita was already moving to attack a second cat-man who was just climbing through the window. She neatly decapitated it before it could get into the room. It slumped on the sill, blocking the opening with its body. Just as the body began to be shifted by something from the outside, there was a bright flare, and even Delno, who was ten feet from the portico, could feel the heat. There were terrible screams from outside as one of the dragons flamed two more Felanxes who were attempting to move the body of the one Rita had killed so they could get in.

Delno had little time to wonder about it all; the first Felanx was on its feet and moving at him again. Even with one arm severed and bleeding profusely from the stump just below the elbow, it was moving with surprising speed and agility. It lunged, and Delno sidestepped and swung his blade again. This time the cat-man's head split in two down to the neck, and it fell dead on the floor.

Delno could hear the clamor of armored footsteps outside in the corridor. Someone pounded on the door and a muffled voice yelled, "What's going on in there? Delno Okonan, are you all right?"

There was a sound of something, probably an armored shoulder banging against the heavy oak. Delno yelled, "Give me a moment, and I'll open it. We're all right."

He and Rita quickly donned robes, and he opened the door to find six guards outside with weapons drawn. "What is happening here?" the guard who had spoken before said.

"Well, isn't it obvious? We're having a party." Rita answered sarcastically, standing next to the body of the Felanx that Delno had just killed.

"We have been attacked by these cat-men," Delno added. Then he looked at the rest of the guards and said, "Quickly, go and see that the healer and my brother are all right."

When the guards hesitated, their leader, who was examining the dead Felanx with a disgusted expression quickly reinforced the order, and the men trotted off to check on Nat and Will.

"That window is twenty feet off the ground, and the wall is nearly sheer," the guard said, "How did they get up here?"

"The wall isn't as sheer as it would seem, then;" Delno responded, "they climbed it. One of the dragons flamed two of them who were trying to get past the body of the one Rita killed while it was still climbing through the window."

"*Delno, are you injured at all?*" Geneva asked, full of concern.

"*I am all right,*" he replied.

"*Did you sustain any injury?*" she asked insistently.

"*No, I am unscathed. Why so concerned?*"

"*Because I smell poison on the blades from the two Marlo flamed on the wall.*"

"*Marlo flamed them?*" he asked.

"That is what I just said. Saadia is the one who alerted me to their presence. She reacted quickly and alerted us all. Then Marlo flamed the two who were still on the wall before they could get inside. I don't know why, but Fahwn and I were unaware of them."

"I will have the bodies searched for magical implements." To Rita, who was examining the body of the cat-man, he said, "Careful, Geneva smells poison on the blades that fell from the two who died outside. They may have poisoned their claws as well." To the guard, he said, "Have the bodies and any weapons they dropped collected and examined by the half-elf Nathaniel, and tell him and your men to be careful: the weapons and possibly the claws have been coated with a toxic substance."

The guard started to protest being sent away, but then looked at the dead bodies and changed his mind. Apparently, he felt the Dragon Riders could take care of themselves. He saluted and strode from the room.

An hour later, the Riders and the king were sitting in the private dining hall. The king was having some stern words with his guards about being more vigilant. The guard outside had now been tripled.

"Well, I don't know how those things got into the city unnoticed, but they won't find it easy to do so again," Dorian said.

"What worries me," Will said, "is that they knew exactly where Delno and Rita were staying. How did they get such accurate information that they were able to go directly to those quarters from the outside?"

"You said that you and Warrick had contact, Delno," Dorian said, "is it possible that he somehow marked you magically so that he could find you when he wished to do something like this?"

"That is a possibility, though I believe it is a small one at best. Those cat-men, Felanxes he calls them, have extraordinary senses; it is most likely that they have somehow scented me before, and then just followed their noses tonight."

"That wouldn't be so hard," Rita answered. "It is fairly common knowledge that Delno and I share sleeping quarters: all they would have to do is find the room in the palace where a man and a woman who both also smell of dragon are sleeping. I've seen hunting hounds who are less intelligent that can perform similarly spectacular feats of tracking."

Delno was only half listening. He had just finished checking himself and the others for magical "tracers." "That is the most likely explanation, since I can find no magical means of tracking any of us about our persons."

"The big question is," Dorian responded, "How did they get past the dragons?"

"Not past all the dragons," Will said proudly. "Oh, yes, Delno, that was Saadia who woke you. She knew your mind well enough from her encounters with you that she took a chance and tried to warn you. It was only partially effective because you didn't actually get her full thoughts, but you did wake in time to fend off the first attack. Then she told Geneva and then Marlo flamed the two still on the wall."

"She was able to rouse me from sleep herself? Without relaying through Geneva? I didn't know that was possible."

"There is no mention of such a thing in any of the books I have read," Dorian said, "but that doesn't mean it can't happen. After all, the dragons can speak to each other using telepathy, and they can speak to their own Rider the same way. I see no reason why they can't bypass the middle step and speak to another Rider if they choose; especially if it is an emergency like tonight."

"Well, any way you look at it, Saadia and Marlo are to be commended for their actions. They have saved both my life and Rita's."

"Speaking of which," Nat said, "the poison that the Felanxes were using is an interesting one. It is extremely deadly. It also is quite hard to find in such a pure form. The Roracks use a crude form when they bother with such things, but they haven't the knowledge or the intelligence to refine it. This fine an extraction must be obtained from elves, or at least their methods have to be used to make it."

"Are you saying that Warrick has Elven allies?" Rita asked.

"Well, that is possible, though highly unlikely," Nat replied. "However, many Riders spend at least some time studying in Elven libraries. It is possible that someone is in league with him who has learned the method of refining this poison. As far as that goes, it is possible that he has learned the method himself. After all, he is over two thousand years old: it is quite probable that he has studied in the Elven lands."

"Why would the elves make such a thing as this poison?" Will asked. "I thought that elves were peaceful and didn't approve of such methods."

"That brings us to the last possibility of how Warrick may have obtained this substance and in this quantity. In its pure form, such as on these blades, it is perhaps the deadliest substance I know of. However, take the pure form and mix extremely small quantities with certain other herbs and chemicals, and it is used for several medicines. The poison itself may be a healing ingredient in one formula, but can also be used in several others to direct the healing properties to certain organs of the body, such as using it to direct tonifying herbal medicines to the heart, or brain. It has many non-lethal, benign uses. It is also shipped out to certain healers in sufficient quantity for them to make medicines with it. Perhaps Warrick has intercepted a shipment."

"All of this is speculation," Delno said, "and distracts us from the important issue here."

Everyone stopped talking and looked at him, waiting for him to continue.

"Warrick is getting more desperate. He has used magic in some way to allow his cat-men to slip past our dragons and try to assassinate me directly. Due to my actions here, his plans for the north are being thwarted. We upset his timetable when we defeated Simcha in Palamore, and he is desperate enough to get back on schedule that he has tipped his hand to us. He is not, however, so powerful that he knows everything about us. He expected us to have the dragons he already knows about on hand, and aimed whatever magic he used directly at them, making them blind to the Felanxes he sent. He was totally unprepared for Saadia and Marlo and they have foiled his plan, which tells me that he sent those assassins before we reached Corice. It also proves my point that the wild dragons are a good choice for allies in this fight because they are the unknown quantity."

"How can you be so sure he sent those creatures before we reached Corice?" Rita asked.

"That's simple deduction, Beautiful; if he had waited for further word before sending them, he would have known about Marlo at the very least, and possibly Saadia as well, and would have been prepared. His Felanxes would not have been caught by them, and we would most likely be dead."

"You don't have to say it in such a matter-of-fact way. We very well could have been killed," she replied.

"That's true enough," he responded. "So Warrick must have sent those Felanxes right after I got away from his little Dream State. If he had waited for a few more days and somehow gotten more information, he would have been prepared for our new companions, too, which also tells me that Paul most likely hasn't returned to Warrick's camp. As it was, he only knew about the three dragons we brought from Palamore. He knows nothing yet about the wild dragons we are recruiting as allies."

He paused before adding, "In fact, I'm willing to bet that he doesn't think it is possible for us to get our new allies to work with us."

"What makes you say that, Brother?" Will asked.

"Because the one thing I noticed about him that really stuck out was his arrogance. He tried to make the wild dragons work for him and failed: he can't bring himself to admit that we may do something he can't. In fact, his dragon, Hella, hasn't been seen in the Dream State since she became angry at Geneva for demanding to know her name. Hella actually threatened Geneva then and was ejected for her disruptive behavior. I'd go so far as to wager that he has simply decided that he has gotten all of the information out of that avenue that he can and has given up on it entirely."

"Well, all of this is certainly interesting," Dorian said, "but I notice that the sun is beginning to shine on the horizon. Since I am up, I am going to have breakfast and then take Will to the libraries to begin reading about dragons and magic. I suggest that you all join me for the meal if you aren't planning to return to bed."

After breakfast, Dorian, Will, and Nat went to the libraries, while Delno and Rita headed off to talk with the refugee soldiers. Nathaniel wanted to get things in complete order in Larimar so he could start his journey to Horne, but he was also quite anxious to get into the king's library and see the books about dragon lore he had never even heard of.

At the refugee camp the news was mixed.

CHAPTER 18

"**I** HAVE JUST OVER six hundred ready to take their chances in Horne with you, Rider, myself among them, but as I had feared, most of the men are more willing to take their chances as refugees then face the beast-men of the south."

"Still," Delno replied, "over half a thousand men is a significant number. I take it most are seasoned veterans?"

"Aye, most of them have seen at least one campaign besides that fiasco out on the plain. However, we've still got a few farm boys with us. Most realize that this is their best shot at making a new life for themselves, but there are some who feel that they showed themselves so poorly outside these walls that they have to do this to make up for it."

"Well, I don't want men who aren't fully willing to fight and prepared for a hard campaign. You did point out the dangers, I take it?"

"I had almost eight hundred initially. Then I went over the dangers again and told them that it wouldn't be held against them if they stayed and gave them a few hours to think it over. Quite a few of them got cold feet and decided that being a refugee isn't such a bad thing."

"Good," Delno replied. "I will make arrangements for you and all of the men who are going to get their weapons and supplies from the quartermasters and then give you letters to take to the man I am going to send you looking for in Horne. He is a commander in the Ondarian army and has need of more seasoned veterans. His name is Winston Eriksson: you will report to him when you get there. I will give you more information when you are ready to leave. If you need anything, send word to me at the palace."

After making arrangements for the Bournese volunteers to get the equipment, he and Rita began walking to the palace. A commotion began on the wall and an alarm sounded.

"*You had better get up here, Love,*" Geneva said. "*I believe that you are not only going to want to see this, but that your presence will be required.*"

Delno looked at Rita who was already turning in the direction of the guard tower nearest the dragons. Apparently she had gotten a similar message from Fahwn. As they reached the stairs, he could sense Geneva's growing anxiety and began running. He took the steps three at a time while Rita yelled for him to wait up for her.

When he reached the dragons and looked out over the plains as Geneva indicated, he was dumbstruck. There on the plain below were at least a dozen dragons, and there were easily that many more circling lazily overhead. He immediately recognized Sheila at the front of those on the ground.

"*Sheila says that they wish to talk to you, but you are not to bring any humans along who are not already Riders.*"

"This is what we've been trying to accomplish," he said to Rita. "I have to go and talk with them; you don't have to come if you don't want to."

"If you think I'm going to sit up here on this wall while you face all of those dragons alone, you are crazier than I ever suspected." Then she smiled and said, "You lead, Handsome, I'll follow."

He smiled and quickly kissed her before climbing onto Geneva's neck. He didn't take time to rig a saddle for two reasons. He didn't want to offend the dragons by keeping them waiting, and, by not rigging a saddle, he hoped to show them that he was not aggressive.

He and Geneva landed quite near Sheila, and Rita and Fahwn landed just behind him. Sheila didn't wait to exchange pleasantries. "I have brought thirty-one dragons, including myself, who are willing to aid your cause. We feel that you are right and this maniac in the south who seeks to control all dragon-kind has to be stopped. Seven of those I bring with me are of the same mind as my daughter and would like to find a bond-mate as soon as possible. Of the rest, seventeen are interested but not sure. The remainder, including me, wish to remain free of such an attachment at this time, though even we admit that the idea of such is intriguing."

"We welcome the aid that is offered," Delno said. "We will begin immediately to look for suitable Riders for those seven who wish to bond with humans now. As for the rest, we are about to have nearly six hundred men camping for several days on this field: I would suggest that those who wish to avoid human contact for the time being stay well away from that camp."

"Very well, Delno Okonan, we will pull back. When will we be leaving for Horne?" Sheila was, as usual, very direct. In a way Delno found it quite refreshing after dealing with high-ranking military and politicians.

"I have business in Orlean soon, and that will take me several days to sort out. Once that business is taken care of, we will then travel directly to Horne from there, I hope. I will begin to instruct the Riders under my command on how to coordinate with your non-bonded dragons, and we will turn this into a cohesive, cooperative force on the way. Tell me; are you in command of these dragons?"

"They look to me for guidance, but they are free to do as they will. We don't see command as you do."

"That is good enough. I will therefore go through you if I need your dragons to do something, and you can go directly through me if you need something from the Riders. That way we won't have any confusion once we actually engage the enemy. You and I will be co-commanders, if that meets with your approval."

Sheila thought about it for a several moments and then began looking around at the assembled dragons. Delno surmised that she was talking it over with them.

"I have discussed your proposal with the others, and they agree we need clear lines of command if we are to do battle. Since both your Bond-mate and I are lineage holders, and you are the owner of a Dragon Blade, we are the logical leaders, so the other dragons agree with you."

"I hope to keep the dragons out of the fight as much as possible. We have lost enough of your kind to this war already. If it is possible to force Warrick's followers to surrender without bloodshed, I would like to do that. Warrick, I'm afraid, will never see reason, but I don't want non-bonded dragons to have to deal with him and his Bond-mate; they are too powerful for a single person to take alone. Hopefully, we will only have to fight against your ancient enemies the Roracks, and the Riders on the other side will see the futility of following a madman."

"We shall see, Delno Okonan. Your concern for our welfare is heartening, but I fear that there will be great loss on both sides of this war.

What dealings we have had with these people show that they are not willing to compromise."

"I am afraid that you are right, Sheila, but I do hope that isn't the case. Now I must go and begin keeping my part of our bargain: you have assembled seven who wish to bond; I must find them some partners."

Delno and Rita mounted their dragons and returned to the city. Delno saw the one person he most wanted to talk to standing on the wall watching all of the dragons.

"Nassari," he called as he dismounted, "I need your help."

"Of course, Del, what can I do for you?"

"There are seven dragons in that group who wish to bond with humans. You should know where to look for likely candidates."

"Me? What do I know about finding candidates for bonding with a dragon? I am a politician, not some school master."

Delno shook his head and said, "Nassari, you know this city and its inhabitants better than anyone I know. Use you sources to find likely young men and women, and they don't have to be that young. In fact, I would prefer they not be children at this point. These are mature dragons, not hatchlings; adults would be best. Bring any likely candidates before Geneva and Fahwn for their scrutiny. If they approve, then we can present the men and women to their potential partners."

Nassari stood there staring at him with his mouth hanging open.

"Really, Nassari, this isn't so hard. Start with anyone who has any connection with the royal lines; they are most likely to be suitable to the process. For seven dragons, we only need a dozen or so candidates."

"I suppose that I should begin with the men and women I grew up with and know to have some royal blood . . ." He trailed off as he walked away. Delno knew that now that Nassari saw it as an interesting puzzle, he would get the job done. Everything to Nassari was just working out the puzzle. That was the real reason he liked being a politician so much; he could work the puzzle all he wanted, and it continually shifted, making it constantly new to him. It was more a game than a vocation to Nassari, a game he got paid to do.

CHAPTER 19

THE NEXT MORNING as Delno made final preparations with the Bournese volunteers before starting them on their way, Geneva told him that Nassari was looking for him. He quickly finished his business with the soldiers and joined Geneva on the field. Before he could mount, however, he saw Nassari approaching him, followed by seven young men and two young women.

"I've found you nine candidates," Nassari said by way of greeting. "Fahwn has examined them all and said they have magic about them. It's the best I could do on such short notice."

Delno looked the candidates over for a moment and noticed that most of them looked more frightened than excited. "You didn't coerce them in any way, did you?" he asked Nassari softly. "Some of them look terrified."

"Delno, I wouldn't do such a thing," he said indignantly. "Besides, Geneva told me last night that if they weren't willing, it wouldn't work, so coercion was out of the question. They seemed fine when we were discussing the idea of bonding back inside the city walls, but now that they have gotten a close up view of a dragon or two," he bowed to Geneva, "they are just having some doubts."

Delno thought for a moment and then said to the group, "You can all come closer. Geneva won't harm any of you so long as you are no threat to me or her."

The group still seemed to hesitate. "Come, come, dragons are just really big people. They are intelligent and have feelings just like you do."

Finally, one girl who looked to be about fifteen stepped forward toward the dragon. Geneva started to smile, but then thought it might frighten more than reassure them and kept her face placid. The girl looked like she wanted to reach out and touch Geneva but was still timid.

"You may touch me," Geneva said. "I like having someone scratch over the small scales around my ear openings."

The girl smiled and obliged the dragon. "I am Nadia," she said.

"I am Geneva, Partner of Delno. The dragons you are here to meet would call the two of us Bond-mates."

Seeing that Nadia was in no danger, the other candidates became braver and approached close enough to touch Geneva. Geneva reveled in the attention as she was scratched and petted nearly to her heart's content.

Delno let them get used to the idea of being around Geneva for about a quarter of an hour before he suggested that they move on to the dragons who were willing to bond. He then had Geneva call the first of the seven dragons to them. The dragon, a green the color of dark malachite named Pina, landed near and began walking toward the candidates. She went unerringly to Nadia and put her head right against the girl's stomach.

While the observers saw nothing special except Nadia's exclamation of surprise and a little pain, Nadia experienced a bright but brief flash of light and few seconds of disorientation.

Nadia and Pina both spoke to each other at the same instant. "You are the most beautiful creature in all the world," Nadia exclaimed, while Pina said, "I had not dared hope that being bonded would be this wonderful."

Nadia nearly lunged at Pina and threw her arms as far around her Bond-mate's neck as she could in a fiercely wonderful hug. Again the two spoke simultaneously, though this time they only spoke to each other, "*I am so glad that I was chosen to come here today,*" Nadia said, while Pina said, "*I have never felt this whole: we are complete.*"

Then, with Nadia rubbing her stomach gingerly, she and Pina moved off away from the group to get to know each other.

"No flying until you have had a bit of instruction, young lady," Delno called after her. To Nassari he said, "I thought you were going to bring adults: that girl doesn't look any older than fifteen."

"Actually, she's twenty-three, and the older of the two young women. The other is nineteen," Nassari responded. "I did the best I could on such short notice, Del. All of the candidates are over seventeen, old enough to make up their own minds about leaving home. There were some younger ones, but their parents had trepidations. I thought it best to get these adult dragons settled, and perhaps we can present the youngsters to Saadia's hatchlings."

"You did well, Nassari," Delno relented, "considering how little time I gave you to accomplish the task. I had just hoped for more mature candidates. I need Riders who are ready and willing to fight when I go to Horne."

As the next Dragon glided in for a landing, one of the candidates, a young man, said "That looked like she got hurt. We were told we wouldn't be hurt."

"The dragon mark that is placed on the Rider by the magic that passes between the two Bond-mates causes some discomfort for a couple of days. It's like spilling a bit of hot tea on yourself. It passes quickly." Delno was a bit annoyed at the youngsters tone: he felt the man was being overly sensitive.

As the dragon, a blue named Terra, landed, the candidates stood ready. It took several moments, during which Terra sniffed all the candidates thoroughly; finally, she made her selection.

She turned to a young man named Raymond and nearly butted him with her snout. Terra had moved so quickly that he at first thought that she was attacking him. Raymond was startled but stood his ground as he experienced a bright flash and felt a burning sensation on the right side of his abdomen. Then he heard a voice inside of his head, "*I am so sorry; I was taking so long I thought that I wouldn't be able to bond. When the magic came over me I wanted to be sure I got the right person. I didn't hurt you, did I?*" The dragon's mental tone was full of concern for him.

"No, you just startled me a bit," Raymond replied. "*I wasn't expecting it to be quite this way. Come to think of it, I don't know exactly what I was expecting.*"

The two laughed together and then they also moved off to get acquainted.

The process continued. Gem landed and bonded with Therese, Cinda bonded with Bard, and then Lena with Gill. Then Wanda landed and looked at the remaining candidates. She seemed a bit confused. Nassari thought it was because the candidates had spread out, so he moved closer to get them into a tighter group. While he was herding them together, Wanda snaked her head around and touched him on the left deltoid.

Nassari felt the burning sensation of the magic and then experienced the light as if he had just come out of a darkened building into the noon sun. He felt a bit disoriented and a voice inside his head said, "*I am so glad to have found you. I am Wanda.*"

"*That wasn't supposed to happen,*" Nassari said, "*I wasn't supposed to be a candidate.*"

"*We are bonded,*" Wanda replied. "*If that is not acceptable, we are going to have a big problem.*"

Nassari couldn't explain why, but he knew that this bond felt right. He had never in his life felt so much for another creature of any kind. He knew that no matter how much trouble this bond might cause, it would be worth it to be the Bond-mate of such a wonderful being, someone he didn't have to prove anything to; someone who loved and cared for him simply for who he was and not what he could do for her.

"*Well,*" he said, "*if anyone has a problem with us being bonded, they will have to just get over it. I am Nassari, Wanda, and I believe that I have been waiting for you to come to me my whole life.*"

"*Then it is good that I have arrived,*" she replied.

Delno had seen his friend's eyes go nearly blank for a second, and then, after the newly bonded pair had had a moment to adjust just a bit, Nassari looked at him in utter shock, but he also looked ready to defend what had just happened.

Delno laughed out loud and said, "Join the other newly bonded pairs, *young Rider,* and no flying until you have had some proper instruction."

Then Keera landed and bonded with a young man named Horace. Delno had them join the others while he turned to address the three young men still standing on the field.

"Don't be discouraged," he said. "The fact that you weren't chosen today does not reflect badly on you. The magic chooses, not the dragon or Rider." That wasn't strictly true, because the dragon did have some say in it, but he didn't want to discourage them from trying again if more adult dragons became willing. "If we have more dragons who decide to bond, you may find a Partner then, if you choose to try."

"I think I was misled," said the young man who had expressed trepidations at being marked. "I do not believe I will try again. I don't see where there is so much advantage to being bonded to a dragon that I am willing to allow myself to be branded in the process." His tone was so peevish that Delno wanted to stand him in a corner like an errant child.

"Well, then," Delno struggled to keep his tone cordial, "thank you for coming anyway. I am sorry that we got your hopes up for nothing." To the other two, he said, "We will keep in contact with you and try to find you partners if you are willing to try again in the future."

The candidates, two disappointed and one relieved, left the field. Delno turned and walked to those who had successfully bonded.

"I swear to you, Del," Nassari said, "I had no intention of that happening. I don't even know how it happened. I have no connection to magic. I've never worked magic in my life."

"Never worked magic in your life?" Delno responded. "Nassari, you work magic all the time. I fully believe that that is how you are so persuasive. Your gift of the silver tongue is your magical talent." Then he spoke to the entire group, "All right, listen, all of you. We have much to do and little time to do it. I don't know how much you understand about our state of war, but let me assure you that there is more to it than you could possibly know. Your Bond-mates are aware of a great deal more of the situation and they will fill you in. In the meantime, Nassari will make sure that you all see the saddlers and get measurements taken for saddles for your Bond-mates. Then we will begin training you in the basics of being proper Riders." He turned to his friend and added, "Nassari, I leave them in your capable hands for now."

Delno turned and strode back to Geneva who was still chuckling at Nassari.

"I am glad that you are so amused at that," he said to her.

"I just find it quite funny that someone who hates flying as much as Nassari claims to hate it has become a Rider. I just want to be there the first time he and Wanda do a barrel roll or a stall-and-reverse."

"You can be sadistic when you put your mind to it, Love," he replied, and they both laughed.

CHAPTER 20

AFTER TALKING ABOUT what had just happened on the field for a few more minutes, the two of them flew back to the city and Geneva settled on the wall overlooking the plain and the new Riders. In the distance, they could see the soldiers forming columns, preparing to begin the long march to Horne. It would take them at least two weeks, if they pushed hard, to get there. Delno had only been able to give them a vague idea of where to find Winston. They had instructions, though, that if they couldn't meet up with the men from Ondar, they were to wait for him and his Riders to get there, and then he would have more specific orders for them. For the time being, Nat would be traveling with the soldiers since he needed to get to Horne to head off any of the Rorack sickness that was sure to be spreading.

As he thought of his friend, the physician stepped onto the wall from the stairs. Seeing Delno, he waved and walked quickly toward him and Geneva. "Well, my friends," Nat addressed both man and dragon, "Marlo is all ready, and I have everything I need. I will be leaving very shortly."

"I'm still not sure you should go alone," Delno replied. "I should send someone with you."

"You are sending more than six hundred soldiers with me. Isn't that enough?" Nat said with a laugh.

"You know very well that I am referring to sending one or more Riders along."

"Have so many that you can spare a few to escort me, do you?" Nat responded. "Delno, we've been over this many times. You don't have Riders to spare right now. Adamus and Rita are needed here to help you train the newly bonded pairs and everyone else is off doing other tasks that have nothing to do with me. I have to go to Horne because most of the soldiers who have answered the call for help are vulnerable to the sickness that nearly devastated Corice. This is the way it must be, my friend."

"I know all of that, but I don't like us splitting up. I think when the Riders go to Horne they should all go together, if nothing else as a show of force. One lone Rider is vulnerable to Warrick's schemes, or outright attack."

"Marlo was raised as a wild dragon; she is better at seeing and avoiding trouble than those raised with humans from hatchlings. Also, I am not completely uneducated in magic; I've just never spent much time doing it. You might remember me mentioning that I was raised by elves. I've been practicing shielding and healing since the plague was brought under control, and I'm not bad at it. In fact, with my knowledge of anatomy, I will rival you as a healer as soon as I've had a bit more practical experience."

Delno smiled at his friend and Nat returned the gesture. Then the half-elf reached out and took Delno's hand to shake. Delno gripped Nat's arm firmly, and then the two men briefly embraced.

"What have I missed?" Rita said as she approached them.

"Nat is ready to leave for Horne, and we were saying goodbye."

Rita walked up very close and said sternly, "You be damn careful, Nathaniel; I expect to find you safe and sound when I get to Horne." Then she hugged him tightly for a moment and kissed him soundly. "Good luck and keep safe, my friend," she added.

Nat smiled once again at both of them before he turned and strode off to Marlo. He mounted up, and Marlo launched off the wall. Delno and Rita watched them for several moments as their friends' silhouette grew smaller.

Delno turned to Rita and said, "One part of the plan is under way. Our physician is off to keep our soldiers healthy. Let us go in and see how my brother is doing with those books."

"Oh, that's why I came looking for you. Will has found even more of the books, and says that the language is a bit archaic, but he can still read them just fine. He believes that he will be able to get a lot of useful training from them."

"That's good, but I still need to talk with him. If what I'm thinking works out, he will be joining us in Horne."

"What are you up to now, Handsome?"

"Sorry, Beautiful, this one I'm going to keep to myself for a bit. At least until I confer with my brother."

Neither threats nor pouting would prize any more information from him as the two of them walked back to the palace to find Will.

Chapter 21

"AH, DELNO, THERE you are," Dorian said as Delno and Rita entered the library. "Hello, my dear, always a pleasure to see you under any circumstances."

Rita smiled and took Dorian's hand as the king led them to the back of the library where Will was so engrossed in a book he was reading that he didn't even notice their arrival. They simply stood and watched him for several moments. He would read a bit then mutter under his breath and then make a note about something. Then he would turn back to the book and start the cycle over again.

"He's been doing that for almost three hours without a break," Dorian said.

At the sound of his uncle's voice, Will looked up as startled as if the three of them just appeared out of thin air. "Oh, where did you come from? I didn't hear you come in."

"Obviously," Delno replied smiling. "I am quite pleased to find you so hard at work, Brother, but don't let your guard down so much. We have had one attempt at assassination since we arrived here in Larimar; it could happen again."

While Delno's smile took some of the sting out of the rebuke, Will was still a bit hurt that his half-brother had chastised him.

"Oh, Delno," Rita said, "can't you see that you've hurt his feelings now? He was just studying hard, like you told him to do. Honestly, you've gotten so serious in last couple of days since we were attacked in our bedchamber. It's not as if we haven't been assaulted before."

Delno looked at her for a moment, and then replied, "You're right; I have gotten more serious since that attack. You and I have both been in danger since the moment we first met. I have had no choice but to get used to that. However, I have never wanted anything for my family other than for them to be happy and safe. Part of the reason I originally left Corice to find Jhren was to take the trouble that seemed to be following me away from my loved ones. Now that I have returned, it has become a direct threat to them."

Will put his hand on Delno's shoulder and said, "Brother, I am safe. I am never out of range of Saadia, and she is doubly vigilant now since those assassins got through the city's defenses. She knew you were getting close, but has been told that you can be trusted. Also, I don't intend to rely solely on her vigilance, though I do trust her completely. I was just reading about how to set wards in place to detect if someone or something approaches. That is what I was studying so single-mindedly." He drew a deep breath and added, "Also, I have studied regularly with the City Guard as a reservist for three years. I don't carry a sword just for show." He patted the scabbard he had taken to wearing since the attack had occurred.

Delno noticed that Will also had a *main gauche* hanging on the left side of his belt, the same side as the foot saber he carried. It struck him that he and Will were as much alike in spirit as they were different in appearance. *Perhaps*, he thought, *Will will make a good lieutenant among the Riders.* Out loud he said, "I am sorry, Brother, I just want to keep my family safe. I guess it's high time for me to start thinking of you as an adult and not as my little brother."

"Apology accepted, and I doubt you will ever stop thinking of me as your little brother; just as I will never stop thinking of you as my big brother."

"So, show me these wards you were talking about. Jhren mentioned something about them, but didn't get the chance to teach me before Nat put him on light duty and I had to leave Palamore."

"Oh, they're very simple, really. You call up the magic and then erect a kind of magical wall. You keep the wall weak on purpose rather than making it strong enough to repel someone. Then, instead of breaking contact completely, like you would if you put up a one-time shield, you remain in contact. When something passes through the wall you feel it immediately."

"So, in a way, it's just an extension of shield magic. I didn't study that much yet because I can do a shield using telekinesis that is better at repelling non-magical attacks and doesn't drain me the way a magical shield does."

"Yes," Will replied, "it is just like a magical shield. I suppose it would drain your energy if it was strong enough to repel, but it is so weak that the drain is negligible. In fact, someone passing through it would never know it was even there unless he himself was an experienced magic user. As for using a telekinetic shield, you'll have to teach me how to do that. I haven't had much opportunity to practice that type of magic yet."

The two brothers had become so engrossed in their conversation that they had forgotten everyone else around them. "Do you two think you can a take a few moments and join the rest of us in the here and now?" Rita asked.

The brothers looked at her like two children who had been caught passing notes by the teacher. Then Delno said, "It is very near lunch time. Why don't we move to the dining hall so we can talk over a nice meal? Things are going to start moving a bit more rapidly now, so this may be our last chance to sit together with our family for a while."

"*Nassari has had Wanda report to me that all of the newly bonded dragons have been measured for saddles, Love,*" Geneva broke into his thoughts. "*I do believe that he is inordinately pleased with himself at being able to report to you in such a way. I get the feeling that he is going to be a pest until he gets used to the idea of being a Rider.*"

"*He will learn, Love, have patience with him.*" Delno chuckled as he replied to Geneva and then had to explain the reason for his mirth to those who were with him in the room.

"The man was nearly insufferable before he bonded," Rita exclaimed, "being a Rider will only make that worse."

"Nassari is a good man at heart, Beautiful. He'll come around in short order." Then he added, "Look at the bright side; now that he's got a dragon of his own to ride, he can't grope you under the guise of being afraid to fly."

Dorian smirked, and Will laughed out loud. The look on Rita's face was a mixture of amusement and relief. He told them about the doings on the field while they walked to the dining hall.

"So, tell me, Uncle," Laura Okonan asked Dorian over lunch: "How is the construction of the new fortifications at Stone Bridge coming? I've always thought that the treaty prohibiting such was good for Bourne but went drastically against Corice's best interests."

"I haven't heard any good news from there since Delno and Rita returned," Dorian replied.

Laura's direct manner didn't offend him at all. In fact, he had come to rely on her as an advisor of sorts. She was very good at seeing what was in the best interest of Corice, and was usually able to cut through the bureaucratic nonsense and get to the heart of a matter. She was a very capable and pragmatic woman, and Dorian was quite proud of his niece.

"Of course," the king continued, "if there were bad news, I'm sure we would have heard it by now. What do you think, Nephew?"

"Geneva is close enough to Beth to have contact. If anything were wrong, she would have informed me," Delno responded. "I do intend to go there tomorrow and see for myself one more time before we head off to Orlean, though."

"So, it is still your intention to leave soon?" Dorian inquired.

"I have no choice, Uncle. We must settle the two eggs that Gina will lay, may have already laid for all we know, and then get the rest of our new Riders ready to depart. I hope to return in less than a fortnight and see to the hatchlings here before we move on to Horne. If all goes according to plan, we will leave here with nearly a dozen Riders plus the dragons who aren't bonded, and still leave enough protection to ensure that Warrick doesn't make another move against Corice."

"Well, I am glad you are leaving us protection, Nephew," Dorian said. "But I thought you sent the un-bonded dragons with the men who marched south this morning."

"Most of them went and will meet up with us later. I was going to keep them all here, but I was also loath to send our best physician off without air support. Sheila and those who have said strictly that they do not wish to be bonded at this time will fly close enough to keep an eye on them without getting close enough to risk bonding." He paused and then added, "As for the defense of Corice, I hate to say this, Uncle, but if Warrick didn't have his eye on these two kingdoms, I wouldn't be leaving any dragons or Riders behind. I am from Corice, but my first loyalty has got to be to the world at large."

At the shocked looks from his father and brother, he added, "If the war here against Bourne were simply a matter of border disputes, I would take every Rider who would come with me to face the threat in the south. Warrick may be a madman, but don't mistake madness for stupidity. He is intelligent and cunning, and he has had many years to plan his attempt to seize power. If he isn't stopped, any who oppose him in deed, or even thought, will be killed mercilessly, and Corice as we know it will cease to exist."

No one spoke for several moments. Finally Delno broke the silence. "Forgive me for sounding melodramatic, but it is the truth. Our enemy seeks nothing less than total domination of the entire world. However, on the bright side, we have thwarted his plans and discouraged and demoralized his lapdogs here in the north. He is weakened and distracted by our efforts. What he thought would be a safe haven for him once he leaves the south is now a hotbed of resistance. And now we have, not only more Riders, inexperienced as they may be, but also two dozen non-bonded dragons he never expected to have to face who will all be going south to meet him and his forces head on." He paused for a moment and then added, "Our victory is by no means assured, but neither is his. Our one big advantage is the element of surprise, and I intend to capitalize on that surprise before it is lost."

There was no further discussion of the war during lunch. Delno's mother seemed determined to have a good meal without the subject of war creeping back into the conversation. Every time it seemed that the conversation must shift in that direction, she would recall some story from her sons' childhoods that would amuse Dorian and Rita while good naturedly embarrassing either Delno, or Will, or both simultaneously.

"I find it quite a coincidence that so many of your friends have become Riders, Nephew," Dorian observed. "If I didn't know better, I would think that you had planned it that way."

"I'm not so sure we know better," Rita said astonishing everyone at the table, including herself.

"Why would you say a thing like that?" Delno asked her.

"Well," she replied, "lately you have been a bit closed about your plans. I thought that perhaps the way that the Riders were being chosen could be part of your schemes that you hadn't mentioned yet." She was obviously still a bit miffed at not being told his plans for Will.

Delno decided to let it drop for the moment and said, "Actually, I have had nothing directly to do with how the dragons have bonded. However, Geneva and I discussed it briefly after we left the newly bonded pairs this morning, and we believe we have an answer.

So many things, such as my friends and family becoming bonded, and even meeting up with Rita and Brock at just the right time to form the strong friendships we have, seem like coincidence, but I have come to realize that very few true coincidences actually exist when powerful magic is at work. Geneva and I have come to the conclusion that her mother is at the root of it all."

"I'm sorry, Brother, but individually the words you just spoke have meaning, but when strung together that way, they don't make sense. How could a dragon who died months before any of these events took place have influenced what happened? Are you saying that she is still alive?"

"No, Will, she is quite dead," Delno responded. "Even Leera felt her death independently of Geneva, before she met us. But Geneva's mother bestowed on me a Dragon Blade."

"So you believe that the Dragon Blade you carry is controlling events?" Dorian asked.

"Almost," Delno answered. "You may correct me if I am wrong concerning the making of a Dragon Blade, Uncle: you know more dragon lore than I," he began. As Dorian nodded, he continued, "It takes powerful magic to make a Dragon Blade. The dragon who makes one must concentrate her fire enough to etch and strengthen the blade while protecting the unhatched dragon who is still in the shell. That protection carries over and gives some measure of the original magic to the possessor of the blade. Geneva's mother not only wished to reward me for my service to her and my willingness to bond with her last daughter, she wanted to help me carry on my grandfather's work. She wanted this partly out of a sense of duty, and partly as a tribute to the Bond-mate with whom she had spent more than three thousand years. She waited until there was no margin of error to make that blade. If she had waited even a few more minutes, she might not have been able to do so. She made it as she passed on her family lineage to Geneva. She infused both the history and the blade itself with that purpose as the last act, besides going off to mourn her Rider and die, that she would ever do in this world. She put everything she had left into my Dragon Blade. She infused this blade with the power to help me on my quest to finish what my grandfather had started. So, Geneva and I believe that since we need all of the allies we can get, the magic of the blade is influencing the bonding process to ensure that those loyal to me are put in a position to help me, and that is why my friends and family are chosen over other candidates."

No one spoke for several minutes after Delno had finished telling them about the blade. Finally, Dorian said, "Well, it's nice to know that there is a perfectly good reason for all that is happening." Though it was meant to lighten the mood, no one laughed at the joke.

After lunch, Delno had Rita meet him on the wall, and they headed off to inspect the Stone Bridge fortifications. As they landed, Rita noticed that it was much dustier than she had remembered from the last time she landed there. Two dragons shouldn't have kicked up that much debris. Suddenly, to her great surprise, Will and Saadia seemed to materialize out of thin air.

"Very good, Brother, very good indeed," Delno shouted to Will. "I wondered if you would be able to hide both yourself and Saadia, but it seems to have worked quite well. I had hoped that your connection with Saadia would strengthen your talent enough to allow you to hide the two of you. The only suspicion I saw on Rita's face was when you kicked up the extra dust landing."

"You could have let me in on this," Rita said. She was a bit annoyed. "I was nearly startled out of my wits when they suddenly appeared out of nowhere."

"We are sorry for startling you, Rita, but if he had let you in on it," Will said, sliding down off of Saadia's neck, "it wouldn't have been much of a test of my ability to remain hidden, would it?"

"So, Rider, you are making bonded pairs appear out of thin air now," General Dreighton said as he walked up to them.

Adamus, who had been informed as to the happenings of the wild dragons through Geneva relaying information through Beth, had been expecting that he would see newly bonded pairs, but he was just as surprised at Will's stunt as everyone else. Delno quickly explained how it had been done.

"So," Dreighton asked, "is this something that all Dragon Riders can do?"

"Unfortunately not, or fortunately, depending on how you look at it," Delno replied. "If all of us could do it, we would all be vulnerable to invisible attacks at any time. Though I would like it if all of our Riders could accomplish the feat, I'm glad that the only one who can is on our side."

"Also, Brother, remember, I can hide Saadia and myself because our connection strengthens the magic. However, like when we were kids, the more people who are concentrating on finding me, the more possibility that someone will see something. Also, if they know I am there, the likelihood of detection is increased as well. It is a talent to be used sparingly and kept secret from our enemies."

"That is why I had us land so far back from the camp, Brother. So far only the five of us humans and the four dragons here know about this. I would like to keep it that way, especially if you are to be valuable as a scout in Horne."

"I thought he was to remain here and study," Rita remarked.

"Adamus will remain behind with the newly bonded pairs. I trust him to watch Corice and instruct those new Riders we leave behind. I am also thinking about leaving Jason and several of the wild dragons. Just the sight of dragons circling overhead will be enough to discourage the Bournese. If the wild dragons fly low enough to be seen but high enough to hide the fact that they have no rider, the soldiers of Bourne won't make the distinction, they will simply behave themselves out of fear."

"I had hoped to prove myself to you in Horne, Delno," Adamus said.

"You have already proven yourself to me, my friend; that is why I am trusting you with guarding my homeland. I don't think that Bourne will be foolish enough to attack, but if they do, we will need one or two experienced Riders here. Also, I need experienced Riders to train the newly bonded hatchlings and their Bond-mates."

Adamus nodded and saluted. "By leaving me alone, you show that you trust me completely. For that I thank you. I won't let you down."

Delno returned his salute and smiled. Then he turned to General Dreighton. "The king is curious about the fortifications. How are they progressing?"

"Better than expected," the general replied. "With the masons and engineers working round the clock, we have done more than we could have hoped for. The men, civilians and soldiers alike, seem to understand the importance of this project and are working accordingly."

He motioned for Delno to precede him to the work so that he could show the Rider what had been accomplished. There were at least twice as many men working as Delno would have figured would be needed, and they all seemed to be making a coordinated effort. The progress was amazing. The work, which normally would probably have taken a year, would be finished within six weeks.

When he mentioned this, the general replied, "We are working double crews all the time, filling in with soldiers when we don't have civilians to do the jobs. It's expensive and tiring, but the men have been promised a good rest when it's done."

"I noticed that the bridge itself has been shored up: why is that?" Delno asked.

"Because we weakened it first," the general answered with a smile. "The Bournese got a new commander; some pock-marked moron who probably would be better at running a supply depot than commanding combat troops. He kept massing their troops as if he couldn't decide if they should try another attack. They weren't actually doing anything more than posturing, so we didn't have your Rider call you. But the threat was still there, so I had the engineers weaken the bridge and then shore it up. The Bournese sent a messenger over to ask what we were doing, and I told them straight out that we would either hold our side of the bridge or knock the damn thing down. Since we did that, they've backed off completely and behaved themselves."

Delno looked at the work done to the bridge itself and shook his head, "I suppose it had to happen sooner or later. I had hoped that the Bournese would see reason."

"I don't think reason has entered into the equation for a long time," Dreighton replied. "Have you seen any of those so-called 'infantry *men*' over there?"

Delno shook his head, and Adamus interjected, "At least half of them look to be nothing more than older boys, and half of those are probably younger than fourteen; some are no older than eight or nine. Even in Llorn, where the harsh climate and small population calls for drastic measures to protect the country, they don't allow boys younger than sixteen to enlist."

"Most of the youngsters can barely lift a sword, let alone actually fight with it," the general added, "They're there as arrow fodder to keep the real soldiers from getting killed long enough to get into the fray. It's a despicable way to run a campaign, but it's not new to the Bournese. And the thing is, you can hear them telling those boys how tough they are and that they can do this, whipping them up with false praise so they'll charge blindly and take the initial brunt of it when the time comes. That's one of the reasons the soldiers are so keen to finish the stone works; they hope that if they get it done, the Bournese will give up and we won't have to kill children. That king of theirs should be made to dangle at the end of a rope."

Delno could only shake his head in astonishment at the tactics that the Bournese had sunk to. Rita was outraged and disgusted. She was all for mounting up and going after the King of Bourne right then before there was even the possibility of any of the young boys being sent into battle. It was all Delno could do to calm her down before she carried out her threat and went alone if no one else would go with her. Several of the men gathered around voiced encouragement and offered to go along, but the general told them to go back to work.

As Rita walked back to Fahwn, Delno told Geneva not to let them do anything unwise, and she agreed to curtail any such action on Fahwn's part.

"I didn't mean to upset her," General Dreighton said to Delno.

"In the culture she comes from, children are revered above all else. Child abuse is the worst crime you can commit on that island, and as far as Rita is concerned, putting children in harm's way like the Bournese have done is nothing more than several hundred acts of child abuse," he replied. "I think it is time we return to Larimar. Otherwise she may try and carry out her threat."

CHAPTER 22

GENEVA HAD REPEATEDLY tried to relay messages from Delno to Rita on the way back to Larimar but Fahwn had told her that Rita refused to respond, even to her. Rita was furious at not being able to do anything to protect those young boys the Bournese had conscripted. Once they had landed, Rita quickly dismounted and ran from the wall, refusing to speak to anyone. She had even neglected to remove the saddle from Fahwn.

Delno got some of the soldiers to remove the gear from both dragons and went in search of her. He found her locked in the bathing room in their quarters. She wouldn't answer when he knocked on the door, and he had to have Geneva, through Fahwn, check and see if she was all right. Geneva also relayed that Nassari was looking for him concerning the newly bonded Riders.

"Damn," he replied, "trouble always comes in sets. Why can't I ever get one problem resolved before another arises?"

"I'm sure Rita will see the logic of your actions earlier today, Love; she just needs more time. Nassari wants to see you about getting more equipment for the Riders. It seems none have any but the most basic supplies. Two of them come from families who are not wealthy and don't even have their own basic weapons."

"Tell Nassari and the others I will be along as soon as I can. I have to talk to my uncle first. Perhaps I can get some funds from him to equip our new Riders."

After giving Geneva Nassari's instructions, he said to the closed door, "Rita, I know you can hear me. I couldn't just let you go off to the capitol city of Karne to take on the King of Bourne by yourself. You are certainly a woman to be reckoned with, but you are not up to taking on an entire kingdom on your own. You would have accomplished nothing, and gotten yourself and Fahwn killed in the process."

He waited for a moment, but there was still no reply, so he went on. "Even if Adamus and I had joined you, we wouldn't have accomplished what you wanted to do. Do you really think that Warrick wouldn't just put a replacement in the king's seat if you killed the man? We would have to take the city itself and hold it. That would require that we have ground troops to hold any ground we take. To get ground troops there, we would have to fight our way through the very children you so desperately want to protect."

He waited another moment and was about to continue when the lock on the door clicked and Rita opened it. She had been crying. She fell into his arms and sobbed uncontrollably for several moments.

"I just want to keep those children safe," she said as she got control of herself.

"I know that, Darling, but the best way to ensure their safety right now is to do nothing."

She looked at him, and he could tell she was about to give him an angry reply, but he cut her off. "If we do anything aggressive, we put them in harm's way. The best thing we can do is make that bridge so heavily fortified that they won't attack. Then the boys on the Bournese side will get nothing more than some exercise. That is what General Dreighton is doing. That is why he weakened the bridge itself and threatened to destroy it. They can't do more than posture, and we don't have to fight children because of the standoff we have created there. Meanwhile, it would be very costly to try and move that large a force to one of the other passes, and they would need seasoned veterans to make an attack in those confined spaces. The boys won't be moved, and they won't attack. It isn't as good as sending them home to their mothers, but it does keep them safe. In the long run, the Bournese will send the boys home because it will simply become cost prohibitive to continue to feed them."

"I hadn't thought the whole thing through," she said. "When I look at it your way, I see that you are right." Then she looked sternly at him and said, "Just tell me that you have a plan to make that callous bastard pay for putting those children in danger like that."

"For that and numerous other crimes he has committed," he sounded so harsh when he said it that she actually flinched slightly. "I am already working on a plan to deal with the Kingdom of Bourne in a way that will stop these wars for all time." At her perplexed look, he said, "I'll tell you about it later; right now I need you to play politics. Oh yeah, you should also let Fahwn know you are all right; she has been a bit worried."

Rita suddenly looked pained and said, "I ran off so fast that I didn't even get her saddle off of her. She must be angry with me."

"Relax; I had some of the soldiers take care of both her and Geneva. I believe that she is waiting for her turn at being washed and oiled by some lads in the central auction area of the stockyards right now. Just tell her you're sorry and that you love her; she'll be fine."

"You really do think of everything, Handsome."

"Fortunately, when I do make a mistake, I have you around to cover for me, Beautiful, so nobody ever notices how fallible I really am."

They found Dorian in the main hall surrounded by the city council members. He looked as though he would rather be anywhere other than where he was at the moment, so Delno said, "Could I have a word with you privately, Uncle?"

The council members looked upset at the interruption, but Dorian looked immensely relieved. He accompanied Delno and Rita to a nearby alcove.

"As much as I appreciate the interruption, Nephew, I can only spare a few moments of my time. Now that the immediate threats of pestilence and war have both been averted, the council wants to get back to the business of running the affairs of state, and I must attend to them."

"This won't take long," Delno spoke directly. "What I need to do is outfit our seven new Riders. You have already authorized their saddles, but they need other equipment as well."

The king was pensive for a moment, and then said, "The council won't like it, but I can authorize you enough funds provided that you do it discretely. Give all of the letters of debt to that sergeant I appointed to act as go between for the Riders, and he will give them directly to me."

"I will also try and go through the military whenever possible to further confuse anyone who might be watching for such purchases," Delno replied.

"I wish you didn't have need to do so, Nephew, but not only do we need to keep the council from getting involved if possible, we can't be sure just how much we can trust anyone. You are trying to keep your new recruits a secret from your enemies, and there may be spies anywhere." He looked around the room as if he expected to see someone trying to gather information for the enemy.

"I'll leave Rita here in case we have any problems; that way she can get the message from the dragons, and we can save time."

"Very well," Dorian replied, "but it might be better if she then went through my newest advisor." At Delno's perplexed look, he leaned closer conspiratorially and said with a smile, "Your mother: I've made the position official."

Delno smiled and saluted before turning to go about his business while the king sent Rita off to find Laura Okonan.

CHAPTER 23

ONCE HE LEFT the palace, he didn't have to look far to find Nassari and the other new Riders. They were waiting right outside the front doors. Delno looked them over and found that while two of them owned long knives, and all but two had good belt knives, none of them owned a sword.

"Normally, I would assume that since you are Corisian you have had at least basic weapons training, but I've learned to assume nothing. Who here has not had any training with sword and bow?"

No one raised a hand and he nodded. "Good then, follow me." He led them off through the twisting streets of Larimar. Even though the city wasn't as big as Palamore, it was still a quarter of an hour before they reached their destination.

The metalsmith's shop was dimly lit as always: the smiths liked to keep it that way so that they could easily judge the temperature of the hot metal by its color, and bright light tended to interfere with that. Elom was hard at work at one of the forges. As they walked further into the shop, one of the apprentices got the master's attention and pointed to the group of Riders. Seeing that Delno was leading the group, Elom stopped his work and walked toward them with the peculiar rolling gate that he was forced to adopt due to the braces on his legs.

"Corporal Okonan," Elom exclaimed, "I thought you had left for good. I heard all about what you and your dragons accomplished out there," he waved one of his massive arms in the general direction of the field outside the northern gates. "It's good to see you again, my friend."

"And it's good to see you, Elom," Delno replied. "How have you been doing since I left?"

"Busier than ever, once word of that blade of yours got around the caravans. I had to take on two more apprentices and hire two men I'd hoped to send off as journeymen just to keep up."

"Well, I've brought you even more work, I'm afraid. I need these seven equipped with swords: shields, too, if they use them."

Elom looked over the five men and two women. Then he said, "Nassari? I thought you preferred to do your cutting with that wicked tongue of yours, not with a blade."

"It seems I find myself in a position where I may have to use both, my giant friend," Nassari responded.

Elom looked a bit confused and then said, "You've bonded to a dragon, too, then?"

"Inadvertently, but yes, I've bonded, and now I find that I may actually be needed to fight in this war."

"Well, you may not have fought in the last one, but you still did your part. I remember lying in that hospital and you working yourself near to death to help care for all of us who had been wounded. I also remember you doing your best to comfort the dying, and then shedding tears for them when you thought no one was lookin'. And you never once complained to anyone about it. You worked and worked until you couldn't stay on your feet any longer and then some doctor would order you to go and rest and you'd be gone for a couple of hours before you started again." He paused for a moment and then added, "It was you that got my father and the doctors to work together to design these braces so I could walk and work. I've never forgotten that. Whatever you need is yours for the asking."

Delno looked at his best friend with new respect. He had known that Nassari had done some volunteer work in the hospitals, but the man never talked about it. Apparently it was pretty much the same way that Delno never talked about his war time experiences.

"Well, we certainly won't take advantage of your generosity, Master Elom. The king has agreed that the Crown will pay for what you supply to us."

"I just said I want no money from you, Nassari," Elom said, somewhat put out by the thought.

"That's all very well, but since I know it comes from your generosity, and it isn't coming out of my pocket, there's no reason you shouldn't at least be compensated for your time."

As Nassari spoke, his eye settled on something on a nearby work bench. He walked over to the bench where there was a blade that was similar to a footman's saber, though about six inches longer, but not quite as wide, and slightly more curved, though not enough to be considered a scimitar. He looked at Elom and asked, "May I?"

"Ah," said Elom as he nodded for Nassari to pick up the blade, "Now that blade was commissioned by a wealthy merchant. I made it to his exact specifications, but he refused to pay the balance, swearing that it was too plain. It's an odd design, and I was sure no one else would want it."

The blade was plain, but quite serviceable. It was strong and light. The guard, though not as ornate as Delno's Dragon Blade, was done in a similar style of bronze and nickel-steel. Instead of dragons designed into the guard, it was done in beautiful scroll work. There was a scabbard on the bench that accompanied the blade.

"Too plain?" Nassari said, "What was he looking for, a sword or a tiara?"

"So, you've met him," Elom laughed. "He was one of those dandies who wanted a jewel-encrusted bauble to hang on his belt at parties. I made him a blade that would keep him and his skin all together, but I doubt he knows more than which end of the thing to aim at an opponent. When I pointed out the fine points of this blade, he stalked out and said he'd find someone who really knew metal. He didn't ask for his deposit back, and I didn't offer, so that blade is all but paid for anyway."

Nassari made a few practice swings. Delno knew that his friend had studied sword like most Corisians, but the two of them hadn't sparred since they were children, and he was pleasantly surprised to see the ease with which Nassari handled the blade.

"Then with your permission, good Master Smith, I will take this fine blade. I already have a *main gauche* of my own that I am comfortable with."

Elom smiled broadly and nodded.

As Nassari and Elom had been discussing the blade, the other new Riders had also been looking among the blades already made. The four young men and the younger woman all chose long swords, and small shields. Nadia chose a footman's saber and ten-inch targe.

"Well, Elom," Delno said as he made out the voucher for the merchandise, "it seems that circumstances once again are going to keep you and I from spending much time together. I have to get these Riders outfitted because I must fly off to Orlean tomorrow morning. From there I don't know if I will be back this way or go straight to Horne to confront the beast-men."

"I have no experience with those monsters, but I wish you didn't have to face them. I heard from a vanner that they already killed one dragon and Rider down there. I don't like the idea of you goin' off into that."

"I go to do what must be done, my friend," Delno replied. "I haven't chosen this war, it's chosen me. I have to see it through."

"Delno," Delno was surprised that Elom had used his given name and not called him Corporal, "I know men who served for thirty years and retired from the army with full pensions who never saw a tenth the action you did. How much does a man have to go through before he can sit back and say it's someone else's turn?"

"For some, Elom, that time may never come. My grandfather fought the Roracks off and on for three thousand years, and in the end they killed him, but it's because of him and men like him that most of the people of Corice have never even heard of the beast-men of the south."

Elom looked as though he was going to argue his point, so Delno laid his hand on the smith's arm and said, "Don't worry, Elom, if this war goes our way, we will put paid to that account, as well as settle other scores here in the north."

"Very well," the smith replied after a moment's thought, "but you must promise me that when it's all over, you will come back and spend a day just tipping a few back in honor of the old unit and the heroes, living and dead, who were a part of it."

"That's a promise, Elom. Until then, take care of yourself."

"That's a good bit of advice Dragon Rider; see that you take it yourself," Elom said as he turned and strode back to the forge.

Since the Corisian Army issued long bows, while Riders needed shorter recurved bows for shooting while mounted, Delno took them to the same bowyer where he had bought his own months before. It had been too much to hope that the man would have another horn bow like his, but they did find suitable weapons for all seven of them. Again, Nadia surprised him by choosing a heavy bow with a ninety pound pull. For such a small, shy, young woman she was remarkably strong, and handled both bow and sword with surprising ease.

"Because of my size and young appearance, I've had to get twice as good as those I practiced with to be taken seriously," she said without conceit in response to his inquiry. "Besides, pulling a strong bow is more an act of personal energy than sheer physical strength."

Their next stop was the quartermaster's storage point. The supply men had been told they were coming and had field packs all ready for them. The packs contained the basic supplies they would need while traveling: mess kit, sleeping roll—which contained a thin, insulating bed cushion as well as a sleeping bag—a small, one-man scout's tent instead of the usual shelter half that would require two people to build a tent, and rain gear in the form of a poncho and large brimmed hat. The supply sergeant offered them dried field rations, but Delno declined. He told the man that the packs already weighed nearly two stone, and he wanted to keep the weight down to spare the dragons, but the real reason was he'd spent enough time eating those dried rations while he was in the army, and he wanted to spare the new Riders the misery.

Once they had everything, they returned to where the Riders were quartered: a small house near the palace that had been turned into government offices and later a storage place that had been hastily cleaned and furnished for their purpose. As the others stowed their gear, he pulled Nassari aside.

"You've spent a bit of time around these young men and women, Nassari. What's your opinion of them?"

"In what way, Del?"

"Well, since Warrick has his eye on the north, we will have to leave some of the new Riders here to protect Corice. All of the Riders have to train, and those who stay will probably get to actually do the most training. Those I take with me to Horne will have to be willing to put up with the travel and be able to learn their jobs as they do so. Therefore, I need those who accompany me to be more mature with the temperaments of soldiers."

"So, you want to know which of the men would be better soldiers in your war in the south," he said thoughtfully.

Before he could continue, Delno said, "Not just the men. We may be Corisian by birth, but we are Dragon Riders by choice of fate. We have to put aside the prejudice of not allowing women into combat. I have been watching that young woman, Nadia, and she seems to be much more than first impression would have you believe."

"I was going to say pretty much the same thing before you spoke up, Del. She would be my first choice. She's smart, she's tougher than she looks, and she might lull an enemy into a false sense of confidence that could just give her an advantage in one-on-one combat. Adding that to the fact that Pina is a mature dragon of forty-four years should give them an edge when they are training as they travel."

"I didn't know Pina was so old; I thought all of the dragons were younger for some reason."

"Most are: except Pina and Wanda, all of them are less than twenty years old. Wanda is forty-one."

"That's quite interesting. So, any other recommendations?"

"Well, I was thinking about Terra and Raymond; they seem pretty level headed, and Raymond's father was a career soldier who instilled discipline into his sons. Other than myself, that's about it, I'm afraid. The others are good folks, but I don't think they have realized their place in the wide world yet. It's probably best we leave them with Adamus and Will to train."

"Actually, Will is coming with me to Horne. I was rather hoping to get you to stay with them."

"After those bastards tried to destroy my home with war and plague, you want me to stay here and train new Riders? I would prefer to go and take this battle to our enemies before they bring it back home again."

"Nassari, this is war, not vengeance. I need to have people who are clear headed and not likely to act because of emotional ties to what has been done."

"I can be clear about it, Del," Nassari said with such steel in voice that Delno was actually a bit shocked by his friend's statement, "but I've seen what happens if we ignore Warrick, and I don't want to give him any more chance to work his mischief. I want to come along, and Wanda is completely with me on this. Since Riders and dragons are not truly under the command of anyone other than themselves, we will not be left behind."

Delno and Nassari stared at each other for a long time. This time it was Delno who looked away first. "Very well," he said, "we will have to figure out how to do this. Adamus will need someone else to help him train the new Riders and watch the borders. I'll discuss it with Rita and Brock and see what they say."

"Good," Nassari responded, "I'm glad you are willing to see my point. I know that the idea of having Geneva order Wanda to stay must have passed through your mind, but Wanda, too, is a lineage holder." At Delno's astonished look, he continued. "Wanda's lineage was scattered because two successive lineage holders died in Horne at the hands of Roracks, so she doesn't have as much authority as Geneva or Sheila, but she isn't as compelled to listen to them, either. To put the dragons' politics into human perspective, she is like a smaller country that has joined two bigger countries. She doesn't have as much authority because she doesn't bring as much to the alliance, but she is still independent and only has to listen so long as she agrees with what is said."

Delno thought about that for a moment and then said, "I don't want either one of you going off in search of vengeance once we get to Horne. She has lost much of her family and history, which is vital to draconic society, and you have seen these enemies attack your home directly. You both feel great hatred toward our enemies, and rightly so, but I don't want either of you getting reckless down there."

"Del," Nassari said with his usual nonchalance, "this is me; have you ever known me to be reckless?" Then he quickly added, "With my own life, at least?" He smiled broadly and added. "Besides, all of those same things could be said of you and Geneva!"

Knowing he'd been outmaneuvered, Delno switched subjects. "How long until the leatherworkers have your saddles ready?"

"They claim a week, but I'd give them ten days due to the fact that there are eight of them to make. Even in a city the size of Larimar, there are only so many skilled craftsmen. Add to that the fact that the plague has killed so many people and slowed down all trade, and I would prefer not to rely on the earlier estimate."

"Well then, we'll have to get you all in the air without saddles until then," Delno said. "We'll rig safety straps and avoid aerobatic maneuvers for now, but I want everyone flying as soon as possible. Once all of the gear is stowed, and you've had a bit to eat, have Wanda relay that you are ready and meet me on the field. I have to inform the king of our progress and have lunch."

He quickly gripped Nassari's arm and then left the house.

CHAPTER 24

ONCE HE REACHED the palace, he was informed that the king and Rita could be found in the private dining hall with Laura Okonan, but he was totally unprepared for what he found there.

Rita and his mother were both present and each was holding a young child. The children were both about two years old and both looked exactly alike. They were fair skinned with blue eyes and curly blond hair. There was a slightly older child who looked to be their sibling playing quietly on the floor near them.

"Nephew," Dorian said happily as he entered the dining hall, "come in, we have new guests." Dorian indicated the children.

"These are Gwendolyn," his mother indicated the child she was holding, "and Gillian," she pointed to the child Rita was holding, "and Marcus," she indicated the boy sitting on the floor.

"Hello," Delno responded, smiling at the children. The little boy smiled, but it was a smile mixed with a lot of sadness.

"Rita says to tell you that these children are orphans. Their parents died of the plague just before we arrived. They nearly died too, but Nat's skill as a healer saved them. The boy is four and the twins are two," Geneva relayed the message to him. He nodded to Rita and smiled at his mother.

Rita gave Gillian to Laura and motioned Delno away from the group. They walked far enough away to hold a private conversation if they whispered.

"The boy pretty much understands that his parents are never coming back, but the girls are just too young to grasp the concept. By the time the girls are old enough to understand about death, they most likely won't remember their parents at all." She hadn't spoken about what was truly on her mind concerning the children yet, but Delno knew it was coming. "We can't just abandon them; they have no other family. Your mother and I were hoping that we could help with raising them."

Delno had thought he'd seen just about every emotion that her eyes were capable of showing, but this one was new, and it left no doubt that she was going to do this regardless of what anyone else might think of the idea.

"We can't drag them off with us now," he responded. "Do you plan on fostering them with my parents until this business with Warrick is settled?" The thought of even suggesting that she turn away from these three was simply out of the question. From the look she had given him, he knew that as far as she was concerned, she had already adopted all of them.

"Your mother seems to think it will work, and your uncle has said they can simply move into the palace now, since they have no place else to go. Your father was a bit shocked at first, but he is really soft-hearted when it comes to children; I wouldn't be surprised if he has them start calling him grandpa by this evening."

Delno looked back and stared at the kids for several moments without saying anything. Then he began to knead his eyes with his thumb and forefinger.

"Delno, we can't turn our backs on them; they have no one, and your parents are willing to help us raise them for now. We have to do this." Her tone was imploring but also set: she would do this whether he agreed or not, and he knew it.

"Of course we can't turn our backs on them," he said. "After all, if we aren't doing all of this for the next generation, then who are we doing it for?"

She couldn't even bring herself to make a sound, she simply jumped into his arms and hugged and kissed him. Finally, after several moments, she said, "The children will stay with your parents here while we go to Horne. Then we will have to decide where we will raise them once this insane war is over."

"Perhaps you could stay with them while I go to Horne," he replied.

The look she gave him at that suggestion would have been answer enough, but she said it anyway. "If you think you are going off to Horne without me, you are sadly mistaken. I don't care if Geneva is Lineage Holder and orders Fahwn not to take me. If Fahwn won't carry me, I will bloody well walk there. I'm going, and that's final."

"I had a feeling you'd say that. It would have solved two problems for me if you had agreed to stay, though. I would know that you were safe and that I have another experienced Rider to train the newly bonded Riders I'm leaving here." Then he sighed and said, "Oh, well, it was worth a try. Now I suppose we should go and spend some time with the children."

After lunch Delno, Rita, and both of Delno's parents brought the children to the field with them. This would be the first time his father had actually gotten close to the dragons. Nassari looked totally confused when he saw the small procession arrive.

Before his friend could ask out loud, Delno quickly had Geneva relay who the children were and that they were just along to see the dragons. Nassari gave an almost imperceptible nod that he understood.

"So then," Delno said as he stepped in front of the group of young men and women, "we have some soft cord that is strong enough to rig safety straps. You have been told to wear heavy clothing to avoid being abraded by your dragons' scales and we have blankets to use for further padding. First, Rita and I will teach you how to rig a makeshift saddle; then we will get you into the air."

"What, no stable boys to saddle our mounts?" Nassari said.

Everyone laughed a little at the joke.

"Well," Delno said smiling, "if you would prefer to let someone else rig your safety straps, Nassari, I certainly won't interfere. After all, it isn't me who's going to trust to someone else's work several thousand feet off the ground."

All of the new Riders were suddenly wide eyed at the thought of how high up in the air they would be.

"Point taken," Nassari replied.

It took a little longer than Delno had anticipated to get everyone rigged to fly, but they were still ready to get off the ground in under two hours.

"Remember," Delno shouted so that everyone could hear him. "You are not flying on young, immature dragons. Your Bond-mates have years of experience doing this. They already know the basics without this instruction. What they need is time to learn to maneuver safely while carrying a rider. If anything happens that really scares you, just lay forward over your Partner's neck and hold on. She will know what to do instinctively. If you start trying to shout orders at her to correct her flying, you will only confuse her and make the situation worse."

"Sir," Raymond held up his hand to be acknowledged.

"Yes, Raymond?"

"What is the likelihood that something like that will happen?"

Delno was pleased to see that the young man was simply curious and not frightened. "It doesn't happen often, but sometimes you can be buffeted by a sudden gust or strong cross wind. Sometimes when that happens you can suddenly drop like a stone; sometimes for several hundred feet. If that occurs, your dragon will know how to react instinctively and keep both your hides intact."

Everyone began raising their hands to ask questions and he realized that if he answered them all, he would be all afternoon just getting airborne. He held up his hand for their silent attention.

"As you learn more about flying, you will learn when you are needed to do something other than hang on. There will come a time in your career as a Dragon Rider when you and she will truly be partners up there. That time, I'm afraid, will come very soon for the seven of you. Today, however, you are pretty much just along for the ride. Enjoy the easy work while it lasts; as was pointed out to me, being a Dragon Rider is more than just parking your arse in a saddle and letting your dragon do all of the work."

They all laughed a bit and then, seeing that he had quelled their questions for the time being, he said, "Let's get this show in the air. I want to do a few very basic maneuvers, but we won't do anything particularly difficult today. Remember to brace yourselves for takeoff or your head can be whipped around and leave you with a stiff neck."

Everyone, including Nassari, appeared to be in high spirits and eager to get started. Delno took off on Geneva first, then the students launched one at a time with Rita watching, then she was the last to join them in the air.

Geneva and Fahwn put the students through a series of basic maneuvers including a stall and reverse, though that was the most difficult of the set. They decided to hold off on barrel rolls until they could be taken up in smaller groups, since that was a much more difficult stunt.

"I'm tempted to have Wanda do a barrel roll, Love. I'd like to see Nassari's reaction. Of course, so far he seems to be enjoying himself. Perhaps all of that complaining about flying was simply a ruse to allow him to get away with groping Rita after all."

Delno laughed at Geneva's comment and said, "Let's keep that observation to ourselves, Dear Heart; Rita might be tempted to take revenge if she also figures that out."

CHAPTER 25

ONCE THEY HAD done the basics and the dragons all sig-
naled that they were beginning to adjust to the added weight
and bulk of a rider, he had them head for Stone Bridge. Adamus and Beth were in full view on the Corisian side of the canyon on
the ground, out of range of any Bournese bows. Delno had the students
each make a quick strafing run on the bridge itself: Geneva went first,
making sure that her flame hit the stone about half way across the chasm
to avoid the wooden barricade; she was followed by Fahwn, and then the
newly bonded pairs each took a turn with Nassari going last. They didn't
flame close enough to be any danger to the Bournese on the other side,
but the run was close enough that the soldiers got to be impressed by the
sight of nine dragons flaming.

Once the strafing run had been made, Delno had all of the dragons
land far enough back away from the canyon that the Bournese wouldn't
be able to see that none of them wore proper saddles.

After introducing all of the newly bonded Riders to Adamus and
the officers stationed at the bridge, he had the human students work in
groups of twos with him and the other two experienced Riders. Nassari
joined his group which also included Nadia and Raymond. They spent
the remainder of the afternoon working on healing and shielding.

Before they got back in the air for the return trip to Larimar, Delno
said to Raymond and Nadia, "I took you two in my group for a reason.
Tomorrow, Rita and I will leave for Orlean to settle the eggs that will be
laid there by Gina. We will also meet up with Brock, who is my teacher

and one of my most trusted lieutenants, and any other Riders he has managed to bring along with him. Most of the un-bonded dragons who have remained up to now will depart, and we will again meet up with them in Horne."

Nadia and Raymond were a bit confused as to why Delno was telling them all of this. He was impressed that they held their questions and waited for him to come to the point.

"The reason I am telling you this is simple. I would like to take as many Riders to Horne as possible. Nassari is going along and will continue training as we go. I have observed you two and believe you both show enough good sense and fortitude to come with us also. The choice, however, is yours: I won't try to order you to go if you wish to remain here to train."

"I will go with you," Nadia said immediately. "I have been talking a lot with Pina and the other dragons, and I know that what has happened here in Corice was all due to the machinations of our enemies in Horne. I think it is better that we take the fight to them rather than stay at home and wait for them to bring the war to our door again. My father nearly died in that plague that was brought to us by our enemies. It was only through the intervention of your friend, the half-elf physician, that he survived. I don't wish to wait around to see if my family will fare better next time. I'd like to prevent the next time from happening."

Delno was nearly shocked. That was more speech out of the young woman at one time than he had heard since he'd met her.

"I'm not as eloquent as Nadia," Raymond added, "but I feel the same. Stay or go, either way we end up fighting the same enemy. I say take the battle to them before they endanger our loved ones again."

"It's settled then," Delno said smiling broadly. "I was going to try to leave directly from Orlean, but my plans have changed because of circumstances here in Corice. When Rita and I have settled the eggs there, we will return here. By that time, your saddles should be ready, and you will have had a few more days to practice flying. We will all travel together to Horne. It's a two-day trip each way to Orlean, and we will most likely need two days there. Nassari will make sure the saddles for the four of you get priority over the others. Be ready to travel in one week."

"Excuse me, sir," Raymond said, "but you've said four. Who is coming besides Nassari, Nadia, and me?"

"My brother Will is coming along also. In fact, I would like the four of you to train together at weapons practice and flight training during the day, and then get together every evening to go over the books on magic he has been reading in the palace library."

There was stunned silence for a moment at the revelation that there were books on magic at the palace, but then all three Riders looked at each other briefly before turning and saluting Delno.

Later that night after he had gone through his gear, a task he had been putting off for a long time, he came into the sleeping chamber that the children shared. His mother and Rita had just gotten the kids into bed, and they were still settling down and getting tucked in. He put the small reed flute he had made so many months ago to his lips and began playing the tune that he remembered from the lullaby that Rita had sung so many weeks past.

The room that had been given over for a nursery had a window looking directly out on the wall where Geneva was perched. As Delno played the flute, Geneva joined in with her hauntingly beautiful multi-toned voice. The dragon was far enough away that her voice was a very soft accompaniment.

Rita started humming and smiled warmly at Delno. Soon she began to sing softly:

> Hush now child, the night is warm,
> Daddy's safe, the sea is calm,
> Tomorrow's sun will bring no harm,
> Hush now chi-l-d and Sleeeeep.
> Sleep my daaar-ling, Sleeeeep.
> Now the moon is riding high,
> The fish swim on the rising tide,
> So Daddy's gone to-night,
> Hush now chi-l-d and sleeeeep.
> Sleep my daaar-ling, Sleeeeep.

The children, tired from their long day, where asleep within minutes.

Laura opted to stay with them while Rita and Delno went off to finish preparing for the trip to Orlean the next morning.

CHAPTER 26

DAWN WAS A faint glow on the horizon as Geneva and Fahwn rose high above the plain on the northern side of Larimar. The dragons were in high spirits as they both strove for altitude.

"Tell me, Love," Delno asked, "why is it that dragons appear to like flying early in the morning so much more than any other time?"

"I'm not sure why, Love," she responded, "but there is just something about flying up to greet the sun as it comes over the horizon. To be the first to see it appear is a joy to all dragons. Even wild dragons like to take wing early when they are rested and awake at dawn. I have no other answer to your question than: because it makes us happy."

"Then that is answer enough," he said with a laugh. "I am glad it makes you happy because your happiness is contagious, and I am pleased to be infected with it."

The winds were strong but blowing in the right direction. They were able to soar quite well and made good time all morning. By the time Delno called a halt at noon, they had already traveled nearly as far as he had hoped to travel that whole day.

"If we can keep this pace up for the rest of the day," he said to Rita as they ate a simple lunch of sandwiches, "we will be in Orlean tomorrow morning instead of tomorrow evening."

"That would be nice," she replied. "I like Larimar just fine, but I was beginning to fear that beating the Bournese had begun to lull us into a false sense of security. I would like to get this business in Horne over with so that we can get on with the rest of our lives."

Delno had the definite feeling that she was a bit put out about leaving the children behind and wanted to get back as soon as possible. "We are on our way, Beautiful; hopefully events will start moving at a brisk pace now. However, we do have to settle the eggs in Orlean and then make sure that we do the same in Larimar before we do anything else. They are as much a part of the next generation as are the human children we are dealing with."

"Am I that transparent to you?" she asked.

"You have just been made a guardian to three wonderful children; it's only natural you would chafe at anything that takes you away from them. When this is all over, Darling, you will have the leisure to raise those children as you see fit."

"Careful what you promise, My Love, but I do appreciate the sentiment."

They finished their lunch and were back in the air in under an hour. Since the dragons had spent most of the morning soaring on the prevailing winds rather than expending energy flying, they were still quite eager to travel. Delno decided to push the limits and kept them in the air until after the sun had gone completely down. In fact, if the humans hadn't needed a rest from riding, the dragons could have finished the trip in one night.

He decided that since the weather was so mild and there was no sign of rain, they would forgo unpacking and just sleep curled up with the dragons. They made a small fire and heated some water for tea, but ate a cold meal of jerky and fruit. Rita was unusually quiet; her thoughts were obviously turned towards Larimar and the children. He leaned back against Geneva's front leg, and Rita lay down with her head on his chest.

He hadn't been practicing using much of what Geneva's mother had taught him because he had been trying to concentrate on Jhren's lessons. Tonight, however, he decided to extend his feelings outward and check the life forces in the area. He pushed out as far as possible and found that he was now able to feel every living creature within a three and half mile radius of their camp. He damped down his sensitivity enough to concentrate on only those big enough to be a threat as individuals. It took him nearly a quarter of an hour to complete the check, but he was sure that nothing within that circle was hostile to them.

"*Have you completed your inspection of the area, Love?*" Geneva asked.

"Yes, Dear Heart, and there is nothing more dangerous than a couple of wild pigs rooting around in the darkness," he responded.

"Then go to sleep, Dear One. I will keep watch even if I doze, and Fahwn will do the same. We are safe for now; enjoy it while lasts."

"Thank you, Love. I will sleep better knowing that my serenity will be temporary. I'd hate to think that my life is suddenly about to get boring."

Geneva chuckled both mentally and out loud. Rita stirred beside him but didn't wake. "Raising children is never boring, and being a Dragon Rider who is raising children should be proportionately more exciting. Good night, Love."

"Good night," he replied. He didn't think he was exceptionally tired, but he was asleep almost instantly.

"Wake up, love," Geneva called softly in his mind. "Brock approaches and he is not alone. Leera says that we are needed, the eggs are laid and we should be there the first time the candidates see them. If you and Rita would like to attend to bodily functions before we have company, you had better get up and do so now."

Apparently Rita had gotten the same message from Fahwn because she got up grumpily and walked toward the relative privacy of the bushes. He decided that similar action was in order. While he and Rita were attending to their individual concerns, the dragons waded into the nearby stream and bathed as best they could.

"Leera has relayed that Brock says you should get bathed and dressed in the best clothes you brought with you, since the boys' parents will be there when the boys are presented to the eggs. Fahwn and I have wallowed out a place that is now plenty deep enough for you and Rita to both bathe comfortably if you choose to do so," Geneva said.

"Thank you, Dear Heart. While I don't relish the idea of a cold bath first thing in the morning, it is very thoughtful of you and Fahwn to accommodate us by making the stream deeper."

"You're quite welcome, Dear One. We try to be thoughtful."

He and Rita quickly gathered soap, bath sheets and clean clothes before going to the stream. The cold water wasn't as bad as he had feared. It wasn't chilled enough to take their breath away, but with fall in the air it was too cool to want to languish there for longer than needed, so it actually worked out well. They were bathed and dressed by the time Brock, Jason, Lawrence, and someone Delno had never met landed.

As the Riders dismounted, Delno noticed that this new Rider was different than what he expected when he thought about Riders in general. First, while the other Riders he had met went to great pains to keep themselves physically fit, this man, though not grossly fat, was well-rounded, more as if he tended to keep to sedate activities rather than sword practice or other such endeavors.

"Craig?" Rita asked. "What brings you out of your libraries and into the wide world?"

"Hello, Rita, my darling, I heard you had taken up with this fine young man," Craig responded. "I had to come and see who had made an honest woman of you."

"Delno Okonan," Brock said, "this is Craig Carver. Craig has been a Rider for about fourteen hundred years and has studied extensively with the elves." Then he turned to Craig and said, "This is Corolan's grandson."

Craig grasped Delno's hand and said, "Well, except that you're a good foot taller than your grandfather, you look enough like him that I have no trouble believing it." Then he looked over Delno's shoulder at the dragon and said, "You must be Geneva; I'm so pleased to meet you."

"I was just going to introduce you," Delno said, "but since you have already done so: Geneva, this is Craig Carver."

Delno wasn't sure exactly what was different about this man. He had a different kind of energy to him. Whatever it was he didn't feel threatened by it. In fact, he felt he rather liked the fellow. It was strange; kind of like meeting an old friend for the first time.

"We will have to hurry," Brock said. "The boys and their parents will be there soon. It wouldn't look good if we were late."

They all helped Rita and Delno stow their gear before mounting.

The flight to Orlean only took about an hour. Delno was surprised when they followed Brock to the garrison.

At his look of inquiry, Brock said, "It's Gina's first clutch. She's a typical over-protective first time mother and insisted on settling her eggs in the garrison courtyard for protection. She almost didn't fit inside, and then we had a hard time getting her out again. I was surprised that she left long enough to go with us to fetch you."

Brock had been right about nearly being late. They had barely arrived at the garrison when the boys and their parents showed up at the gate. All of them were shown inside to the livery stable where the eggs had been moved.

Delno wasn't sure exactly how this should all go and would have been content to let one of the other Riders handle it. However, everyone looked to him to make the first move.

"Brock says that as the Partner of a lineage holder and bearer of a Dragon Blade you should take the boys to the eggs," Geneva informed him. *"Just show them the eggs and let them get close and touch them. Give them a few minutes with each egg and see if there is any reaction."*

Delno nodded to the boys' parents and then led the boys to the clutch. Everyone else stood back a bit and watched. Both boys seemed reluctant to touch them at first, as if they were afraid that this might somehow harm the little dragons inside. After a bit of urging, they finally approached close enough to touch the eggs. At first, as had been pretty much expected, nothing happened. The boys touched the eggs and knelt near them but there was no hint that either would bond. Then they switched which eggs they were kneeling next to.

Tom got pretty much the same reaction, but as Jim got up to leave, he suddenly went completely slack jawed like he had been momentarily stunned. Then he knelt back down and began to caress the shell possessively with one hand while absently rubbing his right lower leg with the other. He had bonded to the dragon while she was still in her shell.

Tom knelt back down next to the other egg hopefully, but again nothing happened. Finally, he turned to Delno with a tear on his cheek and said, "I'm not getting anything, sir."

Delno knelt down beside him and said, "It's all right, lad. We didn't really expect you to. Bonding with a dragon while she's still in her shell is extremely rare, but we give the candidates the chance. It doesn't mean you won't bond to her once the shell cracks. You should come back and spend time with the egg every day until she hatches. Talk to her and try to listen for her to respond. She probably won't, but it could still happen, and when she does come out maybe she'll already be used to you. Just don't lose hope; the dragons all say you're a good candidate. They wouldn't say that if it weren't the truth."

Tom smiled at him and said, "I'll spend all the time with her I can, sir, I promise."

Delno patted him on the shoulder and got up and walked back to the parents.

Jim's parents were elated that their boy had already bonded and were edging nearer to him and the egg he was hovering over. Delno quickly explained to Tom's parents that not bonding at this point meant very little. Bonding with a dragon before she hatched was extremely rare, and they only brought the boys because they always offered the chance to do so. While they were pleased that Jim had bonded today, they actually hadn't expected it from either boy. Robert and Mary were somewhat reassured by his words, but they still had trepidations as they looked at Tom, who was obviously disappointed.

"The eggs will hatch within the next couple of days," Brock said. At Delno's look of astonishment, he explained, "Because it is her first clutch, Gina misjudged her time and actually laid the eggs down south, nearer to the Elven lands, while we were waiting for Craig to join us. We had to transport the eggs here after they were laid."

"I should have made myself available to you in the Dream State so that you could have told me. I would have figured out a way to leave Corice earlier."

Brock smiled and said, "What would you have done? You still would have had to meet us here, and it wouldn't have hastened our trip any, especially since we had to take extra care because we were carrying the eggs." Before Delno could say anything to the contrary, he added, "Relax, everything turned out just fine."

Just then Tom cried out in alarm. Everyone turned back to the stall where the boy was watching the egg wide eyed with worry. "Something's wrong!" Tom shouted.

All of the Riders ran to see what was happening. Tom was nearly frantic as he watched the egg rock back and forth. Brock and Delno, the first Riders to reach the stall, both laughed, and Brock said, "Nothing is wrong, son, the egg is just hatching. Stay close and see what she does as she breaks loose from the shell."

Mary whispered, "What if she doesn't pick Tom once she's hatched?"

Brock was about to make a reply when a long crack appeared in the shell. Everyone watched silently as the egg rocked more violently. Then the young dragon's nose poked through a hole she had just made in the end of the shell. She shook herself fiercely and widened the fissure that was now nearly splitting the egg in two lengthwise. One last shudder and the egg broke into several pieces, and she was free. The little blue dragon took a moment to orient herself to her surroundings.

Tom's parents actually held their breath as they watched. They were obviously worried that their son would be rejected after having his hopes raised so high. The dragon, however, had no trepidations what so ever. She immediately went straight to Tom and butted him on the waistline just above his left hip. The boy went glassy-eyed for a few seconds and then knelt down and cradled his Bond-mate's head in his hands. He looked at his mother and said, "Her name is Karla."

Just then Robbie, who had been called by one of the men when the egg started hatching, came in and said, "I've ordered some men to raid the kitchen stores and bring meat. I remember reading that a newly hatched dragon is usually ravenous. We don't have too much on hand, but two of the sergeants and four of the men have gone to procure enough cattle to keep them both fed for a few days at least."

"Thank you, Captain," Delno said, noticing that Robbie was wearing the new insignia of rank. "Just one of them has hatched so far, but the other will probably break free of her shell soon."

"Just one?" Robbie asked. "How long until the other hatches, do you think?"

"That is quite impossible to tell," Brock replied. "You see, unlike most creatures that hatch from shells, the baby dragon actually has some choice in her time. It usually takes about a fortnight once the egg is laid, but the dragon may decide that she wishes to come sooner or later. I've seen them stay stubbornly in their shell for nearly a month before hunger forces them to hatch."

"If there's one thing I've been able to figure out about dragons," Robbie responded, "it's to never believe you have them figured out."

Brock and Delno both chuckled but also nodded in agreement.

"Well, we had best let Jason and Lawrence help Tom get settled," Delno said to Brock. "We have much to discuss, and I would prefer the privacy of Pearce's house."

CHAPTER 27

AFTER MAKING SURE that the new dragon and Rider were being helped, they walked quickly to the healer's house. Missus Gentry was delighted to see them, and quickly served refreshments in the sitting room. After they had all gotten something to eat and drink, Delno, Brock, Rita, Craig, and Pearce closed themselves in to talk.

"I take it that Connor is flying patrol?" Delno asked.

"Yes," Pearce responded, "he takes his duties quite seriously."

"Good, I have much to tell you all, and I prefer that he not be here for most of it."

Brock looked at Delno and asked, "Do you think the boy might have been swayed by Simcha after all?"

"No, nothing like that," Delno replied, to Brock's obvious relief. "He is just fourteen and anxious to prove himself. We need to make plans to head south, and he will be upset when he finds out that I plan on him staying here." Then he added to Brock, "Of course, you are the boy's father; if you want him to go south with us, I can't exactly refuse to allow it."

"No," Brock sat flatly, "I would prefer to keep him here doing his job rather than risk his life in Horne."

"Hopefully, my friend, we won't be risking his life by leaving him, either."

In response to the puzzled looks from the three who weren't aware of the events in Corice, he quickly explained what had taken place up north. They were all especially astounded about the wild dragons who had found Bond-mates. Pearce was pleased that Nat had bonded, but looked just a little jealous that he hadn't been given the chance.

"So," Delno added, "that is why I plan to leave Jason here to assist Connor with training the new Riders. That way Connor can still do his job while he trains them, and he will have another trusted Rider with him if Warrick turns his attention to this area."

"Do you think Warrick will scatter his forces further to make trouble in this area?" Brock asked incredulously.

"I don't see where it will give him any advantage, but he is so convinced of his invulnerability that he may see doing so as a ploy to divert our attention rather than scattering his forces. He knows who I am and that I am working against him. He may choose to move against places that he thinks I have an interest in to keep me from confronting him directly while spreading our forces thin."

"So how high do you think the probability is that he will try something here?"

"Not very high at all, which is why I am leaving Connor and Jason rather than just transporting the hatchlings and their Riders to Larimar. I believe they are safer here in the long run."

"So, we are now certain that Warrick is alive and the master mind behind all of this trouble. That is very interesting." Craig observed.

"You may as well fill Delno in on everything, Craig," Brock said.

At Delno's nod, Craig began. "As you may have heard, I spend most of my time studying with the elves. I have learned a great deal in their libraries, and even after hundreds of years of study, there is still much where I have not done more than skim the surface. The elves have come to trust me as much as if I were one of them." He paused to give Brock a chance to add something if he wished. When Brock merely nodded, Craig continued. "I have lived among the elves for over a thousand years and been given full access to all of their knowledge. We, meaning the elves and I, have not troubled ourselves much with the outside world for some time. That all changed about three years ago."

At this point, Brock added, "That was near the time the Roracks got very quiet and people in Horne actually started to believe that the beast-men had given up raiding or moved on to someplace else."

"At that time, three young Riders I didn't know came and asked to use the libraries." Craig continued. "The elves don't hoard their knowledge; they simply want to ensure that their books are treated well and not taken away from them. They would even allow everyday humans to read them if they were asked politely. At least, they would have then, but that has changed, and the libraries are now guarded, and access is restricted to only elves or those they have known long enough to trust completely."

"What did these young Riders do that caused the elves to begin guarding their libraries?" Delno asked.

Craig looked pained as he continued. "There was a fire in the section of the library that the three of them were in. We managed to put it out and save the books, though a good friend of mine was killed in the process. When we took inventory, we found three books missing."

Delno asked, "You're sure they were missing and not destroyed?"

"Oh yes, quite sure. The only books damaged by the fire could be identified. The fire was started as a diversion to allow the three to escape with their prizes."

"Let me take a guess," Delno said. "One of the books was on the making and control of magical beasts, another was about wild dragons, and the third was most likely about how the dragons create and maintain the Dream State." He made it a statement not a question.

"Exactly," Craig said, "how did you know?"

"It wasn't really that hard to figure out. I first met Warrick when I was pulled into that Dream State he had created. Though his control isn't as absolute as he thought, he is powerful there, since it is his creation. Then there are these new cat-men; or Felanxes as he calls them. We had thought that he and Orson had gotten the knowledge of creating them from Jhren, but even he is limited in such matters, so that knowledge had to come from somewhere else. Also, that "compelling stone" he mentioned wasn't something Jhren had first-hand knowledge of either. As for the last book, he has tried to "compel" the cooperation of the wild dragons. It didn't work, but the magic he used frightened them enough to make them fight back. So knowing what three volumes he stole is no great feat of clairvoyance, just a bit of deductive reasoning."

"Well, that isn't all that was stolen," Craig said. "When we realized that the Riders had stolen the books, we began looking for other things they may have taken also. They took quite a few medical supplies, including one particularly potent poison. The poison is used in medicine in extremely small quantities. It isn't as dangerous to elves as it is to humans, but it still must be handled with care or the results could be fatal."

"Yes, we've run across some of Warrick's assassins who were using it. That explains where he got it, which is good because we didn't want to believe that he had Elven allies. Knowing he stole it puts that to rest."

"I'm glad that you were willing to give the elves the benefit of the doubt and not just assume that they were working with Warrick," Craig said.

"I don't know any full-blooded elves, but the one half-elf I do know is a man I would trust with my life. He was reluctant to place any blame on the elves, and I was willing to accept his judgment until real evidence to the contrary could be found."

"I appreciate your open-mindedness," Craig replied. "Now then, to finish up with what I am doing here: that poison wasn't the item that upset the elves the most. The worst thing, even worse than the books, was a piece of stone that was a part of an ancient artifact from a time when mages sought to make and control beasts to gain more power through the use of them. The stone had some power over plants and animals. It was used by the elves to make plants grow and mature faster, especially when making new hybrids. If what you have said of this "compelling stone" is true, then Warrick must have found a way, using magical theory from those books, to use the stone to control the beast-men he commands. I have left my studies to seek you out and ask you to help us recover that stone."

"That puts everything into a new light," Delno replied. "I had feared that Warrick had somehow gained some incredible advantage on his own during his six years in hiding."

"Getting hold of those items and putting them to such good use makes him pretty powerful, as far as I can see," Rita interjected.

"Yes, when you put it all together, he has become a powerful force. However, it is because of items in his possession, not because he himself has learned some new way of increasing his personal power," Delno responded to her.

"The difference seems to be a moot point," Brock added.

"No, not really," Delno said while Craig shook his head in disagreement with Brock's last statement.

At the looks of inquiry from Brock and Rita, Craig said, "You see, controlling items is different than controlling the magic you use to make a spell. If you make the spell, then you control it. Someone can attack it and negate its effects, possibly even turn it back on you, but he can't take complete control. He can take control of the energy you send out and even reverse it, but you can then release it and do something else to counter that or shield yourself, and the energy of the original spell will dissipate. That is why a shield has to be overpowered; since you are just maintaining an energy field, the opposing magic user can't take control of that energy, so he has to batter his way through it. An item, however, is imbued with magical power. Someone can control that item, but they can only work within the parameters of the item. Warrick can't use that compelling stone to control humans because it was never meant to be used that way. Also, since he doesn't form the magic that the stone uses, even if it draws energy from him, he can't stop someone else from trying to take control away from him, though if he is more powerful than the person trying to wrest the control away, he will prevail."

"Also, the more he has to control, the more his power is scattered and the more vulnerable he will become," Delno interjected. Brock looked quite impressed with Delno's knowledge, so he added, "Though Jhren accused me of daydreaming during my lessons, I really did pay attention."

"Even with all of that, you can't afford to get complacent," Pearce said. "Remember that Warrick has had two thousand years to practice magic; he won't be easily defeated."

"You're right," Delno replied, "we can't get complacent, but until now, he was an unknown, and we were reluctant to do anything to engage. We now know that, though he is very dangerous, he is still just a mortal man who can be beaten."

Delno thought for a moment and then turned to Craig. "I don't want to be abrupt or sound like I don't appreciate your help, but since I have been handed the job of commander, I need to know: what do you bring to this war?"

"Oh, dear," Craig answered. "You have misunderstood me. I am skilled in magic, and Torin is certainly a mature dragon, but I am not a good fighter. I came to seek your aid and offer whatever assistance I can, but I had thought that assistance would come in the form of advice, rather than actual physical help on my part."

Everyone mulled that over for a few moments as Brock looked on amused at Delno's surprise.

Finally Delno asked, "Do you have enough experience to help train a few Riders?" At Craig's doubtful look, he added, "You'd get a chance to meet some of the newly bonded wild dragons."

Craig's eyes lit up at the prospect. "Well, I certainly would like to spend some time with them and find out their reasoning for bonding since they have grown up wild. Even though we have books on the subject in the libraries, our knowledge of such things is woefully limited. If, while doing some good for this cause, I can learn a few things, where's the harm?"

Delno didn't bother to tell him that about all he was likely to get out of the newly bonded dragons as an explanation was the fact that they bonded because they were lonesome. He figured that Craig could put whatever spin on that he wanted, so long as he was around to help Adamus train those new Riders. As he finished that thought, Warrick's words ran through his mind. "You see, we're more alike than we are different, you and I. You and I are tools of fate. Those I use are just extensions of that; their lives only have what meaning I give them. On your side, you have taken the role of leader in opposition to me. You would sacrifice your allies as willingly as I if the need arose."

He shook his head slightly to clear those thoughts away. Because of this insane war, he might have been forced to use people as tools, but he wasn't trying to send Craig unawares into danger. What he was doing might be manipulative, but he was merely using Craig's desire to learn to get the man to help out in a way that wouldn't put him in harm's way: he wasn't callously sending the man to his death. Also, there might be something different about Craig, but lack of intelligence wasn't one of his problems; the man had to be one of the smartest people that Delno had ever met; if he was being manipulated, he had to be aware of it and didn't seem to mind.

Still. The ease with which he had so easily shifted tacks to use the man had unsettled him somewhat. He would have to be cautious about that in the future, especially if lives were really at stake.

"So, I can count on you to travel with me to Corice and see to the newly bonded pairs, then?" Delno asked aloud, wanting to make absolutely certain there was no misunderstanding.

"Of course," Craig responded, "I had planned on traveling that far to find you anyway. The chance to actually speak with formerly wild dragons just makes the trip more worthwhile. As for training, as I have said, I'm not a great fighter, but I know the basics and can probably be quite useful in that role. I would also like to help in this war against Warrick in some small way and this gives me the opportunity. So you see, dear boy, you aren't tricking me into coming along: I'm going willingly."

Delno was a bit abashed that his thoughts might be so transparent, but very relieved that Craig was so willing to go.

"Well, since that is settled," Delno said to Brock, "what news do you bring to this meeting, my friend? How many Riders have we added to our forces, and have you heard any more news out of Horne?"

"With everything else that we've been over, I hadn't gotten to what is probably the most important news," Brock replied. "There are nine more riders on our side in Horne now. Also, there was another magical attack on one of our Riders and his dragon. This time the pair survived, though it was a near thing, and he saw the two Riders who attacked him. I sent word that our Riders should start patrolling in groups of three whenever possible and never alone."

"Who was attacked, and did he know those who attacked him?" Rita asked."

"Daevid was the Rider, his dragon is Marra. No, he had never seen the two young Riders before."

"But Daevid is over three hundred years old; surely he knows all of the other Riders?" Rita said.

"I'm not surprised that he didn't recognize them," Delno responded. "Warrick disappeared for six years before he started acting overtly and risked his identity being discovered. Hella is certainly a mature dragon, but she isn't so old that she wouldn't rise to mate. In fact, when Geneva was talking to her before we knew who she was, she left the Dream State one night in search of a male who had gone there to display his readiness to breed. I believe that Warrick has been very busy for the last six years. Not only has he stolen elven artifacts, his dragon has been breeding and placing those eggs with his own chosen candidates. I'd bet that every one of those young Riders, including that young man Paul we captured, is rider to one of Hella's offspring. He has tried to augment that force with outside dragon blood by convincing teachers to join him, as in Simcha's case, but he has had only limited success. He can so easily control the Riders and Dragons under his command because his dragon is their mother."

"I wonder why none of us has thought of that until now?" Rita wondered aloud.

"I had, but I needed to have more evidence to support the theory," Delno responded. "Remember when you told me that you had been around for a hundred years and knew every Rider?" When she nodded, he continued. "Well, you didn't know Paul when he presented himself. Between you and Brock, I would have thought that there wasn't a hatching that occurs in our territory that wasn't known. Warrick had to be getting his Riders from somewhere, and being in control of their mother is the final link we need to understand how he can control them so completely that they readily work with their ancestral enemies in so short a period of time."

"If that is the case, how does he get Hella to cooperate then?" Rita asked.

"I suspect that he has two things going for him there. One is that he probably keeps her far enough away from direct contact that she isn't constantly being insulted by the presence of the beast-men. The other thing is that he has had a thousand years to plan this and has probably been working on getting her to accept his plans for a long time. Also, I don't think he would have any qualms about using the compelling stone on her if she was uncooperative."

"It certainly makes sense," Brock responded. "I know for a fact that it was never unusual for Hella to lay three eggs at a time and sometimes four, so he could have quite a force of Riders he has total control over."

"Ah, but once again, though, his control is not as total as he thinks," Delno replied. "He thought he had total control over Paul, but the man was so furious at being used like a pawn that he gave up on his mission. Also, his control over those dragons is limited by how far away they are from that compelling stone."

Before they could continue, there was a knock on the door. Missus Gentry was smiling broadly as they opened it. She said, "I'm sorry to interrupt, but I just got word from the garrison. The other egg has hatched."

"I suppose we had better see to the new hatchling and then make plans to head back to Larimar as soon as possible," Delno said.

They all got up and headed out the door and off to the garrison.

CHAPTER 28

THE NEXT MORNING the five Riders, Delno, Rita, Brock, Craig, and Lawrence, rose into the air as one at dawn. Connor, as expected, was a bit upset about being left behind yet again, but he settled down when he was told that he wasn't being left as Jason's subordinate but as his equal in the task of training Tom and Jim. He was happy that he was being trusted with such adult responsibility. Also, his sword practice was coming along nicely, and he appeared to have his father's keen physical abilities, but he still needed more practice before either Brock or Delno would consider him to be a true swordsman.

"Are you sure of your choices regarding who goes and who stays?" Geneva asked.

"I've thought it over carefully. It isn't necessarily ideal, but it's the tiles we've been dealt; we have to play them. Craig is not a really good swordsman. He prefers to use words over blades when dealing with problems. I personally think that the man might just be on to something, but Fate seems to have decreed that many of my own problems can only be solved with the Dragon Blade I carry. Craig, however, is good at magic, both theory and practice. His knowledge is nearly on par with Jhren in that respect, and, because of his bond with Torin; his power exceeds Jhren's by quite a bit. He will make a good teacher for the new Riders. In fact, I wish I could stay for some of those lessons myself."

"What about Lawrence? I don't dislike the man specifically, but I find him lacking in general. I don't know that I want to go into combat with him watching our flanks," she responded.

"Lawrence always deferred to Adamus before the pair was separated, and Adamus had always been the brains for both of them. Part of the reason for separating the two of them was to give the man the chance to begin to develop some independence while traveling with Brock. Lawrence, however, still hasn't shown any particular interest in growing a brain. He has simply substituted Brock for Adamus and follows Brock around the way a stray puppy follows someone who throws it scraps of meat and occasionally pats it on the head. I had briefly considered leaving the man in Orlean with Connor, but Connor has enough to handle with his work for the garrison, his own training, and the training of the two new Riders. Leaving Jason behind will give Connor someone to help him, while leaving Lawrence behind would just have given a fourteen year old one more kid to care for."

"We could always leave him in Larimar when we travel south, Love."

"No, I separated Adamus and Lawrence for good reason. While they seem to be friends and work as a unit, the two of them diminish each other's strengths rather than make up for each other's weaknesses. I think it is best we keep them apart, at least until this is all over," he replied.

"Well, I can see your point, Love, but I don't like him along on this excursion. I have spoken of my concerns to Leera and told her not to rely on Rhonna and Lawrence to cover them in a fight. After all, they were the weakest link in Simcha's forces over Palamore."

Delno was surprised that Geneva had taken the responsibility of telling Leera not to rely on the pair. However, he was also relieved that she had taken it on herself to do so. He liked the fact that although he was the leader of the humans, he wasn't necessarily the only one in charge. Often he felt that he was alone in his position of responsibility, and while he didn't want to put any stress on Geneva, he was glad to have a co-leader to help him. He suddenly bent forward and hugged Geneva's neck and said, "I love you, Geneva."

"I love you, too, Delno, but is there any particular reason for this show of affection—not that I am complaining—or do you just need the contact?"

"It's just good to know that because I have you, I am never alone. I always have someone who loves me and cares for me. Thank you, Dear Heart."

"You're welcome, Dear One, and I thank you for the same."

They flew on until nearly noon. When they stopped for lunch, they made a fire and settled down to rest for a couple of hours. While they weren't fighting strong head winds, the prevailing winds weren't with them, so they had to fly rather than soar, and the dragons needed the rest, especially Torin.

Delno walked off by himself to relieve his bladder. After he was finished, he decided to sit alone for a bit. He got about a quarter of an hour to himself, which was a luxury he was rarely granted these days.

"There you are, Handsome. I was wondering if you had gotten lost," Rita said as she approached.

"I'm not that lucky," he replied.

"I can leave you alone if you like," she said, a little hurt that he didn't seem pleased to have been found.

"No, you and I get so few moments alone these days that I cherish each and every one of them."

At his words of encouragement, she brightened. "Would this be a good time to talk about the children we seem to have adopted?" she asked sheepishly.

"I don't see why not," he said.

"I really do want to raise those children right, Delno. I want them to actually come to think of me as their mother." She paused to give him to time to respond if he wished, but he was content to let her get to her point. "I would also like for them to come to think of you as their father."

The comment hung in the air for a few moments. Finally, she continued, "You just seemed a bit aloof with them before we left. I had hoped that you would be happier that we had children to raise." Her statement was almost a plea for his affection for the children.

"You're right, I was a bit aloof," he said. The look on her face told him that this wasn't what she wanted to hear, so he quickly explained, "I love children, and those children are wonderful. If I didn't have the responsibility of commanding our side of this war, I would like nothing more than to settle down and raise them properly. However, I am not the type of commander who can sit back and give orders from a safe distance. I have been in direct danger since I first became bonded to Geneva. I don't complain about that, it just is, and there is nothing I can do to change it besides get this issue settled. However, I don't want those children to get attached to me and then be orphaned again if I don't return from Horne. I am aloof for their own good."

"Delno, you are coming back from Horne!" she said vehemently. "We will win this war, and those children will live a good life. You will have the opportunity to move on with 'Delno's Grand Scheme' like you planned. You won't orphan them again, and you won't leave me alone!"

Her words were as much a plea for reassurance as they were an oath. If it was within her power to make them happen, she would. He had been beginning to feel that events were spiraling out of his control, and that he might be fated to die in Horne like his grandfather before him. Her words, however, had the effect of a slap in the face or cold water thrown on him. They woke him up, and he again felt the sense of grand purpose that had driven him to this point.

Delno took Rita in his arms and pulled her very close, "I love you, Rita. I can say that now with conviction. I have never known any woman as wonderful as you and cannot imagine a better human partner for me in this life. I love you and want to raise those children with you."

"I love you too, Delno. I know that you have said that you weren't sure that people were capable of falling in love in only a few short days, but I have known that I love you since our first night together. We will be together for a long time, my darling, and nothing, not even cataclysmic war, can stop that."

"Very well," he said. "There is much still to be done in Larimar and little time to do it. I won't be around much to spend time with the children because everyone seems to look to me for everything. The one I seem to be able to rely on most is the one I would have thought the least likely."

She stepped back and looked at him, "I know you aren't talking about me. I would like to help you more, but I know my limitations. I'm not good at organization. I'm much too impulsive. So, who is it that has suddenly become so reliable?"

"Nassari," he answered nonchalantly.

"Nassari!" she almost shouted. "Since when has he become reliable?"

"Well, partly since Warrick sent both a plague and an invading army to slaughter the people of his home, and partly since he bonded with a lineage holder."

"Wanda is a lineage holder?" she asked as if she had been struck on the head with a heavy object and not quite knocked unconscious.

"Yes, with everything that happened at the bridge, and after with the kids, I didn't get the chance to tell you about it. Wanda's line has been a bit scattered because of deaths from Roracks in the south, but she is the youngest surviving daughter of her line, and that makes her the lineage holder. Because some of her lineage has been lost, she doesn't have quite the same status as Geneva or Sheila, but she is still a lineage holder and, therefore, has authority of her own. Nassari has stepped into the role as if he has simply been waiting for the right partner all of his life. He has taken complete charge of the new Riders, and they all defer to him without question. Even the young woman, Nadia, who is so competent, defers to him like she's his lieutenant."

"I wouldn't have thought that Nassari would bond with a lineage holder, but then I wouldn't have thought that Nassari would bond with a dragon at all. Now you tell me that he is acting as though he takes his position seriously. I'm sorry, Handsome, that is almost more than I can believe."

"Well, it's all true. Nassari took charge and has been dealing with all of the little tasks that have to be accomplished to get them settled into their roles. He wouldn't even have needed me to get their weapons and equipment if I had thought in advance to get him the vouchers. He is also insistent on coming to Horne with us."

"Nassari? A warrior? He doesn't seem the type," she responded.

"No, he doesn't seem the type, but he certainly handles his weapon as though he knows how." He then told her what Elom had said about Nassari. "So you see, my lady love, there is more to our friend Nassari than meets the eye."

"I had no idea he had served such a vital position in the war. He has never spoken of it. I would have thought that he would brag about such heroic deeds even if they were in the hospitals and not of the field of battle." The way she spoke Delno could tell that her opinion of Nassari had just gone up considerably.

"Since he does not speak of it, we should respect that privacy and not mention it again, either," he said. At her nod, he added, "Come on, we've spent enough time by ourselves that the others are probably getting worried. We had better get back and be on our way again."

As if on cue, Geneva said, *"Brock wishes to know if you are all right, Love."*

"I am fine," he replied. *"Tell Brock that Rita and I are on our way back to the clearing and we will be leaving soon."*

The winds had shifted and the dragons were able to soar for most of the afternoon. Since they were making good headway, and they all wanted to get to Larimar as soon as possible, they stopped briefly for a cold meal after about five hours and then flew long into the night. When they finally stopped to rest, it was near midnight, and no one even bothered trying to make camp. They simply divested the dragons of their saddles and packs before pillowing their heads on their Bond-mates' feet and went to sleep.

The changing red hues told him that he was in the Dream State. He looked around and saw some dragons soaring. He just stood next to Geneva and, together they watched for a while.

"We have company, Love," Geneva said.

Delno sensed more amusement in her voice than annoyance, so he knew it wouldn't be an unwelcome interruption. A dragon materialized into view, and he immediately recognized the light blue female and the blonde rider.

"Brother," Will said, "isn't this place amazing? This is only my second time here, but I am completely thrilled with the place."

"Yes, I have been here often, but I am always taken by the beauty and serenity."

Will turned to watch the other dragons soaring for a few moments. They stood shoulder to shoulder, and Delno suddenly felt closer to his younger sibling than he had ever felt before.

Will turned to him suddenly and exclaimed, "Standing here in all of this beauty while watching the dragons soar, I almost forgot I came with news. Six more un-bonded dragons—they really do prefer that term over calling them wild—have joined our cause. They showed up and presented themselves to Nassari, who was drilling the new Riders on the plain the afternoon of the day you left. Two of them wished to be bonded, and they each chose one of the two candidates who weren't picked the first time. Nassari saw to the whole thing, and he has them 'settled in and geared up,' as he put it. He really has taken charge; I never would have thought of him as being so capable."

"That is good news," Delno said smiling. "Tell me though, what of Saadia? Is she close to laying those eggs? Gina laid her eggs early. I understand that dragons can tend to misjudge the time of the laying if it is their first clutch."

"I believe I have misjudged my time," Saadia spoke from close behind him.

"I'm sorry, Saadia, I didn't mean to speak of you as if you weren't here. I thought you might be communing with the other dragons and didn't want to disturb you," Delno said, thinking he might have offended the dragon.

"I was a bit perturbed, but your reasoning is most courteous, so I forgive you," Saadia replied good naturedly. "I do believe now, and my mother concurs, that the signs are showing that my quickening will come sooner than I expected. I will probably lay these eggs within the next few days."

"Then we will make sure that you are comfortable for the event. I will speak to the king personally about it when we arrive in Larimar."

"You are most generous, Delno Okonan, I thank you."

Delno bowed at the formal compliment.

"How are your magic studies coming, Brother?" he turned to Will.

"Nassari and I have been reading and practicing quite a bit. It's funny, for someone who claims to have so little connection and knowledge of magic, he certainly takes to it well enough."

"Well, Brother, that probably has something to do with him having a strong bond with a lineage holder."

"A lineage holder? Wanda? That certainly explains a bit. Now I understand why he struts around the practice field like a drill instructor ... and why we obey him so willingly."

"Practice field?" Delno asked, somewhat amused.

"Oh, yes, he has us all up at the crack of dawn with practice blades in our hands studying with the weapons masters. After that, it's magic practice, where he and I drill the others on what we've learned. Of course, he pushes himself harder than he pushes any of us. In fact, by the time we all arrive on the practice field, he is already there and has been practicing for an hour or so."

"It sounds like he is filling in for me quite adequately. I'm glad to hear that none of you has neglected your studies in the three days of my absence. I worried that if I had been gone longer, you might have slipped into complete laziness," he joked. "Now, of course, it looks like I shall have to ask Nassari's permission before I commandeer any of *his* troops."

Both brothers laughed, and then Will said, "Well, Brother, dawn comes early, and I must be ready for training, so I will leave you now. See you when you get back." With that he faded from view.

"Nassari certainly seems to have changed for the better," Geneva observed.

"Yes, I always knew that he was a good man deep down. He has always been sensitive and driven to succeed, but that public face he cultivated kept most people from seeing it. He may be just the lieutenant that I have been looking for. With him and Brock, I will have enough leaders among the bonded pairs to keep our attacks and defense coordinated. With Sheila as commander of the wild—excuse me, *un-bonded*—dragons, we will be able to fit them in as part of a cohesive whole. All in all, we will take a formidable force to Horne when we go."

"I hope it is enough, Love."

"So do I," he responded, "I have one last thing I want to try for, and then we will be off, and the game will be in play."

"Care to fill me in on that little bit of information, or are you still keeping secrets?"

"I think I will keep this one to myself for now, Love. I know you won't betray me, but there is just something that seems right about keeping my own counsel this time."

"All right, but I can't help you if I don't know what you are doing." She tried not to sound upset and almost succeeded.

The next morning Delno was up before anyone else. He spent the time writing a letter. When everyone else was awake, he called them all together and made an announcement.

"Lawrence is not going to Larimar with us. I have an urgent task for him that requires he fly to Palamore immediately. The rest of us will continue to Larimar; if we leave quickly, we should be there by this afternoon."

The rest of the group exchanged glances, but no one asked what this was all about. Brock, Craig and Rita busied themselves with packing and saddling the dragons for the remainder of the trip. Delno took Lawrence aside and handed him the letter.

"You are to take this letter to Jhren in Palamore. You are not to get involved with any of the Queen's plans or schemes while you are there. If she tries to get you to do anything or go anywhere, you must simply apologize for not being able to do as she asks. Tell her that you have specific orders from me and cannot do otherwise."

"What are my specific orders, other than delivering the letter to Jhren?"

"Very simple: make yourself available to Jhren and do as he tells you." As Lawrence nodded, Delno added, "You do whatever he tells you, including taking him where he tells you to go. Do you understand?"

"No, I don't understand, but I do know that I am to follow Jhren's orders," the man said with a puzzled look.

"Good, you have no need to know more for now. Just remember that Jhren is in charge." Delno then waited until Lawrence mounted before adding, "You may feel better knowing that this isn't just make-work, Lawrence. This is a vital task I have set for you. Jhren will probably need you to transport him soon after he has read that letter. Go now, and don't let anything or anyone distract you from your task."

Lawrence nodded once, saluted, and then Rhonna launched into the air. Delno watched until he could no longer see them before he turned and walked back to the group. They all mounted up and took off. Everyone remained quiet for the rest of the trip and he was grateful for the solitude.

CHAPTER 29

"**W**ELL, LOVE, THAT was a short trip. The stones of the wall are almost still warm from where I was resting before we took off."

"*I know you have done quite a bit of flying recently, Dear Heart, but we still have much to do.*"

"*Yes, but unless you intend we do it right now, I am going to lay here on the wall and rest while you handle the human end of our situation!*"

Delno laughed out loud. "*You rest, Love, I will call if I need you, but I promise to only call if I need you.*"

"Is Geneva getting settled all right?" Rita asked. "Fahwn is a bit grumpy. She says it is because we pushed them so hard on the trip, but I think she likes it in Orlean better than she likes it here."

"Geneva isn't exactly grumpy, but if I were one of the guards here on the wall, I'd walk softly while she's resting," he replied.

""Well, they don't have any more to complain about than the other dragons do," Brock observed as he joined them. Leera had taken a place on the wall nearest to Geneva, automatically fitting into that place reserved for a trusted second in command. "Leera and Torin have spent a good deal of time flying over the last couple of weeks, also." Then he turned to Delno and added, "It might be a good idea if we give them a few days to rest and eat before we head south."

"I was thinking the same thing, but also think that the exercise is good for them." He held up his hand to forestall protests from either Brock or Rita. "I know you wish to defend your dragons and tell me that they are hardworking, but they are not in nearly as good shape as the wild, excuse me, un-bonded dragons who have joined us." Again he had to stop them from speaking up. "At least, they weren't before we started all of this. Look at Torin. She's the newest member of our team and, though she put a brave front on it and didn't complain, she was barely able to keep up with Geneva on the trip from Orlean, and Geneva set a light pace because she was along. We have pushed our dragons hard, and they sometimes complain about it, but show me a soldier who doesn't complain about the physical exertion expected of him. They are in better physical condition because we have pushed them to do more than would normally be expected of them."

Rita was thoughtful but Brock was simply staring at him with his mouth hanging open.

"Why are you looking at me like that?" he asked Brock.

Brock had to visibly shake himself to break the spell that had come over him. "Because, my friend, for a minute there, the way the light was playing on your features and the tone of your voice, I thought that I was looking at and listening to your grandfather. Many was the time that he railed against dragons and Riders neglecting physical conditioning in favor of a more sedate life style. He gave me the last couple of lines of that speech nearly word for word many times."

Delno smiled. He wasn't sure why he liked being compared to Corolan so much. He knew his grandfather was a good man and a great Rider, but he had never met him, that he remembered anyway. However, he always felt a real sense of pride when one of the older Riders compared him to the man, but it wasn't just pride: it made him feel more kinship with his grandfather, and that made him somehow feel less alone as a leader.

"Well," he said in a softer tone, "when we get to Horne, we will be facing dragons and Riders who have kept hidden for the most part. Hopefully, they have been letting themselves get slack, and our physical training will give us another advantage."

"I hadn't thought about that, Handsome," Rita was never one to be left out of a conversation for long. "I was just getting a little bit annoyed that you were pushing us so hard. I hadn't realized that part of your motivation was to give us a physical advantage over our enemies."

"It really is part of my upbringing and military training," he replied. "Here in the north, the climate is harsh and can kill you if you aren't prepared for it. Not just the cold either; the whole country is just reluctant to give you a living: you have to scrape that living out forcefully. Children are pushed hard to achieve, both mentally and physically. In fact, the children of Corice are some of the best educated in the known world. Then the army's training regimen is big on stamina as well as weapons and hand-to-hand combat. The Battle of Stone Bridge that I am so famous for was won partly due to the bravery of the men who fought there, but also due to the fact that we were able to fight on longer even though fatigued because of the emphasis on building stamina in the Corisian Army. Since it has served me so well in the past, it is only natural that we prepare ourselves in a similar manner now. Because we all mesh so well together, I tend to forget that we all come from such different backgrounds. I guess I should explain my actions more often."

"You are the commander, and we have accepted that, so perhaps we shouldn't question you so often. What you say makes good sense," Brock responded. "It is always better if we and our dragons can outlast our opponents as well as out fly them."

"Well, you've done pretty damn well by us up to this point, Delno," Rita said seriously. Then she smiled and added, "You lead, Handsome, I'll follow."

"Well, I may understand why you are pushing us so hard, Love, but Brock is right about one thing. At this level of exercise, I am going to need to eat soon. Please remember that when you speak with your uncle."

"I will remember, Love. I will try to have enough food beasts for all who are hungry available by the time you have finished resting."

Craig joined them and Delno said, "I suppose it's time I take you and Brock to meet the king."

The "palace" wasn't all that palatial; it was originally built to house the officers of the garrison that protected the docks, and the city sort of grew up around it. Once Larimar became the capitol, the building was taken over by the royal family and had been called the Palace ever since. It consisted of kitchens, the main hall, a couple of small offices, the main dining hall, the king's private dining hall, and the library, as well as fifteen small apartments. It did have indoor plumbing for both the refreshers and the baths. While the mountains in Corice were rich in gold and other minerals, the Corisians weren't people who squandered their wealth. They preferred to use the money to take care of their people rather than build elaborate government structures to impress visitors.

Delno led Brock and Craig into the main hall while Rita went to check on the children. Dorian was easy to find. He was, as usual, dealing with some city council members in the main hall. The conversation was on one of the very subjects that Delno needed to speak with his uncle about.

"Why does Corice, and the city of Larimar in particular, have to bear the brunt of feeding those colossal beasts?" one of the council members asked in a nasally voice.

"Partly because those 'colossal beasts,' as you put it, are responsible for the kingdom of Corice still owning the city of Larimar. We owe them our freedom and most likely our lives." Dorian responded tiredly as if this subject had worn thin from over use.

"Well, they are now just lying in the open field or perched on the walls like stone gargoyles doing nothing. Couldn't they go somewhere and hunt for their food?" the man responded.

"They could," Delno said coldly, "but if they all hunted locally, the area would be so depleted of large game it would take years for the deer and wild pig population to recover."

The councilman was startled by the unexpected appearance of the Dragon Riders. He looked to the king for support and found none.

"Also," Delno continued, "dragons usually only eat three to four times a year. Sometimes they will feed more if they are working hard enough to need the extra food. By nature, dragons are quite frugal with their resources. Most of the dragons who are here have not fed and will not need to do so for quite some time. By the time they do need to feed, they will most likely have finished fighting your war for you and returned to their own lands so that they won't over burden this area. They know how to be good guests even if you aren't willing to be a good host."

He knew that saying that last bit would further alienate the man, but he was sick of the whining about providing for loyal allies, especially when they came in answer to his call for help, not because they saw the opportunity for a free meal.

"You have no right to speak of what we should do here in Corice," the councilman spat. "You are one of them. We have our own problems, and you swoop down and add to those problems by burdening us with, not just more mouths to feed, but giant appetites attached to them. You claim that these beasts eat so daintily, but that blue monster devoured a whole cow and two large pigs. Then what did she do, she flew back to her perch on the wall and . . ."

"Set up watch over your city, you pompous ass." That may not have been the way the man had intended to finish the statement, but Will, who had just come in and heard the man insulting Saadia, had decided that he liked his ending better. "She, pregnant, flew all night to come to our aid because she had been asked to do so, and you fault her for a few scrawny beasts? Your selfishness amazes me and makes me sorry that you come from the same homeland as I."

"I . . . you . . . he. . . ." The councilman was so enraged that he could only splutter nearly incoherently.

Delno put his hand on his brother's shoulder to quiet him, but Will ignored him. He had apparently been putting up with this nonsense since he moved into the palace, and he was through holding his tongue.

"As for my brother being one of them and not one of us; if it weren't for this man and the few brave souls who stood shoulder to shoulder with him on Stone Bridge during the last war, you would be lucky to be a beggar in a land ruled by the Bournese rather than a wealthy merchant and politician in Corice. Even if you don't feel obliged to admit your debt to the dragons, you owe this man more than you can ever repay. He was born and raised in Corice and served honorably in the Corisian Army and was decorated with the highest award our kingdom can give for his bravery and service to all of us. The least you can do is acknowledge that much."

The councilman's anger was still apparent, but Will's last statement hit home. No matter how miserly or greedy a Corisian he might be, he was, first and foremost, a loyal citizen of Corice and was raised to honor those who Corice chose to honor. Now that his slight of a Corisian hero was brought to his attention, there was a great deal of shame mixed in with his anger. He hung his head and said nothing for several moments.

Finally he looked at Delno and said, "I have wronged you. I have allowed my position of keeping track of the kingdom's money to cloud my good sense. Your brother is right, of course, and all I can offer is my apology. I am deeply sorry and deeply shamed by my words and actions."

No one spoke for a moment after the formal apology. Then Delno said, "I accept your apology and feel that we can put this matter to rest. Let us be friends." Then to complete the formal acceptance of the apology, he extended his hand to shake.

"Well, then, that's settled," Nassari said, stepping forward. Nassari didn't have Will's magical talent for not being seen, but spending so much time in public life had taught him the ability of being inconspicuous in a crowd when he wanted to be: he had heard the whole exchange.

"You are very lucky that Delno is a forgiving man, Walter," Nassari said to the councilman. "He is one of the best swordsmen there is. He didn't win the Battle of Stone Bridge on luck alone. Also, there are a lot of people, myself included, who might invite you onto the field for giving insult to him. I'm glad we can put this all behind us and work cooperatively."

There were, of course, several other council members present, and they began to speak out all at once. Nassari silenced them with a wave of his hand.

"Before we go on and I have to start challenging the whole council to duels, let me say something. You all know that I worked in the hospital during the last war. Many wounded men came into that hospital from the field with one name on their lips. They all talked of how Delno Okonan had saved their lives. If Delno Okonan hadn't risked his own life to save theirs, they would never have survived. Over a score of men had personal stories of how Delno had saved them and their comrades from being slaughtered. He was decorated with the Corisian Medal of Valor and given a small pension for his services. If he had received medals for all of his feats of bravery and a pension for each, he could most likely cover a wall with the awards and his monthly stipend would bankrupt the country."

Delno was amazed to watch the change come over the politicians as Nassari spoke. His friend really did have a magical talent for speaking. Even Brock, Rita and Craig seemed thoroughly enthralled as Nassari warmed to his subject.

"After saving this kingdom, he didn't try to use his fame and notoriety for his own personal gain, he found and helped a distressed dragon and bonded with her offspring. Then he left and stopped a war in Palamore that would have eventually spilled over into the north. After that, he didn't sit back and rest. He headed north and once again took it upon himself to save his beloved homeland by this time bringing Elven healing techniques to cure the pestilence and Dragons to fight our war."

The council members began to shift and twist like young children who were being scolded for teasing a playmate.

"And now, when he is preparing to take this war to its source in the mountains around Horne, he finds that those he is trying to protect are treating him as an unwanted guest in his own home. I am ashamed to say that I used to think of you all as friends. Spare him your miserly condemnations and loosen your purse strings so that the Riders can be about the business of keeping you safe and happily ignorant of the dangers you still face."

"Again," Walter said to Nassari, "I offer my apologies. I will support whatever the Riders need. I understand that there is much happening that still endangers us that we don't have knowledge of." He then turned to Delno and added, "If you have any further trouble getting supplies, see me directly. If the funds aren't available from the Corisian coffers, I will call on all of the merchants personally and see that you get what you need, including enough meat for your dragons." Then he turned to the other council members and said, "Since our only business here today concerned the dragons and Riders, and that is now settled, we should go and let the Riders confer with the king. We are obviously still at war, and since I am reluctant to vote for our surrender at this point, we have no further business here until the war is concluded."

He turned to leave, and when the other council members seemed reluctant to follow, he simply snapped his fingers to get their attention and bade them to come along. They were confused but followed in his wake.

Once the council members had gone Delno said, "Uncle, let me introduce you to two more Riders." He turned to Brock and Craig and said, "May I present my uncle, the King Dorian Corice of the Kingdom of Corice. Uncle, this is Brock Ard, once my teacher and now my most trusted lieutenant; and this is Craig Carver, Senior Dragon Rider, who usually lives with the elves."

"Delno, you make me sound so formal," Craig said, "I am pleased to meet you, Your Majesty." Craig bowed slightly to Dorian.

"I, too, am pleased to meet you, sir," Brock said, nodding his head in place of bowing.

By now Dorian had definitely gotten used to Dragon Riders being his equals, so he took no offense.

"I have seen your name in one of my books, Rider. That particular book came from the south and is over five hundred years old," Dorian said to Craig.

"That is entirely possible, sir; I am more than fourteen hundred years old."

Dorian smiled and turned to Brock. "I have heard so much about you from my nephew. I feel as if I almost know you already."

"I am glad to be of service in this cause," Brock responded.

"Now then, gentlemen," Dorian said, "I am sure that you didn't just come along to rescue me from those politicians you sent packing. What can I do for the Dragon Riders?"

"Well, Uncle, Nassari is handling the new Riders quite adequately, so the only thing we will need that he isn't taking care of is food for the dragons and a place for Craig to hold classes for his new students." His uncle looked puzzled at his last words, so he added, "Craig has left his home among the elves to help train the new Riders: those who have bonded with the mature dragons as well as those who will bond with Saadia's hatchlings."

"As for food for the dragons, Nassari can see the same sergeant I have been sending you to see. Tell me, can a dragon carry off a whole cow?"

"As long as the distance they have to fly with it isn't far and the cow isn't too big. A dragon will fatigue carrying the weight of a Rider and passenger if she has to fly for long distances. But for a very short trip, a dragon can carry eighty or ninety stone. Of course, with that much weight, they won't be able to do much more than a short flight of about half a mile, and they won't be able to get much altitude," Craig said while Brock nodded in agreement.

"That is probably enough. We can have some cows brought out to the plain and the dragons can come one at a time and take their pick and then carry them off to eat in privacy. That way we get them fed quickly without having the delay of tying each animal out separately." Dorian then turned to Nassari and said, "Since you seem to be in charge of such things among the Riders, I will leave you to see to it."

Nassari simply nodded his agreement and turned to Craig and said, "Since you will be staying in Larimar to train the Riders, I can get you settled while I am making the other arrangements, if you like."

"Oh, yes, I would like that very much," Craig said. "I am not used to long trips, and I would like to get a hot bath and a full meal as soon as possible."

As Nassari led Craig out of the main hall Dorian said, "So, tell me, Delno, how long do you anticipate staying in Larimar this time? Not that I am trying to get rid of you—I especially don't like the idea of you going off to fight—but I would like to know what to expect."

"Well, I am glad you are not in a hurry to send my sons off to war, Uncle," Laura Okonan, who had just joined them, said sternly. Then she turned on Delno and asked, with even more emotion, "What is this I hear about Will going with you?"

"Ah, so you've found out about that. I am sorry, Mother, I knew you wouldn't like it and had planned on breaking the news to you gently."

"Gently?" She nearly shouted, "How can you break such news to a mother gently? It's bad enough that one of my sons is going off to fight this insane war, and now I find out that I could lose both of you to the same bastard who killed my father!"

Both the brothers were shocked to hear their mother use such language, and in such anger. Delno looked to his brother, and Will only smiled sheepishly and looked at his feet like a child caught at something he shouldn't be doing. Apparently, Will had already endured his mother's wrath, so he wasn't even going to offer Delno much in the way of moral support.

"Mother . . ." Delno began.

"Don't you 'Mother' me," she said cutting him off. "I am furious with you about your decision to take your brother along. I nearly died when you went off to war against the Bournese the first time. Each act of heroism that was reported of you was like a cold knife in my heart. I worried continually that the next time you risked your life to save the lives of other men, it would be the last thing you ever did. May all the gods forgive, or even if they don't, I wished you would just let those other men die and keep your own head down and be safe."

"Mother!" he said, shocked at her oath, "I don't believe you said that."

Laura Okonan looked at her son and then slapped him across the face with all of the force she could muster. Then, with tears in her eyes, she said, "If you must go, then leave your brother here." Then she said in a hoarse whisper, "I can't risk losing both of you."

She began to weep uncontrollably. Delno, stunned at being slapped, not by the pain but by the fact that his mother, who had never raised a hand to either of her children and didn't believe in such, was moved to such an uncontrolled act of emotion, put his arms around her. She nearly fell against him, and he held her. Will put his arms around her also, and she was nearly lost between the two men. She huddled there in the protection of her sons' arms and cried for nearly a quarter of an hour.

Finally she stopped sobbing and pushed the two young men apart enough to look up at Delno first, and then turn and look at Will. "I am so afraid of losing you both that I wish we could just run off and hide from this trouble. I don't care about the rest of Corice in this matter. Even if the war is lost, it will still be several years before the average Corisian sees a change in his life. But if we lose, then I lose both of my sons to the same madman who had my father killed. I lose my life to his insane plan to rule the world. Why is it my sons who have to go off and risk death in a faraway land to save this kingdom?"

"Mother," Delno said gently, "it is we who have to do this because we are who and what we are. None of us asked for this. When I left the army, I had hoped to put wars and fighting behind me. I left my home in part to get away from all of this, but it followed my every move. Fate has delivered a cruel lot to this family, and we have to fight this war because there is no one else. The Riders look to me as their leader, and Will has the skill I need to observe the enemy while remaining unobserved himself. All I can offer you as consolation is that we will both be careful. However, neither of us will forfeit his duty to the people we have sworn to protect, and we will also avenge the murder of our grandfather."

Laura dried her eyes on a handkerchief and looked her eldest son in the eyes for a long time. Then she straightened herself and nodded once. "Your father and I raised you to do the right thing when called upon to do so, and to recognize the call when it comes. I cannot, then, rightfully ask either of you to stay. I will not have what could end up as the last words I speak to you be the harsh words of a bitter woman, but rather the loving encouragement of a concerned mother. Keep safe and don't take unnecessary risks with either of your lives. Come home safely to me when you have won this war."

Laura suddenly noticed a small trace of blood on the side of Delno's face where the family ring she wore on her right hand had cut him slightly just under his left eye. She suddenly began crying and trying to wipe away the blood with her handkerchief. She kept repeating "I'm so sorry."

Delno reached up and stayed her hand and said, "Mother, it's nothing. I've cut myself worse shaving. If I wanted it healed, I could do so in a second. I prefer it to be left as a reminder to me that emotions are running high, and I need to take other people's feelings into consideration."

She stopped trying to dab at the cut and looked at him. She then laid her hand on his cheek and, with tears still flowing, said, "You have grown into such a good man." She reached out with her other hand to Will and pulled him to her also. "You both have grown into such good men. I tend to forget that you are both fully grown and not my little boys anymore."

"Well," Delno replied, "perhaps this afternoon we can both be your little boys again, at least for a while."

Laura brightened and even laughed some.

Brock said, "Since we are regressing to our childhoods, I could use some cookies and a hug."

All three of them turned to the older Rider and laughed.

Brock said, "Hello, Laura, you've grown a bit since the last time I saw you."

Even Delno was shocked at this revelation. Brock had never mentioned that he knew Laura Okonan.

"The last time I saw you was when I was visiting your caravan while I was traveling with your father," Brock said. "I believe you were about five or six."

"I vaguely remember a dark man who came with my father a couple of times when I was young." Then she brightened and said, "Your Bondmate is blue with an orange star on her face, isn't she?"

"You always liked Leera's orange marking," Brock responded.

"I remember that I liked those exotic candies you always brought with you, too." Laura's smile broadened, and she extended her hand to Brock.

Brock kissed her hand in the way of a gentleman and she laughed and said, "I also remember that you had a way of charming all of the older girls. I believe the candy was to bribe us younger children to go away and leave you alone with them."

Brock's eyes went wide and he affected a look of total innocence and said, "Would a Dragon Rider do such a thing?"

"In the wink of an eye," Rita replied as she joined the group.

Everyone else laughed as Brock feigned an indignant protest.

The high tension and worried mood had completely lifted. Dorian suggested they all move to the private dining hall and have lunch.

"So Brock, what have you been doing since the last time I saw you?" Laura asked once the meal had settled down to light nibbling and conversation.

"Oh, I traveled more with your father off and on. Unfortunately, I was dealing with other business farther south when he was killed in Horne. I owed him my life several times over and wish I could have been there to help him that day," he said sadly. "So, when I met his grandson, I figured I could best repay some of that debt by helping Delno learn how to take care of himself as a Rider."

"You cannot be faulted for not being there for Corolan," Laura replied. "He was a strong man, despite his small stature, and he traveled where and when he pleased, as he pleased. If he had not wanted to be traveling alone, he wouldn't have been, and since he wanted to travel alone, the choice was his, not yours." She paused for a moment and then added, "As for helping my son, you have my thanks. It makes me feel better knowing that he has brave, competent friends who stand by him."

Brock smiled and nodded and the whole group settled into a comfortable silence for several minutes.

Rita broke the silence, saying, "The children are with your father, Delno. The twins are beginning to grieve, in their way, for their parents. They are coming to understand that they won't see their mother and father again, so they will not allow themselves to be left with anyone they don't know. I would have brought them to lunch with us, but Marcus had just fallen asleep and the girls were tired, so we put them down for a nap. They should awaken soon."

Brock looked completely confused, and Delno realized that with everything else that had gone on, they had not told him about the children. He quickly filled Brock in on the whole situation here in Corice.

Brock was about to comment when Will straightened and said, "Saadia!" before jumping up so fast that he knocked his chair over. He further surprised all of them by running for the door without even stopping to right the chair before he left. The entire group quickly followed.

Since Laura and Dorian couldn't keep up with the magically enhanced musculature of the Riders, even Rita, whose short stature usually put her last in such contests, outpaced them slightly. Eventually they all caught up with Will at the stock yard where he was standing next to Saadia looking a bit distressed.

He looked at Brock and said, "She is ready to lay her eggs, but she is in so much pain! What is wrong?"

Brock examined Saadia and then spoke mentally with Leera and then turned to Will. "All is normal, lad. She is just in labor. The egg is moving through the passage normally and should be out soon. Then there are the second and third to be laid. It will all be over shortly."

"Should it hurt this much?" Will asked. He was obviously in direct contact and sharing Saadia's pain.

"Hmm," Brock snorted, "son, if you were passing a small melon that was nearly the size of your head through one of your orifices, would it hurt?"

Will thought about it and then nodded.

"The pain is not as extreme for a dragon as for a human female in labor, but it is quite uncomfortable. Just lend her your strength, and she will get through this just fine," Brock said gently, laying his hand on Will's shoulder and giving him an encouraging shake.

Will smiled and turned back to Saadia. "I'm here, Love. Do you need anything?"

"You being near is all that I require, Love," Saadia responded out loud. "My mother is circling overhead, and she has told me just what the older Rider has told you. We will be fine. This will all be over soon."

It wasn't long before the tip of the egg appeared so that all could see it. Once it had reached the opening, it moved faster and slid out in only a few seconds. It lay on the ground gleaming. The shell was hard and mottled, and glistened with a faint coating of the fluid that lubricated the passage.

"Now that the passage has been forced to relax to allow the first egg through, the second should pass much more easily," Saadia said.

She was right, of course. Within several minutes the second egg appeared at the opening and then slid rapidly out onto the ground beside the first. The third egg repeated the performance of the first two and the laying process was over. Then, even though she had only three eggs, which was a big clutch for a dragon, Saadia spent a great deal of time arranging them near her until they were set just the right way to her satisfaction. She kept one of them slightly apart from the other two. In fact she placed it on the other side of her body.

"Why have moved the one egg to the other side of your body from these two?" Will asked.

"Because that is the male," she replied. "He will hatch very soon and he will be much more mature than either of his sisters." At Will's perplexed look she explained. "Male dragons aren't as intelligent as females, but they are born much more fully developed. They are still small at hatching, but they are immediately capable of flight and hunting small game. Once he hatches, I will feed him lightly, and he will leave in search of a suitable territory as far from any other intelligent beings as he can get. However, if I didn't separate the eggs, he might attack the un-hatched females before I could stop him in his effort to find food before he leaves. At this stage in his life, he would see them as nothing more than a source of nutrition."

"We will make sure that he has food when he hatches," Delno said.

After listening to Saadia's explanation, Brock said, "We may as well go and see those children you spoke about. Being a first time mother, Saadia will spend a great deal of time tending these eggs, and won't settle down as long as there are too many people around."

Will stayed with Saadia, and everyone else went back to the palace to see if the children were awake.

CHAPTER 30

THEY FOUND THE children in the nursery playing: John Okonan was watching them. As they entered, the girls, who had been playing with dolls, came running to Laura and Rita. Marcus, who was building something out of wooden blocks that Delno recognized as the same toys that he and Will had played with, looked up for a moment but went back to his toys rather than interact with any of them.

The girls were anxious to show him their new dolls, and he took a few moments to look at them and make appropriate compliments. Then he moved to Marcus and sat down on the floor with him.

"What are you making, Marcus?" Delno asked.

"A fort," the boy responded.

"That's very good. Are you going to keep an army there to protect it?"

"No, armies can't protect forts. This fort will keep out sickness so children's mothers and fathers won't die."

Delno's heart almost skipped a beat, and he was immediately engulfed by the enormity of the boy's situation. He nearly cried.

"You know, Marcus, that would be a good thing if we could do it. I wish we could have done that for your mother and father." As Delno spoke, he realized he had suddenly gone a little hoarse and was having trouble speaking around the lump in his throat.

The boy looked up at him angrily and said, "You're a Dragon Rider. You're supposed to be able to protect people. Why didn't you protect my mother and father?"

"Marcus," Laura said softly, "dragons can't fight sickness the way they fight armies. Delno and the other Riders brought the healers as soon as they could. They tried very hard to protect your mother and father."

Tears began to flow down Marcus's cheeks, and he yelled at Delno, "I wish you had died instead of my parents."

At first, no one spoke. Then Delno, with his own tears starting to flow, said, "So do I, Marcus, so do I."

The boy hit Delno several times on the chest. Delno made no move to defend himself or stop the boy from venting the pent up frustration. John Okonan started to move to stop Marcus, but Delno stopped him with a wave of his hand.

After striking the Rider about dozen times, Marcus threw himself into Delno's arms and sobbed uncontrollably. He held the boy and rocked him. The girls were a bit distressed by the scene, and Laura and Rita took them out of the room. Delno continued to hold Marcus until he was beginning to worry that the sobs that wracked the child's body would do him harm. In the end, Marcus settled down into soft crying, which eventually abated completely. Still he clung to Delno, and Delno held him, trying to convey the feeling of safety and love the boy needed.

"Rita says to tell you that that is the first time the boy has wept for his parents. He has been trying to put on a brave front, but it's good to see that he has finally let some of it out," Geneva relayed to him.

"I'm glad that he has also. Now maybe he can begin the long process of healing," he responded. "Where are Rita and the girls now?"

"In the main hall. The girls are playing some game I don't understand. In fact, I think the girls are the only ones who do understand it. These children are extremely intelligent, Delno. It's too early to tell, but they might make good Riders someday if the magic stays with them."

"Stays with them?"

"Yes, sometimes a child with strong magic loses some of that connection as he grows. Sometimes they simply suppress it as they get older. Hopefully, with you and Rita raising these children, they will do neither."

"Well, that's very interesting, Love, and I would enjoy talking about it further with you, but right now this boy really needs me to be with him. I will talk with you later. I love you, Geneva."

"Give the child all the time he needs, Dear One. I love you, too."

As he finished talking with Geneva, Marcus sat up in his lap. "I'm sorry I hit you," the boy said.

"It's all right this time. You had all of that inside you, and it needed to go somewhere." Then he looked the boy in the eyes and joked, "I'm glad you stopped when you did though; it kind of hurt."

He and Marcus both laughed a little, and Marcus hugged him. The boy was still sad and would miss his parents terribly for a long time to come, but he had finally started to heal.

Delno looked around and saw that everyone had left the two of them completely alone. "Are you ready to go and join your sisters and the others?" he asked.

Marcus thought about it for a second and then said, "I need to finish my fort first." Then he again looked at Delno and asked, "Would you help me?"

"Of course I'll help. Let's make it a big, strong fort."

"With dragons to guard it?" Marcus asked.

"If you'd like, we'll have a whole army of dragons to guard it."

Marcus gave him a big smile, and they spent the next hour building the fort out of blocks.

CHAPTER 31

"I DON'T KNOW IF this is going to work, Love," Geneva said. "I haven't seen Marlo here since she bonded with Nat."

"You did say that all dragons always kept an awareness of the Dream State, even when they are awake, right?"

"Yes, I said that. I also said that because of that, I will have to sift through all of the consciousnesses that are present to find her while dampening my search methods enough not to alert our enemies. This is no easy task."

"I'm sorry, Geneva, it must be rather like looking for a needle in a hay stack."

"No, it's like looking for a needle in a haystack while blindfolded and wearing mittens, and it's a very large haystack. Now if you don't leave me to it, it won't get done," Geneva replied testily.

Delno had no choice but to sit back and enjoy the view in the Dream State while Geneva tried to locate Marlo and pull her and, hopefully, Nat, in with them. Delno wished for the thousandth time that he had insisted that Nat and Marlo wait for the rest of them. He needed to speak with them, and this method was too iffy. They had already tried and failed on the previous night. If he had known it would be this difficult, he would have had Geneva start trying the night he sent Lawrence off to Palamore.

"I have them, Love," Geneva said triumphantly.

As she finished her statement, Nat and Marlo came into view as if they had been standing there all the time and had just become visible.

"Delno, isn't this place magnificent?" Nat asked by way of greeting.

Delno couldn't suppress a chuckle. His appeal to Marlo and Nat to join him had been most urgent, but his friend couldn't help but let his curiosity get the better of him.

"Nat, my friend, when this is all over you may spend all of the time you like studying dragons and everything associated with them, but right now I have to talk seriously with you about the war."

"I'm sorry, Delno, I forget that you have been here enough times to be used to it by now."

"Nathaniel, every time I come here, I find it new and beautiful, as well as mysterious. However, time is short, and we have much to discuss."

"Yes, you're right, of course. I haven't gotten to Horne yet. I am still following your orders and staying with the men you sent. It will be at least another week before we actually get there. However, we did meet several messengers on the road, and they were carrying news and seeking aid for the same sickness that afflicted Larimar. I told them about the sickness and how to treat it, and sent them back to the healers in Horne at double speed. The sickness should be under control by the time we get there. As for the rest of it, well, the messengers were glad to see our force of men going, but they had hoped for more. It seems that the Roracks have been massing by the hundreds and sometimes even by the thousands."

"Well, the news about the sickness sets my mind at ease. Perhaps we should have just sent word instead of tying you up with the job. As for the Roracks, that will be more difficult, but I think we will be ready," Delno replied.

"I could have sent word, but I still feel better going. I don't want to leave anything to chance," Nat said.

"Neither to do I," Delno said. "That is why you are going to divert back north."

"What? Divert north? Why would I do that? I've spent a week sleeping among sweaty soldiers to get less far than Marlo and I could have flown by ourselves in a day. Now you want me to turn around and come back?"

"No, I don't want you to come back. I want you to fly to Orlean and meet Lawrence and Rhonna. They are traveling with Jhren, and I want you to see to him personally. Even in a weakened state, he is a powerful magic user, and he is willing to help in Horne. However, I don't want to risk his life needlessly. I need you to see to him and find out if he really is strong enough for the trip."

"When did you send for Jhren, and why?" Nat asked.

"I sent a message to him the morning after I left Orlean after seeing to the Hatching of Gina's eggs. That was four days ago. I got new information on this whole situation while in Orlean, and because of that, I called for Jhren's advice. I had thought that he might come here to Larimar and talk with me directly, but he's a stubborn man. He decided to go directly to Horne and see the situation for himself. Geneva and I spoke with Lawrence in the Dream State last night, and Jhren is adamant about this. I should have sent someone with a stronger will than Lawrence, and now I am trying my best to deal with that mistake by sending you to see to the old man before he exhausts himself right into a grave."

"Delno Okonan, if you would talk about these things before you act, we could all advise you better before the situation turns into an emergency." Nat paused and thought for a moment and then continued. "Yes, there's nothing for it; I'll have to divert. If he and Lawrence have been traveling for four days, they should be closer than Orlean. Why don't I wait for them here? Then we could all continue on with these men."

"That might be a good idea, but he didn't leave until yesterday. It seems that he had some things to see to that might be helpful and that took time. As for meeting them in Orlean, I told Lawrence that he is to wait for you there no matter what threats Jhren makes to try and convince him otherwise."

Nat laughed and said, "It's Lawrence I'm going to have to see to. He'll be so torn between obeying you and obeying Jhren that he will have developed stomach problems from the fret by the time I get there. Very well, I will leave as soon as we finish our conversation."

"You can wait until morning," Delno replied. "There's no need to exhaust yourselves over this."

"Oh, isn't there? If we don't get there soon, Jhren will take it upon himself to find alternate transport. Besides, Marlo and I have been traveling lazily because we have had to wait for the men to catch up. We like to fly in the dark, and it will give us something to do beside circle this army like an overlarge bird of prey."

"Very well," Delno said. "The newly bonded dragons and Riders who are coming with me will be ready to travel in a day or so, and we will all meet up in Horne. I will look for you here tomorrow night. Until then, keep safe."

"We will; you do the same," Nat said as he and Marlo faded from view.

"Fahwn and Rita are here, Love. I have kept them waiting because I know that you haven't told her about Jhren, and I wasn't sure if you wanted her to hear."

"Thank you, Dear Heart."

Rita and Fahwn came into view and Rita joined him. He was always impressed with how solid this psychic realm felt.

"You've been very secretive in here for several days now, Delno. Care to tell me what you are up to?" she asked.

"I may as well. That letter I sent off with Lawrence was to Jhren. I wanted his advice about the compelling stone and other magical means that Warrick may possess. The problem is that Jhren is so damned stubborn that he has insisted on joining us in Horne."

"But he is too weak for such a journey. How does he plan to get there?" As she asked the question, it dawned on her and she said, "He is flying with Lawrence. You told Lawrence to make himself available to Jhren so that Jhren could join us in Larimar, but the old conjurer beat you at your own game and used Lawrence's lack of insight to get the man to take him to Horne instead." She looked at him the way she had taken to looking at the children when they were doing something they shouldn't, and then added, "What do you intend to do about it now that the deed is done?"

"Well, at least Lawrence did take enough initiative to contact me last night and tell me of Jhren's plans. I have given him strict orders to take Jhren no farther than Orlean until Nat or I arrive and pronounce the old man fit enough for the trip." He then quickly explained his meeting with Nat just before her arrival. "So, you see, My Love, everything has worked out. The soldiers in Horne will get the medical treatment they need, and I have diverted Nat so that I know he is in no immediate danger."

"I hope your luck never runs out, Handsome. Because if it does, you will have a lot of debt to pay from all the times it's saved your hide and your reputation," she said with mock severity.

"Don't worry, Beautiful, this isn't over; there is still plenty of time for luck to fail me. Hopefully, when it does, my loyal followers will be there to save my arse."

"So," she said, "Nassari has the saddles and supplies for those new Riders who will travel with us. Are you still planning on leaving day after tomorrow?"

"Actually, since it's almost dawn, it will be tomorrow, and yes, we will be leaving at dawn that morning as planned."

They were silent for a moment and then Delno said, "The last four days with you and the children has been more than I ever hoped it would be. I have really grown to love those kids. I also love to watch you with them."

"Delno," she said sternly, "I know where this is going, and I won't be left here. I am going with you to Horne and that is final."

"The children would much prefer that one of us stays here, and I have to go because I am in command . . ." he began, but she cut him off.

"That is not fair!" she said angrily. The landscape shimmered and blurred for a moment because of her angry outburst. They waited until the changing hues of the Dream State settled down and she said, "Also, it isn't going to work."

He looked like he was about to respond, but she hushed him and said, "I know why you want to leave me behind. Damn it, if I could leave you safely behind, I would do the same. I appreciate why you want me to stay, but you have to understand why I can't."

They stared into each other's eyes for several moments. Finally, she said, "You lead, Handsome, I'll follow." Then she added, "To the ends of the earth if necessary."

"Well, for now, how about following me to breakfast? It's time to get up anyway. I have a lot to do today to make sure that we are ready to leave tomorrow."

"It's funny," she remarked, "I am usually a slave to my stomach. Here in the Dream State, however, I never feel the hunger that I know my body must feel. It seems strange that I have complete sensation of everything here, but I have no sensation of my body lying next to you in our bed."

"You can get a sense of it if you spend enough time here and practice. I've worked on being able to stay in contact with my physical body so that I can remain aware of my surroundings. I've even been able to come here and find Geneva without her pulling me in. Now if I can figure out how Warrick is able to come and go while he is awake, as well as pull in someone else who is also not sleeping, this could be especially useful to us. I suppose in time I will, but time is a luxury I don't have at the moment."

Saying that, he faded from view and came fully awake in his bed, with her lying nearly on top of him. He gently shook her and she woke up. She smiled at him, and they got out of bed to start the day. Dawn was still about an hour away, but they bathed, and he went in search of Nassari.

When he stepped into the hall from his bedroom, Brock was just coming out of the room that had been provided for him.

"Good morning, Brock. I'm glad you're up early. I need to talk with you while we still have a few moments with no one else to listen to us."

"I was just going to go and see to Leera. She is a bit moody because she is coming into season. She mated last year, but it didn't take, so, with so many hatchings going on around her, she is a bit upset about not being allowed to go in search of a male this year." At Delno's look of concern, he quickly added, "There's no need to worry about her performance when we get to Horne. It's all of this lying about that is getting to her. If she had other distractions, she wouldn't be upset. Dragons are capable of ignoring such urges for a time, and, as I said, she did mate last year."

"I can certainly sympathize with her on that point," Delno replied. "Don't worry, I won't keep you long. I just want to know what you think of the new Riders who will be going along."

"Ah, those four." Delno started to ask what that meant, but Brock held up his hand to stop him. "They are good, and they work well as a unit. Will is extremely good at not being seen. He and Saadia can disappear from view while you're watching him, and if you aren't trying very hard to pay attention, you won't see him again until he is ready for you to. As for the others, they play on that quite well. And the three of them have worked themselves into quite a fighting squad. They will be very effective against ground troops, but they haven't had enough practice against other dragons in the air. So far that's all been mostly theoretical. Leera and I have flown maneuvers against them, but we've only had four days to practice. All in all, though, I think they are quite competent."

"Hopefully, because they have had to stay hidden so much, our enemies won't have a lot of experience either, but we can't count on that. I would much rather expect the worst and be pleasantly surprised than hope for the best and be disappointed, especially since disappointment in this case will probably mean the death of one or more of our pairs."

"Perhaps we can set up some kind of drill routine during our trip to give them a few more days of training. Let them fly contests against you, me and Rita to give them time against dragons and Riders who have experienced aerial combat."

"That's a good idea. I'll leave it to you and Nassari to coordinate, and then let me know the particulars once we are in flight. In fact, I would like you and Nassari to see to it that they are ready to leave by this evening."

"This evening? I thought we weren't leaving until tomorrow."

"We aren't, but I want everyone ready. No last minute preparations. Tonight we all bed down with our dragons at sundown and get a good night's sleep. Tomorrow morning we wake before dawn and gear up. After that, we rise with the sun."

Brock looked at Delno for a moment and then asked, "Do you want to inspect the Riders who are staying?"

"No," Delno replied. "My day is full. I have to speak with Adamus and make sure he is ready to take charge of the defense of Corice: I believe he is, but I want to hear it from him. Then I have to talk with my uncle and mother, and then, I want to spend a little time with the children before the day is over."

Brock looked like he was about to say something, but he changed his mind and simply saluted. Delno would have liked to indulge his friend with more explanations of his plans, but he needed to eat and then fly to Stone Bridge, so he returned the salute and strode off toward the dining hall.

CHAPTER 32

"I HAVE TOLD BETH that we approach, Love; Adamus is expecting us."

"Good, I want to finish up here and get back to Larimar as soon as possible," Delno responded. "I still have to speak with my uncle about provisions, and I want to again press the point that the Riders aren't in Corice as a Corisian fighting force."

"Delno, when are you going to trust that the man won't try and use the Riders the way that some others would do? He is your uncle, and he cares about you, and he would like to see the dragons and Riders restored to their former glory."

"He is my uncle, but he is the also the King of Corice. I am Corisian; we are a pragmatic people. Now that he has been presented with dragons to solve any problems that may arise, he can't help but want to take advantage of the opportunity. Remember, Lark is my cousin, and she had no problem at all trying to lay the entire leadership of Palamore on me. I have grown quite fond of my uncle, and I truly believe that he means well, but I can't take the chance that we will return to another mess when we finish this business in Horne. If there is one thing I have learned since your hatching, it is that you are the only one I can completely count on. Everyone else has his own agenda. I believe I can trust Brock and Rita, and I have a good deal of confidence in Nassari, but I can't even confide everything in them. Hopefully, when this is over, things will change for the better."

"Careful, Dear One, you're starting to put yourself apart from everyone." He started to protest, but she cut him off. "I know you are not doing it *because it is what you want. You are in command, and you may find yourself in a position of having to choose which of your friends you have to send to their deaths. I feel that pressure also. You are not the only one who has others looking to you for leadership. However, one of the biggest distinctions between us and our enemies is our compassion and our love for our fellows. That may seem like a weakness at first glance, but I believe that, in the long run, it is one of our greatest strengths. You won't sacrifice your friends needlessly or callously, but they will willingly sacrifice themselves for you if the need arises: that is a big distinction.*

Delno considered her words carefully and then said, *"You're right, of course. I know that we will all do what must be done and that Adamus and Craig will see to the new Riders while we are gone. It is just hard to keep that in perspective sometimes. I am distancing myself so that I can continue to function if one of my friends, my extended family, dies under my command. I will try to not shut off my emotions so much, Dear Heart. If you see me doing so, remind me of this conversation."*

"I will do that, Love. Now sit tight, we are about to land."

As Geneva touched down, Adamus ran up to meet them. "It's good to see you, sir. I was hoping that I would get the chance to do so again before you left for Horne."

Delno slid down from the saddle and said, "Well, besides wanting to make sure that you have everything that you need, I did want to see you just to say goodbye. We started off together as enemies, but I think that we have truly become friends."

"Yes, I still can't believe that we were so easily taken in by Simcha, and by default, Warrick. I am just glad that you were able to show Lawrence and me the error of our ways. The outcome could have been much worse."

The two men looked at each other for a moment and then Delno said, "So, you know that you will be working with Craig. You and he will be rotating the new Riders between aerial practice here with you and theoretical instruction in both being a Rider and doing magic with Craig. He will try and be the one to coordinate with the king's people to make sure that both dragons and Riders are well supplied."

"Yes, I've spoken with Craig several times, once when he came here to look over the situation, and then we have had relayed conversations through our dragons. We have everything in hand."

"Good," Delno said. "How is everything going here?"

"The stone works are progressing just fine. The iron workers are already setting the gates. The whole structure will be ready in less than another month. Also, if all else fails, we can pull the supports and let the whole thing fall into the canyon. The Bournese are going to stay on their side of the bridge this time."

"Excellent. I can't stay long; I have other things to do today, and we will be leaving at dawn tomorrow."

"Well, there is one more bit of good news." Delno looked at the man with open curiosity and Adamus continued. "The Bournese have apparently come to realize that the children they were using aren't going to be needed and have sent them home. The only soldiers on the other side of the bridge now are full grown men, and about a third of their original number have gone too. It could be that they have moved them to the other access points, but it is more likely that they just don't want the expense of feeding them anymore."

"Well, I thank you for that news. My life will be so much easier when I tell Rita that those children are no longer being used as troops. Just in case though, as you put the newly bonded pairs to work up here, widen your search patterns so that all of the passes are covered. Also, the Bournese are good mountaineers; don't neglect to keep watch on the slopes near all of the border points to make sure that no sappers get through to do acts of sabotage in our rear areas."

Adamus nodded. "I hadn't thought of that. Where I'm from the land is flat, and I look around and think of these mountains as impossible to climb. Now that you mention it though, a squad of well-trained men could do quite a bit of damage if they could get past our initial defenses. I'll also instruct the others to look for signs that hostile Dragon Riders are in the area, too. Beth hasn't felt anything, but the newly bonded dragons might be more sensitive. I don't expect to find them, but better safe than sorry."

"Good man. I knew I was right leaving you in charge of defense here."

Adamus straightened proudly at the compliment.

"I know that we may be a bit paranoid about the Bournese getting more help from Warrick," Delno continued, "but it has been my experience that a little paranoia in warfare is sometimes a good thing."

"I wish we had a time table of how long you will be down in Horne." Before Delno could say anything, Adamus added, "I know it's impossible to tell at this point, but I can still wish."

"Yes, we can all wish," Delno said. "I wish that this weren't happening. Unfortunately, the only way to make my wish come true is to get down to Horne and settle this account."

Both men stood looking over at the Bournese camp for a moment and then Delno said, "One last thing, and I'll be on my way." He paused and made sure that no one was within earshot of their conversation. "I served with General Dreighton when he was a captain. He is a good man and has a good military mind, but he is a Corisian military man. His supply lines are secure and his rear lines are in no danger. Now that he has strong fallback points at all of the border crossings, he may start thinking about pushing forward. You are not to let him commandeer you or your Riders for such a push. Your job is to protect these outposts. Unless you have to do so to fend off enemy dragons, you are not to cross the border."

"Yes, sir. You have nailed a potential problem. His staff officers have been wondering why we aren't taking this fight to the Bournese. Apparently some of them are anxious to get some revenge. I have told the general that the dragons aren't to attack on the Bournese side unless we are attacked, and he has been satisfied up until now. I won't move forward without specific orders from you."

"Good," Delno said. "In that case, I have to get back to Larimar and finish preparations for leaving tomorrow."

They saluted each other and Delno climbed back into the saddle. Geneva crouched and pushed off as her wings beat down and they were again airborne. Delno just sat and enjoyed the ride for a few moments. The mountains, rugged but beautiful, diminished below them slightly. The tallest peaks were snowcapped even in high summer. Delno had always loved to look at these mountains, and viewing them from the air only made them appear more majestic.

"It won't take long to get back to Larimar, Love. The winds are with us, so even soaring, the trip will be short. Should I circle for a while and let you think?"

"Am I so transparent?" he responded.

"No, but I have learned how to read you. You are enjoying the view and not thinking of this war. It is good for you to do that from time to time. It seems to give you better perspective when you once again return to the task at hand."

Delno laughed out loud. "Geneva, I love you. I think we can afford a quarter of an hour just for ourselves."

"I love you, too, Delno. Let's give ourselves a real treat and make it half an hour!"

"I like a strong-minded female. Very well, Love, half an hour."

CHAPTER 33

"OH, THERE YOU are, Nephew. I am glad that I found you," Dorian said as Delno entered the main hall of the palace. "I was hoping we could talk again before you and your forces set off for the south."

"I wouldn't have left without seeing you, Uncle. In fact, I have made specific time in my schedule to see you today. Besides wanting to say goodbye, I want to make sure that all arrangements are made concerning the housing of the new Riders, and food for any hungry dragons."

"Well, you know, Delno, the dragons and Riders have my total support." Dorian paused for a moment and then said, "Which brings me to something I wanted to speak with you about."

Delno was suddenly suspicious, but he simply waited for his uncle to speak his mind.

"I have been considering this alliance we seem to find ourselves in," Dorian continued. "I have thought about these constant wars between Corice and Bourne. I am starting to think that perhaps leaving the descendants of House Bourne to rule that land is not a good idea. With the help of the Riders and the dragons we could . . ."

"Uncle," Delno said sharply, "we have discussed this very thing, and I have told you that the Riders are only involved because of Warrick. I cannot allow the Riders to get involved in Corisian expansion."

"Corisian expansion? Nephew, the Bournese have tried to take over this kingdom by force at least once a generation for hundreds of years. The current king of Bourne is particularly determined to control Corice

and its resources. I am merely asking the Riders for assistance in protecting our own people. I have come to believe that the only way to ensure
the peace in this area is to stop the Bournese by consolidating both
kingdoms."

"Uncle, few people are more acutely aware of the Bournese determination to conquer this kingdom than I. However, I cannot allow my
Riders to become embroiled in local politics, especially with a war of
our own to fight in Horne. I have left two fully trained Riders and seven
newly bonded pairs to help protect the borders while I am gone. As far
as anything further, I cannot allow the Riders left behind here to participate in a push into Bourne: I have specifically ordered them not to
comply with any such request. Unless Dragon Riders from our enemy's
camp show up and make overt acts of aggression, my Riders will not fly
into Bournese air space. That is the way it must be, at least until I return
from Horne."

Dorian regarded his nephew for several moments and then said, "So,
that is your last word on the matter?"

"I'm afraid it must be, Uncle." Dorian shook his head and Delno
added, "When I return from Horne, I have every intention of settling
matters in Bourne."

Dorian raised an eyebrow as an invitation for his nephew to expound
on his statement. Delno, however, had no intention of saying more at the
moment. "We will discuss this further after the Riders have settled with
Warrick. For now, your newest advisor seems to have found us."

Both men turned to Laura Okonan who had just come into the main
hall.

"Mother, I am glad you came now. We can have lunch together." He
didn't add that he was also glad that her appearance saved him from his
uncle's questions.

Will, John Okonan, Rita, and the children joined them for lunch. The
conversation was a bit strained because of the fact that the three Riders
would be leaving for the war in the morning. That subject was specifically, and somewhat obviously, avoided by all.

After lunch, he and Rita took Marcus and the twins for a long walk,
and then spent the remainder of the afternoon with them.

"How do you play the tiles?" Marcus asked Delno.

"There are several games that can be played with tiles," Delno
responded. "Most of those games involve some form of betting on the
outcome of how the tiles are dealt." Delno had quickly found out that

while Marcus was still a child emotionally, he was quite a bit older intellectually, so he made sure not to try to talk down to the boy. "I'll tell you what: I'll go and get a set of tiles and try to teach you one of the games. I'll be right back."

"I'm not sure your mother would approve of you teaching the child to gamble, Love," Geneva said. She had become quite fond of the idea of helping to raise three human children.

"You could be right. She was a bit put out when my father taught me when I was Marcus's age."

It didn't take long for him to find a set of tiles and return. The tiles were in a wooden box: this set was made of ceramic, but most were made of wood or bone. Delno shook the box gently to make sure the tiles were mixed up.

"Each tile is inscribed with a number or a symbol," he explained. "There are forty-eight numbered tiles. They are numbered one through twelve." He paused and asked, "Do you know your numbers?"

"My mother taught me those last year," the boy said. There was still a bit of sadness in his voice whenever he talked about his parents, but he didn't dwell on it.

"Good, then I won't have to explain all of that and we can get on with the game," Delno replied. "Now then, there are four sets of numbered tiles and each set is a different color: Usually red, green, yellow, and blue. Some homemade sets use different colors because the person who made them used what was available to paint them. There are four sets of tiles that have animals on them that are also painted the same colors as the number tiles. The animals are dragons, which are the highest ranking tiles; the swans come next, then horses, then dogs."

Marcus was picking through the tiles and identifying each one as Delno spoke.

"Then there are three last tiles in the set: two are blank and one has a skull painted on it. Sometimes people remove those three tiles before they play."

Marcus found the three tiles in question.

"The two blank tiles, sometimes referred to as open tiles, can be used in place of any other tile. Depending on the game and the rules agreed upon, the skull tile either completely kills the hand of the person who draws it, or it can just block that player from drawing more tiles."

"How does it kill his hand?" Marcus asked, looking from his own hand to Delno a bit suspiciously.

Delno chuckled. "Not the person's hand," he said, wiggling his fingers. "The tiles you are dealt are called a hand by some people because some of the tiles are held in your hand. Some people call the tiles that you are dealt a spread instead of calling it a hand."

"What do you call it?" Marcus asked.

Delno shrugged and said, "I sometimes call it a hand, and sometimes call it a spread. It doesn't matter what you call it, the people playing will know what you are talking about. Now, as to your question about killing the hand: if you get that tile and it kills your hand, you simply lose because that tile means you can't play that hand."

The boy looked at the tile a bit dubiously and then shrugged and waited for more instruction.

"If it is used as a block, then you can still play that hand, but only the tiles you have drawn up to that point. Since only six tiles are counted, and some spreads, or hands, deal eight tiles, you can still possibly win the game if you have already turned over enough tiles to have a good enough hand to play before you get to the skull."

The boy looked confused so Delno said, "Why don't we just play a few hands and see how it goes?"

Marcus nodded in agreement.

"The first thing we must do is mix up the tiles."

He dumped the tiles out onto the floor and began turning over any that were face up. Once the tiles were all face down he started sliding them around and shifting their positions randomly using both hands. Once they were as thoroughly mixed as he could get them, he said, "I'll deal," then he paused and added, "This would be better if we had something to wager. The men who play this wager coins, but we could bet anything small enough."

"I know," Marcus said. His face brightened and he got up and ran across the room. He returned with a small basket about the size of a drinking mug: it was full of brightly colored buttons. He handed the cup to Delno. "Will these work?"

"These will work just fine," Delno replied smiling. He took the buttons and divided them evenly between the two of them. "Now I will begin dealing. The game I will teach you today is very simple. It involves dealing six tiles. The skull tile is called the death tile, and if you get that you lose. One tile is dealt face down and only the holder of that tile gets to look at it until all the tiles are dealt."

He picked up one tile without looking at it and placed it in front of Marcus and then placed another one in front of himself. "Now, you can look at the tile I dealt you but don't show it to anyone. Well, I may ask to see it because I am teaching you, but that tile is called your hide tile because you hide it from everyone else until all the tiles are dealt and the betting is over." He started to reach back to the tiles and then said, "Oh, I almost forgot, put in one button between us as the opening bet." After they had both put one button on the floor between them he continued. "Now I deal the other five tiles one at a time face up."

He placed a six in front of Marcus and an eleven in front of himself. "Well, it would seem that I have a higher score than you so I get to make the next bet." He put another button in the pot and Marcus did the same. "The way you win is to get the highest hand, but it isn't just numbers. The picture tiles with the animals are worth fifteen for the swan, dog, and horse, and twenty for the dragon. However, a pair is worth more than a high-numbered hand. Two pairs are worth more than one pair, three of a kind is worth more than two pairs, but six tiles of all the same color are higher than two pair or three of a kind. Six tiles in sequence are worth more than six tiles of the same color. Three pairs are worth more than that, and three of a kind plus a pair is worth more than three pairs. Two sets of three is the next highest hand. The next is four of a kind, followed by four and a pair. The highest hand is six tiles of the same color in sequence. If you have two similar hands, such as you have a pair of something and I have a pair of something else then the higher pair is the winner. Do you understand all of that?"

Marcus looked totally confused and started to nod but stopped and shook his head.

"Good," Delno said, "I'm not sure I did either. The quickest way to learn is to play for a while and see how it works. I'll help you figure out what you have as we go."

They spent the next hour and half playing the tiles until Rita and his mother came in with the twins.

"Delno Okonan!" his mother exclaimed. "Are you teaching that child to gamble?"

"No," he replied flatly. "He is teaching me not to gamble. He claimed to have no idea how to play the tiles, and he has taken every one of my buttons away from me by thrashing me at the game he pretends I was teaching him."

Marcus smiled broadly, and proudly displayed the pile of buttons in front of him, and then pointed to the three lonely-looking buttons left in Delno's stack. "I won them from him," he said.

Laura tried to remain stern but the puzzled look on her son's face combined with the triumphant look on her adopted grandson's was too much for her: she couldn't contain the laughter that bubbled up and spilled out.

CHAPTER 34

ELNO HAD SPENT the night sleeping with Geneva on the wall. He woke up shivering. Summer was all but over and, despite the heat of the day, the nights in the mountains had turned cold. The sun wasn't even a vague hint on the horizon at this hour. He took care of his bodily functions and began readying his equipment while avoiding making noise to allow the others to sleep as long as possible.

He began to pull out a piece of hard bread and some jerky when a soft voice behind him said, "Here, at least eat a warm breakfast and drink some hot coffee: I made it with cream and sugar the way you like it."

Delno smiled at his mother. "Thank you. What are you doing up at this hour?"

"Besides making sure you don't fly off without eating? I am making sure you don't fly off without me getting to see you before you go."

"Mother," he said softly, "we've said our goodbyes. This won't make it any easier."

"Hush. I know it won't make it easier, but I am your mother, and I want to be here. You know that parents aren't supposed to have favorites among their children, but I do, and you are mine." Then she added in her sternest parent's voice, "If you ever let a hint of that slip to your brother, I will deny it and tell him you are delusional."

Delno smiled at her. She shivered in the predawn cold, so he draped the blanket he had been folding over her and put his arm around her shoulders. They stood for a few moments just looking out over the plain and sharing the steaming mug of coffee she had brought him.

She looked up at him and said, "You look so much like your grandfather that I have to wonder if the magic has something to do with it. I wonder if magic and fate have conspired to put you in this position right from the day you were born. Not only do you look like my father, you are beginning to act like him. His visits were always too short and his absences always too long. I miss him, and I already miss you. I want my father avenged, but not if it costs me my son."

"Mother, I am coming back from this. I will avenge Corolan and make Corice safe. I will ensure that we help stop these nonsensical incursions from Bourne, and in the process ensure that my people have a safe place to come home to when they need it. I also have plans to help prevent future Riders from getting delusions of grandeur. I can't do any of that if I don't return."

He wiped away a tear that was trickling down his mother's cheek, and she smiled at him. Then she threw her arms around him and said, "You will do what must be done in Horne, and I won't tell you not to take unnecessary chances because I know you won't. However, I also know that you will take any risk that you feel is necessary. I love you Delno, as much as any mother could ever love one of her children. Please come home safe."

There was a slight scraping noise behind them, and Delno turned to see Brock walking toward them. Brock was far enough away that he might not have heard the conversion between Delno and his mother, but Delno was pretty sure the man had heard and moved farther away to give them privacy and then deliberately dragged his boot to let them know he was there. Somehow he felt a little better knowing that his friend and second in command had heard everything. In a way it made him feel more like Brock was part of his family, and not just a fellow soldier.

Laura quickly composed herself and retrieved the large jug of coffee she had set down earlier. "I brought enough coffee and warm food for everyone."

She poured Brock a cup and offered him some of the cream and sugar. Brock declined the sugar but added a splash of cream to his cup. "Oh, that's good," Brock said after sipping from the cup. "This is wonderful, Laura, thank you. I had expected to have hard bread and cheese washed down with water this morning."

"That may be what you eat tomorrow, but I won't see you off today on less than good food and hot drink. It was cold last night and will be cold in the air this morning when you start your trip; even if you are immune to disease, you still need to keep warm," she responded.

"Is that real coffee I smell?" Will asked.

Everyone was waking up, and they ate as quickly as they could without wolfing down the food. They again said their goodbyes while they loaded their gear onto the dragons. As they were getting mounted, Dorian joined them and added his good wishes. Then, since dawn was only about a half hour away, and there was no possible reason for further delay, Delno gave the signal to take off.

The four dragons on the wall rose slightly ahead of the three on the ground, but Wanda beat the air furiously to catch up with Geneva. The other two with her were quickly outdistanced. Wanda settled in at Geneva's left in the customary position of the second in command. Delno looked back at Brock and could barely see him shrug his shoulders.

"Leera says that, as a lineage holder, the position is traditionally Wanda's anyway," Geneva said. "She also says that Brock has no problems with Wanda and Nassari taking that position, but they should be told that he and Leera are more experienced at working as a team. When we get into battle, Nassari and Wanda might do well to remember that."

"Very well, Love. Relay that to Nassari through Wanda, but please be tactful. I don't want to start this trip on a bad note."

"I have already done so, Love. Wanda and Nassari both say that they understand, but since there are no enemies about they will keep the position for now," Geneva replied. "Wanda has a good heart, but she has a strong will and her ego pushes her to show that she and her Rider are important members of this team. She apparently feels that some of those we fly with see her and Nassari more as a pair you have good-naturedly included rather than serious members of the group."

"You tell Wanda that I have known Nassari for over two decades, and he is my closest friend. Also tell her that Nassari is my third in command. He is third only because Brock and Leera have five centuries of experience at the type of warfare we are going into. If anyone else on our side has any problem with her or Nassari's place in the chain of command, they are welcome to see me about it, and be set straight. She has no reason to doubt that they have been included because of their competence."

After a few seconds Geneva said, "I have relayed your message and Wanda gives her thanks as well as relaying the thanks of her rider. They both appreciate your confidence in them." She paused before adding, "Rita wants to know why we aren't veering more west and are not making a more direct line toward Horne."

"I want to swing a bit toward Orlean to see if we can hook up with Nat and Marlo. I would like to have them along with us. Also, if Nat has pronounced Jhren fit to travel, we would be better off if we had him along to back us up magically."

After giving Geneva time to relay his response to Rita and the others he asked, "Love, can you contact Marlo from here?"

"I can feel her on the edge of my consciousness, like almost seeing an image out of the corner of your eye, but I am not close enough to speak with her yet. She and Rhonna are a bit west of Orlean, and I am adjusting our flight to try and intercept them. As soon as I can contact them directly, I will tell them to wait for us to catch up."

"Well," he responded, "apparently if Rhonna is with them, Jhren has decided to push on to Horne whether Nat has condoned the action or not. Hopefully, he isn't pushing himself so hard he causes harm."

"It is my opinion, Dear One, that Jhren will do as he pleases regardless of what anyone else thinks he should do."

"Yes, I've noticed that tendency in him myself. Tell me, Dear Heart, have you had any contact with the un-bonded dragons who have joined us?"

"Yes, I spoke with Sheila last night in the Dream State."

"You spoke with Sheila and you didn't tell me?" he asked accusingly.

"Calm yourself, Love, there isn't much to report. I didn't want you to get excited and wake earlier than you did because of the conversation since nothing is really happening that required your attention. I love you and don't want you to over exert yourself."

"I appreciate your concern for me, Geneva, but please let me make those decisions for myself."

"Well, I have to admit that it wasn't completely altruism on my part, Love. I care about you and want you safe, but you are half of this team, and you keep me safe also. You can't protect us with magic very well if you are beyond exhaustion, and I prefer to keep both our hides intact."

"Point taken, Love, one for you," he said. "Now, what did you learn from Sheila?"

"She and the others—they have had more dragons join them and now number twenty-nine—are still watching over the men we sent, and they are still nearly a week's march from any real danger in Horne, though they are making better time than we had expected. They seem to be pushing themselves harder than need be, and Sheila is a bit concerned that they may be too spent to fight when they get there." She paused and then added, "From the images she gave me of them, I don't believe there is a problem. She is used to seeing only a few people from the south, and then only at a great distance. She has no experience with you northern mountain people and how hardy you all are. I believe the men will be fine."

"I'm sure the men will be all right. Most are trained soldiers and the captain in charge won't be foolish enough to push his troops so hard that they will all be killed from exhaustion. It is also good that more un-bonded dragons have joined us. With the four we left in Corice, that makes a total of thirty-three un-bonded dragons we have contact with, and that means that it is possible that we will eventually have that many more bonded pairs."

"I wouldn't hold out too much hope that Sheila and the other older dragons will change their minds any time soon and choose a partner, Love."

"True enough, Dear Heart, but for some reason, today, I feel that anything is possible."

"I want to get more altitude, Love. The sun is just now coming up, and I want to be the first to greet it!" she said as she beat down hard to get higher.

"Then push hard, Dear Heart, because it looks as though Wanda wants to beat you to it," he said, and laughed.

Geneva and Wanda both drove themselves to their limit to get higher while turning farther to the east. Seeing the two vying with each other to be the first to see the sun appear on the horizon, the other dragons joined the race. It was Geneva who first roared triumphantly as they saw the thin crescent of the flaming orb appear. Her roar was accompanied by Wanda's a half a second later, and then all of the others joined in at once. Delno, not caring that his own voice would be drowned out by the bellows of the dragons, whooped along with them, as did everyone else.

CHAPTER 35

DELNO STOOD WATCHING the changing reddish hues of the Dream State as Geneva reached out to contact Marlo. She had said it wouldn't take long tonight, because Marlo was close to them, and she would be watching for Geneva to make contact. Time always seemed to pass differently here than it did in the waking realm, but Delno still felt a sense of urgency.

"I have found her, Love. She and Nat are coming."

As Geneva finished speaking, Marlo and Nat became visible to him. They simply appeared next to him rather than having actually moved toward him spatially. Delno wondered yet again why sometimes the people he wanted to speak with here would actually move toward him, but other times they would simply appear as if materializing out of thin air.

"Ah, we have found you. I can't help but wonder how the dragons navigate this place," Nat said mirroring his thoughts.

"I would love to have long philosophical discussions about it sometime, my friend, but tonight we have other matters that are more pressing," Delno replied. "I take it Jhren is in good enough health to travel and is with you?"

"Well, I would like to have had him rest for a couple of more weeks, but he is a stubborn man. I decided that since he would go anyway, it would be better if he traveled with his physician than if he simply went alone. So, yes, he is with me."

"Yes, several people have noticed that characteristic about Jhren," Delno said. "I'm glad he will be helping us, but had I stopped to think before I sent word to him, I would have realized he'd do something like this, and I wouldn't have sent the letter to Palamore. He is a powerful magic user, but even his magical expertise can't save him from his own folly."

"I think he will be all right, Delno. I have examined him, and he has been drinking the herbal teas I prepared before I left him. He is doing quite a bit better, and sitting at the palace in Palamore dealing with Lark's constant bickering with her advisors was wearing on him."

"That would be enough to wear on anyone. It wore on me enough to make me flee to the safety of another war," Delno said. He chuckled a bit before continuing. "Nat, the reason I wanted to find you tonight is simple. We, meaning Brock, Rita, Will, Nassari, and two others you haven't met, are now traveling to Horne. Since we are close to you, I think it is best if we travel together. Geneva knows where you are in relation to where we are now, so if you will wait for us, we will join you sometime tomorrow."

"It will do us all some good to rest for a day. We will wait for you here. We are camped by a little stream and there are pan-sized fish for catching. There is also plenty of game, and the dragons have hunted and eaten well. Waiting shouldn't be too bad, and it will give Jhren another day of rest, though he will not like it."

"Like it or not, he will wait," Delno replied. "One last thing, my friend; if Geneva can find you, then other dragons can, too: be damn careful about keeping watch. Now is the time for Marlo to use all of that superb skill she developed for spotting other dragons before they spot her."

Marlo, who had been conversing with Geneva, said, "No dragons will approach that I don't know about, Delno Okonan. You may set your mind at ease on that count."

"I am aware of your prowess at detecting nearby dragons, Marlo, and that makes me doubly glad that you are one of my friends and bonded to Nat. Remember though, I don't want you and Nat to engage unless there is absolutely no alternative. You are both too important to be common soldiers in this war. Nat is the best healer in all of the human kingdoms." Both Nat and Marlo nearly glowed with pride at the compliment. Delno added, "I have specific plans for your incredible abilities also, Marlo, so don't risk injury in a skirmish if it can be avoided: I need you to gather intelligence once we actually find our enemies."

Marlo puffed up proudly and said, "I will keep my Rider safe and be ready when you need me, Delno Okonan."

"Very good, I knew I could count on you both," Delno responded. "Now I will let you get some sleep. Geneva and I need to see if we can contact the un-bonded dragons who are watching over our ground troops."

"Damn me for an easily distracted fool," Nat exclaimed. Delno looked at him quizzically. "An un-bonded female showed up in our camp when we stopped this afternoon." Then he quickly added, "Marlo, of course, saw her coming long before she saw us. Since she was not carrying a rider, and Marlo had met her before, we let her join us. She is older and has heard of our mission in Horne. She has lost two sisters to Roracks and, most interesting of all; she also lost one sister to bonded dragons and was injured in the battle. She has quite a story to tell about how that happened, but I will let her tell it when you get here."

"Nathaniel," Delno said, "I love you like one of my own family, but we have to do something about that associative memory of yours. Start tying strings around your fingers or something. . . ."

"I tried that once," Nat replied. "I forgot to look at the strings."

Delno laughed out loud. "At any rate, my somewhat absent-minded friend, had you started this conversation with that bit of news, I would have already been in the air for ten minutes by now. Any chance I have to gather more intelligence on our enemies must be exploited at once. Oh, don't look so down, Nat, I'm not angry with you, and you did tell me the news. A few minutes delay won't actually make any difference. I really am quite proud of all that you have done so far; you and Marlo both." Nat smiled sheepishly and Delno added, "I will take my leave now, and we will get airborne."

Nat waved and faded from view as Delno pushed hard to wake himself up. He came fully awake as if he had been dowsed with cold water. Rita was startled out of her sleep and bolted up reaching for her sword.

"Relax," he said, "It isn't that kind of an emergency." Then he said out loud to Geneva, "Wake Leera and have her rouse Brock. We will need to discuss this immediately."

"I have already woken Leera. Brock is walking toward you now."

"Wanda woke me," Nassari said from a few feet away. "What's all the commotion about?"

"I'm only going to explain this once, so wait until Brock gets here."

"I'm here, Delno," Brock said coming up behind him. "What is going on?"

Delno quickly told them of Nat's news concerning the new un-bonded dragon.

"Is this something that has to be handled now?" Rita asked. "Surely she will still be there when the sun comes up in the morning."

"Yes, she may be there with Nat, but the bonded dragons who attacked her sister may move to prevent themselves from being found now that they have given away their position," Nassari said, before Delno could explain it.

"Exactly," Delno replied. "I want to get Will into the area as quickly as possible to do some scouting: perhaps Marlo, too."

"Marlo?" Brock asked. "I thought we wanted to keep Nat out of harm's way as much as possible."

"Marlo doesn't have Will's talent of disappearing, but she is superb at scouting without being detected. She has honed her skills at spotting other dragons before they spot her for over a hundred years. She is a logical choice to go on this mission. With the two pairs flying in separately, and from different directions, we double our chances of getting some useful information."

They all just stared at him.

"Damn it! Don't stare at me like that. Do you think I don't know that I am talking about ordering my brother and one of my best friends to go on a mission that could result in their deaths? This is war. We need the information this sortie could give us to save lives. If I could go myself I would, but the mission is too vital, and Geneva doesn't have Marlo's skills, and I don't have Will's talent. I don't like it any more than any of you, but that is the way it is, and I don't have a choice."

"No, Brother, you don't have a choice," Will said as he suddenly appeared nearly in the middle of the group. "You don't have a choice because I would go regardless of what you said. So, since I am going anyway, I may as well do it with the blessings of my commander rather than against his orders."

Will smiled at the astonished looks of both Nassari and Brock who had not had the opportunity to see his talent at work before at such close range. Rita had been mildly surprised but recovered quickly.

"Well," Nassari, who had recoiled only slightly from the shock of see-ing Will suddenly appear like that, said in his nonchalant manner, "I guess that settles that."

Delno turned on his brother and said, "We don't know for sure that there will be a mission yet. I have to talk to this new dragon first. If there is a mission, you will stay in contact with me, or Brock, or Nassari." Will nodded and Delno added, "Oh, and Brother, remember I can heal injuries quite well, so if you ever use your talent to sneak into one of my commanders' meetings again, I will break one of your legs. You won't be incapacitated long until I heal you, but the pain should teach you a lesson."

Will smiled at his older brother and said, "I'm sorry, Brother, old habits die hard. I used to follow you and Nassari for hours when we were kids. I guess I just slipped back into that tonight." Then he added seriously, "It won't happen again, I promise."

"Good," Delno replied. "Well, since the leaders of this troop are already up, I suggest that we wake up the rest of the soldiers and get into the air and find Nathaniel."

"No need to wake me up, sir." Nadia said from the shadows. She stepped into the half light of the dying fire, but with their dragon-enhanced sight they could all see that she was indeed awake and armed to the teeth. Her powerful recurved bow was in her hands with an arrow nocked but not drawn. "When I saw my commander," she indicated Nassari, "get up quietly and slip around the camp, I armed myself and moved to cover his back."

"Nadia, you are a constant source of amazement to me. There is definitely more to you than first meets the eye. I am glad you came along and didn't stay in Larimar," Delno said.

"I grew up in a home with my father and five brothers, so I'm a good fighter. I was the youngest and my mother died while giving birth to me. My brothers and I shared the household duties, so I can cook too. Therefore, since my gear is all ready to go, why don't I get us some breakfast while the rest of you pack?" Saying that, she put the arrow she had nocked away in her quiver and moved toward the fire and the supplies to make food.

Fifteen minutes later, Delno sat down to a meal of jerky sautéed in coffee and herbs served with hard bread. There was also coffee to drink, though they had no milk or cream to lighten it. Everyone was surprised to find that the coffee gravy was actually quite good. The beverage was much milder when used in cooking than they would have expected.

"Yes, Nadia," Delno said while mopping up the last bit of gravy off of his plate, "there is more to you than meets the eye. This is delicious, thank you."

"She really is quite a gem, Del," Nassari said. "She is one of the most competent people I have met in a long time. I'm glad she is on our side, or we would be hard pressed to beat her, *at anything.*"

Nadia hadn't done more than nod at Delno's compliment, but she straightened noticeably when Nassari praised her. Delno just smiled. Normally he would discourage a relationship between two such soldiers, but he couldn't very well tell Nassari not to get involved with a subordinate when *he* was having just such a relationship with Rita, especially since Nassari was Rider to a lineage holder himself.

Ten minutes later they were aloft. The predawn chill on the ground had been nippy but it was downright cold several hundred feet up in the air. Delno had Geneva relay his thanks once again to Nadia for the hot meal. Then they made a straight-line course toward Nat's camp. The sun wouldn't be up for at least another two hours, and they should meet up with Nat and Jhren well before noon.

Chapter 36

"**M**ARLO HAS JUST informed me that she has spotted us and that we are the only dragons in the sky for at least five leagues," Geneva said. "She really is quite good at spotting any dragons approaching. Even knowing they are near, I can only get the faintest trace of Rhonna at this distance. I wish I knew exactly how she does it."

"*Perhaps I was wrong about it being a learned skill, and it is an inborn talent,*" he replied. "*Perhaps, it's a little of both. Whatever it is, it is a useful skill, and it makes me glad that she is on our side.*"

"*I wonder why our side appears to be getting humans and dragons with such skills. I would have thought that Warrick would be glad to find help like that.*"

"*It's possible that he has teams who can do such things and is just too arrogant to notice,*" Delno answered. "*It's also possible that he discourages such talents because he fears that he may be overthrown by his own troops. What we need to watch out for most, though, is that he does have talented teams he plans on using, and we don't know about them yet.*"

"*Yes, Dear One, you are right. If we want to keep our assets a secret, so would he. We will have to be doubly on our guard now that we know such things are possible. We'll be landing in less than a quarter of an hour at this rate. I will relay that everyone should get down quickly and disturb the surroundings as little as possible.*"

Once they were on the ground, Nat came to greet them at a trot. "You made good time," he said. "It's still three hours before noon."

"We had favorable winds for the trip, though it was cold up there. If you have anything hot to drink, we could all use something," Delno responded.

As they all gathered around the fire and Nat poured tea and coffee, Delno made introductions. Jhren was conspicuously absent.

"Where is Jhren?" Delno asked, "I would have thought that he would be here to yell at me for holding him up and wasting time."

"Ah yes, Jhren," Nat said, while Lawrence pointedly found something to occupy himself rather than look at Delno.

"Now what?" Delno asked sternly.

"Well, it seems that our good magic user decided to spend some of his leisure time talking with the un-bonded dragon. Sometime during their conversation, she bonded with him."

"She what?" Delno and Brock both exclaimed.

"Jhren is nearly a hundred years old!" Brock sputtered.

"Carra is over a thousand years old, but that didn't seem to prevent them from becoming bonded," Nat replied.

Brock thought for a moment and then said, "Well, I believe it's possible, but I'm just not sure I like the idea of a magic user that powerful bonding with a dragon."

"Afraid I might take it into my head to kill Warrick and take his place?" Jhren asked as he approached the group. Delno noticed that the old man was walking a bit straighter, though whether that was due to the bond with Carra or Nat's herbal medicine, he didn't know.

To his credit, Brock stood his ground, "To be brutally honest with you, Jhren, yes. I do believe that magic should have its limits, and a magic user with your abilities increasing his power by bonding to a dragon is, quite simply, scary."

Jhren was silent for a moment, and then he spoke very carefully. "I have to admit that if our positions were reversed I would probably feel the same way, Brock. There are limits on magical power because humans and elves put them there to prevent people from doing just what Warrick is trying to do. With my power, I could possibly bide my time and wait until you destroy him or he destroys you and then seize control of what's left. Fortunately, I don't want that kind of power. I've seen what it does to men, most recently my own apprentice."

"Still," Brock said, "what is to keep you from changing your mind?"

"Only this: I've had nearly a century of life to observe the people of this world. Many of them want to be ruled. But they want to be ruled by benign leaders. I have no interest in ruling anyone. Not only do I think it's high time I start giving back to the world, but I just don't have the patience to put up with the politics. However, all I can give you is my word that I don't want power. If that isn't good enough, then I guess you will have to kill me now before I become a threat."

"That is enough!" Delno said. "No one is going to be killed here today. Jhren, I'm glad you see our concerns and accept that they have some validity." Before Brock, or anyone else, could object, he added, "Of course we will watch you; we watch each other all the time. Simcha, who was always a good man and a good Rider, was corrupted, and we didn't want to believe that he had turned so far against us. Not seeing the truth that was staring us in the face led to the deaths of three dragons, and their Riders. I believe those persons could have been saved if we had not let ourselves be blinded because of the fact that Simcha was once a good Rider. The power that the Riders wield can be used to do great things, but it can also corrupt if the wielder of that power if he is not careful. For now, we welcome you as we would welcome any new Rider."

"Very well, Delno, I accept that. I didn't set out to get myself bonded to a dragon. In fact, I have steadfastly avoided dragons for a long time for fear that my magical connections might result in something like this." At everyone's astounded looks he continued. "Oh yes, Corolan and I talked about it. Geneva's mother said I should be presented as a candidate at a hatching. I was twenty-three at the time, and even then I knew that I was afraid of that much power. I refused to go anywhere near a hatching after that, despite repeated attempts by Corolan and Geneva's mother to get me to do so."

"So, what changed your mind?" Nassari asked.

"My mind was changed for me. I just wanted to talk with Carra and get some information concerning how she and her sister were attacked by those bonded dragons. I figured that at my age, and in my state of health, I was well beyond bonding," the old conjurer replied. "Carra has always stayed as near to her sisters as they would allow because she feels the loneliness so badly. For over a thousand years she has sought companionship among her own kind even though her instincts told her not to. As we talked, it just kind of happened. I didn't really notice anything other than a brief flash of light, and my left shoulder felt like I'd gotten hot water splashed on it. Then it dawned on both of us that we were together and would be until death. I spent the rest of the night just being with her."

As Jhren said the last sentence his features softened and he suddenly looked more like someone's kindly elderly grandfather than the taciturn old wizard Delno had come to know. Seeing that change and the caring in Jhren's eyes was even enough to allay some of Brock's fears about the old man's motives.

"Well, if you would lead the way, I would like to meet Carra and talk to both of you," Delno said.

There was definitely a spring in the old man's step as he walked ahead of Delno toward Carra. Perhaps the magic was working on him and making him feel younger. He glanced at Nat as he walked by and realized that the half-elf's hair was a bit more platinum-blonde and less gray. He wouldn't have noticed if he hadn't been looking for it, but it was there.

"*The magic is changing their bodies to come into line with their new life spans,*" Geneva said, reading his thoughts. "*Nat had spent about half of his life by the time he bonded with a dragon who is only a little over a century old. He now has well over half of his current life span left, so instead of being a middle aged half-elf, he is a fairly young Rider. Don't be surprised when all of the gray is gone from his hair. As for Jhren, he has bonded to a dragon who is over one thousand years old. He is walking straighter because instead of being an old man with a few years left to live he isn't even middle aged any more. Carra had four to six thousand years left to her and Jhren has received half of that, his body will also adjust to match his true age.*"

"*That is very interesting, Love. Now if you could tell me before I walk into this, is Carra a lineage holder?*"

"*No, Dear One, she is not even close in the line of succession as far as I can tell. Despite losing so many of her siblings, she has four younger sisters between her and that title. I don't wish to sound arrogant, especially since Carra seems like such a nice person, but if the need arises, she won't be difficult for me to control.*"

"*That is good,*" he replied. "*I hope that it doesn't become necessary to control her forcefully, but Jhren can be extremely strong willed and may have to be reined in from time to time. We will do so as diplomatically as possible,*" he stressed, "*but I won't have him going off on his own once we get to Horne.*"

"*I know how to be diplomatic,*" she said a bit indignantly.

"*Yes, I noticed that when you first met Brock and Leera, and later at the jailhouse when we rescued Jhren.*" Delno couldn't resist teasing her.

"I did what I had to do on those occasions. Even you complimented me on how I handled the two situations," she said defensively.

"Peace, Dear Heart, I was only teasing you. You have become quite adept at handling delicate matters well. I have every confidence in you."

Geneva chuckled, "I still haven't completely forgiven you for that comment about being attracted to movement. I think you owe me another good back scrub."

"As soon as we have the time, Love, I promise," he responded, laughing softly to himself.

"Delno Okonan," Jhren said as they got close to a smallish red dragon. "This is my Bond-mate, Carra. Carra, this is Delno Okonan, the commander of this little excursion, whom I've already told you about."

"I am pleased to meet you, Delno Okonan. I am glad to be with your group. Jhren has told me that our bonding may cause some problems. I hope that is not so, because I am looking forward to helping you with this war that has killed three of my family."

"So long as you and Jhren both realize that we are here to fight a war as a cohesive unit, and that there is no room for individual vengeance, I cannot see where you and Jhren being bonded will be a problem." Delno knew that his gruff speech might alienate the dragon, and thus the wizard, but he also knew that priorities had to be spelled out now to avoid real trouble later. "If that condition is agreeable, then the only problem we have will be finding Jhren a saddle to save wear and tear on both of you."

Carra considered his words for a moment and then said, "That is a rational condition, and I agree that it is necessary if we are to stop our enemies. I will agree to that if it is suitable to my Bond-mate."

Jhren laughed and said, "Dear, I didn't come all this way to get myself killed playing at damn fool heroics. I have no problem with being part of the team so long as I'm not the one in charge."

"Then it's settled," Delno said. "I welcome both of you into our little army."

"I will say this," Jhren spoke up, "I sure do hope that there are more of us hiding someplace. I've been doing some calculations, and, knowing that Hella lays large clutches of up to four as the norm, I figure we could be facing as many as two dozen other Riders just from her offspring. That would put us at a definite disadvantage if all we have are the ten of us that I see here."

"Oh, we aren't alone in this," Delno replied. "Brock sent nine more Riders south before he and his group veered north to meet us. Add them to the seven who were already there, and we total at least twenty-six. Then there are all of the un-bonded dragons who are traveling there with the ground troops I sent: there are over thirty of them."

Jhren whistled, "That, Delno, is a lot of fire power on our side."

"Yes, it is," Delno replied. "However, there is a problem that I have yet to come up with a solution for." Jhren raised one of his bushy eyebrows. "As you know, bonded pairs fight as a unit. They are a team with the dragon doing the flaming while the Rider shields her and watches for airborne threats. It doesn't take that much, just maintain shields to protect her eyes and wing membranes from missiles while watching for enemy dragons. As long as the dragon isn't fatigued, her scales will stop any arrows that actually hit her body."

"So," Jhren replied, "the un-bonded dragons don't have anyone to shield them from ground attack or watch for airborne threats while they are distracted with flaming the enemies."

Delno nodded. "That is something I was hoping you could help with. I don't want you to completely distract yourself shielding them, but if you could help the un-bounded dragons as much as possible, it would reduce casualties on our side."

"Not an easy task you have set for me, Commander, but I will do my best. The problem is not just shielding them, but doing so without interfering with them. As you know, dragon flame is hotter than most other forms of fire. Those paintings in the south of dragons diving down and flaming everything in their path might look good on canvas, but they're a crock. If a dragon flamed directly in front of herself she'd fly right into it, once the air slowed it down, and burn herself to death. The flame weapon is actually fairly easy to block magically, so I will have to make sure that any shielding I do doesn't inadvertently protect our enemies, or worse, blow it back in the dragon's face."

"Remember, you only have to shield her eyes and wing membranes. The rest is heavily armored. Also, and I hate to say this, but, if it comes down to it, the un-bonded dragons have all said that they are joining us willingly and they know the risks. You are not to risk yourself fighting the Roracks. I will need all of the magical help I can get once we have drawn Warrick out. I don't intend for this to be some one-on-one battle of honor if I can avoid it. He killed my grandfather and loosed war and pestilence on my homeland; however, this is war, and I will hit him with everything I have to throw if I get the chance, and settle this once and for all, for the greater good, not personal vengeance."

"Good," Jhren said. "I was hoping you'd feel that way, but I was worried that you might be here for a bit of payback yourself. I knew Corolan better than just about any other person on this planet, even Brock. I bet you didn't know that I traveled with him for about twenty years when I was younger, did you?" As Delno's stunned look answered the question, he continued, "Besides saving my life more times than I can remember, he was a good friend. I want revenge for his death just as much as you do, but I don't want it at the cost of the lives of anyone on our side if that can be avoided, and neither would he if he was still around."

"I'm glad we see eye to eye on those points," Delno said.

The old wizard switched the subject, "I met Warrick when I was traveling with your granddad. Warrick learned some of his skills from me, but he was always impatient. He was already two thousand years old, and thought that a mere magic user was a bit beneath him, so he didn't pay attention to his lessons, and his magic work was always sloppy. Hopefully that, and his over confidence, will give us the edge when we finally confront him directly."

Delno told Jhren about Craig and everything the older Rider had told him about the theft of the elven property. Their conversation took much longer than Delno had expected, and it was nearly noon when they finally got around to the subject of where the attack on Carra and her sister had taken place.

"I have always felt the loneliness more than any of my sisters, and they tolerated me being near them so long as I didn't hunt in their territory. I had gone far south to be with one of my sisters, and she was coming close to her time to mate. I offered to watch her territory if she didn't want me to travel with her, but she was willing to have company until she found a ready male. We were flying toward the northeast and were attacked near the border between the lands you call Horne and Tyler."

"Tyler is just north west of Orlean and just southwest of Corice. It's a small kingdom like Trent, its southern neighbor. Tyler and Trent together act, by chance, not design, as a buffer between Corice and Horne. I wonder if Tyler is Warrick's next target as he pushes forward. If he could conquer Horne, then Tyler, he could move directly into Corice and then join up with the Bournese, with whom he has already allied himself. Then he would be in a perfect position to again turn his attention southward."

"Well, fortunately," Jhren interjected, "he hasn't conquered Horne yet. I believe he may have originally planned to squeeze Orlean between Tyler and Palamore, but your defeat of Simcha thwarted that plan. So now he will try and go at it from the other direction."

"I'm sorry, Carra," Delno said to the dragon, "we didn't mean to cut you off. I would still like to hear the rest of your tale, but Jhren and I are also distracted with trying to plan for our enemy's ultimate strategy. If you would, continue, please."

"My sister and I were flying along and not paying much attention to our surroundings. We had expected no trouble, since my sister was the only un-bonded dragon living that far south. We had heard of the trouble in Horne, but thought it didn't concern us, since we would be staying out of Rorack territory. Suddenly, my sister spotted three dragons and their Riders on the ground. We were seen before we could get out of the area. We weren't immediately concerned, since Dragon Riders aren't usually a threat. The three quickly mounted, and then a bolt of magic hit my sister, and she was knocked from the sky. I realized that the Riders had done this, and I turned to attack rather than try to fly off. It was a foolhardy thing to do, but it saved my life. They expected me to try and fly off rather than turn on them. They tried to use magic on me, but the magic missed me by inches, or I would have fallen too. I folded my wings and dropped much faster than they expected. I was within range of them before two of them could get airborne. I flamed at them and killed one pair while wounding another. The pair who were already in the air flamed me, and I was burned, but not badly enough to bring me down. I used my flame to make them stay back and flew away. I am smaller than most dragons, but very fast and maneuverable. I would have continued my attack, but the pain was bad, and I needed to find healing: dragons can perform such magic, but don't usually need to do so on themselves since we heal faster than other creatures, so my skill at such things is not good. I flew this way and felt the presence of the younger dragon. As I got closer, I contacted her, and she told me to come and land. The half-elf healed my wounds, and then I bonded with Jhren while he and I were talking."

"I am sorry for your loss, Carra," Delno said. "I know that your sister was also your friend, and I mourn her with you."

"I will miss her, Delno Okonan, but her death has shown me that I cannot remain neutral in this fight. If I don't do something, the trouble will only follow me wherever I go. However, it is the Riders who attacked us. Their dragons' reluctance to attack me for no reason is, I believe, why I was so successful in my attack and my retreat."

"I am not happy with the loss of any dragon. I believe that our enemies have no problems with using their bond with the dragons in their camp to achieve their goals regardless of whether or not it is good for the dragons or the rest of the world. They have forced their dragons to go against their natural instincts and actually work with Roracks. The deaths of the dragons who are with our enemies is one of the most unfortunate aspects of this war. I believe that many of them are being coerced with magic to act against their will, and I regret that some of those, perhaps many of them, will die as a result. They are innocent pawns, and I would like to save them if possible, but I won't do so at the risk of our own."

"Jhren has told me that you are a good man and wise beyond your years, Delno Okonan. I wanted to believe him because he is my Bondmate, but I needed to meet you to be sure. I see now that he is right about you. I was glad to have found this group at first, because I needed the healing skills of the half-elf. Then I was happy beyond measure to have found a human to bond with. Now I am glad to join you, because not only am I fighting in a just cause, I am also following a good-hearted person who is wise enough to make the decisions that will need to be made in this war. Thank you for allowing me to a part of this."

"I am glad to have you, Carra. I hope I can live up to all of the good things you have said about me."

CHAPTER 37

"I DON'T LIKE DIVIDING our forces," Brock said flatly. "As has been pointed out by nearly everyone here, Warrick has had six years to assemble a formidable fighting force of fully mature and trained dragons. If we split up, we could be leaving ourselves vulnerable to attack by superior numbers."

"Since it is highly probable that our enemies are watching the borders, it will be difficult to sneak by them with ten dragons and Riders," Delno responded. "Even with Marlo's abilities, we will be hard pressed to slip by them with half that number. The time is coming when we will no longer need to hide our strength from Warrick, but that time is not here yet."

"I would prefer to stay with you and your group so that the chain of command isn't broken."

"I would prefer to have you along with me also, but, while Nassari has proven himself quite reliable, he hasn't your experience as a Rider, or your first-hand knowledge of the terrain. You will have to go with him and Will. Nadia and Raymond will fly with you as back up. After Will scouts the area where Carra and her sister were attacked, the five of you will then make a straight line flight to join up with us and the men I sent from Corice."

"Why do we need to join up with ground troops?" Rita asked. "Won't that slow us down?"

"Yes, but any victory we achieve in the air must be consolidated by having ground troops to hold the ground we take. Otherwise, as soon as we leave the area, Warrick will simply send in Roracks to retake it," Delno replied. "Also, I sent enough leather supplies with them to repair gear and even manufacture some equipment if needed. We can't expect Jhren to be effective if he doesn't have a workable saddle of some sort, and he will be needed, not only against Warrick, but he will also try to keep the un-bonded dragons shielded as much as possible. With his bond to Carra, his power has increased enough that he should be quite effective if he isn't distracted by the fear of falling off her neck during skirmishes."

"Won't it take a week or more to make a saddle?" Nat asked.

"For a proper saddle, yes," Brock answered, "but I have drawn up plans for a smaller version that has no provisions for passengers or gear to be carried. A moderately skilled craftsman can make it in a day. It won't be as comfortable, but it will be serviceable."

"Won't that be a hindrance for an inexperienced Rider?" Jhren asked. "I don't mean to complain, but I am nearly a hundred years old and quite new to warfare on dragon back. I can live with any discomfort, but I don't want to hinder the rest of you if I can't do what needs to be done because I'm slipping all over the place."

"That is why I will be using the smaller saddle," Delno replied. "I have seen the plans, and I have no problem with it. The saddle that I have is the first one that was made for Geneva before she attained her full growth. While it was made with growth in mind, none of us ever figured on her becoming one of the largest female dragons on the planet."

He paused while everyone looked over at Geneva to confirm his statement. Now that they were looking with a critical eye, they all realized that she was huge. She dwarfed Leera, Carra, and Saadia, and while Fahwn was certainly a well-grown dragon, even she was noticeably smaller than Geneva.

"That saddle has served us well, but it was made at a time when Geneva was no larger than Leera, and it is at the limits of its adjustment. It now impinges on her flame bladder when she fills it. I should have had a new saddle made in Corice before we left, but I had so many other things on my mind that I simply forgot about it until we were gearing up to fly here this morning. When we all leave tomorrow, I will help Jhren put that saddle on Carra and rig a temporary pad with blankets and rope for myself until we can have the new saddle made."

"I don't like the possibility of you being caught in a fight with a temporary rig!" Rita exclaimed, and there were nods all around the camp fire.

"I have flown quite a bit of aerobatics with nothing but a temporary rig," he replied. "If it is done right, it is quite secure. I will be fine." Then he added, "Besides, I have every intention of remaining hidden for the time being."

"I still don't like splitting up," Brock said stubbornly.

"Brock, we have been through this several times already," Delno responded tiredly. "We have to know about the Riders who attacked Carra. If they were simply border guards, then they can be ignored for the time being. I don't like leaving any enemies behind us, but I don't want to alert Warrick of our presence by preventing his guards from reporting in yet, either. If, on the other hand, they were on their way north to carry out some mischief, I would like them stopped before they get there. It would be nice to question them also, but only if we are forced to engage. At this point, I wish to remain unnoticed by our enemies until we have gathered in sufficient force to draw them out without putting us at a definite disadvantage. In any case, the information you get from this mission will tell us much."

"If Warrick is guarding the borders won't that deplete his forces?" Rita asked. "It seems that guarding that much territory would take a lot of Riders."

"Yes," Delno answered, "that would also tell us that Warrick believes he has the troops to spare. I would like to know if that is the case, because that will raise another vital question." Everyone looked at him expectantly. "If Warrick's Riders are ranging so far out, who is guarding his rear lines? If he, himself, is poorly guarded we might be able to take him with overwhelming force and get that damned rock away from him. Then taking care of his Riders will be much easier, partly because we will not have the Roracks distracting us, but also because their dragons will be less willing to fight. I still hope to do this with as little loss of life on either side as possible."

"I hope that attitude doesn't get you into more trouble than you already have," Brock said.

"Don't worry, my friend, I have no intention of letting sentiment keep me from killing our enemies if it must be done, but I will do it only if it must be done. If they offer to surrender, I will accept."

Brock nodded along with everyone else gathered around the fire.

"Good, everything is settled," Delno said. Marlo and Saadia have hunted for Carra to replenish her since she used so much energy when her wounds were healed, and she has eaten. We will all be ready to go tomorrow morning."

"I still don't understand why a simple healing requires her to have food," Lawrence observed, "and why she couldn't hunt for herself." He was a bit resentful of having had to be Jhren's errand boy, and he resented any privilege that Jhren seemed to get now, and by extension he passed that resentment on to Carra.

Delno sighed. Could the man really be that thick? "Lawrence, if you injure yourself, your body heals. That requires a small amount of energy constantly to rebuild the tissues until the wound is healed completely. You don't notice because you eat and drink and breathe anyway so the little bit of energy your body puts into the rebuilding process isn't noticed over a period of days or weeks. However, healing the body magically is simply a process of speeding up and augmenting what is occurring naturally. Since that happens in moments, it uses that energy all at once and you need to eat to replenish yourself. As for why she didn't hunt for herself, Marlo is very adept at not being spotted, and with Will on her neck, Saadia is invisible. They hunted for Carra to avoid detection by our enemies." Delno paused but then, after thinking a moment, he added, "If you don't get over this resentment you have for Jhren and Carra, I will send you back to Llorn. I can't have my Riders getting caught up in personal disputes that could endanger the rest of us. Is that clear?"

Lawrence looked at the ground and blushed. He was embarrassed at being chastised in front of everyone, but he simply nodded and said nothing.

"Good," Delno said, "Now, I suggest that we let the dragons maintain a watchful sleep while we all get some rest. Jhren, if you would put up a ward to warn us of incoming danger, that would help us rest more peacefully."

Jhren nodded and set to work while everyone else settled down to sleep.

CHAPTER 38

WILL CIRCLED THE remains of the two dragons again. This time, he was low enough to be sure that the bodies of their riders were with them. It was obvious that one of the dragons had died nearly instantly, and her Rider had perished at the same time. The pair was burned so thoroughly that he had no doubt that they had borne the brunt of Carra's flame. The others appeared to have moved enough to make it obvious that they had lived for a while after the battle had ended. The Rider, burned over about half his body, had been removed from his saddle and laid out next to his Bond-mate, though Will doubted he had been able to manage the feat of unsaddling himself in that condition. There was no sign of the third Rider at the camp site. Carra's sister had fallen several hundred feet away, and her body was completely undisturbed. Will had Saadia relay his findings to Brock and Nassari.

"*Leera says that we should land, and they will join us here. Brock wishes to examine the camp himself,*" Saadia *relayed.*

"*Very well, Saadia; make sure that we keep a watch on the sky. That third Rider may come back.*"

They landed, and shortly Brock, Nassari, Nadia, and Raymond appeared in the air overhead. Brock had all four of them circle a wide pattern to make sure they were alone. Will began looking through the remnants of the camp. There were three tents and some gear, but it was all burnt. The area of char was impressive. Will began to get a sense of the power contained in a dragon's breath.

He shook himself to break through the awe he felt at the devastation and then began to sift through the ashes. At first, it was a fruitless, smelly job. But just as the others landed, he found a small leather pouch deep inside the remains of a saddle bag that had been somewhat protected by the gear piled on top of it. He opened the pouch and found two pages of written instructions addressed to King Torrance of Bourne. As Brock approached, he held up his prize for the older Rider to see.

Brock took the pages and read them. "If this is all, we have to get back in the air. Delno will want to see these."

They quickly searched the ruined gear one more time and then mounted. Brock had Leera set as nearly a straight line toward Geneva as was possible. They flew hard while keeping watch for enemy dragons.

"Marlo says that there are many un-bonded dragons about, Love," Geneva said. "We are near the men you sent and the dragons are watching over them. I can sense Sheila if I push to my limits. She can feel me reaching out and has acknowledged. She has a report for you, but doesn't want to get too near the men. She will meet you near the camp, but not near enough to risk bonding with anyone."

"Very well, Dear Heart, have the others land near the camp, and Rita can have the Commander find his leather worker for me while I meet with Sheila." After thinking about it for a moment, he added, "Have Jhren stay with me for now: the fewer people who see him initially the better. If Brock and his group arrive as quickly as you believe they will, then having ten bonded dragons and their Riders might keep Jhren from being seen and possibly recognized if the camp is being watched."

"As you wish, Dear One, but it is only mid-afternoon. Because of their mission, Brock's group will be at least three hours behind us. You and Jhren may be kept out of camp for a long time waiting for them."

"That can't be helped, Love. The Roracks and most of Warrick's Riders may not know of Jhren and his abilities, but the significance of his inclusion in our forces won't be lost on Warrick himself. I would like to keep the wizard a secret as long as we can to cut down on the possibility of more visits from those damned cat-men."

"I understand, Love, I don't disagree in theory, but I know that you have been flying for several hours with nothing between your flesh and my scales but a few thin layers of cloth. You must be sore and tired. I was only thinking of you."

"My comfort and rest can wait for a couple of hours, but I appreciate your concern. Thank you, Geneva."

Delno and Jhren went in search of Sheila. They found her about a mile from the soldiers' camp.

"Greetings, Delno Okonan. I am glad you have come. I have news of our enemies. At least, I have news of the Roracks. I have seen no dragons or Riders yet," Sheila, as blunt as ever, said.

"Any news is more than I knew before, Sheila," Delno replied. "I thank you for the effort. Tell me what you have discovered."

"A group of nearly fifteen hundred Roracks are waiting for your soldiers less than three leagues from here. These Roracks are indeed different than those I have dealt with in the past. They are organized, and they are patient. Those I have seen before had no patience for such an ambush when gathered in large groups. In fact, they had no tolerance for each other when gathered in groups of more than fifty or so, and were likely to turn on their fellows. They would have attacked by now, but these are content to sit and wait for our troops to walk into their trap."

"Then we will oblige them, but not the way they think," Delno responded. "Their controller believes he has caught a force of soldiers unawares. But the Roracks, even though they are organized, are still not very intelligent. They have no idea that they will be facing three dozen or more dragons in the air while being cut down by over half a thousand seasoned veterans on the ground."

"Good," Sheila replied. "I don't wish to become reckless, but I am anxious to begin collecting on the debt that is owed by these beast-men."

"We need to wait a little longer, though," Delno said, "the rest of my group hasn't arrived, and I need to re-outfit myself and Geneva. Also, while the dragons see better at night than most men see in daylight, and the Riders' night vision is magically enhanced through their bonds with their Partners, the men we fight with have no such advantage. If we move at night, they will be hampered in their efforts to assist us."

"Delno," Jhren spoke up, "it's me you want to hide here. Why don't you go and see to that new saddle while I stay here and see what I need to do to coordinate my magic with these Ladies' fighting skills?"

"I am sorry to you both. I should have introduced you. Sheila, this is Jhren, and his Bond-mate, Carra." Then he turned to Jhren and Carra and said, "This is Sheila; for all intents and purposes the leader of the un-bonded dragons who fight with us."

"I know Carra," Sheila responded. "We have spoken many times in the Dream State over the years. It is good to see that she has finally found a way to end her loneliness."

Delno looked at Jhren and said, "I don't want to just leave you out here like an errant child."

"You aren't leaving me, youngster; I'm sending you off to do the work you need to do," Jhren replied. "I will be fine. Carra and I will hide among the dragons here and find out the best way to help them when we fight. When the others show up, we'll sneak in unnoticed. Now go; you're useless this late in the day, anyway."

Jhren said the last part with a smile, and Delno saluted both the wizard and Sheila, and then he and Geneva left to join the others already in camp.

CHAPTER 39

ELNO READ THE letter to the King of Bourne again. He had read it at least five times since Brock had given it to him earlier that evening, but he was nervous about Will's mission, and it gave him something to do.

Warrick promised Torrance that as soon as he had finished his business in Horne, he would come in full strength to settle matters in the north. Of course, Torrance would most likely miss the point that Warrick had no intention of sharing power with any non-Rider and would, therefore, relegate the present king to the position of something akin to court jester. The letter further stated that Torrance had nothing to worry about because the Riders who were causing him trouble would all be leaving to fight in Horne soon, and his way to Larimar would again be open once they had gone. Warrick admonished Torrance not to fail in his mission to take Larimar because it was a vital trade center. He made vague threats of what would happen if he had to handle the situation himself when he finished in the south. He closed the letter by saying that soon the House of Bourne would become the ruling house of all of the lands of men and that those who helped him would be rewarded generously while those who opposed him would be crushed without mercy.

Delno put the message away and said, "I think I will keep this safe for now. It is interesting, but really doesn't bear on our doings any more. Warrick is posturing to his underlings. He will soon find that he is not facing the small force he had planned on us bringing. I would actually have preferred that this letter had gotten to Torrance. It would be interesting to see how he reacts to the fact that the Dragon Rider kin he places so much faith in has made such grave errors in judgment: though I am glad that the three Riders carrying the message didn't get through unscathed. Adamus might be hard pressed to handle three experienced Riders with only new recruits as backup. If the one Rider continued on, he is alone now and won't be so eager to join in battle again."

"Since he felt the message was destroyed, he most likely returned to his master to get new orders," Brock observed. "We may be facing him down here, and he will have reported that he and his fellows were attacked by un-bonded dragons. Even though Carra wasn't with us at the time, and it was simply happenstance that put her and her sister in proximity with Warrick's troops, it may still have inadvertently tipped our hand."

"I'm not as worried about that as I had been. Our forces have been watched and expected, though they don't expect all of our firepower, yet. The time of our secrecy is very close to an end, my friend. By the time we have finished with the battle that is coming, Warrick will have an idea of what he is facing, and we will be hiding no longer."

"Then you intend to meet these beast-men head on?" Lawrence asked.

"What would have us do, Lawrence?" Delno asked. "We have to make our way deeper into Horne and draw out our real enemy. These beast-men are just pawns he is throwing in our path to slow us down and thin our numbers. By defeating them in large groups like this, we leave Warrick no choice but to face us or have us hunt him down like an animal. He is too proud to allow the latter, so he will choose the former."

"Saadia approaches, Love. She and Will have returned from their scouting trip."

Apparently Brock had received the same message from Leera, as he was looking to the sky to spot Will. Will didn't wait until he was on the ground to stop cloaking himself. That way any lone spies who might be about would not see the trick: he un-cloaked while he was still so high in the air that none but a very alert dragon might have noticed. He glided in for a landing and dismounted.

He saluted Delno and the other leaders as he walked to the fire. "The Roracks that the un-bonded dragons saw are still there. I found it odd that they were waiting in ambush so openly and on the low ground. It looked as if they wanted us to spot them and attack from the high ground. I figured that even the beast men couldn't be that stupid, so I began looking more carefully. When I examined the area magically, I found that someone had glamoured it, and I believe that is why the dragons haven't seen the Roracks body heat. There are about fifteen hundred of them waiting in that obvious ambush, but Saadia and I were able to penetrate the glamour and discovered that there are nearly two thousand of them hiding in those black trees on the slope just beyond. They are hard to spot because they are managing to hide their heat signature from the dragons, while their skin is roughly the same texture and color of the trees. They blend in quite well, and we almost missed them, too."

"No Rorack is capable of doing a spell like that," Jhren said. "Roracks are resistant to magic, but not magically active creatures. That's why the idiots who created them didn't use them. They are hard to control because they resist any spells to compel their behavior, and, unlike dragons, they don't do a damn thing to add to the magic user's power. Warrick must be expending a tremendous amount of energy into that compelling stone to control such a large group of them at once. Especially if he isn't close at hand and is doing so over a greater distance. Then add to that the glamour to prevent the dragons from seeing the body heat, if he is the one doing that, and he must be near his limit."

"Is it possible that other Riders could be forming the glamour?" Delno asked.

"It's possible," Jhren answered. "It's not really high level magic. A glamour like that is a simple illusion. It's the scale of the thing that is difficult. The person maintaining it has to be covering an area the size of a small city to cover that many beast men and keep them hidden from so many dragons. Remember, the dragons are naturally resistant to falling for such tricks."

"That's true," Will interjected. "Once I had used enough magic to penetrate a small area, Saadia just began to see all of the beast-men hidden as if the glamour had fallen away. However, when I checked the area again magically, I could see that it was still in place. I had feared that I had disrupted it and alerted our enemies, but that wasn't so."

"That's pretty typical of glamour magic," Jhren said. "Once you see it for what it is, it tends to become completely transparent. You know, boy, you should study with me some. You strike me as a much more attentive student than your brother. You say you learned all of this in a couple of weeks reading books in your uncle's library?"

Delno cleared his throat loudly. "Will's magical training, as well as mine, can be discussed at some other point in time," he said, and couldn't keep the annoyance out of his voice. "Now—we were discussing the beast-men and the magic they are using before I lost control of this meeting."

"Could one young but somewhat experienced Rider cast such a glamour, Jhren?" Brock asked.

Jhren considered the question so long that everyone began to wonder if he would answer at all. Finally he said, "I don't think so. I could do it, but I've got a lot more experience than some young Rider who's had only a few years of practice. Glamours are funny things and take some concentration and practice. The bigger it is, the more it takes. If it's Riders under Warrick's command, then I'll bet there are three or four of them working together on this."

"Well, we need more reconnaissance," Delno said. Then, as Will began tying his coat shut for flight, he added, "You're staying, Brother. Nat and I are going."

Everyone looked at him, and Brock said, "Suppose you are seen?"

"We won't be attacked. Our enemies want their false ambush to be seen and scouted; otherwise they wouldn't have bothered putting it there. We don't care if we are seen because the enemy expects us to do just what we are doing. What they don't expect is that Marlo will use her senses to detect any bonded dragons hiding in the area."

"I don't like it," Brock said. "Suppose it's a trap to lure you out into the open so that they can take out our commander?"

"Then they will find that they have more to deal with than they expected," he replied. "Besides, as commander I have to know the lay of the land to see how best to use our forces, and this will give me a chance to try that new light-weight saddle that was made for me this afternoon."

Without another word he turned and strode toward Geneva with Nat following in his wake.

"*Be ready for anything, Love; this could be dangerous,*" Geneva said as they took off from the ground.

"*I am ready, Love. However, I don't think the enemy will attack. They will be expecting us to scout their position, and we will act as if we have seen only what they want us to see. That way, they will give us free passage while Marlo uses her senses to locate the Riders who I am sure are out there. While she is doing that, I will survey the land and see if I can figure the best means to frustrate their real ambush.*"

"*That's all well and good, Dear One, but just remember, that saddle you are using was made very quickly and has not been tested.*"

"The reason they finished it so quickly was that they had a riding saddle for a horse that they were able to adapt for our purposes. They triple stitched everything with strong thread. I supervised the operation, and Brock said the work looked quite good to him. The saddle isn't even particularly uncomfortable, though it isn't as heavily padded in the seat as the saddle I gave to Jhren."

"It certainly is more comfortable for me. That other one had gotten so small that I felt as if I were choking when I filled my flame bladder. This one seems to ride in the right place and won't interfere with my flame or my wings."

"I'm glad it works better for you, Love. I'm sure I will adjust to having less padding just fine," he replied. "We are getting very close, and I can make out the low ground where the false ambush is situated. Tell Marlo to concentrate on the area beyond that and see if there are any dragons we don't know out there."

"Done, love. Tell me though; wouldn't Marlo have sensed any dragons long before now? After all, she sensed our approach from nearly fifteen leagues away."

"Yes, her senses in that respect are acute, but she may have been unconsciously dampening them because there were so many dragons to sort through on our side. Remember, it's not just the ten of us she is feeling in camp, but thirty or so un-bonded dragons as well. That's a lot of background noise to filter out to see the enemy. Marlo is good, but I suspect that even she has certain limits that we might have exceeded."

"I don't know about that; it sounds like guessing to me." She paused and then said, "All right, Love, point for you. Marlo just informed me that she has detected seven dragons who are with Riders just beyond the Roracks hidden in the trees."

"Well, since she has done her job, and I have seen the lay of the land, I suppose we should get back to camp and make some plans. I think I have found a way to deal with situation, and I would like to get the game going."

CHAPTER 40

"**I** DON'T SEE HOW *flaming those trees will help us, Love,*" Geneva said. *"The Roracks that are hiding in them are spread out. We won't get many of them this way."*

"You are forgetting the terrain, Love." Delno replied. *"It was a wet winter followed by a dry spring and summer. The trees and the underlying brush are like a tinderbox. When we set those trees burning, the fire will then take on a life of its own. The Roracks may be fast, but they will find themselves facing a wall of fire between their hidden reinforcements and the bait they set for us. We will then concentrate on the false ambush, and then when we are finished the soldiers will mop up anything we missed."*

"But the fires won't burn forever, Delno. What happens when they die down?"

"Dear Heart, you have never walked in the hills after a forest fire. The carcasses of the animals that tried to outrun the fire litter the forest floor. The beast-men may be a bit faster than an average human, but even they can't out run a fire that is burning uphill and has plenty of fuel to feed it. I doubt any will survive, but if some do, they will be in no shape to fight."

"I hadn't thought about that. Now that you have explained it, I see the logic of your strategy."

"I am not surprised that you hadn't thought of it. You are a winged creature. It isn't in your nature to stay on the ground and try to outrun a fire. You would simply fly away, and therefore don't see forest fire the way that flightless creatures do. After all, one thing I have noticed about the bodies of the animals on the ground is that there are darned few birds among them."

"Well, that is why dragons and humans make such good Partners, Dear One. We augment each other's skills and instincts."

Delno had been waiting for the sun to rise just a little higher before giving the order to attack. It was an hour past dawn and the sun was just reaching the position that would have the dragons flying down to flame the tree line with the sun glaring directly behind them. Hopefully, this would help to blind the enemies on the ground to their intentions until it was too late. As he realized that the time had come, he had Geneva relay the order to commence the attack.

Sheila led the un-bonded dragons in the first wave. They flew straight at the trees and flamed them. As one dragon emptied her flame bladder, the one behind her would slightly overlap her strafing run and continue the line, then the next would repeat the performance. Soon, to Delno's satisfaction, and also to his horror, the line of trees was burning for nearly a mile, from one side of the slope to the other. As expected, the fire caught quickly and began to climb the hill with incredible speed.

As the un-bonded dragons were lighting the slope on fire, the bonded dragons began their runs on the false ambush. This group of Roracks may have been the bait but they certainly weren't helpless. As the dragons swooped down, the beast-men immediately hit them with a hailstorm of arrows. Literally thousands of the missiles were flying in the air. Most missed their mark, but the shields the Riders erected were put to the test.

The shields held for the first round, and hundreds of beast-men died in the conflagration. However, hundreds more were still alive, and they seemed to have no real fear of the fire that consumed their fellows. They began to spread out, and Delno had Sheila use her forces help to ring the Roracks in flames so that they wouldn't break out of the low area they'd set up in.

Delno saw that the reinforcements were, at first, frustrated that they couldn't get through the flames to attack the dragons and Riders. Then, as many of them started dying, they began to realize the reality of their predicament. They turned and began to race the fire uphill, and they quickly lost the race. He knew that they were Roracks and that they were merciless killers, but he still couldn't help but feel sorry for those on the slope, and for the rest of them that were now ringed with fire and dying by the score.

"Coming down from top of the ridge, Love," came Geneva's urgent warning.

He looked where she had indicated, and there were the enemy Riders. They were grouping for attack. Delno sensed that at least two of them were massing energy in preparation for using magic. He had, of course, been expecting this. That was why Jhren had been kept in reserve. Carra quickly rose high, and the old wizard cast a bolt of magic at the seven enemies. One of the opposing dragons screamed as she was knocked from the air onto the slope, and she and her Rider were quickly lost in the flames: the others scattered.

Delno tried desperately to figure out which of the pairs of enemies was the obvious leader. They were flying in a spiraling formation that wove a somewhat intricate pattern and made it hard to keep track of any one of them. He was having trouble deciding who to go after when Geneva said, "I have them. *The large green and her Rider are giving orders.*"

"*Then they are our target, Love. Inform Jhren, but make sure he knows that he isn't to confront them directly. I want him as backup, and he's too important to risk his life trying to fight directly without training.*"

"*Done,*" she said. "*I am going to close on our quarry.*"

Geneva circled around and made a straight line for the large green dragon. The green's Rider was so busy directing the others that he didn't look up until it was too late. He managed to shield himself from the magical bolt that Delno shot directly at him, but Geneva simply grabbed the other dragon's wing with both sets of her front claws while passing at full speed. The green's wing was not only horribly torn but also pulled out of joint. She desperately tried to arrest her fall, but, with one wing completely useless, she fell spiraling faster and faster until she hit the ground hard enough to break her neck, and nearly every other bone in her body. As she hit, she flipped over on top of her Rider, squashing him like a bug.

"*Two down; maybe the others can be reasoned with at this point.*"

"*That would be nice, Delno,*" Geneva replied, "*but I don't think they are ready to give up yet. Keep your shields up, Love; they have decided to come after us.*"

"*Call for back up!*" Delno said as he poured more energy into the shields he was maintaining around himself and Geneva.

Delno blocked one magical attack while Geneva maneuvered out of the way of two others. Then one dragon got close above them and flamed directly into their faces. Delno redoubled his shields and felt extra energy being poured into them from somewhere else, most likely from Jhren. Then Brock and Leera made a strafing run on the attacker, and she was forced to veer off.

It was still a second or so before Geneva came out of the smoke and flame and they could see clearly again. When they could see, they found that the last of the five remaining enemies hadn't been deterred, and the pair was bearing down on them. They had no time to avoid the attack. Geneva began to roll so that she would take the attack on her heavily armored underside and be able to deal some punishment with her own claws, while Delno braced for the impact and began readying a magical retaliation of his own.

Just before the other dragon hit there was a blur and Geneva's attacker was knocked about fifteen yards off course. She had been hit by another dragon from the side, and the impact was such that the noise of it was audible even above the roaring of the wind and sounds of the dragons screaming. The two dragons were now locked in mortal combat and falling rapidly. Delno then realized that his rescuers were Rhonna and Lawrence. The man wasn't creative when it came to tactics and had opted to simply hit the other team as hard as possible. Unfortunately, Rhonna's wings and other limbs were now so entangled with her semi-conscious foe that she couldn't break free. Both Dragons hit the ground so hard that they were knocked apart. Rhonna and Lawrence were killed instantly on impact, and, as if to leave no doubt of the outcome, the other dragon's flame bladder ruptured and the explosion engulfed both pairs.

Lawrence had died saving Delno's and Geneva's lives. The young Rider had simply followed Brock as he had been doing since leaving Palamore and used the only tactic he could come up with in the situation. Delno couldn't bring himself to believe that Lawrence could possibly have been so dull witted that he would have thought he could survive such an encounter. The pair had deliberately sacrificed themselves to save their comrades.

"That was a very brave act, Love," Geneva said. "I will make sure that all dragons remember it. I would like to take time to mourn and celebrate the act, but we still have four more enemies to deal with."

"Then let's put this matter to rest. I want those Riders on the ground as soon as possible, and at this point I don't care if they are alive or dead when they land. We need to end this before we lose any more from our side."

A dragon screamed in pain to their left and Delno turned in time to see one of the enemy pairs trailing smoke from the dragon's hide while they were desperately trying to get away. Four un-bonded dragons had attacked them simultaneously, and they had been unable to avoid all of them. As they were trying for altitude, a fifth un-bonded dragon was waiting for them. Delno realized that the first four had herded the unsuspecting pair into a trap. The fifth dragon flamed them, and the bonded dragon's wings were crisped. She fell like a stone. She fell right in the middle of the Roracks who were still alive at the point of the false ambush, and her flame bladder exploded when she hit. Not only did that reduce the number of opposing dragons to three, it killed several score of the Roracks who had formed a protective ring on the ground while disrupting their formation.

Delno saw nearly a hundred Roracks, all relatively unscathed, form up and begin advancing toward the only opening in the flames that were consuming the dry grass and nearly surrounding them. He quickly had Geneva report the movement to Sheila, and several un-bonded dragons dove on the Roracks and closed the gap before they could escape. The Roracks screamed in rage and charged the flame wall as if they were insane. The charge amounted to nothing, and the beast-men who participated died in the useless attempt to get past the wall of fire.

The three enemy dragons had pulled back and were holding in confusion. Apparently, this was going so far against what they had envisioned they were unable to even regroup. Delno took the respite to survey the slope. It was completely involved in the fire and would probably burn for a day or more. Geneva confirmed that there were no living Roracks to be found on the ridge. The two thousand beast-men who had waited in ambush there had been low enough on the slope so that they would have been able to get quickly into the battle; therefore, none of them were close enough to the top of the ridge to get to the down slope on the other side before the flames reached them. They had all died without even getting the chance to return fire at the dragons who had killed them.

"Try and contact those Riders and tell them that if they surrender, they won't be harmed," Delno said.

There was a pause while Geneva relayed Delno's message. "One of them says that he will personally kill you, and one says he is willing to surrender, while the third is completely confused as to what to do, and is waiting for the other two to decide."

"Tell the one who has offered to surrender to land behind us. Have Will and Saadia, and several un-bonded dragons ensure that he really doesn't try *something. If he is not aggressive, they are not to do him or his dragon any harm."*

The pair acknowledged the instructions and moved to comply. The Rider who had made the threat was furious. He immediately moved to attack the pair who were surrendering, but found his way blocked by over a dozen un-bonded dragons and four bonded pairs. Then he made the colossal mistake of trying to flame his way through them. All of the un-bonded dragons returned fire for fire, and the pair were dead before they hit the ground.

The last enemy dragon turned and flew away from the scene of the battle as fast as her wings would carry her. Several dragons moved to give chase, but Delno called them back.

"Tell them to let that pair go," he said to Geneva. *"Let them return to their master and report on what has happened here today."* He looked down and saw that his soldiers were moving in and finishing off the Roracks who were still alive. In most cases, it was more an act of mercy than an act of aggression. *"There may be a lot of Roracks out there, but the loss of nearly four thousand of them without any appreciable gain against us will be a blow to Warrick. Add the loss of six of his dragons, and he will be hard pressed to make up the deficit."*

"We should get on the ground, Love," Geneva replied. *"We have some injuries on our side and a prisoner to interrogate. Also, I wish to mourn the loss of a brave pair who died defending us."*

Delno suddenly had a bit of trouble with a large lump that popped up in his throat so he simply let Geneva take control, and she began gliding down to land. Once on the ground, the two of them just stood together for a moment gathering themselves before they moved on to do what must still be done.

Once he felt his composure return, Delno moved to the injured dragons who had been burned or pierced and began healing them. It didn't take long; casualties were light on their side, and the bonded dragons had their own Riders to heal them if they had been injured. A few of the dragons had gotten a bit scorched, and three had actually gotten arrows in their mouths, while one had taken an arrow in the flesh surrounding her eye where the scales were the thinnest.

If the arrow had been an inch higher, she might have lost her eye. As it was, he had to pull the arrow out, which was quite painful because the Roracks used barbed arrow heads that tended to work the dart in deeper rather than facilitate removal. The dragon stood stoically though while he pulled the thing free. Then he healed the injury completely within a minute or so.

Many of the uninjured dragons remained aloft and watched the skies in case more enemies showed up, but the air remained free of threats. Those dragons on the ground gathered with Geneva around Rhonna's body and set up that same eerie keening that Delno had heard Geneva use when her mother had died. The sound was echoed from those still circling above. Then the dragons soaring overhead all began to flame while flying in a spiral pattern as a tribute to Rhonna's and Lawrence's sacrifice.

CHAPTER 41

"YOU CAN'T DO anything to me. I surrendered today, but Warrick will soon take you out of the picture, and I will be back where I belong!" the young Rider they had captured, Kurt, said defiantly.

"There are several reasons you shouldn't be so quick to put any further faith in your master, Warrick, boy," Delno responded. "First; he will not take lightly to you surrendering. As far as he is concerned now, you are a deserter. If he catches up with you, he will treat you accordingly. Second; he has consistently underestimated us since we joined this war. What happened today is simply a large scale version of what has happened every time we have faced his forces. We lost one dragon and Rider, while his losses number five Riders and their dragons dead, and one captured. At the same time, he lost nearly four thousand of his beast-men without so much as making our ground troops break a sweat. He has over extended himself and now doesn't have the resources to keep his captured territories. He is losing ground continuously in every kingdom where we have moved against him to this point. Now that we have arrived in Horne, he will lose ground here as well." He paused and let that sink in. "No, son, don't look to your former friends to swoop down out of the sky heroically and rescue you from our clutches. You are our prisoner and will remain so until I say otherwise."

"*There are six dragons approaching, Love,*" Geneva reported. "*Marlo says that two are bonded and four are not. She also says that she knows the un-bonded dragons and believes that they are not hostile. She is puzzled though, because they travel with a large group of people who are on foot. That is all she can get from so far away."*

"Ask her to keep watch. It is possible that we are getting reinforcements that have come unlooked for, but I don't want to let our guard down this deep into Warrick's home territory."

"Now then, why don't we start again, Kurt," Delno said more softly. "We need to end this useless fighting. Warrick has no compunction against letting us kill every Rider who is under his command if it serves his purposes. He made you, and he can make more. As long as he is free, he will feel that he has a chance to succeed and will not give up his plans to conquer all of the kingdoms of men. Forgive me for sounding melodramatic, but Warrick seeks nothing less than total world domination and won't give up so long as he is free to pursue that goal. What I would like to know is where exactly he is hiding now, so that I can take the fight directly to him and end the needless bloodshed on both sides."

"If you are so powerful," Kurt replied sarcastically, "you should have no problem finding him yourself."

"Let me try and get some useful information out of him, sir," Captain Jameson, the commander of the Bournese troops under Delno's command, said. "I'll deal with that haughty attitude of his."

There was a warning growl from the direction of the dragons, followed by over a dozen other dragons responding with growls of their own. Jameson blanched.

"No, Captain," Delno replied. "Even if I condoned such methods, his dragon would try to come to his rescue, and we would then end up killing them both. This boy is just young and a bit impressionable. He is enamored with being one of Warrick's lieutenants in the world that Warrick has described will come about when his forces have taken control. The boy is just foolish enough to believe that that madman will ever share power with anyone. Keep him under control and away from his dragon, and we will gather other intelligence. Warrick can't hide forever."

"As you say, sir," the captain responded. "We have some safety chain for the wagons that our smith can fashion into shackles: that should keep this young man from getting into mischief without doing him any harm. I'll see to it."

"Good, Captain; now, if you will excuse me, we are going to have company, and I have to see to any arrangements that must be made." At the man's puzzled look he added, "I'll explain later when I have more information; for now, all I can tell you is that it looks as if more dragons will be joining us."

As he said the last bit, Delno glanced at Kurt, and saw the young man pale visibly at the thought of more dragons joining with those already opposing Warrick.

"*The young Rider is desperately trying to reestablish contact with his Bond-mate, Love. What did you say to him?*"

"*Not to him, but I let him overhear me telling our good captain that we have more dragons joining us. He seems upset by the information.*"

"*We will continue to prevent him from contacting his Partner, then.*"

"*That sounds like a good idea. Later, when we have more information about the new dragons approaching, we will let his Partner know just what we want her to know and then let them resume contact. For now, let his own imagination work on him for a while.*"

Delno stepped out of the command tent that had been erected in camp and was nearly blinded by the mid-afternoon sun. So much had happened so quickly he had just about forgotten that it all took place that morning and not some time ago. He knew it was an illusion caused by being raised to battle awareness then left to come down from that without a break, but it seemed like the events that were taking place were altering time as well as the political make-up of the world.

"*Interesting news, Love,*" Geneva broke into his thoughts. "*One of the bonded dragons coming toward us is Mariah. She is close enough to speak to her, and she has relayed a message from Paul that he has thought over what you said and wishes to join us. I have told them to halt and wait for further instructions. Should we let them proceed or keep them at a distance until we can be sure of their intentions?*"

"What do we know of the other dragons with them? Also, who are the people they travel with?" he replied.

Geneva took a few minutes to get answers to his questions before responding. While he was waiting, Brock and Jhren joined him.

"*Hold your answers until I get to you, Love. Brock and Jhren are with me, and they may as well hear this too.*"

He motioned for the others to follow, and they walked quickly to where Geneva was waiting, far enough away from Indigo, the midnight blue dragon who was bonded to Kurt, that they wouldn't be overheard.

"Mariah says that the people are a mixture of men and elves," Geneva said. At the looks of astonishment on the men's faces, she added, "Apparently, the elves have left their home to come and help find the compelling stone. There are about seventy of them, and they are traveling with about two hundred dark-skinned men from the extreme south.

"Those would be men from my homeland of Iondar," Brock said. "It lies even further south than Trent, close to the Elven lands. When we were down there I sent word that we needed help, and these men must have come in answer to my call. I would have preferred to have more, but two hundred is still better than none. The seventy elves is quite a surprise, though my people have always gotten along with them. I know the elves have people who actively hunt the Roracks, but I didn't expect them to send any to us."

"The other dragons," Geneva continued, "are four un-bonded females who have heard of our plight and want to help, and Deena and her Bond-mate Chad, who both know Brock."

"Chad is one of my former students, and he has fought the Roracks with me in the past. I haven't seen him in nearly three years, but he is a good man and a good Rider. We should let them come ahead. The only ones in question are Paul and Mariah."

"Tell them to come to us," Delno said. "I will speak with them here and make the final determination for myself."

CHAPTER 42

"WELL, PAUL, IT appears that you have come around to our way of thinking after all," Delno observed as the two new Riders dismounted.

"It was Mariah who started the process. After we left you, she wouldn't even talk to me for three days. Then all she would do was give me fits about forcing her to work with Roracks. She told me your theory about how Warrick had been using that compelling stone on our dragons and how angry she was that I hadn't seen it. I finally began to see the truth of it myself. We decided to fly off and get ourselves sorted out before we made any further decisions. We weren't specifically heading toward Elven lands but ended up down that way. We met Chad and Deena, and then the three of them ganged up and made me see that all of that nonsense I was spouting off about was just Warrick's brainwashing." He turned specifically to Nat and added, "I sure did make an ass of myself."

"The dragons have all talked with Mariah, and she is of the mind that you have gotten your head put right, so I welcome your help," Delno said. Then he turned to Chad and added, "Brock has spoken highly of you, Chad; I'm glad to have here you, too."

Then they all shook hands, and Delno told them that refreshments were available at the main tent.

"Tell me, sir," Paul asked, "the Rider of that dragon, is he hurt?"

"No, he is fine physically, but he is being kept under lock and key as a prisoner."

"May I speak with him? He is my half-brother." Then he added, hastily, "I don't expect to be left alone with him."

Delno led Paul to the prisoner, but stood near to make sure that neither got crazy ideas.

"Well, Kurt, it's at least good to see that you are still alive," Paul said as he stepped up to his half-brother.

Kurt sat up, not fully believing his eyes. "Paul? Warrick told us that you were dead. He said you'd been killed in an unprovoked attack by this man while on a diplomatic mission."

"That's certainly not the first lie that Warrick has told, Kurt. I was on a mission, though 'diplomatic' isn't how I would describe it. I was sent to try and intimidate this man into joining Warrick. However, the real reason I was sent was to be captured so that I could spy on Delno and his people. Delno realized what was going on immediately and still refused to allow me to be killed, or even threatened. I traveled with him for a few days and then was allowed to go my own way once I came to realize that I was on the wrong side. I wasn't ready to join up with these people yet and went farther south to do some soul searching. The more I traveled, the more I realized that Warrick is a maniac who must be stopped."

Kurt looked at Paul like he had suddenly gone mad. "Paul, do hear yourself? You are talking about the man who saved us from certain death and then made Riders out of us. Warrick not only gave us our lives, he raised our station in life far beyond what we could have achieved for ourselves."

"Yes, he saved our lives. He saved us from Roracks. Of course, now that I see the situation clearly, I realize that he is the one who sent the Roracks to murder our parents and take us prisoner." Kurt shook his head in disagreement, but Paul went on. "You were only thirteen, brother. I was nineteen. The Roracks had been attacking in small uncoordinated groups before, but these attacked our village and killed everyone but you and me. They slaughtered our family and friends but took us prisoner. Why was that, brother? And why did it happen so soon after that Rider stopped in our village and talked to all of the younger men and women?"

"Why would Warrick do such a thing?"

"Why? You have to ask that? Do you remember how that Rider was treated? The villagers wanted nothing to do with him, and our parents certainly weren't about to let him take both of their sons off to be candidates. Hella had a clutch ready to hatch and Warrick needed candidates for the hatchlings. So he had his own Roracks attack the village and kill everyone but us, because that Rider and his dragon had identified us as potentials. Then he staged that rescue so that we would feel grateful to him. He had us standing at the hatching less than two days later."

"But there were nearly two hundred people in our village . . ." Kurt whispered.

"Yes, Kurt," Paul said softly. "Two hundred people, including our parents, who had become inconvenient to him. So he had them killed to get what he wanted. Then he brainwashed us into working with the beast-men, perhaps even the same beast-men who killed our parents. I know I can't tell one of them from another, can you?" As Kurt shook his head, Paul continued. "The last insult is that he has used that same damn compelling stone to help us control our dragons and make them work with their instinctive enemies."

"I don't know what to say, Paul. I had volunteered to be part of that ambush out there to avenge your death. Then, when we were beaten so badly, I surrendered in the hopes that I would get the chance to kill this man," he indicated Delno, "to get that vengeance. Now I find you alive, and you make a very logical argument about Warrick being behind the deaths of our parents." Kurt started to cry and looked at his older brother. "Paul, I don't know what I should do anymore."

Paul moved closer to Kurt and said gently, "I know what you should do, Kurt. You should stop fighting these people, to start with. Then, if you still can't bring yourself to join us, you should go off away from here and keep yourself, and especially Indigo, as far away from that compelling stone as you can until both your heads clear."

CHAPTER 43

"THE MEN OF *Iondar and the elves who travel with them have arrived, Love. They are waiting a half a mile out to avoid being mistaken for enemies in the darkness. The elves were able to get the message to Deena and she relayed it to me. They wish to come forward and meet with us.*"

"Very good," Delno replied to Geneva, "*but the bulk of their forces may as well make camp for the night. Even though the ground fighting was light today, many of our troops have worked hard and are getting what sleep they can. No sense disrupting both camps this late. We will fly there and meet with them. Have Jhren, Nassari, Nat, Brock, and, of course, Chad get ready to come with me.*" He started to move to get his gear and then added, "*Oh, and Love, ask Brock if he will transport Captain Jameson. I was going to do it, but then I remembered that our saddle isn't built with passengers in mind. The man should be there if his troops will be working with the newcomers.*"

"*I'm sure one of the others can carry him, Love.*" Then she chuckled and said, "*It's not our group I'm worried about; it's whether or not you can get the man to actually consent to ride on a dragon. He is still terrified of us ever since our performance on the plain outside Larimar, and that showing this morning, even though we were on his side, doesn't seem to have allayed his fears much.*"

Delno remembered the horrified look on the man's face when Indigo had growled because Jameson had tried to scare Kurt. Even with all of the other dragons to prevent trouble, the man had gone white as bleached linen. He chuckled and said, "*Yes, we have made quite an impression on the*

Bournese, haven't we? Still, tell everyone I wish to leave as soon as we can get the saddles in place."

"Already done, Dear One; I await you near our gear."

They were right about Jameson not wanting to get too close to the dragons, but the man was a soldier first, and he put his fears aside and climbed up behind Brock. Once airborne, the trip only took a few minutes since the newcomers were camped so close. They landed, and two men walked up to meet them.

"Delno Okonan," Chad said, "this is Captain Rand Ard of Iondar, and Walker Longleaf of the Elven Kingdom."

Delno shook hands with both men. "Ard? Are you any relation to Brock here?"

"Rand is my grand-nephew, but don't ask us to figure out exactly how close or distant the relationship is, or how many generations removed, because we don't keep track of such things in Iondar. Where we come from, family is family no matter how many generations have passed," Brock said as he moved forward and embraced his kinsman.

"Well, Keem, don't you have a greeting for your family member?" Nat asked the elf.

Walker's eyes went wide as he recognized the half-elf. "Nathaniel!" he shouted as he nearly threw himself at Nat. "It's been so long, and I never expected to see you in a camp of war."

"I'll wager that you never expected to see me bonded to a dragon, either." Nat replied and laughed.

Walker looked at him in complete shock and said, "That will take some explaining, Cousin." Then he looked at the rest of the people there and said, "But we are being poor hosts. Come let us get you all some refreshments, and we can discuss everything." Then his smile broadened, and he added, "Who knows, we may actually get around to talking about this war and what we are going to do about it."

"Your new name may take a bit of explaining also, Walker," Nat replied. "Congratulations, even if it is a bit late."

Nat and Walker moved quickly ahead of the others, and Brock and Rand held back with Delno and Nassari. As they walked, Brock spoke in a low voice. "Which of you is in charge here, Rand?"

"Well, Uncle, that is complicated. I am the commander of the Iondarian troops. However, Walker's real elven name is Keem Longleaf. Walker is his Hunter's name."

Brock seemed to grasp the importance of what Rand had said but it was lost on Delno and Nassari, and it showed on their faces.

"The Longleafs are the main ruling family of the elves." Brock explained. "Walker, that is the name given to him by his hunting clan for his prowess, is the son of the head of the most powerful family in the Elven Kingdom. Him being here is akin to your uncle sending his own son if he had one. Think of him as a prince rather than a common soldier."

"I see," Delno replied softly. "That is all well and good, and I am glad to have any help I can get, but I won't coddle him because of his political status. The fact that he is a skilled hunter doesn't make him a soldier."

"Ah, I see that we have confused you," Rand said defensively. "The Elven Hunting Clans are not there to provide meat for the table; they are soldiers. The term 'clan' refers to their specific unit, not their family. In fact, they are the most elite of the Elven soldiers, and what they hunt is Roracks. An elf doesn't earn his name among his clan until he has killed one hundred enemies, and every kill must be witnessed or it doesn't count. Most hunting clansmen don't earn the honor. Walker has earned his name by spending a good many years hunting Roracks in their own territory. He is not only the leader of the Shadow Clan, but a superb fighter and highly skilled tracker. The only ones who possibly know the Roracks' lands better than he are the beast-men themselves, and it's likely that even they don't."

"My apologies," Delno replied. "I am from Corice and only recently became involved with dragons. In the north we are so far removed from all of this that many people don't even believe that elves still exist in the world. I meant no offense; I only wish to do what is best for the troops and dragons under *my* command. Since Walker is so skilled and his knowledge so valuable, I will treat him accordingly."

"Good save, Del." Nassari quipped in low whisper. "Of course, if you had waited longer to speak up, you might not have put your foot in it in the first place."

"Politics is your forte, Nassari," Delno responded. "Perhaps if you had nudged me I wouldn't have spoken out of turn."

"Perhaps if you would stop holding Wanda and me back in battle and let her take charge of some of those un-bonded females like a lineage holder should do, I wouldn't be so put out that I let you get into such predicaments." Nassari smiled at him and then stepped out more quickly to catch up with Nat and Walker.

Brock chuckled softly as Delno stared blankly at Nassari's back. He held Delno back and let Rand get ahead of them, so he could speak privately with him for a moment. "Nassari is a good man, Delno, and he has a right to be a bit miffed at you. You should have used him more in a leadership role earlier. I was going to talk to you about it, but never got the chance with everything else happening. You have to start delegating more authority. That's why you have me and Nassari along as lieutenants. I've watched the man in the air, and I believe he is competent; give him a chance to prove it."

Delno started to make a heated reply, and Geneva growled both in his mind and audibly. He looked back, and she glared at him without saying a word. The flash of anger he had felt growing abated completely, and he said to Brock, "You are right. I do need to delegate more. If I recall, it was your group that saved my arse when I overextended myself this morning. And it was Nassari and his group that kept the Roracks busy on the ground while you were doing it. I will remember that next time. I can't fight this war alone; we are a team, and I am only one of the leaders."

"*That's better, Love,*" Geneva said.

"I'm glad we've settled that, then," Brock replied. "Now we had best get ourselves to that meeting." He strode forward toward the central camp fire.

As Delno joined the group, Walker said, "First, let me apologize for being rude and ignoring you all when we first met," he waved in the direction of where the southerners had met them by the dragons. "I haven't seen my cousin, Nathaniel, since the last time he visited the Elven lands with his father. I was so surprised and happy to find him here that I forgot my manners, and now I must beg your forgiveness."

"There is nothing to forgive," Nassari said. "We all understand."

There were nods all around the group, and Walker smiled. "Very well, then," he turned to Delno and said, "I have traveled extensively throughout the lands. I have even made it into Corice on occasion." Delno was taken aback by this news, but Walker continued as if he didn't notice. "It isn't easy for an elf to disguise himself well enough to travel in human lands undetected, but I am fairly good at it. While in Corice, I heard of the exploits of Delno Okonan. I must say that I am impressed. If you were Hunting Clan, you would have your name for your deeds in the war between Corice and Bourne, and now I find that you are a Dragon Rider and traveling in such prestigious company," he bowed to Brock. "I am glad we have found you and your group."

"I must say," Delno responded, "that I am not familiar with the elves and their ways. I wasn't suitably impressed with you, Walker, when we met, because I didn't understand who you were and what you had done. Now that I know, I am also glad that we have met here. Perhaps when the trouble in Horne is settled, and I have put paid to accounts in the North, I can travel to the Elven lands and learn of your people and their ways."

Walker laughed, "Well said, Delno Okonan. I accept that and offer to be your guide when you visit my homeland. Perhaps you can even persuade my cousin to join us and visit his relations who miss him so much."

"Done," Delno replied. "I look forward to it. But for now, we must deal with this unpleasant business here."

"You are right, my new friend. I bring seventy elves; all from my own Hunting Clan. All have traveled with me in the beast-men's territory and all are well blooded, though not all have earned their names yet. We bring our skills with bow, sword and long knife; as well as our tracking abilities. We are quite capable of supplying ourselves as we go and will require no provisions other than what we can gather." He turned and bowed to Rand.

Rand stood and said, "I am Rand Ard of the Iondarian Elite Forces. Traditionally, we are the King's Guard and don't leave our own borders. However, our king has decided that he will keep his main army in Iondar and has sent two hundred of his best warriors in response to Brock Ard's call for assistance. We travel light but bring most of our own supplies. We could use some fresh food to augment the hard rations we carry, but won't complain if those we join have none to spare."

Rand bowed to Delno, and, when Delno hesitated, Brock nudged him. He stood and said, "I am Delno Okonan, Rider to Geneva, lineage holder of her line." Everyone was suitably impressed with both Geneva's name and her title. Apparently, Corolan was well known in both Iondar and the Elven lands. "I bring a dozen Riders and their dragons as well as nearly forty un-bonded females who have offered their aid in this war. I also bring over six hundred seasoned veterans from the north. We are provisioned and need no supplies. We offer to share what we have and will forage with everyone else if the need arises. We are moving to join forces with other soldiers, who number in the thousands, many of whom are known to us and are counted among our friends."

"Very well met, indeed," Rand said. "Now we simply need to work out a suitable chain of command and how we will coordinate with each other before we can get this army of ours back on the move."

"If we are going to do that," Delno replied, "we should include Geneva, Sheila, and Wanda." He nodded almost imperceptibly to Nassari. "As lineage holders, they have authority with the dragons and will be vital in coordinating air assaults, and support for ground troop activity."

It was well past midnight when the commanders' meeting ended. It had been decided that each commander would retain command of his own forces. The Elven forces would be the lead shock troops since they were so skilled at tracking the Roracks, and had such good, first-hand knowledge of the terrain. The Iondarians would be their immediate back-up since they were also elite and the two groups knew each other and had worked well in cooperation thus far, even though they hadn't actually fought together yet. Finally, the Bournese troops would be the backbone of any operation, supporting both elite groups while moving in to hold any ground that was taken.

The job of overall commander again fell to Delno. He had been willing to give the job to Walker or Rand, but it was pointed out that he had done quite well so far, and, being high in the air on Geneva, he would have a much fuller picture of everything that was going on in a battle. He accepted as graciously as he could, and then they adjourned for the night.

Later, Delno once again found himself in the Dream State standing on a ledge with Geneva looking out over the landscape and shifting clouds.

"Hella is here with Warrick, Love; they wish to talk."

Delno had thought something like this might happen now that they had dealt such a crushing defeat to Warrick's forces, but he was still shocked. "You seem rather blasé about this development, Love. Aren't you concerned at meeting them here?" He was thinking about how Warrick had attacked him the last time the two met in a psychic realm.

"Hmph," she snorted. "Warrick may have some control in his own realm, but here he is more of a guest than you are. The other dragons have only allowed him because I thought you might like to talk with him now. If you prefer not to have this meeting, they will eject him and Hella without a second's hesitation."

Delno thought for a moment and then asked, "Could you pull Carra and Jhren in and let them witness this meeting without Warrick and Hella knowing they are here?"

Geneva was quiet for a time and then answered, "I can do it with the help of the other dragons. Many of the un-bonded dragons are supporting us even though they have chosen not to get directly involved. They have decided that what we are doing is important enough that they are bending the rules of the Dream State to accommodate us. Jhren and Carra are here, but Warrick can't see them. Unfortunately, neither can you for the moment."

"Very well, Love, I don't need to see them anyway, not until this meeting with our enemy is over. Me not being distracted with their presence may keep Warrick from suspecting that they are here. Let Warrick through."

Warrick was soaring on Hella. Once he could see Delno, the pair glided down to land on the ledge. Delno was keenly aware that he couldn't physically touch Warrick in this place and was a bit frustrated to be so close and not be able to do anything to end this other than talk with his enemy.

Warrick looked as if he hadn't slept in a week. Even in his psychic persona, he was disheveled and his eyes were sunken. He was looking around as if expecting enemies to jump out and attack him at any moment. Through it all, though, he still had that same haughty look of someone who just can't imagine himself losing at anything.

They stood regarding each other for a moment, and finally Delno said, "Well, Warrick, you requested this meeting. What's on your mind?"

"What is on my mind, youngster, is that I may have been hasty with you before now. You obviously are more resilient than I thought you would be, and I see now that I should have done more to bring you into my camp rather than try to eliminate you. I have come to again offer you the chance to join me. If you do, you will be second only to me."

"Second only to you," Delno said thoughtfully, and Warrick smiled. "Let me see now. Paul has told me that Hella has laid a total of twenty one eggs in the last six years, counting the last clutch this year. That means you started with less than two dozen Riders and their dragons that are under Hella's control, and three of them are still immature. Even if you have managed to get another half dozen or so from outside your little group, that still means that you had less than thirty bonded pairs after we defeated Simcha." Warrick's smile faltered as he began to suspect where this line of thought was going. "Paul left your side when he came to realize what you had done to him and Mariah." At Warrick's sneer he said, "Oh, you didn't realize that I was able to figure out your little talisman and project our conversation so that all of those present, including Paul, heard every word you said? I'm sorry, Warrick, you really should learn to watch what you say; it can get you into no end of trouble."

"You should take your own advice, whelp!" Warrick said angrily and the fabric of the Dream State wavered.

Delno said to Geneva, "*Try to hold the contact, Love. Apologize to the others, and make them see that it is in their best interest to allow Warrick to stay for a little while longer.*"

He looked back at Warrick and continued, "Let's see, where was I . . . ? Oh yes, Paul deserted because he came to realize that you were megalomaniac who cares nothing for the people he uses. He has convinced his brother of the same. So that is two Riders lost from your camp to defection. Then there was the un-bonded dragon who killed those two idiots who attacked her and her sister for no reason when they should have kept to their mission of delivering your letter to Torrance of Bourne. He won't receive that letter, by the way." Again Warrick looked angry enough to kill, but Delno continued before the man could explode and get himself ejected. "Then there are the five we killed outright yesterday morning, not to mention the nearly four thousand Roracks who died."

Warrick regained a bit of his composure and said, "At least one of your Riders was killed also."

"Yes, that is, unfortunately true. Of course, he was one of your former troops who was flying under Simcha's wing. He was so eager to get clear of you that he was willing to sacrifice himself to save one of us." Warrick looked as though he might explode, so Delno pressed on quickly. "Add to those numbers the magic user you sent to help, who I killed in Bourne," Warrick paled visibly, "and that brings the number of your important troops that have died or defected up to ten. That means that you may have less than twenty left. I, on the other hand have recruited the un-bonded dragons you failed to control. They augment our forces quite well, and we greatly outnumber you. Your control is beginning to slip, Warrick; it shows on your face. Give up this madness, and you may live through this. Return the compelling stone and the books you have stolen from the elves and surrender before more people die on either side."

"You are quite mistaken," Warrick shouted. "My control is not slipping. My control is absolute, and you will be the one who will die. I won't even use my Roracks to kill you. I will enjoy doing that deed myself."

Warrick raised his hand as if to strike like he did in his own psychic realm, but nothing happened. He stared at his hand as he had never seen the appendage before. Then he again pointed at Delno, and again nothing happened.

"As I have said before, Warrick, your control is not as absolute as you think. I am done with you, be gone."

Warrick started to protest, but was ejected before he could get a word out. Geneva reported that Hella was trying desperately to get back into the Dream State but was being blocked. Once Geneva was certain that Hella could not see what was going on, she opened the contact with Carra and Jhren.

"Well, Old Wizard," Delno said to Jhren "what are your observations about all of this?"

Jhren considered his answer carefully and then said, "Well, as you have most likely figured, he has greatly overextended himself. He's so far gone that he can't even maintain a better psychic image; he just doesn't have the energy to spare. He is gaunt and hasn't slept. He is also starting to lose his hold on reality; not that his hold on reality was all that strong to begin with. However, all of that only makes him more dangerous for us. It's possible that he will simply kill himself trying to maintain control of the beast-men and his dragons, but I doubt it. When his control falters to the point that it is an immediate threat to his life, he will most likely give it up, and fight like a cornered animal. If he does that, he will go directly after you because he has focused on you as his main antagonist to the point that doing so has become an obsession. You had best be careful, Delno; that man wants you dead, and when the time comes, he won't care what it takes to accomplish the feat, even if it means he dies with you."

Delno smiled sardonically and said, "That's what I like about you, Jhren; your cheery disposition and your upbeat advice."

CHAPTER 44

THE VILLAGE WAS unnaturally quiet, and Walker knew that meant trouble. He held up his left fist as a signal to halt. The nineteen elves with him stopped instantly, alert for the slightest sign of danger. If the village had been taken, there should be Roracks present. If it had not, then where were the villagers? Every instinct told him that this was a trap.

His arm was still bent at a ninety degree angle, and his fist was still closed in the sign for STOP. He spread his fingers as a sign to spread out to five yards apart: close enough together to come to each other's aid while separated enough to prevent being targeted en masse. Then he held up two fingers before gesturing back over his shoulder with his thumb, meaning that he wanted them to fall back by two's. He and his team partner, being the pair in the lead, began to move back the way they had come as everyone else nocked arrows to cover them.

As the elves began the retreat, the beast-men, who had been hiding in the buildings, began swarming out of the shadows through the doors while screaming out their fierce war cries. The elves at the edge of the village suddenly found themselves outnumbered nearly seven to one. Those who had readied their bows now loosed their arrows and each missile found its mark. A dozen beast-men fell dead, some with more than one arrow piercing its hide.

The Roracks seemed not to notice that their fellows had fallen, and continued to charge. It was only due to the fact that they had to come out of the buildings one at time because of the constraints of the doorways that they hadn't closed the distance yet. They saw twenty elves and were sure they had lured easy prey into their trap. However, more elves jumped up from the sandy ground. As they rose, they threw off the dun colored cloaks they had been hiding under. Their camouflage was so good that from a distance it looked as if they had sprung out of the earth itself in a shower of dust. They all began firing arrows at the beast-men.

Walker and the elves nearest to the buildings were close enough now that they were forced to drop their bows and draw their swords because those Roracks who had made it out of the doorways alive were nearly on top of them. The elves cut their enemies down like scything wheat. For a moment, it looked like an easy victory for Walker and his clansmen. Then over two hundred Roracks appeared at the end of the village's main street, and began to run headlong at the elven Hunters.

Before the Roracks could get close though, a light blue dragon appeared, seemingly out of thin air, and flamed those that were at the head of the main group. Saadia's flame not only killed the beast-men in the front, but also set the buildings on either side of the street on fire. The Roracks had no choice now; if they wanted to continue to attack the elves, they would have to come right down the middle of the pathway, which was just what Nassari had in mind when he had given Will the order to flame them.

More dragons appeared in the sky. Three bore riders and six more did not. The dragons quickly closed the distance to the village, and the large, orange dragon in the lead flew directly along the main street and began flaming as she reached the Roracks who were just beginning to regroup after avoiding Saadia's breath. Right behind Nassari and Wanda came Nadia and Pina, followed by Raymond and Terra. The bonded pairs were quickly followed by the un-bonded dragons. By the time the last dragon had made her first run, most of the beast-men were dead or dying.

The elves hadn't been idle while the dragons had been about their task. They had killed so many of the initial group of Roracks who had been hiding in the buildings that those left were having trouble getting through the doors over the dead bodies of their fellows. The dragons flamed the buildings to kill the Roracks inside while the elves finished off those who escaped the fires. Within minutes of the start of the battle, there were none of the foul creatures left alive.

Wanda landed and Nassari dismounted. "It worked just like we planned," he said to Walker.

"Yes, my friend, you and your dragons did a fine job. We had a feeling that there was an ambush waiting, and your plan worked flawlessly. We had no injuries on our side, and there are nearly four hundred beast-men dead."

A large shadow passed over them, and they both looked up to see huge bronze dragon gliding down to land. Once Geneva was on the ground, Delno dismounted quickly, and joined them.

"Nassari's plan went well, Delno," Walker said. We have thwarted the ambush that was laid for us and destroyed the beast-men. He and his other Riders, and all of the dragons, did their jobs well. There was little left for us to do when they were through."

"I wouldn't go that far," Nassari responded. "Walker and his elves acquitted themselves quite well. Their camouflage was so good that I couldn't see the bulk of them until they moved, and I knew they were there. They are amazing."

Rand and his troops were marching into view, and behind them came the Bournese, as more dragons began to land on the fields around the village. All of the buildings in the village were now ablaze.

"It seems such a waste to fire the buildings," Delno said. He turned to Walker and asked, "I suppose it's foolish to ask if any villagers survived."

"From the scant evidence we found before we had to withdraw from the flames," Walker replied, "it looks as if there were no survivors. It appears the ones who died in the initial attack were the lucky ones. There was ample evidence that those who survived were subjected to the beast-men's perverse cruelty. We are allowing the fires to burn unchecked and saying prayers over the ground in the hope of cleansing the area and giving the victims some peace."

Delno was raised to believe that once a person was dead, their body was simply an empty shell. Many of the elves, he discovered, believed the spirit stayed with the body for a time before moving on, and some of them felt that the bodies of people who were murdered should be cleansed by fire to release the victim's spirit so it could find peace.

Delno saw no harm in allowing the elves to take a few moments to pray for the Roracks' victims. He found that, as a human being, he appreciated the respect. The more time he spent around elves, the more he found about them that he liked. He wouldn't call all of the elves he had met friends, but most seemed like good people.

"I didn't mean to imply that you shouldn't carry on with your observances, my friend. Of course you and your elves should do what you feel is right for these poor people. I was merely thinking that one day we will rid this land of these foul creatures and men will return here." He paused for a moment in thought and added," Perhaps it is best they will have to rebuild and not use these buildings. When I think about it, the ruins will stand for a time as a fitting reminder of what happened to these unfortunate folks."

Walker put his hand on Delno's shoulder and smiled. "We might make an elf of you yet, my friend."

Just as Rand and Captain Jameson arrived, Geneva said, "*There are troops moving this way, Love. They are coming from the direction we are heading. Sheila says it is a large group of men. She hasn't made an exact count, but estimates their strength at about a thousand.*"

"*That's too many to simply allow them to get close without finding out their intentions first.*"

"*I didn't know we had to worry about men attacking us,*" Geneva replied, "*I thought we were hunting Roracks.*"

"*I will leave nothing to chance. Warrick may be a mad-man, but he can be persuasive. It wasn't Roracks who marched from Llorn, and it wasn't the beast-men we faced in Corice.*"

"*You're right, of course, Love. Who do you want to send to meet this army?*"

"*You and I will go. We will take Brock, Rita, and Nat. I think Paul should come along since he may recognize these men if they are Warrick's troops. Also, ask Sheila to provide half a dozen of her dragons as back-up.*"

"*Kurt will be unhappy if his brother goes and he isn't allowed,*" Geneva responded.

"*He can take that up with Rita. She is adamant that Kurt is not to be involved with anything that might put him into combat. He is fifteen and is still a boy. The only two reasons she left Connor to work in Orlean are that he needs the training that he is getting at the garrison, and when he is flying patrols he is so high off the ground he isn't in any danger.*" Then he rolled his eyes and added, "*That boy tried to kill me, but as soon as she found out that he is a fifteen year old orphan, all was forgiven. The woman has appointed herself mother to the world!*"

Geneva laughed, "*I won't tell Fahwn that you said that, Love.*"

"*Thank you, Love. Now if you could get the others assembled, we will fly out to meet our incoming guests.*"

Even from nearly two thousand feet off the ground, Geneva could make out the faces of Winston and Sergeant Smith. She reported to

Delno that they had apparently found the joint forces sent from Ondar and Palamore. He and the other Riders began to glide down for a landing. As Geneva got close to the ground, Delno could see that Winston was wearing full Colonel's insignia, and Smitty was wearing a Captain's collar.

"Well met!" Winston said as Delno and his Riders approached the soldiers. "We were beginning to despair of ever seeing you again, my friend." Then he looked in surprise at Nat and added, "When did you become a Rider? I thought that only young boys or girls were presented to hatchlings."

"Marlo is no hatchling; she is over on hundred years old," Nat responded with a smile. "However, the whole story will have to wait for another time. I think you and Delno have much to discuss first."

Winston tilted his head and looked at the half-elf curiously, but then shrugged his shoulders and turned back to Delno and said, "Something big must be happening to have kept you so long. I had expected you over a week ago."

"We were delayed by a war in the north that was perpetrated by our enemies here. Though Warrick has his eye on that region; it is still unclear whether he was simply following his timetable, or specifically trying to delay us from coming south," Delno responded. "We got here as quickly as we could." Then he added, "We also bring six hundred ground troops from the north, and we have been joined by a joint Elven and Iondarian force of nearly three hundred."

"So, we've managed to finally put a name to the mind controlling the beast-men, huh? I have heard of Warrick. He was reported killed some years back. I had always heard that he was a good Rider."

"It would seem that he has been scheming to take control of all of the lands of men for a long time. His disappearance was simply a feint so that he could ready his forces without anyone noticing. Now he has revealed himself and his plan."

"Well, at least that is more information than we had before," Winston replied. As for the troops you bring, we can certainly use all the help we can get. As you can see, the eighteen hundred we left Palamore with has been reduced to just under a thousand. These beast-men fight like demons. They seem to have no fear of dying, and none have yet to even attempt to surrender. Also, they are smart enough to specifically target our officers. As you can see," he pointed to Smitty, "I've had to make some field promotions."

"I noticed that," Delno replied. Then he turned to Smitty and said, "Congratulations."

"I appreciate the sentiment," Smitty responded, "but the way these damn Roracks have been targeting our officers, I'm not sure this collar is such a good thing."

Delno turned back to Winston and asked, "Why are you headed in that direction?" He pointed toward the smoke coming from the morning's battle. "I thought the main fight was the other way."

"We were pursuing a somewhat large force of Roracks that way. From the signs we saw, we estimated their numbers at about two to three hundred. They destroyed a small village back the way we came, and we had hoped to catch them before they could do more harm." Then he looked at the smoke and said, "I suppose that you and your force have put paid to them, then?"

"Yes, we were tracking a group of them that was about a hundred and fifty strong. Apparently, the two groups joined forces at the village back there, and then set an ambush for us. They are all dead, but they had already killed the villagers by the time we arrived."

"Well, it's good they're all dead. Damn shame about the village though. I have been pushing these men hard, and they've been giving me their best, but they just can't keep up with those bloody beast-men. Those creatures seem nearly tireless when they get in the mood for killing. We forced marched right through the night, but the Roracks were running, and I mean literally running, ahead of us."

"Yes," Delno replied. "Walker has mentioned that. While Roracks do get tired eventually, they push themselves to physical injury rather than give in to the fatigue. It can make them hard to fight on the one hand, because they will fight until they are killed no matter how exhausted they are. However, if you catch them when they are tired, it can make them easier to kill because they can't fight as effectively due to pushing themselves beyond their limits."

Everyone was silent for a moment, and then Delno said, "All that remains now is to coordinate how we will join our forces and take this fight to the enemy's camp. I suggest that since you and your men have been traveling through the night, and we need to head back the way you came, your forces wait here while ours come and join them. You and your men get what rest you can while we advance. Then we can get all of the commanders together and decide on our next move."

CHAPTER 45

"WHAT CONCERNS ME is that we haven't met with more resistance," Walker said. "We've been steadily moving deeper into Horne for four days, and we've only been involved in minor skirmishes. The reports the elves had said that the beast-men were moving in large, organized formations, hundreds strong. Aside from those in the village this morning, the only enemies we have seen have numbered no more than three score and haven't been any more organized than the Roracks I have seen in the past."

"I agree," Delno responded. "Our intelligence said that the Roracks were attacking towns and killing everyone in their path. We've passed two other small villages, and they were completely untouched. The residents there hadn't seen more than a scouting party of beast-men since this whole war began. Of course, there were those beast-men we destroyed on our first day in Horne. I'd say that nearly four thousand of them constitutes a large force, and they were organized enough to set a complicated ambush and coordinate with the seven Riders who were providing air support for them. They were also completely single-minded in their mission, since they bypassed those untouched villages to get to the ambush point."

"Well," Winston responded, "I can certainly attest to the fact that there are, or were, many of them when we got here. We've gone up against three large groups, the smallest still over five hundred strong. I started out from Palamore with eighteen hundred troops. The men I have left number less than a thousand, and we've had so many officers killed I've had to field promote my non-coms."

"I'm not saying that you haven't seen your share of fighting, Colonel," Walker said. "What I am saying, though, is that the resistance seems to be tapering off some. It worries me that as more forces make their way into Horne, fewer Roracks can be found. The signs of them moving in large numbers are there, though they are not fresh. It is as though they have been pulling back in an organized manner. If that is the case, I have to wonder what we will find when we reach our enemy's main position."

"Yes," Delno replied. "I am with Walker on this one. I would prefer that we were meeting steady resistance and thinning them out in smaller groups. As it stands, I have to believe that we will find a large force waiting for us when we finally catch up with Warrick. I believe, and Jhren concurs, that Warrick is overextended and is having trouble maintaining separate groups in any significant numbers, which would explain why the smaller groups we have encountered are disorganized; they have managed to escape from Warrick's control. We think that because of that, he has pulled his remaining Roracks back and has surrounded himself with a force in numbers not before seen. We could very well be facing ten thousand or more of them when we get there. Of course, I don't expect us to be completely alone. Nearly every country has sent men and arms to this fight, and there must be some from Horne still alive, so I think we will find more allies as we move ahead."

"If he is losing control, wouldn't keeping so many of them in line tax him even more?" Captain Jameson asked. Smitty and Winston nodded their heads in agreement with his question.

"Not necessarily," Jhren replied. "Have you ever seen the jugglers who balance bowls of water on sticks?" Everyone nodded affirmation, so he continued. "Well, ever see one of them get about ten bowls balanced and then get distracted?" He didn't give them time to respond before continuing. "Everything is fine until something in the audience catches his eye, and then the bowls start falling, and the water ends up going all over the audience and no one throws him any coins because they are wet and upset. Now, the smart performers use bigger bowls, which looks more impressive, but they use fewer of them, so they don't have to expend as much energy to keep each one on its stick. This magic is the same way: the more scattered it is, the harder it is to keep track of everything and keep it from falling apart. So, since Warrick can sense the whole thing coming apart around him, he just puts one big bowl up and doesn't have to disperse his remaining energy so much to control it."

"Then if we can take him, we can completely confuse the beast-men and make our job easier," Captain Smith said.

Jhren nodded thoughtfully and said, "Yes, *if you can take him*, that would be the case. However, don't expect him to be gallantly leading his troops into battle and conveniently putting himself into the path of an arrow. He may be exhausted and nearly psychotic, but he still isn't stupid. He cares nothing for anyone other than himself. He will expend every one of his Roracks, and his Riders, in an effort to protect himself. Then, when we are fully engaged, he will find an opportunity to go directly after the person he sees as his main enemy in all of this. He will attack Corolan's grandson. He will do everything in his power to kill Delno, even if he ends up killing himself in the effort, too."

"But, surely he must know that, while Delno is a valued commander, and we would miss him sorely if he were killed, we would still fight on even if that happened?" Walker said incredulously.

"No, he doesn't," Jhren replied. At the looks of disbelief from Walker and several others he explained. "Warrick sees this whole war as nothing more than an epic battle between himself and Corolan. He killed Corolan, but Corolan managed to come back, as far as Warrick is concerned, through Delno. Especially in his deteriorated state, he believes that we fight for Delno, and ultimately Corolan, and that if he can kill Corolan again by killing Delno, he will win."

"That makes no sense," Captain Jameson said.

"Sonny," Jhren replied, "I started studying magic and human nature at the ripe old age of four. I've been pursuing those studies without a break for nine decades. I've seen just about every aspect of human behavior there is to see. I never said Warrick's delusions make sense. After all, there's a reason we've been calling him a mad-man."

"Well," Delno said, "there's nothing we can do but play the tiles that have been dealt to us. According to both Paul and Kurt, Warrick's main camp is less than two days' march from our current position. If we veer more north, toward the mountains, and push hard, we can cover much of that distance by tomorrow evening. Since we are no longer trying to hide, I see no reason not to advance to nearly within reach of the enemies' position and be ready for battle the next day."

"Doesn't that leave us exposed to attack?" Jameson asked. "I have no problem with fighting, but I don't want my troops to suddenly find themselves facing a huge group of beast-men who are supported by dragons when they are exhausted. We came to fight, not to commit suicide."

"It won't be suicide," Nassari responded. "You and your men will be supported by dragons also. Not only do we have our bonded pairs, but since Delno had his conversation with Warrick in the Dream State, over a score of unbounded dragons who were not participating have flown here and joined us. Your men will be covered by more than sixty un-bonded dragons, as well as our Riders. Also, do not forget that Brock had gotten the word out and at least another dozen Riders are already here in Horne, and we will most likely join up with them as we get nearer to our enemies."

"I suppose that will make up for lot of the deficit I expect we'll find in our respective ground forces," Winston replied. "Still, we've only seen one enemy Rider since we arrived in Horne, and you only met seven. That leaves Warrick an unknown number of dragons and Riders to throw at us." He turned to Delno and asked, "Didn't those brothers have more information as to how many Riders fly for their former master?"

"Paul thinks there are about two dozen left, though he can't be sure, and Kurt agrees with him. We would know more, but one of the reasons Warrick is so exhausted is that he controls everything down to the fin-est detail. He is so afraid of someone from his own camp trying to usurp his power that he keeps the Riders separated as much as possible. None of them know all of their comrades, or even the exact number of Riders under Warrick's command."

"I can't understand that way of thinking," Winston replied, "but it does make our job harder, because we have no idea what to expect."

"It can also work to our advantage," Nassari interjected. "Our Rid-ers are used to coordinating with not only each other, but also with our troops on the ground. We have worked out signals so that even the un-bonded dragons can see immediately if a ground unit is calling for air support." He paused and looked to Walker, and said, "Those flags you came up with for communicating are a wonderful idea, as are the hand signals you have taught us."

"The beast-men may not be extremely intelligent, but they aren't fooled by false bird calls, either. My people are used to working without support in hostile areas and the beast men have extraordinary hearing. We've had to come up with ways to communicate over these relatively short distances without giving away our positions by using sound."

Nassari nodded and went on with his train of thought. "The Riders on Warrick's side aren't used to working as a cohesive fighting force, and they see their ground troops as nothing more than grist for the mill. Even if the Roracks were bright enough to call for help it is doubtful that any of their Riders would heed that call. Also, they have been kept from working together by their master because of his paranoia. Where we coordinate with each other and shift our tactics constantly to adapt to each other's needs, they simply fly at us as single units with little or no support, unable, as a group, to adjust to our attacks and defenses. We have a definite advantage: providing, of course, we don't throw it away by getting over-confident."

"That's a good point," Brock stated. "One of our biggest concerns is that our Riders will get cocky. The men on the ground won't have that problem, because, I believe, they will be out-numbered by a determined force of Roracks who will fight to the death. It's in the air where we can still lose this war." He paused and looked at all of the commanders. "Notice that I said that we can lose, not that they can win. We need to make sure we don't get too full of ourselves and turn victory into defeat. No matter how badly we beat the other Riders, if our own ground troops aren't able to consolidate that victory, we win nothing."

"It's our job, as Riders," Delno said, "to make sure that the enemy dragons don't harass our army. Remember, Sheila and her un-bonded dragons have been told to target the Roracks and leave the Riders to us. They have specifically been warned that they are in great danger if they attack enemy Riders and shouldn't do so unless they have overwhelming numbers on their side. Therefore, we have the responsibility of keeping the enemy Riders from doing to our ground troops what our un-bonded dragons will be doing to theirs."

"There is one last question," Nassari said. "What about those Felanxes? They are smarter than the Roracks, and they seem to have an inborn hatred of us. They are harsh enemies. How many of them will we be facing?"

"According to Paul and Kurt, there aren't many. Warrick keeps six near his quarters as guards, and they are completely loyal to him, but only to him. It seems that Warrick, Orson, and the magic user I killed in Bourne had to work together to make those they had. They used large wild-cats and magically blended them with men. Somehow the men turned into the Felanxes, and all that remained of the cats were the dried carcasses."

"Si-shorn!" Walker exclaimed. Very few of the men present under-stood the elven swear word, which literally translated, meant "Gods' Excrement," but in reality meant so much more. However, there was no mistaking the emotion behind it. The elf was highly upset at the pros-pect of magically bonding unrelated species in such a way. Walker looked around, and then said, "Foul deeds by foul men."

"I tend to agree with you," Delno said to the elf, "I have personally dealt with three of the creatures, and have found that they are indeed foul works, with an unnatural feel to them. Fortunately, there are only six left. Hopefully, none will escape us."

"There are dragons approaching, Delno. Marlo says that she doesn't know them, but that they haven't readied flame. They claim to be friends and want to land."

"Very well, Love. Find out who they are before we allow them to get closer."

Delno told the non-Riders present what was going on, while Geneva ascertained the identity of the new comers.

"They are Derrick and Reena, and Chureny and Pauline. They are the bonded pairs who have lived in Horne for centuries. They have news about our enemies."

Delno exchanged looks with Brock, and the older Rider nodded. *"Very well, Love,"* Delno said, *"ask them to land and join us."*

CHAPTER 46

"**B**ROCK," DERRICK SAID as he and Chureny entered the commanders' tent. "We had hoped that you would come. I see that you have also brought reinforcements. How many ground troops, and how many dragon Riders have placed themselves under your command?"

Delno was immediately reminded of Simcha by Derrick's mannerisms. He quelled the urge to set the man straight forcefully. He was just about to speak when Chureny beat him to it.

"Really, Derrick, you must learn to be more diplomatic. It is obvious by looking around that we are in the company of a group of commanders who have formed a coalition, rather than one Rider who is in command of this entire camp. Brock may be a good Rider, and he may still have some influence over his cousin who holds the throne in Iondar, but I certainly doubt he is in command of all of these northern men. Also, I am sure that the Elven contingent of this force is under *Elven* control."

"Well said, Rider," Walker said to Chureny. "I am Walker Longleaf, and I am in command of the elves in this company. Colonel Winston Eriksson is in command of the men who have come from Ondar and Palamore. Captain Jameson is in command of those from the northern lands of Corice and Bourne. Our overall commander is this man," he bowed toward Delno, "Delno Okonan, Rider of Geneva, lineage holder of her family."

The significance of Geneva's name and title was not lost on either man. Nor was the meaning of Delno's name. They both knew that Delno bore Corolan's very unusual middle name.

Chureny turned to Delno and said, "I apologize for my friend. We are not used to working closely with the men of Horne. Over the years, they tended to forget that it is we who have kept them safe until this war started. Then, when the rulers of Horne realized that they weren't up to the task of keeping these Roracks in check, they basically turned their forces over to us to lead. Derrick simply made the assumption that the oldest Rider present would be in charge because that is what has been thrust upon us up until now."

"Very well," Delno said, "we are here to deal with Warrick and his Roracks, not make new enemies. Let us get down to business and see how we can work together to defeat our common foe."

He didn't exactly accept the apology, but he had made it clear that he didn't want to pursue the matter. Both of the new Riders looked at each other for a long moment.

Finally, Chureny shrugged and said, "Very well. We have just over two thousand troops who are still alive and capable of fighting. Most of the men we have left are not from Horne. However, their commanders have been killed, and they have joined under our banner. Our enemies are holding at a position less than two days march from here, but we haven't the strength to attack. The Roracks are not moving against us, but they have massed—over seven thousand strong—and are simply waiting, as if they expect something to happen that will stir them into action."

Delno nodded, and then began telling Derrick and Chureny everything, bringing them up to date. The tale took over an hour to tell.

"So, you see gentlemen," Delno said, "what the beast-men are waiting for is me. When Warrick thinks he has me where he wants me, the final battle of this war will commence."

"So you bring a dozen Riders, one of whom is a powerful magic user," Chureny said, "as well as over three score wild dragons. That is quite a feat. Your grandfather talked about the wild dragons being an untapped resource, but I never thought it would be possible to get them to work with us."

"Corolan made the initial contact quite some time ago, but he was killed before he could consolidate his ties with them. Oh, they really do prefer to be called un-bonded, rather than wild. They feel that the term wild is demeaning, and makes them sound uncivilized."

"Very well," Derrick said. "We will call them whatever they wish to be called. But we must get this force moved as quickly as possible. If the Roracks attack our forces now, while your troops are lounging here, this war will be lost."

"First," Delno let the annoyance in his voice come through clearly, "our men are not merely lounging here. Colonel Eriksson's men are resting after having force marched through the night. The rest of our troops engaged a force of about four hundred Roracks this morning and then force marched nearly fifteen miles to join up with the Colonel's soldiers. Our men are getting some much needed rest if they are to be of any use when we do reach the enemy." He paused and Derrick moved to speak but Chureny silenced him by stepping on his foot. "Second," Delno continued, "as we have told you, the beast-men won't move against you so long as Warrick perceives me as being the greater threat. He will hold his forces around him like a shield until we get there."

"So you have told us, but what makes you so sure you are right? The Roracks have shown no sign of such restraint in the past," Derrick said.

"We know we are right," Jhren said, "because we have seen the direct evidence when Warrick threw nearly four thousand Roracks at us in that failed ambush, even though, numerically speaking, we posed no big threat to him and his forces. Then, after that failed attempt, he tried once again to get Delno to join him. When that didn't work, he tried to use magic, in the Dream State, to attack Delno. He is obsessed with Delno as the leader on our side of this war. He believes that if he can kill Delno, he will be victorious, regardless of how many dragons or ground troops we array against him."

"The man would have to be completely insane to think that," Derrick replied.

"Yes," Jhren said seriously, "he has gone utterly, raving, mad."

CHAPTER 47

"WELL, DERRICK," DELNO said as they all conferred once again to finalize the plans for the upcoming battle, "it took us two days to get here and merge with your forces, but as you can see, the Roracks haven't attacked yet. My presence is being kept hidden for the time being, so that this battle will run by our time-table and not Warrick's. Our forces move into position even as we speak."

"Hmmph," Derrick snorted. He and Delno had not learned to get along any better in the two days it had taken to get Delno's combined forces into position, but they had come to terms with their mutual dislike and could work together. "I see that you have inherited your grandfather's arrogance; I just hope that you also got enough of his common sense that your plan doesn't get our troops killed wholesale."

Before Delno could respond hotly to Derrick's comment, Chureny spoke up. "Really, Derrick! Stop making an ass of yourself. Delno has done extremely well, thus far. We have no reason to believe that he won't continue to do so." He turned to Delno and added, "You see, Delno, the problem is that so many people tend to see Riders as something somewhat above royalty, but just below the status of godhood. After nearly eight centuries of such deferential treatment, it is easy to forget that you were once the son of a humble craftsman and have no real military training of your own. When someone comes along who makes you realize all of that, even if he doesn't mean to do so, it can put you off until you can get used to the idea that you are a man, and that there may be others more suited to command than you."

"Enough," barked Brock. Then to Derrick he said, "Chureny is right, though. Delno knows what he is doing. Also, even though Jhren has a delightful personality, and his sparkling conversation is always intriguing," nearly everyone, including Jhren, laughed at that, "those are not the reasons we brought him along. He will help cover the un-bonded dragons while watching any enemy Riders to make sure they don't use magic we can't handle. The un-bonded dragons have become much more adept at shielding themselves, though they aren't as strong magically as those bonded with us. Once that part of his job is under control, he will use his own magic to help as needed." He paused and looked around, giving anyone who wished to add anything time to do so.

Delno spoke up, "We have had eleven more un-bonded dragons join us in the last two days, which brings their total strength to over eighty. Three more Riders have arrived to augment our bonded forces, bringing our total there up to thirty-one. All in all, we will have a very large, impressive force in the air. Once the un-bonded dragons have done their work on the beast-men, our ground forces will move in and mop up any who remain, while our bonded pairs keep the enemy Riders from causing trouble for our army."

Delno waited to see if anyone wanted to add anything or clarify any points. When no one showed any such interest, he said. "We all know what we must do in the morning. I suggest that we retire from this meeting and enjoy what rest we are able to get. I fear that dawn will come long before we wish it to."

Those assembled moved to vacate the command tent. Derrick held back and motioned for Delno to do the same.

After everyone else had left, Derrick said, "Chureny is right. I've never been a military man. My father was a simple leather worker. I was chosen as a candidate by Geneva's mother. It was an accident that she even met me in the first place. Then, after I was trained, I spent my time here keeping the Roracks at bay. My strategy was pretty simple. Whenever I found a large group of them, I would shield Reena while she flamed them. They were usually too damn stupid to even take cover. It's been hard having this command thrust upon us. I've been so afraid of losing men due to my own incompetence that I have probably held them back too much. I just don't want to get them killed."

Delno looked at the older Rider for a moment and then said, "I understand. I feel the same way. However, I've been placed in command, and it's not the first time. I led men in Corice against the Bournese for two years. I don't like losing men either, but men die in war, and someone has to order them to fight."

"How do you get used to it?" Derrick asked.

"You don't," Delno said. "Sometimes, when I lay down to sleep, I still see the faces of those men who died under my command in Corice, and that was a while ago. I'm sure that there will be more faces added to those rosters after this is all over."

The two men just looked at each other for several moments. Finally, Delno said kindly, "Go now, Derrick. Get some sleep if you can. Tomorrow we hold Warrick accountable for his actions."

CHAPTER 48

DELNO MADE A final address to the Riders who had placed themselves under his leadership, as well as the commanders of the other forces. "Since Warrick will be specifically watching for me," Delno said, "I will remain out of sight until the battle is well under way. Even seven or eight thousand Roracks can't stand long against eighty or more dragons flaming them. Remember, an un-bonded dragon may not be as strong magically as a bonded dragon and her Rider combined, but her flame is just as hot and burns just as long. Once we attack the beast-men, Warrick will send most, if not all, of his Riders to reinforce his ground troops in order to protect himself. Our Riders will engage them, but not in single combat. I have no intention of fighting on Warrick's terms. We will hit them hard, and we will fight in coordinated groups. If you are in a group that has lost members and is no longer effective, then join another group. Don't go after any enemy alone. We are not here for personal vengeance. We are here to end this war decisively. Once we have taken the advantage and totally enraged Warrick, I will show myself and lure him out, and then we will end this. Once Warrick is down and we have possession of the compelling stone, the rest will, hopefully, be nothing more than mop-up."

Everyone looked around at their fellows, but no one spoke.

"Since there are no questions, and we all know our jobs, we had best be about it," Delno raised his fist in a sign of victory.

The Roracks were crowded onto a plain that was nearly a mile across. They surrounded a stone building that was situated on the only high ground on the field. Most were reclining, as if they had been asleep and were reluctant to wake up.

The building was all that was left of a fort that had been part of the original outposts built on the edge of Rorack territory to try and contain them. The building was large enough to house three dragons. According to Marlo, the structure was occupied by Hella and two others. She also reported that, as near as she could tell, there were about twenty other dragons in the rocky hills on the north side of the plain. The men of Delno's command were in position on the south side of the plain, waiting for the dragons to do their damage and withdraw before they would advance.

Jhren and Delno had worked together and crafted an illusion that kept Delno hidden from view. That, and distance, would, he hoped, keep him out of the fray, but still allow him to see what was happening so he would have first-hand observations to use in making command decisions.

The first wave of un-bonded dragons flew down and began flaming the beast-men. There were eighty-one dragons in the formation, and they all hit their targets at once. From Delno's hidden vantage point, it looked as if a quarter of the plain suddenly erupted in flames. Many of the beast-men died before they could even get on their feet. The dragons rose as a unit, looking almost like some colossal beast rather than individuals. They circled around to make another run.

Delno expected the dragons hiding in the rocks on the hills beyond the plain to take flight and protect the field, but they stayed hidden while the un-bonded dragons made their second pass. He had no idea why the enemy Riders waited so long, but it wasn't until the un-bonded dragons were pulling up from their third pass, and nearly half of the beast-men on the plain were dead, that they flew into view.

Nineteen enemy dragons gained altitude as the un-bonded dragons began to circle around for a fourth pass. It was clear that they intended to intervene, but as they rose into the air, a sudden, hurricane-force wind hit them. Most of them dropped like stones as they retracted their wings to get beneath the dangerous crosswind, before opening their wings again and arresting their fall. Four were not so fortunate; they misjudged and were killed when they hit the sharp rocks on the slopes.

"Jhren says he doesn't know if he will be able to do that again without depleting himself, but that he got four with that wind he conjured," Geneva *relayed* Jhren's report.

"*Acknowledged,*" he replied. "*Tell the others that now is the time for our Riders to earn their keep. Attack the enemy Riders and protect our un-bonded comrades.*"

"*Done, Love. What about us? Should we begin moving out of hiding yet?*"

"*Not just yet. There are still enough Roracks on the field below that Warrick will feel too safe to come out. We will move soon.*"

Delno was pleased to see that, though the enemy Riders had risen as one, they had not regrouped well after Jhren's crosswind had scattered them. They flew in mostly ones and twos. There was one group of five, but they were simply milling about as if unsure what to do next. Apparently, at least some of Warrick's Riders had believed that all they would have to do was make an appearance and everyone in their path would surrender or run away. Those Riders were confused about their next move now that they faced determined foes.

Meanwhile, the un-bonded dragons made a fourth pass. This time, they took their flame right up to the walls of the building itself. This opened a clear path all the way from the southern end of the plain to the old fort. However, the Roracks on the other side began running to fill the gap. Over half of the Roracks were now dead, and the remainder were beginning to break into smaller groups, but this was no easy rout. Those beast-men still alive were not separating because Warrick had lost control of them. They were breaking into smaller groups so that they would no longer be one large target for the dragons to flame.

"*Tell Jhren that the beast-men are preparing to begin counterattacks on the dragons. They have used arrows sparingly so far, but the initial surprise has worn off and they are regrouping. He must do what he can to help our un-bonded comrades.*"

"*I have relayed the message, and Jhren says he sees it. He will use his magic, but he wants to hold some in reserve for when Warrick shows himself.*"

"*I don't like the thought of facing Warrick without him, but if we don't make Warrick feel truly threatened, he will not show himself at all. Tell him to do what must be done to make those beast men either die or run away.*"

Geneva said nothing for a moment and then relayed Jhren's response, "*I will do what must be done to accomplish your orders, but I hope that doesn't leave you swinging in the wind when Warrick comes out to play.*"

Delno was about to reply when a dragon screamed in agony. Two of the enemy Riders had gotten through and managed to flame an un-bonded dragon who had strayed from the group. She was burned badly and fell mercifully quickly to her death. As her last heroic act she managed to angle her flight right into a tightly-packed group of over a hundred Roracks. She crashed right in the middle of the beast-men, and her flame bladder burst, incinerating over half of them.

Delno aimed a bolt of energy at the nearest pair of the enemies who had killed the un-bonded dragon. He used as much energy as he had used that day he split the small boulder outside Orlean while training under Brock. The dragon pulled up in obvious distress and then went completely slack. Her head hung and she fell, tumbling like so much debris. She was dead before she hit the ground, and her rider joined her when her body crushed him as they crashed. Their companion looked for the source of the attack but could see no one and retreated.

Nassari's group, which now included Paul and two others, charged at and killed two Riders who were also trying to attack the un-bonded dragons. The enemies were making a run at their prey and didn't even look up to see if they were in danger. Wanda and Pina led the group, flaming one before they knew what hit them. The other saw the attack at the last second and tried to avoid it and ran right into the flame streams from Mariah and Saadia, while Terra and Raymond acted as rear-guard.

Five other enemy Riders simply turned and flew away as fast as their dragons could fly. Apparently, they had had enough. Delno was actually beginning to feel that this might just go as planned when Geneva screamed a warning.

"*Two enemy dragons bearing down on us! Hold on!*" she *shouted* as she folded her wings and dropped out of range of the other dragons' flame.

Delno chastised himself for not paying closer attention. He hadn't even been maintaining a shield. He was far enough back that these two shouldn't have found him.

"*They aren't part of the original nineteen who rose up, Love. I don't know where they came from, but they were apparently looking for us.*"

"*Watch out, Geneva,*" he said, "*they're trying to get above us.*" Then an idea struck him and he said, "*Slow down slightly; let them think they are going to make it, but make them work for it.*"

Geneva trusted him and slowed just enough that the other dragons started to pull up and would soon be ahead of her if they pushed themselves hard enough. Just as the lead dragon of the two was getting into position to try and flame them, she ran into an invisible wall. The sound of her neck breaking was audible even over the roar of the wind in Delno's ears. She pitched forward and crushed her rider between her body and the shield that Delno had erected in her path. He had once used the same trick to save Rita's life back in Palamore.

The second dragon ran into the first. Though she wasn't killed by the impact her wings tangled with the dead dragon's wings, and they both fell. The live dragon struggled as she and her Rider plummeted. Finally, less than a hundred feet off the ground, she freed her wings. However, the effort to free herself caused the dead creature to pitch, and its head hit the live dragon's rider. The man went limp and hung over his dragon's neck. Delno didn't know if the Rider was dead or just knocked out, but either way, his dragon withdrew.

During this time, Jhren and the un-bonded dragons hadn't been idle. The Roracks on the plain now numbered less than a thousand. The dragons had made seven strafing runs, and Jhren had used his magic to intensify the fires. The men on the ground were rapidly moving in to attack those beast-men who remained. The rest of the enemy's Riders were engaged with Delno's Riders, but they were heavily outnumbered.

Just then three dragons rose above the walls of the old fort. Delno recognized Warrick and Hella, but had never seen the other two before. Apparently, when Delno had been found, his position had been relayed to Warrick. Warrick and his two companions quickly strove to gain altitude to pursue Delno.

"Careful, Love, that one dragon is nearly as old as Leera. She and her Rider are not novices. I'm calling for help."

Before he could respond, movement on the hills caught his attention. Roracks were pouring out of hiding places like ants from and ant hill. He realized that there must be at least three thousand of them. He now understood Warrick's strategy. He had used seven thousand of the beast-men as bait, and allowed them to be killed. The un-bonded dragons had made seven strafing runs, using up most of their fire. Some might be able to make as many as five more passes before their flame gave out, but most would be lucky to have enough chemicals left for three. The dragons would be doing well if they could get half of these new beast-men before they closed with the army of men who had already committed themselves to the fight on the plain.

Delno was angry. He was angry that Warrick had so callously used his forces, but mostly he was angry with himself for being so easily duped into committing his whole force before he had made sure that his enemy had done the same.

He redoubled his shields and was just about to direct Geneva to go after Warrick when a bolt of magic hit them. If he hadn't just increased his shields, they might have been knocked from the sky. As it was, they had still been hit hard enough to knock Geneva back nearly as far as the length of her body. Geneva grunted, almost stunned by the impact, and Delno saw the older Rider frown in frustration. Apparently, this man had been sure that his magic would kill the dragon and thus the Rider, and was surprised when it didn't. The man looked drained, and Delno was sure that he wouldn't be able to repeat the trick for a while, though he was still dangerous.

Delno called up a bolt of energy and aimed it directly at the Rider and not his dragon. The bolt hit the other Rider's shield. The shield held, but barely. Apparently the man was better at the attack than he was at defense. He was rocked in his saddle, and there was a trickle of blood coming from his nose. The look of surprise on his face told Delno that the other Rider had expected Delno to attack the dragon like he had done to Geneva. By going for the smaller target, Delno had been able to concentrate the bolt.

The man grimaced and readied for another attack. Suddenly, there was a blue blur and the enemy Rider was nearly knocked from the sky as Leera raked his dragon's wing with one set of her front claws. The Rider turned to go after Brock and Leera, but as he did, Fahwn hit them. This time the attack came from the other side, and Fahwn raked the other wing. Just as the Rider tried to turn to face the new threat, an arrow suddenly appeared in the man's shoulder. Delno looked in the direction the arrow had to come from and saw Nat astride Marlo with a bow in his hands.

The arrow had to penetrate the man's shield before it hit, so it wasn't in deep, but it was still a good distraction. The Rider turned to face the new threat, and Leera nearly decapitated him while he was occupied with Nat. The Rider, realizing he now faced an attack by three coordinated opponents, fled to get some maneuvering room.

"Tell them to be careful," he told Geneva.

"Brock says you had damn well better do the same," she responded.

There was a younger Rider with Warrick; Geneva had said his dragon was one of Hella's offspring about fifteen years old, and he hadn't been idle. The dragon had closed the gap between them considerably and was now nearly close enough to flame Geneva. Delno could see her flame bladder expanding and was strengthening his shield when a light blue dragon appeared to materialize out of nowhere and flame the pair head on. The enemy dragon retracted her wings and dropped to safety, but not before getting singed. She screamed as she extended her wings and caught herself. She turned on Will, but Nassari and Wanda flew at her from the side and nearly got her. She managed to avoid Wanda by inches, but was almost hit by Pina. This pair, too, was force to abandon their original target and retreat. Paul and Raymond were hot on their tail as Nassari, Will, and Nadia circled around to get another chance at them.

Warrick was so busy directing the other two he had apparently forgotten Delno and Geneva momentarily; it nearly cost him his life. Geneva dived directly at Hella trying to get the older dragon's wing with her claws. At the last possible second, Hella noticed what was happening and swerved to avoid the collision. Geneva managed to rip a small hole in Hella's wing, but it was nothing serious. She was still aloft and now she was doubly alert for such an attack. Delno put more energy into his shield.

Warrick turned and aimed a bolt of energy right at Delno, just like Delno had done to the other Rider earlier. Delno's shield, however, held fine. It also held as Hella suddenly turned and flamed them, though they felt the heat this time.

He managed a quick glance and discovered that the un-bonded dragons were actually doing quite well against the new Roracks who were joining the fray. Apparently, they realized that they only had a very limited amount of flame left, and were using that only on the large groups that were massing in preparation of charging the men. Also, it looked as though the flames were burning especially hot, so Delno figured that Jhren was helping with the ground war. That was all of the time he could spare for such observations, and he turned back to Warrick.

Warrick and Hella made another pass. This time Geneva avoided them and used her own flame as they went by. Warrick hadn't been shielding as well as Delno had, but they weren't in the flame long, either. Hella screamed, but it was more in anger than pain. The pair circled for another try, but Geneva matched them move for move. Again and again they made passes and flamed at each other. Again and again the flame burned harmlessly on the other's shield, while Warrick and Delno both fired bolts of energy at each other while diverting enough energy to maintain their shields. It was a standoff.

Delno had deflected so much energy with his shield that he was hard pressed to gather enough to reinforce it. He was forced on the last pass to use his own personal energy to shore up the shield against the joint attack of Hella's flame and Warrick's magic. He realized that his battle with Warrick would not be decided with this maneuvering for position. Both he and Warrick were getting fatigued, and neither could continue to maintain their shields and their attacks much longer. He had to admit, though, that the man had reserves Delno had not thought would be there.

"Get above them, Geneva!"

"Delno, you can't; he'll kill you."

"He may very well do that, anyway, unless we end this soon. I am running out of tricks, and you are running out of flame. Now, get me above them!"

Geneva didn't like it, but she realized that he was right. She tried to maneuver herself above Hella. Hella, of course, thought she was trying to get above to flame them, and kept maneuvering to stay on level. Just as it was beginning to look hopeless, there was a red blur that flew right between them and distracted Hella. Delno was about to tell Geneva to relay to Rita to keep herself and Fahwn out of this, when he saw Fahwn out of the corner of his eye helping Brock force their opponent down to the ground.

As Geneva suddenly used the distraction to gain altitude without Hella compensating she said, "There's more than one red dragon here, Love. Thank Sheila if this works."

"Thank her for me, Love, I'm too busy at the moment."

Saying that, he pulled the quick ties loose and launched himself at Hella's back. There was a moment when he was suspended in the air between the two dragons that seemed nearly timeless. Everything moved in slow motion until he remembered to widen his field of view. The world returned to normal speed as his left hand neared his goal.

The dark green dragon didn't even see it coming. She had just realized that Geneva was above her and had started to move out of flame range when Delno grabbed Warrick's collar and pulled himself into a crouch nearly on top of her flame bladder. Hella was totally unsure what to do and hesitated.

Warrick wasn't so easily shocked. Delno was on one knee, crouching just behind him. He quickly thrust Corolan's Dragon Blade into Delno's thigh. Delno felt the blade enter above his knee and travel along the bone and emerge out the back side of his leg just below his hip. Geneva screamed as the blade pierced her Partner. She dove at Hella's face to keep her distracted, so that Delno would have time to recover and attack Warrick.

The pain was incredible, and he wasn't sure why he didn't lose consciousness. He let loose of Warrick's collar and grabbed the man's hand in an iron grip. He could hear several of Warrick's fingers break under the pressure of his dragon enhanced strength. Warrick yelled in pain, and, his right hand pinned in place by Delno's grip, drew his dagger with his left hand and tried to swing it around behind himself and stab the younger man. Fortunately, Delno was positioned too far to Warrick's right, and Warrick couldn't get the blade around as long as Delno was still holding Warrick's right hand pinned to the hilt of Corolan's saber.

Delno drew his own Dragon Blade, and Warrick tried desperately to shift to prevent him from being able to stab or slash him. Delno realized that it was still a standoff, but in this standoff he was at a definite disadvantage. Even if Hella didn't overcome her shock at suddenly finding him crouching on her back and roll to dislodge him, he would eventually bleed to death. As Delno looked for some way to end this, he saw the compelling stone hanging on a cord around Warrick's neck, and he knew that this had to end. If it he didn't do something decisive now, Warrick would kill him, and this could go on for years.

Warrick was just beginning to get a look of triumph on his face, and he could feel Hella preparing to do a roll. He reversed the saber in his hand and raised it high. Just as Warrick realized what he was about to do and started frantically trying to get around to stop him, Delno plunged the blade straight down.

Brock had told him months ago, that, in his hand, his Dragon Blade could break steel and even penetrate the scales of a dragon. Delno plunged the blade straight into Hella's flame bladder nearly to the hilt. Warrick's eyes went wide and Delno released the man's broken hand from his grip. Warrick let go of the hilt of the Dragon Blade that was impaling Delno's leg and Delno worked his own blade back and forth, widening the tear in Hella's flame bladder. Then, as Hella screamed in pain and anger, he *yelled* to Geneva, "*Catch me, Love,*" and launched himself from Hella's back.

As he pulled his own blade free of the dragon's hide, a gout of flame erupted and his arm, shoulder, and the right side of his face blistered. Somehow, he managed to hang on to his own sword despite the pain from both the burns and the leg wound. He was free falling and wondering what it would feel like to hit to the ground when he felt clawed feet encircle his torso. The claws didn't penetrate him, so he figured it must be Geneva and not an enemy dragon who had caught him.

At the same time that Delno was pushing off, the flame that erupted from Hella's flame bladder surrounded Warrick. He had tried desperately to rid himself of the safety straps that held him in place, but failed. He also couldn't get a shield up in time. He was dead before the pressure let up enough to stop the jet of flame. Once the pressure let up, the gas burned inside the bladder and it exploded, but with so little of the gas left it didn't blow hard enough to dislodge the dead body of the Rider. It did, however, cause the dragon to fall screaming from the sky. Dragon and Rider plummeted down and landed with a sort of muffled explosion inside the walls of the old fort. A reddish-green shock-wave traveled from point of impact out to the walls, and then shot into the air several hundred feet.

Geneva set her semi-conscious Rider on the ground, and then landed a few feet away. Because Geneva had called to Marlo, Nat was already on the ground waiting for them. He quickly ran to Delno and began examining his injuries. Geneva, who had had to dampen down the contact between herself and her rider so that she wouldn't be overwhelmed by his agony, had managed, despite her anxiety, to use magic to stop the bleeding. Nat pulled Corolan's Blade from Delno's leg and immediately started healing the wound. Once Delno's leg was healed, he turned his attention to the nasty second-degree burns. Even after being healed, it was still nearly a quarter of an hour before Delno regained full consciousness.

He came to his senses with his head cradled in Rita's lap. She was staring at him through the tears that were running unchecked from her eyes. He reached up and put his hand behind her neck and pulled her to him, and they kissed each other deeply.

"Is there some reason that you refuse to keep your arse in that saddle?" Brock asked. "We were just finishing up with Kern. If you had simply kept Warrick at bay for a few more minutes, we would have been able to come and help you."

"I don't think I could have lasted a few more minutes," Delno replied. "I was running out of tricks, and had been forced to use my own energy to reinforce my shield once already by the time I decided to go after Warrick directly."

Delno moved to get up and Rita held him where he was. "You just lie still," she said. "Nat will see you again soon, and then you can get up."

"Nonsense, woman," he said. "I am fine now. I need to get back into this war. The last time I looked, and it couldn't have been that long ago, we were holding our own, but it was still a contest." He looked around and then added, "Why is everyone standing around? There are still Roracks to deal with."

"Relax," Brock told him. "As soon as Warrick died, the Roracks ceased fighting cohesively, and began to break up into small groups. Most of the small groups turned tail and ran with our men chasing them all the way to the hills. There are no beast-men left alive on the plain, and those who escaped have scattered."

"Still," Winston said as he walked up, "between the dragons and our ground troops, we killed nearly nine thousand of them today. It will be a long time before they return in sufficient numbers to cause problems again. And with that compelling stone gone, it isn't very likely they will organize if they do recover their numbers."

"The compelling stone is gone?" Delno asked.

"Yes, my friend," Walker said. "Wanda flew me to the fort and I went in to look for it. It is the reason that my clansmen and I were sent to this war. I was to recover the stone or destroy it. We found the remains of Warrick and Hella in the fort, along with those cat-men that you and Nae-sah-rae told us about." Walker and Nassari had become such good friends that the elf had insisted on changing the man's name to make it sound more Elven. "However," he continued, "the man and dragon, as well as the foul creatures, have been . . . changed. Jhren is still examining them."

Before Delno could ask any more questions, Geneva said, "*Love, are you all right now?*"

"I am fine, Dear Heart, there's no need to worry."

"*I wasn't worried. Well, I was before, but I saw Nat heal you, so I knew you were fine physically. What I mean is, Nat and the others are healing the injured on our side, but there are many casualties, both human and dragon. Most of the Riders and dragons are assisting in the efforts, but most of them have not studied anatomy as you have, so Nat has asked for your help with some of the more serious cases if you are up to the task.*"

"I am up to it, Love. Take me to them."

CHAPTER 49

"I'M NOT SURE exactly what happened to cause this," Jhren said, as he and Delno examined the remains of Warrick and Hella. They were, quite literally, turned to stone, and had become part of the bedrock on which the fort was situated. The six Felanxes had also been turned to stone when their master had crashed into the old fort. The cat-men were standing around the central courtyard of the fort just as they had been standing when the dragon and Rider had hit. They were still gripping the vicious-looking, heavy blades that they carried, though those had been altered just like the bodies of the creatures.

"What's your theory, then?" Delno asked.

Jhren seemed reluctant to answer. Finally he said, "Well, I'm pulling this out of my hat, because I only have limited experience with things like the compelling stone. . . ."

"I'm not going to hold your feet to a fire if you're wrong, old man. I would just like to get an idea of what has happened," Delno said.

"You always have been too damned impatient for your own good," the wizard replied. "As I said, I'm just working with a theory here. I will need to do more study before I can be even marginally sure of anything."

Delno looked at the conjurer for a long moment before Jhren finally relented, "All right. This is what I think happened. That compelling stone, if you shade the area you can still see it glowing faintly." Jhren paused for a moment while he spoke to Carra.

Carra nodded, and extended her wing to shade the large raised area where the bodies of Warrick and Hella had fused to the stone of the huge central yard inside the old fort. Delno could see through the semi-transparent rock that had once been a dragon and her rider that there was indeed a faint glow coming from about the area where Warrick's body would have been situated on Hella's neck.

"Reach out and use your magical senses," Jhren said.

Doing so, Delno realized that the energy he could see coming from the stone within the rock extended well down within the earth. His surprise showed on his face.

"Yes," Jhren said softly, "that energy goes all the way down, and seems to be connected to the energy of the earth itself."

Delno said nothing, but continued to examine the phenomenon with all of his senses.

"I managed to learn a few things while I was traveling with your grandfather," Jhren said. Delno gave Jhren his attention, but couldn't help but continue to study the stone. Jhren went on with his ideas, "This is the area where the mages who originally made the magical creatures—trolls, Roracks, and dragons—did their work. One of the reasons this fort stands here is because the energy of the place lends itself to controlling such creatures. The compelling stone itself comes from around here somewhere, perhaps from this very place."

Delno stared, wide-eyed and open-mouthed, at Jhren.

"Oh, the compelling stone came from this very place, my good wizard," Walker said as he approached. "This book that I have recovered from Warrick's quarters confirms that." He displayed a very old tome he was carrying. "This is one of the books that was stolen from our libraries. There are references to this plain, and specifically to this building. This book clearly names this as the place where the compelling stone was made."

Jhren looked at the book the way a greedy man would look at a precious gem held just out of reach. Walker smiled at him and let him look at the pages he had opened the book to. Jhren read as quickly as he could, as if afraid the book would be taken away without warning.

"According to this," Jhren said, as Walker allowed the mage to take possession of the book, "this place didn't start off as a fort. It was the site of the original experiments to create a magical creature that would bond with a person and combine powers with him. It is hinted at here that this place may even date all the way back to the Mage Wars." Jhren was obviously in awe of what he was reading.

"That is not a confirmed fact, but it is possible," Walker interjected. "Whether or not this building survived the Mage Wars that nearly destroyed everything cannot be proven. This building, however, is the oldest standing man-made structure in the world."

Delno looked around with a new perspective. It was awe-inspiring to think of the age of the place.

"The mage, or possibly mages, who made the magical creatures made many beasts that were unfit, or completely uncontrollable, and had to be destroyed," Walker continued. "The arrogance of those people is astounding. To treat their fellow creatures such. . . ." He shuddered and then switched back to his subject. "They finally made the trolls, which were little more intelligent than the stupidest of beasts. The trolls were highly resistant to magic, but were not magically active. They could be controlled through training and conditioning, the way a circus trainer controls dangerous beasts. However, the mages saw no point in trying to use them since they were worthless for the intended purposes. They didn't destroy the trolls outright because they thought that they were heading in the right direction. While they experimented on magically bonding human and Elven stock with them, some of the trolls escaped and moved off into the wilderness to establish themselves as viable species, or were later released. That point isn't exactly clear in the book."

Delno shook his head. "I've heard much of this. The species they got from those experiments are what we call Roracks, or beast-men. They, once again, found that they didn't get the characteristics they were looking for, and then went on to create the dragons."

"That's partly right," Walker said. "The beast-men were uncontrollable, and magic resistant. However, they at first thought that by controlling this new creation they might still salvage something. Also, regardless of whether or not the Roracks ever proved useful, they felt the need to have better control over any future creations." He paused for a moment and looked at Jhren to see if the wizard wanted to add anything. Jhren, however, was deeply engrossed in the book, so Walker continued. "They used the magic of this place and created the compelling stone."

"I thought they continued their experiments on creating a species they could bond with, and made dragons next," Delno said.

"No," Walker replied. "They abandoned the Roracks completely after a short time, when they learned that they couldn't increase their powers by using the foul beasts. They did continue to use elves and humans as unwilling participants, but it is unclear what other species they added to get dragons."

Jhren looked up and said, "That stone was drawn up from the very bedrock where it now, once again, resides. It seems to have fused itself back into the bones of this place when Warrick and Hella fell here, and it has fused them into the rock with it. I believe that Warrick poured so much of himself into the stone controlling the Roracks, that he, and Hella, in the end, simply became part of it, and now share its fate."

"That sounds like a good theory," Walker replied. "At any rate, as regards the dragons, they weren't created until after the stone. When the mages did get the dragons, they thought that they had achieved success, until they found that the dragons were highly intelligent and morally resistant to being used as mere slaves to the mages' desires. The mages then tried to use the compelling stone to control the dragons. Unlike their earlier creations, the dragons were not only intelligent enough to realize what the mages were trying to do, they were also able to use magic to defend themselves. The mages didn't count on the dragons being as powerful magically as themselves, and the resulting battle caused the stone to be damaged. There were losses on both sides of that war and, in the end, the mages were weakened enough for the humans and elves to put a stop to the mages quest to create a magical creature to increase their power. This building was left to rot, while the dragons went their own way and disappeared from history for over a thousand years."

"If this place was left to rot, why is it still so intact?" Delno asked, looking at the walls around him.

"Well, much magic was used in the construction of the place. It was, after all, owned by powerful mages. Later, when the Roracks resurfaced and began causing troubles, this place was converted to a fort since it was so conveniently close to the beast-men's territory. For thousands of years it was manned by the ancestors of the people of this land. It was a fort for so many generations that those who manned it forgot that it was ever anything else."

"Most interesting," Delno said almost to himself as he walked around looking at the structure. Then he looked at the mound of new stone that had once been Warrick and Hella and said, "Most interesting, indeed."

CHAPTER 50

WILL STEPPED UP on the small flat spot of rock at one end of what had become known in the last few days as Rider's Mound. It had taken the combined efforts of Jhren and Delno, as well as Geneva and Carra, to turn this spot into a flat platform. The platform was now situated right over the glow from the remains of the compelling stone. It had also taken the combined efforts of the two Riders and two dragons to magically inscribe the words Will was about to read. The entire mound looked like obsidian, but was harder than diamond. Apparently, the magic that fused the bodies of Warrick, Hella, and the cat-men, into the stone had also hardened it.

Will raised his right hand to take the oath of the Legion of Riders. "I solemnly swear to serve my fellow creatures to the best of my ability and to uphold the just laws of any land I find myself in. I swear that I will not participate in any attempt to usurp power from the rightful and just rulers of any sovereign nation in an effort to gain power for myself or any master I have chosen to serve, and will make every effort to protect the sovereignty of any nation that is rightfully and justly ruled. I will abide by the just edicts laid down by the Council of Riders, membership in which this oath entitles me. Lastly, I swear that I will always do my best to act in a manner that will bring honor to me, my draconic partner, our respective families, and The Legion of Riders - which I now join freely and without coercion."

Will went slightly blank for a second while the magic that Delno and Jhren had worked into the oath surged through him. Then he smiled at his older brother as he stepped down. He was the seventh Rider to take the oath. Delno had been the first, and Jhren had been the second. Then Brock, followed by Rita. Nassari had stepped forward at that point and he had been followed by Nadia.

For the next two hours, the Riders who had flown against Warrick stepped up and took the oath, one after another. As each person who took the oath stepped down, the platform glowed for a few moments before returning to its inert state.

Finally, after all had finished, Delno called for the prisoners to be brought forward. There were five Riders who had flown for Warrick who had not either fled outright or been killed in the battle. Chief among them was Kern. Kern had been a Rider nearly as long as Brock, and the two had often found themselves at odds concerning their duties as Riders over the years. Brock had usually found Kern to be harsh when dealing with non-Riders, and Kern had time and again accused Brock of being soft-hearted to the point of being soft-headed.

"Kern," Delno said, "Step forward from the others. Your fate is to be decided first."

Kern sneered, "Upstart! I was a Rider before your father was more than a wicked thought in his father's mind. I do not accept your authority here."

"Save your haughty speeches," Brock said. "Our authority here comes from beating you and your master in your bid to take over the freely governed lands of men. We have beaten you soundly, and you now stand next to what is left of your former Leader." Brock pointed at Rider's Mound. Kern visibly flinched and refused to look at the rock formation. "Now be silent," Brock continued, "and you may find some measure of mercy here."

"I seek none of your mercy," Kern said belligerently. "I am a Rider and, therefore, not responsible to you, or anyone else. Riders are independent, governed by none but themselves."

"If you were a wise, compassionate man, I might agree with you," Delno said. "However, you are a murderer."

"I killed in war. Can you say that you did any differently?"

"I killed only those enemies who had openly declared war on me," Delno responded. "Quincy had not openly declared war on you. He was merely trying to protect the people of Horne from the beast-men. You blasted him out of the sky from ambush before he even got a chance to know you were there. You laid in wait for him, and killed him with premeditation. We know this because Geneva and the other two lineage holders here were able to draw that information from Serrin's mind. You may be able to convince yourself that you are something more noble than a backstabbing assassin, but your dragon actually feels regret over the incident."

"I am a soldier, and I demand that you either free me or kill me now," Kern replied. "I have no desire to listen to any more of your accusations."

"Your dragon was injured . . ." Delno began, but Kern spoke up and cut him off.

"You mean she has been crippled, by you and your lap dog." He indicated Brock.

"Serrin's wings were injured when you and she fought with us. She refused to allow anyone to get near her to heal her. Dragons heal much more rapidly than humans do, and her injuries have set. She is crippled as a consequence of her threatening to kill any who got close enough to help her while the injuries were still fresh. She has since come to accept that she is to blame for her infirmity. She is incapable of anything more than short clumsy flights at this time, and she is completely incapable of carrying your weight. However, there may be hope for her."

Kern looked up sharply. He was bitter that his dragon hadn't been healed, and that her injuries left her disabled, but now Delno could see hope in his eyes as well as the underlying defiance.

"There are healers among the elves who have studied dragon anatomy much more extensively than anyone here. Walker thinks it is possible that, even if they cannot restore her completely, they may be able to help her. Such will take a long time, quite likely years." He paused for a moment before continuing. "You have shown no remorse for all that you have done, and your deeds could be punished by death, and no one would fault us for such." Kern stiffened, but didn't say a word. "However, Serrin, now that she is no longer in proximity to the compelling stone that was being used against her, has shown great sorrow and regret for her part in all of this. She is still basically a good person. Perhaps it is unfortunate that she is bonded to you, for we would like to be rid of the threat that you might find a way to pursue vengeance. We can't execute you, though, without sentencing her to the same. Therefore, since the Elves have offered to take custody of you while they try to help Serrin, Jhren will magically place a stone over your heart. The stone is one of a pair. If you try to stray too far from the mate of the stone you bear, you will be killed by the magic. If you remove the stone that is placed on you,

you will be killed by the magic. The only way to remove the stone is if the person who holds its mate freely releases you."

Delno nodded to Jhren, who stepped forward with a small bundle in his hand. He walked to Kern and stood in front of him expectantly.

"If you agree to this, Kern," Delno said, "you will travel to the Elven lands with Walker and his clansmen. If you refuse, then we have no choice but to keep you here in chains, quite possibly for the rest of your life. So you see, you can accept this, and face the prospect of redeeming yourself, which will give Serrin a chance at getting the healing she needs; or, you stay here as a prisoner and condemn her to a life of disability. Which is it to be?"

Kern stood straight, and for a moment, everyone thought he would refuse. Then his eyes went slightly blank, and all of those gathered understood that he was in contact with Serrin; when he looked back at Delno, much of the defiance, though not all of it, had gone from his eyes.

"I accept the terms," he said, and hung his head.

Jhren opened the bundle and pulled out a small flat stone. There was no cord by which it could be suspended. Jhren said, "Remove your shirt."

Kern looked at him coldly for a moment, but then pulled the garment off over his head.

"There will be some pain," Jhren told him. "We didn't make it painful on purpose, and we take no pleasure in your discomfort."

Kern nodded his understanding. Jhren brought the stone up to his lips and said the words that would complete the spell that he had placed on it. He then held the talisman in front of Kern's chest, right over the man's heart. It shimmered for a few seconds and then became somewhat fluid and moved onto the man's skin. Kern screwed up his face to resist crying out as the stone bubbled and shifted until it was imbedded into his flesh. The stone solidified, and Kern looked down in a mixture of curiosity and disgust, while Jhren moved to Walker and handed him the pouch that contained the master stone.

"The Elves have accepted custody of you, Kern," Delno said. "They are your jailers, and hopefully, they will ultimately be your saviors; for it is our hope that you will learn compassion and humility while you live among them. We would like to, in the future, welcome you back as a contributing member of Dragon Rider society."

Kern said nothing as Raymond and Nadia stepped forward and led him away to the Elven camp just outside the walls.

"Now then," Delno said, "the rest of you have to be dealt with."

He looked at other prisoners. Two were barely older than Paul's brother, and the older two were no more than in their early twenties. One of the younger two rubbed his chest and stared directly at Jhren, looking to see if the wizard had any more bundles with him.

Delno drew a deep breath. "You have all been part of the war effort in Warrick's camp, but we can connect you to no specific crimes; you haven't committed murder, or even stolen anything, as far as our lineage holders can tell from questioning your dragons. You killed no one during the last battle, and your worst offense is that you have acted as lookouts and scouts for Warrick. Your dragons have displayed remorse at any part they had in this whole affair, and they believe that you are basically worthwhile human beings. Therefore, it is the decision of this council that you are to be released. We require that you separate from each other, but you may join any group of Riders here with whom you wish to travel, providing you stay clear of Kern. This council will meet once a year from this time on, and while you may return and be present at those meetings, you won't be eligible to join us for three years. If you agree to those terms, you are free to go."

None of the four refused to accept the terms. They left quickly, as if half expecting to find out that the offer had been a cruel joke, and they would be brought back and punished. They didn't immediately leave the area, though they did stay away from the Elven camp where Kern was settled.

"Now our last bit of business," Delno said to those still present. "I am obligated to go back to Corice and deal with the problems that have plagued my homeland for generations. I must go back and put an end to the cycle of war between Corice and Bourne. Any Riders who will go with me will be welcome. I would like to take such a show of force that the Bournese will feel compelled to talk rather than try to fight. However, I also understand that some Riders must remain here in Horne to ensure that the beast-men that got away don't somehow regroup and again threaten the people of this land."

"I will stay," Chureny spoke up. "I have lived here so long that I consider this land to be my home anyway. I can't see myself leaving." He turned to Derrick expectantly.

"Before I met this company and took that oath, I might have said the same," Derrick intoned. "Now, however, I realize that I have come to resent the people of this land for their slights over the years. I cannot stay and serve them to the best of my ability while that enmity is still within me. Therefore, I believe I need to travel for a time to put such pettiness behind me. If they will have me, I will travel with the Elves for now. Perhaps I, too, can find healing in their fair lands."

"I would like to stay," Raymond said. "I have never been far from my homeland, but I find that, despite the harshness of the country itself, these mountains give me a strange sense of peace. Terra likes it here, too. I have only met a very few people from Horne, and they have, thus far, treated me well. While I understand Derrick's sentiment, someone should stay in his place." Then he nodded and said, "Yes, I will stay, at least for a time. I trust that Delno, and those who accompany him, can handle the situation in the north without my assistance."

"I too, feel compelled to return to Corice," Nassari put in. "When we've settled things in the north, I believe that I will return here and organize this fort properly as the 'Headquarters of the Legion of Riders' should be organized. Once that is done, I intend to travel south and see the marvelous lands of the Elves that my good friend, Walker, has told me so much about."

It was another two hours before everyone had declared his or her future plans as Riders. Then they all retired to their respective camps. Delno and Rita had taken Warrick's old quarters. There was even a bath, though the water had to be drawn from the pump in the central yard, heated, and carried by the bucketful. Delno found that he could use his magic to heat the water once it was in the tub, which saved time.

"So, explain something to me, Handsome," Rita said as Delno moved the sponge back and forth over her back.

"If I can, Beautiful."

"Why didn't you just force Kern and the others to take the same oath the rest of us took?"

He was thoughtful for a moment before answering. "Jhren and I thought about that. However, binding someone with magic is similar to binding them with rope. The magic is stronger, but the bonds can still be cut if you work hard enough at it. If we had forced Kern to take the Rider's oath, he would have simply started looking for a way to break that oath without incurring magical consequences, and he would eventually have succeeded. Then he would be free to seek revenge."

"Ok, I'll give you that one. But what about the others? Now that Warrick is gone, they actually seem like decent young men."

"Yes, they do," he replied, "and that is why we didn't give them the opportunity to take the oath right now." She leaned forward and gave him a look over her shoulder like she thought he was crazy. "Look at it this way," he went on, "if those young men were sworn to service now, they might begin to resent it. However, we sent them on, and they are now traveling with others from our original group who have taken the oath. They want to be part of the group, and they will see the oath as a way to get that. So, taking the oath becomes a desirable thing. In the meantime, those men, still young enough to be influenced, will begin to work at becoming worthy of taking the oath so that by the time they are sworn to service, service will be second nature to them."

"Ok, then," she said, "Why take an oath at all? It is only binding so long as the person taking it is serious about it."

"Well, this oath is binding on a slightly deeper level than that, but essentially you are correct." He paused while he rinsed the soap off of her back. "I originally wanted to work a spell that would bond all Riders to service and completely eliminate the possibility that someone like Warrick would be able to try to take power again. After talking with Jhren and Brock about it a few times during our trip, I came to realize that there are just too many variables to do that. No matter how specific you think you are, you will always have some kind of loophole. So, we settled for creating a cohesive group of Riders who are willing to swear an oath that binds them to service. This way we create a group of Riders who have a strong bond with each other. Hopefully, when the next threat comes, we won't have as much problem putting together a response to it, and the enemy won't get as strong a foothold before we get organized."

"That sounds a bit off from what you originally said you wanted to accomplish," she said.

"Farther off than you think." She gave him another 'look', and he said, "Remember that part about loopholes?" She nodded, so he continued, "Well, the loophole in this oath is in the intent. We have sworn service to uphold the 'just and rightful' rulers and the 'just laws' of the land. So, if we see a ruler as unjust, or think a law is unjust, we are not going against our oath if we act."

"I had actually wondered about that," she said.

"Yep," he said as he grabbed a towel and held it for her, "that's how I intend to get away with removing Torrance from the throne of Bourne."

He paused and watched while she wrapped the towel around her head, then handed her a second towel to dry her body. Then he began drying himself.

"If one of your first acts as a member of the Legion of Riders is to remove the rightful heir from the throne of Bourne—not that I'm complaining, mind you," she said, "then why did we go through all of that out there today?"

"First, no man can be considered the rightful ruler of a land if he is willing to send two hundred children under his rule to their deaths in combat simply because doing so will help him further his ambition to subjugate his neighbors." She nodded her agreement, and then wrapped the towel around herself for warmth before starting to dry her hair. "Also, I don't intend to '*participate in any attempt to usurp power from the rightful and just rulers of any sovereign nation in an effort to gain power for myself or any master*'. I have no master, and I don't intend to try and hold power in Bourne myself. I simply want to stop this insane ritual of Bourne trying to conquer my homeland every generation or so. That will stop the killing of hundreds of men from both sides, and stop them nearly bankrupting both kingdoms every time it happens."

He remembered that he hadn't pulled the plug from the tub and did so before continuing. "The main reason for all of that today is to bind us together as a group. The council will meet once a year, more often if it becomes necessary, and we will work out policies that we all agree to abide by. Also, before now, the Riders didn't even try to keep in close contact. Craig is an extreme example of it: this is the first time he's left those Elven libraries in over a century. The only reason you ever met him was that you traveled to the Elven lands with Brock, and then again over a decade ago when you took some correspondence to the Elves as a favor to the King of Trent. However, even in the less extreme instances, many Riders go decades without seeing other Riders. There's no peer pressure to do the right things, or even just be good people. This way, we stay in touch, and help keep each other honest."

"And you said you weren't any good at this kind of thing," she said.

"No," he replied, "I said I wasn't any good at lying, and I'm not. This isn't a lie, it's subterfuge." At her raised eyebrow, he added, "It's a fine line of distinction, but there is a difference."

He paused for a moment and then added, "Joking aside, though, the magic is still binding. Also, remember that each Rider who takes the oath is part of a bonded pair, and therefore brings the powerful magic of the pair, which strengthens the magic of the oath itself. Therefore, I wouldn't plan on trying to take over the world any time soon if I were you."

"Well," she said, "you promised me more than a bath tonight, and that better not have been *subterfuge*."

He smiled and let her lead him to the bed.

CHAPTER 51

T HE WHITE FLAG blew gently in the wind as Delno and General Dreighton, along with Brock, Nassari, Rita and Adamus, waited halfway across Stone Bridge. The flag had been hung on the massive iron gate of the fortification a quarter of an hour before they walked out on the bridge, and since they had come out from the gate, they had been waiting that long again. Finally, a group of Bournese approached the other side bearing their own white flag, indicating that they were willing to talk peacefully. Delno recognized the pock-marked face of the general who had taken command after he and Geneva had killed the former commander during the last failed attempt the Bournese had made at taking the passage.

Delno and his group had flown straight across the mountains on the south-western edge of Corice to Stone Bridge from Horne. They had pushed hard, stopping only long enough to rest at the end of each day, and the trip had taken three and half days. Then, using the dragons to relay messages, Delno had gotten Dorian to place the Corisian forces gathered on their side of the bridge under his command. He was now ready to push forward and get this whole affair over with.

"Have you finally regained some measure of good sense and decided to surrender?" the Bournese general said. "If so, open those gates and have your men stack their weapons and ready themselves to be taken prisoner."

"Enough nonsense!" Delno snapped. The Bournese general took a small step back. "I have not pushed myself for more than three days to get here from Horne to listen to any of your posturing. Be silent and pay attention if you want to avoid many needless deaths."

"You have no right to speak to me that way!" the man replied. "I don't have to stand here and listen to this."

"No, you don't have to stand here and listen," Delno retorted. "You can turn and leave, and I will be left with no choice but to rain fire down upon your camp until you, and all of your men, are dead."

"You have neither the authority nor the means to do such thing," the general sneered.

"Oh, don't I?" Delno looked behind him and Geneva and all of the other bonded dragons present moved to the edge of the Corisian side of the canyon. He looked at the men from Bourne and asked their commander, "Does that do anything to change your mind?"

The Bournese general's staff officers visibly paled. The general himself wasn't so easily intimidated, though. He had taken over the command after his predecessor had been killed and had no first-hand knowledge of what dragons could do. "I see nine dragons. That is hardly what I would call an overwhelming force."

"That is because you weren't there when just three of those dragons killed five hundred of your troops and forced the remainder to surrender on the plain outside Larimar. Nor were you here when those same three dragons put an end to the first and only attempt to take this bridge since we began construction of the fortifications. It is because your predecessor was foolish enough to believe that he and his pet magic user could stand up to our dragons that you were given this post. You may have seen his remains in the burned out command tents when you arrived."

The Bournese staff officers inched away from their commander as if to prevent being considered guilty by association, or possibly killed by accident if the man continued to anger the Dragon Rider.

"Who is posturing now?" the man said. "You may have won some temporary victories, but we will soon be reinforced with dragons also. Then it is you who will be at a disadvantage."

"Do you refer to Warrick and his Riders?" Delno asked. "I wouldn't hold my breath while waiting, if I were you." The Bournese's eyes widened. "Do you not recall me saying that I just came from Horne? What exactly do you think I was doing down there?" Delno gave them a moment to absorb the implications of the question before he removed any doubt. "I killed Warrick two weeks ago. He is interred at the old fort on the edge of the Roracks' territory. Those of his Riders who weren't killed or taken prisoner were scattered and will be a long time recovering before they will be a threat to anyone. His mighty army of beast-men is destroyed."

"You lie," the general responded.

"As I once told your predecessor, I never lie. I've never been any good at it," Delno replied. "However, just in case you think that your forces would stand a chance against the nine dragons you have seen. . . ." Delno looked at Geneva for a moment and she nodded.

More dragons began stepping up to the edge of the canyon. Within minutes, the nine bonded dragons had been joined by twenty-seven more who wore no saddles. They were, of course, the remnants of the unbonded dragons who had been part of the dragon army in Horne. These twenty-seven, most under three decades old, had traveled with Delno and his group from Horne to help Delno, but also to get help finding Bond-mates. Although Delno had not made helping with the war a condition for finding them human Partners—in fact, he was emphatic that he would help them regardless—they all volunteered anyway.

Delno turned to the Bournese men, many of whom had gone the color of bleached linen: even the general had visibly paled at the site of nearly forty dragons set against him. "As you can see, we have more than nine dragons." He paused to let them look at the dragons for another few moments. "What you see arrayed against you on our side of this canyon is more than enough firepower to kill every man on your side within moments of beginning our attack. We have no desire to kill you or your men. Our quarrel is with your king. However, make no mistake about our resolve. Tomorrow, our troops will advance across this bridge. The dragons will lead the way and annihilate any resistance that lies between our army and your capitol. If you oppose us, your men will not die honorably, killed in battle by enemy men. They will die horribly, burned to death by dragon fire before our soldiers even step foot on the bridge."

"You can't do this! This, this, this . . ." The Bournese general was having difficulty making coherent speech. "It simply goes against every rule of warfare we have ever agreed upon."

"Are you speaking of the rules of warfare that your king so callously sets aside when it is in his interest to do so?" Delno asked. "Let me assure you, we only have one rule for this war; secure the unconditional surrender of Bourne at all costs. We will settle for nothing else. Either your men will lay down their arms, or they will be killed."

The Bournese general started to say something, but Delno held up his hand and said, nearly shouting, "Silence! There is no more to be said here today. We will have your answer, one way or another, tomorrow morning when we start our advance."

He turned and strode back to the iron gates. The rest of Delno's party turned, one at a time, and followed.

"Do you think that Bournese popinjay will tell his men to lay down their arms?" Dreighton asked as he poured wine for himself and the Riders after dinner that evening.

"It's hard to read the man," Delno admitted. "He is terrified at the prospect of facing the dragons, but he is anxious to prove himself. Also, I think that he is still hopeful that we are lying about events in Horne. However, his staff officers were keen to do what is necessary to avoid facing us. It was the younger officers who delivered up the last commander and surrendered back in Larimar."

"I believe," Brock said, "that tomorrow will be here all too damned early. We have pushed ourselves, as well as our dragons, hard over the last few weeks. Since our plans are set, I am going to finish this glass of wine and go to bed."

Nassari laughed and added, "I wish we could have spent the night in Larimar. It would be nice to have a real bed before we start another campaign. However, Brock is right: tomorrow will not wait for me because I am tired. Bed, of any kind, sounds quite good."

He got up and bowed to those present. Then he left the fire and headed off into the darkness. Delno did notice, however, that Nassari had headed in the same direction that Nadia had gone a few minutes earlier.

Delno drained his glass and took Rita by the hand. They would do nothing more than sleep tonight, but he was still glad that they no longer felt the need to take the precaution of sleeping in separate tents to avoid assassins.

Delno observed that the Bournese had indeed stacked all of their weapons away from their camp, and they were presenting a completely non-aggressive attitude as he and his Riders led the way across the bridge the next morning. Just when he thought that this really would go smoothly, two of the young staff officers approached swinging a white flag almost wildly. They came within about fifty feet of Geneva and stopped. Delno dismounted and waved them forward while Brock and Rita covered him in case this was some trick.

The men stood frozen in place. They were obviously afraid to come closer. "Well," Delno shouted, "come ahead; if I wanted to harm you we wouldn't be talking now, you'd already be dead." His choice of words didn't seem to give them much more confidence. "Come on; you won't be hurt if you don't do anything to threaten me or my partner."

The taller of the two looked at his companion and shrugged. Then he moved forward with his fellow following closely behind. When they were within five feet of Delno, they stopped and the taller man said, "We have a bit of bad news, I'm afraid, sir."

Delno shook his head gently. After waiting a moment he prompted, "Well, what's the news?"

"It's General Parsins, sir, our commander."

Delno put his thumb and forefinger on the bridge of his nose and shook his head. "He hasn't decided to lead a force against us, has he?"

"Uh, well, no sir. Nothing like that, but he and two other officers ran off during the night. I'm sure he went to Karne to warn the king. I'm afraid they will have troops waiting for you when you get there."

Delno sighed. "Well, thank you for the warning. I suppose something like this was to be expected." Then he looked at the officers and asked tiredly, "You men weren't told to attack once the dragons had gone by, were you?"

The man looked a bit uncomfortable for a moment, and then he shrugged. "I may as well tell you. We were supposed to wait until the dragons had gone by and then grab up our arms and attack your troops. The general said you wouldn't be able to attack with fire if we were close to your own men."

"What did you tell the general?" Delno asked.

The man smiled and said, "I took a page from your general's book, sir, and told him to go pound salt up his arse. Then I told him that if he wanted to continue this insanity, he could do it himself. As far as I'm concerned, the best thing we've done for Bourne since this whole thing started was surrender this morning."

The smaller man finally found his voice, "What's to be done with us, sir? We've surrendered as you said. Are we to be kept as prisoners?" There was no mistaking the concern in his voice.

"As long as you act accordingly, you won't be harmed," Delno replied.

"It's not that, if you pardon me, sir. But most of us aren't soldiers. We're conscripts. Most of us are just farmers."

Delno looked around at all of the men and then asked, "If the farmers are here, who's manning the farms?"

"Well, that's just the problem now, isn't it, sir? Our farms are being managed by our lady folk, but there aren't enough of them to do the job properly. There are crops lying in the fields rotting because no one is there to harvest them."

"Damn that Torrance!" Delno exclaimed. "It's bad enough he conscripts his men for the sake of ambition. Then he compounds that by conscripting children. Now I find that he is willing to leave his people to starve this winter as well, all because of his insane desire to conquer Corice."

Delno thought for a moment, and then he looked at the taller man and said, "You seem to be in charge of your side at this point, so I won't try to change that. Get your men organized. Those who have farms to return to need to move out as quickly as possible, and those who have no farms need to move out with them so that whatever can be brought in from the fields is harvested as soon as possible. Fall is upon us: if this isn't done soon, all of Bourne will starve this winter."

The men nodded and turned to carry out Delno's orders. As a parting shot, Delno said, "I will tell our soldiers what you are doing. So long as your men stay away from those weapons, they won't be harassed."

The two men stopped and the taller man said, "If we didn't have to get these men to their rightful jobs, I'd offer to come with you to Karne." Then both of the men saluted and turned back to their task.

CHAPTER 52

"WELL, GENERAL," DELNO said as he looked out at the capitol city of Karne, "it looks as if Torrance has managed to find some men who haven't seen what dragons can do to ground troops. Get your men ready to push forward, and let the Bournese see you, but don't advance yet. We'll try and talk with them, and if that fails, the dragons will have to convince them of our sincerity. I want your troops to hold until we've taken care of any major opposition: then you and your men will move in and deter any counter attack."

Dreighton surveyed the city. It had taken one whole day and night to move the men to this point, which had given the Bournese over twenty-four hours to prepare for them. The capitol itself wasn't walled, like Larimar, but low fortifications had been hastily constructed out of whatever materials could be found on short notice. The main road in was blocked with logs, stones, and sharpened stakes pointing outward. It was manned by both archers and infantry, but that was the most heavily fortified spot, and could be easily circumvented if necessary. Most of the streets had nothing more formidable than a wagon pulled across and then tipped up on its side. Some places had stones or other debris hastily piled up. All in all, it wasn't particularly impressive. None of the barricades, including the one at the main entrance of town, would stand long against a determined force, especially since a generous estimate put the Bournese troops in the city at no more than four hundred.

"We can take this city without the dragons. I have nine hundred and fifty men who are eager to give these Bournese a taste of what they had planned for Larimar," Dreighton said.

"That is precisely why I don't want your men to move in yet," Delno replied. "We aren't here to punish the Bournese for the crimes of their king. I don't want these men slaughtered if we can avoid it, and I damn sure don't want this city sacked."

"After what these people tried to do to us?" a staff lieutenant asked incredulously.

"We intend to put this entire country under Corisian control to prevent future wars," Delno shot back. "Once we take the city, it then becomes the responsibility of Corice to keep everything running. It will be much easier and a great deal less draining on Corisian resources if we leave the governmental infrastructure mostly intact." Delno looked at the officers assembled and added, "Unless you want Larimar to have to feed and house several thousand starving refugees, mostly women and children, I strongly suggest that you make sure that the men under your command do not move into this town looking for vengeance. There is to be no looting in Karne."

Delno then turned away from the men and walked to Geneva. As he was mounting, she said, *"Brock is concerned that the Corisian soldiers will have difficulty keeping themselves under control."*

"Tell Brock that I have issued orders that the men are to be kept in check, and there is to be absolutely no looting. We are going to advance with the dragons and see if we can talk them into handing over Torrance and any senior officers who stand with him. If that fails, we will have to strike, but we will do so very selectively."

Geneva relayed the message, and Brock looked at him for a moment and then nodded. Then Delno gave the signal, and all of the dragons rose and flew to within three hundred and fifty yards of the main entrance to the city. They all landed and spread out in a line. Nearly forty dragons arrayed themselves in full view of the Bournese manning the barricade. Delno pulled a large piece of white linen out of his shirt and waved it over his head. It was only a few minutes before a man appeared on top of the barricade waving a white flag of his own.

Delno, Brock, Rita, Nassari, and Nadia advanced only about fifty feet and waited. The Bournese were reluctant to approach, but Delno and his party simply stood patiently. Finally, one of the officers of Bourne simply walked forward. His fellow soldiers hesitated for a few seconds and then joined him.

"I am Captain Phillip Saunders of the City Guard of Karne," the man said when he was close enough to be heard without shouting. "I have only heard vague rumors of what those beasts can do," he pointed at the dragons, "and I do not want my men to have to face them and find out first hand if the accounts are true. However, my men and I are sworn to protect this city and its residents. Even if your dragons are capable of leveling every building here, we will not forsake our oath and turn the city over to be looted. If you intend to make Bourne pay for the recent incursions into Corice by destroying our capitol, we will fight you to the last man."

Delno considered the man's words for a moment before responding. "Captain, our troops have been specifically ordered not to loot. While some of our men lost family to the plague that was visited on Larimar by agents of your king, they have been told that it is Torrance and his senior military officers who are responsible. We do not seek the destruction of Bourne. We seek to remove Torrance from power and replace him with someone who can rule this land in cooperation with Corice. Torrance has waged war against our homeland repeatedly. This last war has left many of your men dead by the breath of our dragons. Many more men are now fugitives because they saw the futility of fighting us and surrendered. Also, because of Torrance's ill-advised conscription of your farmers and tradesmen, Bourne may face drastic shortages this winter."

"I know that what you say is true because my brother is a farmer and was conscripted and sent to Stone Bridge as part of the reinforcements who were sent after your beasts' devastating attack there," Saunders said. "Tell me, please, what has happened to the men stationed at the bridge?"

The man's concern for his brother was clearly evident.

"It will ease your mind to know that the men at Stone Bridge were sent home to salvage what they could from the fields. Hopefully, they will still be able to save enough to keep Bourne fed this winter, though I am afraid that more will have to be brought in from Corice to offset the shortages. Hopefully, none of your people will starve before first harvest next year."

"You sound more like a friend than a conqueror, sir. I thank you for the good news about my brother and the men who were with him . . . although . . . well, their general said they were left to fight and would weaken your forces so that we could protect Karne. I don't know who to fully believe anymore."

"You must do as you see fit, Captain," Delno replied. "None of the men at Stone Bridge were harmed when we crossed yesterday morning. They all laid down their arms, and we sent them back to their farms as soon as we heard about the harvest rotting in the fields. As I have said, we have no quarrel with the honest, hardworking people of Bourne. Our business is with your king. If you and your men step aside, I will have our soldiers coordinate with you concerning the protection of Karne. You and your men will retain their positions as City Guard and the only thing that will change is the name of the ruler of this country. There is no need for bloodshed here today. If you would truly serve Karne, and ultimately Bourne, then allow us to proceed. The choice is yours."

"The choice is not entirely his to make," said a pudgy little man standing near the captain. "I am Lieutenant Errol Gant, of the Bournese Army. My orders come from General Parsins, not the Captain of the City Guard. The bulk of the forces here are under my control, and we have been told to hold this city against you."

Delno sighed loudly. "Lieutenant Gant, I have nearly forty dragons arrayed in direct opposition to you. If you choose to fight, when the dragons are finished, a thousand soldiers will then move into Karne and take the city. Those soldiers are being held in check by my orders. Do you want to see this city turned to a pile of rubble?"

"The Bournese military will give you no problem, sir," Saunders spoke up.

Gant looked at the Captain and started to speak, but Saunders cut him off. "If you protest, Gant, I will cut you down right here and now."

He drew his sword and menaced the man with it. Geneva growled and moved closer, but Delno had her and the other dragons hold back.

Delno could see that Saunders was frightened by the growls of the dragons, but he was impressed that the man stood his ground and kept his sword leveled at Gant's chest, ready to run the junior officer through.

"I am not threatening you, Rider, please call your beasts off," Saunders said.

"I have spoken to my dragon, Captain. They are waiting to see what happens." Then almost as an afterthought he added, "By the way, they are intelligent creatures and don't like being referred to as beasts."

"My apologies, to you and the dragons: I had heard that they were even capable of speech, but I didn't know how much was real and how much was embellishment on the tales."

Delno chuckled, "When dealing with dragons, Captain, almost anything is possible."

It took the rest of the morning and part of the afternoon to coordinate with the City Guard and secure the surrender of the remaining soldiers in Karne. There were only fifty City Guards: the bulk of the forces really were Bournese Army. However, the prospect of facing forty dragons and a thousand ground troops quickly discouraged those men from fighting. The Bournese military were disarmed, and those who were conscripted farmers were sent back to their farms. The remainder were put to work pulling down the defenses that had been hastily constructed.

"I'm not sure the men like working with the Bournese, Rider," General Dreighton remarked.

"I don't need them to like it, General," Delno replied. "I simply need them to do it."

"It just chafes, if you take my meaning. My men have fought against these men. They think of them as the enemy. It's hard to put that aside and work with the people who tried to conquer our own country."

"Then it's up to you and your officers to make them understand that it isn't these people who are our enemies." Delno paused for a moment to collect his thoughts, and then addressed the general's staff officers as well as Dreighton. "Look at it this way: in Corice our rulers are somewhat restricted by the laws of the people, and we have a parliamentary council to see that those laws are followed. If our king became a tyrant, he could actually be forced by rule of law to abdicate in favor of his successor. If he has no successor, the council is then obligated to choose a successor by vote."

Two of the younger officers began muttering to each other.

"Do you have something to say?" Delno said to them sharply. "If not, pay attention!" Delno nearly smiled when he realized that he almost sounded like Jhren when he said that. "As I was saying," he continued, "as we have moved deeper and deeper into Bourne, it has become obvious that this country has no such system to keep the rulers in check. Here the nobility and the wealthy tread on the lower classes as they please. The working classes are seen by those who govern them as little more than chattel property. In fact, they probably wouldn't misuse their property as badly as they have the common citizens. The king, his top advisors, and his high ranking military officers have not only spent most of the country's treasury on this last war, but they have left entire crops to rot in order to conscript the farmers so that they would have enough soldiers to fill their ranks. They have stores of food for themselves and simply don't care that the people they should feel responsible for, and to, will most likely starve this winter because of their actions."

Delno could see that his words were getting through. The officers were beginning to shift their own enmity from the common soldiers to the leaders of Bourne.

"But, that just doesn't make any sense," one of the junior officers said. "Even if they don't care about their people, if they don't feed them, they will have no army next year. You'd think the people would see what is going on and rise up against him."

"The people are beginning to see it. That is why they so readily surrender to us when they realize we are here to help. However, revolutions take time to gather momentum. We don't have time if we are to stop this insanity and try and prevent mass starvation in Bourne this year," Delno responded. "That is why we must make our soldiers see that we are not here to conquer these people. We are here to rescue them by removing the current government and putting our own replacements in power. Anything else, looting, arbitrary destruction of property, especially government buildings, will only hamper our mission. Likewise, the killing of bureaucrats will hamper the distribution of food and other vital supplies. Winter will be on us soon here in the mountains: we don't have much time. It is much easier, and faster, to work with an existing system than it is to set up a new one."

"Well, we can now see your point, Rider," Dreighton said. "What are we to do then? I have nearly a thousand troops to keep busy. I'd rather they had a definite purpose than just have them waiting around outside the city getting bored. Idle hands leave entirely too much time for armed men to come up with ways to amuse themselves."

"They won't be idle, General," Delno answered. "Bourne does not have a large population after losing so many men to this war already: remember, the men who weren't killed during the siege of Larimar are in exile on our side of the border. Most of the people, primarily women and children now, are gathered in and around the three main cities, Karne, Alton, and Lowell. Alton and Lowell are both overseen by the nobility of those cities. You are to divide your force and send one third to each of those cities to make sure the nobility of each of them also abdicates in favor of a better government. You will take those soldiers of Bourne who haven't been sent home to their farms and intermingle them with your troops. With Bournese troops and a contingent of dragons going to each city you should encounter little resistance. Brock and Adamus will lead one group and Nassari and Nadia will lead the other. Hopefully, we can get the nobility taken out of power before any of them get delusions of grandeur."

Just then Captain Saunders ran up and saluted Delno. "Two of my men have been shot near the palace. Apparently, they got too close, and a couple of those officers up there decided to use them for target practice."

"Damn it!" Delno swore. "I said no one was to go near the place until I was ready. Are both men dead?"

"No, sir. Both are still alive, though one is hurt beyond the skills of our leeches, and will likely die soon."

"Not if I have anything to say about it. Quickly, take me to the men who were hurt."

CHAPTER 53

"THERE, THAT SHOULD take care of that," Delno said as he finished healing the second man. He had healed the worst injury first. The men of Bourne didn't know whether to be awed by the fact that he had healed the men, or frightened of the use of magic. "I should recommend that you both pull extra duty for disobeying orders and getting so damn close to the Palace: but I think we can let the pain you suffered serve as punishment enough, this time." He smiled and patted the man on the shoulder.

Captain Saunders stared wide-eyed at Delno. "I never would have believed that such a thing was possible if I hadn't seen it with my own eyes. To heal a man who is so close to death as to make no difference...."

"Oh, there is a big difference, Captain. If the man had been dead, the only help I would be capable of would be to assist with digging the grave. It's magic, but it has its limits." Delno paused and looked back at the palace. The structure was quite similar in size and layout to the palace in Larimar. "Now then, it's time to finish this business before we risk any more of our men getting hurt, or worse."

All of the Bournese made remarks of agreement. Some of them nearly cheered. Delno realized that these men had now come to think of him as one of them rather than an outsider. Some of that was because of the magic that, as a Rider, naturally surrounded him. However, it was mostly because these men had been down trodden so long that they were glad to follow someone who cared about their welfare and the welfare of their average countrymen.

"Captain, how many people are in that building? I know you may not have exact figures, but give me your best guess."

"Well, sir, we know that most of the servants fled when General Parsins came in the middle of the night and woke everyone. He was going on about dozens of dragons breathing fire and killing everything in their path, and how they were going to burn all of Bourne. There might be one, maybe two servants still in there, but most fled to go and try to protect their families. As for any others, the soldiers were under my command, and we were all sent to build and man the barricades. The only other people in there now are a few of the king's advisors and the high ranking officers. If I had to put a figure to it, I'd guess less than a score."

"I wish I knew for sure about the servants," Delno said. "I don't want any innocent people hurt. If it were earlier in the year, I'd just starve them out, but we need to get the rest of the government back up and running if we are to make sure the people of Bourne are fed this winter, and it will be much easier to get the bureaucracies working again once there is no doubt that Torrance has been removed from power."

They stood watching the building for a few moments. Finally, Delno said, "Oh well, nothing to do but go and talk with them."

All of the men within earshot looked at him like he was insane. Hadn't he just had to heal two men who had gotten close to the Palace?

There was just enough room for Geneva and Fahwn to land in the large central hub of the city, outside the palace. As they landed, three men appeared at the windows facing them. All three fired arrows at the dragons. Delno and Rita quickly stopped the arrows with magical shields, and Geneva roared and breathed a cone of fire that spanned the fifty feet between them and the building. The men who had fired the arrows screamed as they dived for cover. One of the three was standing in the middle of the large window in a hallway, and was unable to get safely aside. Fortunately for him, he died quickly.

Once the fervor had died down, Delno called out loudly, "Torrance, come out and surrender yourself. If you do, you won't be harmed."

"You have no right to make demands here!" The reply came from inside the palace, but the speaker didn't step into the open.

"You're wrong; I have every right," Delno responded. "Why don't you show yourself?"

"So that you can have that beast kill me the way it did Colonel Rollins? I think not."

"Well, if you don't come out, we will come and get you. Would you prefer to surrender honorably or be dragged from your hidey hole like trapped animal?"

"You will find that the walls and doors of this palace are strong. All I need do is keep you at bay until my kinsman arrives with his own dragons to reinforce my position. Then you will see who the trapped animal is."

"Are you referring to Warrick?" Delno said in a conversational tone. "I'm afraid he won't be joining us. Being killed in Horne has put a damper on his plans to travel north and take control of this land."

"You lie," the voice screamed. "My kinsman is much too powerful to be defeated. He will come, and then I will finally grind Corice under my boot heel."

"I am not lying, Torrance." Delno reached up and got a long bundle that he had tied to his saddle. He unwrapped the contents and said, "Do you recognize this saber? This is the Dragon Blade that Warrick carried. He touted it as the symbol of his power. I took it from Warrick just before I killed him and his dragon Hella. Their bodies lie in the courtyard of the old fort he used as his headquarters. That fort is now in the hands of Riders who are loyal to me and pledged to protect people from men like you, Torrance."

"That can't be Warrick's blade; again, you lie!"

"You are partially right; this is not now, nor was it ever, Warrick's blade. It belonged to my grandfather, Corolan. Warrick had Corolan ambushed and murdered by Roracks and claimed the Blade for himself. It is now in the hands of Corolan's heirs, where it belongs."

"I don't believe you! You are trying to trick me into surrendering."

"I am growing tired of this, Torrance. However, I will indulge you for just a few moments longer. Look out here at this Blade. Even from this distance, you can clearly see that it is not only a Dragon Blade, but a saber. Of the scant handful of Dragon Blades in existence, only two of them are sabers. Corolan had one, and I have the other." He pulled his own saber and held both blades out as proof. "As you can see, I now hold both blades, and we both know that Warrick wouldn't have freely relinquished my grandfather's blade." Delno held the swords out for another moment and then lowered them and said, "Now, Torrance, my patience has run out. Come out, or we are coming in."

The only reply from the palace was a long, drawn-out wail of despair that receded as the person apparently withdrew deeper into the palace.

Delno waited only long enough for all of the Riders who were present in Karne to join him before moving to the entrance portal. The double doors were very thick, iron-bound hardwood. Geneva simply thrust her claws into them and yanked them completely out of their frames as she had done with the doors of the jail in Llorn. Even Brock was impressed with Geneva's strength.

"That's a neat trick," Brock commented. "Leera couldn't have done it so easily. Even Fahwn would have had to work a bit to accomplish the task."

"Yes," Delno replied. "It saves us a great deal of time over waiting for a locksmith."

There were just over a dozen Riders and five military leaders. They entered the palace cautiously with their weapons drawn. When they reached the main hall, the doors weren't barred as they had expected. The Riders filed into the hall in pairs. They found eleven military men, all above the rank of Colonel, including General Parsins. All of the men of Bourne had stacked their weapons and were standing near the throne with their hands in plain sight. Next to the officers were four of Torrance's advisors. Every one of them stared at the floor rather than look the Riders in the eye.

Delno walked forward, flanked by Rita and Brock. Nassari was right behind him with Nadia, Will, and Paul. Adamus, along with several of the new Riders Delno had previously kept in reserve, stood rear guard.

As Delno approached the throne, the first thing he noticed was that there was a large amount of blood on the floor. Torrance was sitting back in the seat leaning to his left. His eyes were open but glazed and would never see anything again. There was a long-bladed knife still held loosely in his right hand. The blood had come from the slash he had made in the inside of his own left arm. Unable to face being dethroned and taken away to answer for his actions, he had severed his own brachial artery and bled to death rather than allow himself to be captured.

EPILOGUE

"**G**OOD NIGHT," RITA said. She kissed Marcus on the forehead as she and Delno tucked the boy into bed.

The girls were already asleep when they had carried them to the nursery. Marcus had managed to stay awake long enough for Rita to sing him a lullaby and pull the covers up to his chin. He was slumbering peacefully before she and Delno got all the way to the door.

"They've had a big day," she said as they entered their own room. "We caused such a ruckus on our return that they woke early from their naps, and then we spent the whole afternoon playing with them. They are exhausted."

"We didn't cause that much ruckus," Delno responded as he began lighting candles in the bathing room. "They are all sensitive to the dragons, and the twins are so much so that they woke up when Geneva and Fahwn got near."

"Really?" she said. "Fahwn hadn't mentioned that to me."

"Geneva told me that, providing they don't suppress it as they grow older, they will probably be good candidates someday."

He began pumping water as she gathered the things they would need for their bath. Once she had put the soap and sponges on the edge of the tub, she began undressing. He watched her while he continued pumping the water.

Once she was in the tub soaking, she asked, "Why did you put your mother on the throne of Bourne, Handsome? Her only heirs are both Riders, and you don't want Riders to rule any country."

"Well, she's not Queen, Darling. Bourne has been reduced in status to a duchy, and she is Duchess. Bourne is a small territory with a harsh climate and a small population; it really should have been downgraded from a kingdom long ago."

"But, still. Your mother?" she asked.

"Well, it's true that my mother has no heirs who can take over the Duchy, but that could change. We have adopted our three. If they don't become Riders, they will be eligible heirs. There again, it is always possible that Will could father a child who will take the position. Also, I don't know if you noticed, but Dorian took a fancy to a woman who is still of child-bearing age while we were in Horne. He may yet produce heirs of his own. Only one of them could sit on the throne of Corice, so if he has several children, one of his offspring could be placed as duke or duchess to succeed my mother."

She was about to speak when there was a knock at the door. The caller was Brock, so they decided to get out of the tub. Once they were dried and had donned robes, Delno opened the door and let Brock in while Rita poured wine for all of them.

"So, have you settled affairs here in the north to your liking?" Brock asked Delno.

"As far as I can tell, yes," Delno responded. He ticked off each point on his fingers as he spoke. "I have eliminated the threat of Bournese invasion. I have helped to ensure that none of the citizens of either country will starve this winter, and I have secured enough funds from my uncle that Nassari will be able to outfit the headquarters of the Legion of Riders for the next year or so. All in all, I believe I've accomplished what I set out to do up here."

"So, why your mother?" Brock asked. "She's a good-hearted person, but what does she know about running a country?"

"I was just asking him the same thing when you came in," Rita said.

"Great minds think alike," Brock said with a smile.

"All right, I'll answer you," Delno said. "When we first went into Bourne and began to see the situation, we found that the people were basically looking for salvation. They might have revolted on their own eventually, but that was unlikely: the people of the north are bred to look to a king. That is why the parliament, although it has the power to do so, has never removed my family from the throne of Corice even when the king or queen wasn't a good ruler. The Bournese weren't looking to remove their king and set up their own government. They would, more likely, have waited until Torrance died of old age and hoped for a better man the next time around. When they were presented with someone who would remove their king and govern them justly, they were willing to follow. They know me as a Rider, but they also know and respect me from the last war. They were willing to accept Delno Okonan when they might have defended Torrance against a stranger."

He stopped to sip his wine. Brock waited patiently, but Rita pressed him. "Your reason for putting your mother in charge of Bourne," she prompted.

"Well," he responded, "my mother is a superb manager and has plenty of common sense. Also, it's not like she has to attend to every little detail: the bureaucracy is still mostly intact, and Dorian has said he will help as well. The main reason I chose my mother, though, is that she is Laura Okonan: since I am now the savior of Bourne, the name will carry much weight even if I am not here. By putting my mother in the position of authority, I have, hopefully, headed off any trouble that might otherwise crop up."

"So, why not your father?" Brock asked.

Delno gave him a surprised look and said, "You've talked with my father. He's a good and generous man, and I love him, but he is so honest that he can't imagine anyone else being otherwise. The politicians would play him like an instrument. My mother has always had to look out for his business interests so he doesn't get cheated any more often than he does."

"Delno!" Rita exclaimed. "Your father is a good man, and he's wonderful with the children. How can you say such things about him?"

"It's no more than he'd say about himself," Delno responded. "He is a great man. I couldn't have asked for a better father." Brock was chuckling, and Rita still looked scandalized. "You weren't there when my father first found out about my mother being an heir to the royal family. He spoke then about being a simple man and not suited to palace life. One of his greatest strengths is his awareness of his own limitations. That makes him very secure in his abilities."

Rita looked like she still wanted to defend John Okonan, but she let it drop as Brock spoke up. "What will you do now? Do you plan on going back to Horne with Nassari?"

"Rita and I have talked about that," Delno replied. "We believe we should return to Horne for a short time, but Nassari is a very good organizer; he can handle the fort. We will, of course, begin working on the attitudes of the people and planting the idea of exploring the unsettled lands. However, for a time, I believe we have earned a short rest. Therefore, when we go, we will take the children with us. Then, once Nassari is doing what needs to be done, we will continue south and take Walker up on his invitation to visit the Elven lands."

"What about you, Brock Ard?" Rita asked. "What are your plans for the immediate future?"

"Well," Brock replied, "like you, I want to rest before we begin to actively carry out Delno's plan to expand human settlement. For a now, though, I was reminded by my kinsman that I haven't been to Iondar in a long time. I think I will first travel to Orlean and see if my son would like to accompany me to my homeland."

"I believe," Delno responded, "that is a good idea. It will be good for both of you. Also, though I agree that Dragon Riders should be neutral, I believe that having a sense of home gives us a connection to the people of the world. That is a connection that we need to strive to maintain."

"I can't argue with that sentiment," Brock said. "However, it's getting late, and I must also be off to bed." He bowed to them both and turned toward the door, motioning for Delno to stay seated, "No need to see me to the door; I'll make sure it is closed behind me."

Later, as Delno lay in bed, he reached out to Geneva. *"Are you awake, Love?"*

"I am awake. What is troubling you, Love?"

"Nothing is troubling me. I just wanted to be with you for a while."

"I am always with you, Dear One," she replied. *"However, you have had a hard day. You should sleep. I will not leave you. I will never leave you."*

He smiled as he lay in the darkness and thought about that. *"Thank you, Geneva. I love you. Good night."*

"I love you too, Delno. Good night."

About the Author

J.D. HALLOWELL has been, among other things, an automotive mechanic, a bouncer, a soldier, a dog trainer, a cowboy, a jeweler, a tow truck driver, a stereo installer, a battery salesman, an after-school program counselor, a psychiatric technician, an EMT, a phlebotomist, a paralegal, a medical coder, a photographer, a self-  defense instructor, and a massage therapist. He lives and writes on the Space Coast of Florida.

A Portrait of the Author with Indie the Wonder Dog and a Hawk

CPSIA information can be obtained at www.ICGtesting.com
Printed in the USA
LVOW07s0255111115

462015LV00001B/57/P

9 781629 270081